Ritual of Fire

D. V. Bishop is the pseudonym of award-winning writer David Bishop. His love for the city of Florence and the Renaissance period meant there could be only one setting for his crime fiction. The first book in the Cesare Aldo series, *City of Vengeance*, won the Pitch Perfect competition at the Bloody Scotland crime writing festival and the NZ Booklovers Award for Best Adult Fiction Book. Book two in the series *The Darkest Sin* won the Crime Writer's Association Historical Dagger. He teaches creative writing at Edinburgh Napier University. *Ritual of Fire* is the third novel in the Cesare Aldo series, following *The Darkest Sin*.

By D. V. Bishop

City of Vengeance
The Darkest Sin
Ritual of Fire

Ritual of Fire

D. V. BISHOP

PAN BOOKS

First published 2023 by Macmillan

This paperback edition first published 2024 by Pan Books
an imprint of Pan Macmillan
The Smithson, 6 Briset Street, London EC1M 5NR
EU representative: Macmillan Publishers Ireland Ltd, 1st Floor,
The Liffey Trust Centre, 117–126 Sheriff Street Upper,
Dublin 1, D01 YC43
Associated companies throughout the world
www.panmacmillan.com

ISBN 978-1-5290-9650-7

1 3 5 7 9 8 6 4 2

A CIP catalogue record for this book is available from the British Library.

Map artwork by Hemesh Alles

Typeset in Adobe Caslon Pro by Palimpsest Book Production Limited, Falkirk, Stirlingshire
Printed and bound by CPI Group (UK) Ltd, Croydon, CR0 4YY

Visit **www.panmacmillan.com** to read more about all our books
and to buy them. You will also find features, author interviews and
news of any author events, and you can sign up for e-newsletters
so that you're always first to hear about our new releases.

For readers, librarians and booksellers everywhere –
you keep our stories alive

*The injury that is to be done
to a man ought to be of such a kind that one
does not stand in fear of revenge.*

Niccolò Machiavelli, *The Prince*
translated by W. K. Marriott (1908)

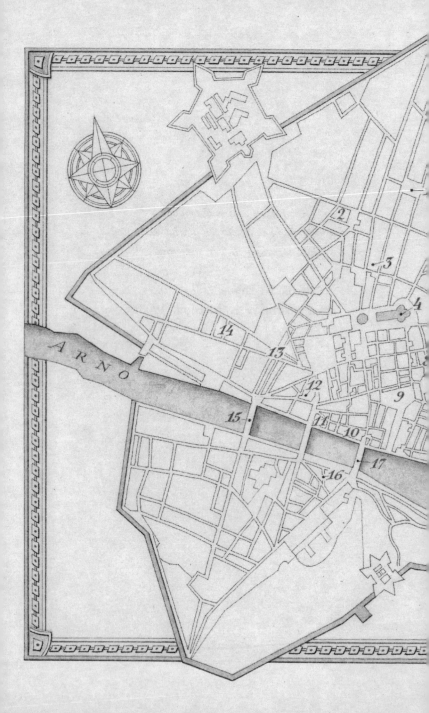

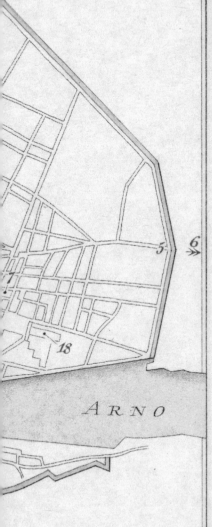

FLORENCE
(FIRENZE)

1. Piazza San Marco
2. Palazzo Uccello
3. Palazzo Medici
4. Duomo
5. Porta la Croce
6. To San Jacopo al Girone
7. Le Stinche Prison
8. Palazzo del Podestà
9. Piazza della Signoria
10. Palazzo Dovizi
11. Palazzo Ghiberti
12. Zoppo's Tavern
13. Palazzo Ruggerio
14. Strocchi's home
15. Ponte alla Carraia
16. via dei Giudei
17. Ponte Vecchio
18. Santa Croce

ARNO

Chapter One

❧

Thursday, May 23rd 1538

Cesare Aldo could still smell flesh burning, even from this distance.

In Florence it would have been one scent among many, easily missed in the city's overwhelming assault of stenches and sounds and sights. But here in the Tuscan countryside there was time to inhale unexpected aromas, to deduce where they were coming from, and to follow an acrid odour across a hillside to its source.

Even in the meagre light of a sickle moon, Aldo had not struggled to find his quarry. Few people roasted meat over an outdoor fire this long after midnight, not unless they were fools or banditi. Looking down on the inept cook hunched in the hollow of a rocky slope, Aldo knew this was no bandit. Any doubts about their foolishness were banished when the stolen capon fell into the fire, prompting a string of curses. The panicked thief failed to retrieve the bird but almost set his sleeve alight. More curses filled the air.

Aldo had seen and heard and smelled enough. Pulling the stiletto from his boot, he chose a careful path down the hillside, avoiding fallen branches and tinder-dry twigs that would signal his approach. His quarry was too busy pushing the charred capon out of the fire with a stick to notice until Aldo stepped into the light.

'What are you doing here?' the thief asked.

'I could ask you the same question,' Aldo replied, 'but the answer is at your feet, Lippo.' The thief had been a successful pickpocket in Florence until he was arrested by Aldo and sent to Le Stinche. Repeated rule breaches inside the prison led to Lippo's favoured right arm being cut off as a punishment. 'Things aren't going well, are they?' Aldo asked. 'Reduced to stealing farmyard fowls from peasants in the countryside.'

'I wouldn't take food from peasants,' Lippo protested, jabbing a stick through the charred capon and lifting it in the air. 'This came from that grand villa further up the hill.'

The grand villa belonged to Girolamo Ruggerio, one of the most ruthless merchants in Florence, but Aldo chose not to mention this to Lippo. Not yet. 'I know where the bird came from,' Aldo said, 'but thank you for confessing where you took it from. Saves me having to gather any more evidence.' He pointed his stiletto at the ground in front of Lippo. 'Sit. It won't be sunrise for a few hours, so we'll be waiting here a while.' Lippo scowled but did as he was told. Aldo leaned against the trunk of a stunted olive tree, blade still in hand. The prospect of chasing the thief in the weak moonlight was not appealing.

'Can I at least eat the bird?' Lippo asked.

'If you wish,' Aldo said, 'but most of it is probably still raw. Better to leave it in the embers until the flesh cooks through, otherwise you'll be sick all the way to Florence.'

'You're taking me back? For stealing a capon?'

'For stealing three capons, one barrel of wine, half a sack of millet you abandoned a mile from where you took it, plus that doublet and the boots you're wearing.'

Lippo looked down at his clothes. The doublet was made of black embroidered silk and the boots were of the softest brown leather, while his woollen hose were a patchwork of tears and stains. 'Have you been following me all the way from the city?'

Aldo laughed. 'Far from it. I am the Otto di Balìa e Guardia's representative for the lands east of Florence, enforcing laws and hunting criminals for the court. I spent the past two days investigating a supposed dispute between two farmers in a village twenty miles further east of here, after someone sent me a letter claiming the quarrel was about to turn bloody. But when I finally got there, both men denied having any argument, or knowing who sent the letter. I returned to a message from the Otto containing an order for your arrest. It said you were released from Le Stinche after serving your time and went straight back to thieving.'

'I didn't go straight back to thieving,' Lippo protested. 'Well, not the same day.'

'Perhaps. But trying to steal the purse from one of the Otto's own magistrates?'

'It was a mistake,' the thief conceded.

'So was fumbling the job and letting him see you were missing an arm . . .'

'That was shameful.' Lippo stared at his stump. 'Never would have happened before.'

'When I read that you had fled into the dominion, I knew it wouldn't be long before you got into more trouble,' Aldo said. 'So I offered coin for reports of any petty pilfering in this area. You obligingly left a trail of thefts all the way here from Florence.'

'A man's got to eat.'

'Half a sack of millet?'

'That was also a mistake.' Lippo sighed, giving the capon a prod. 'You working in the dominion now? Wondered why I didn't see you at the Palazzo del Podestà last time I got arrested.'

Aldo smiled. 'Consider it fortunate I'm the one who caught you out here.'

'Why? You're taking me back to Le Stinche. I won't last a month in there.'

'I'm surprised you survived a week out here. The Otto has branded you an outlaw. That means any other outlaw can capture or kill you and get their own offences reduced as a reward. That's better than any bounty. Most of them would kill you.'

Lippo shook his head. 'I didn't know.'

'You wouldn't . . . until they found you.' Aldo folded both arms across his chest but made sure the stiletto was still visible in his grasp. Lippo had many flaws, but he was far from lacking in guile. If there seemed any chance of escape, he would take it.

'So,' the thief said, 'why are you out here?'

'It's a long tale . . .'

'If we're going to be here till sunrise it might help to pass the time.'

'It's a long tale,' Aldo repeated, 'but not one I care to share with you.'

'Fair enough,' Lippo said, holding up his one hand in surrender. 'I understand, I do. Leaving the city that you love, it tears at a man. Makes him feel—'

'You can be silent, or I can make you silent.' Aldo stood upright, unfolding his arms so the stiletto caught the firelight. Lippo opened his mouth to speak, but closed it again.

A wise choice.

You wait. Everything is prepared, everything is ready. The cart is lined with tinder, oil poured over it to be sure the dry hay and twigs burn fast. The gibbet you nailed to the cart is sturdy, strong enough for the weight of two men. You have several flints to start the fire, should one of them fail. You have more dry hay and discarded paper to catch the spark.

You wait. It will be time soon enough.

You know the patrols that wander the streets of Florence during curfew, the long hours between sunset and sunrise. The men seem lazy and witless, wandering the same circuit through the murky gloom each night. They pass once as the bells chime for the end of the day, a second time near midnight, and a third as the first hints of sunrise lighten the sky.

You wait. Your fingers itch.

Luring your target here was simple. You delivered the letter a day ago, along with a full pouch of coin and the promise of secrets. One was true currency, but secrets are always more valuable in this city. The target came willingly, without guard or escort. Greed and his lust for knowledge were too potent a snare. One blow of the cudgel took his senses. Another ensured he stayed silent while you bound him to the gibbet.

You wait. Your mouth is dry.

You know the target's name but do not speak it. Not when you tied the gag across his mouth. Not when you accused him, the words hissed in his face. He shook his head, offering nothing but denials. You cut away his clothes and shaved his scalp while he raged at you, anger causing cuts to his scalp. When you said what was to come he whimpered, begging for a way out. He offered names, and you took them. As the night passed you told him it had become May 23rd, and he wept.

You wait.

You wait.

Now, at long last, it is time. You go to him, struggling not to breathe in the foulness that has fled his body. You lift his chin and stare in his eyes one last time. He seems to search your gaze for hope; you offer *nothing but righteous resolve. He screams into the gag, and you silence him with the cudgel.*

You peer outside the stable. There are no lights at any windows overlooking the narrow alley. You move the cart through the doors, grateful for the sacks you tied round its wheels to hide their noise. Pushing the cart with the target bound to the gibbet is not easy, but you will not fail. You made a vow.

You reach the end of the alley where it meets Piazza della Signoria, the most important square in all of Florence. This is where citizens gather to celebrate and protest. This is where the people come when they want to change the way things are in their city. This is where it happened all those years ago. This is where it must happen again.

You smile. The piazza is empty.

You push the cart into the centre of square, ignoring the looming silhouette of the Palazzo della Signoria, a symbol of the power held by so few over so many in Florence. No doubt those few will judge what you do here, while others may applaud. No matter.

You strike the flint, sending sparks into the dried hay and paper and tinder.

The sparks catch to become a flame, and the flame becomes a fire.

You stay until tongues of heat are licking the target's skin.

Carlo Strocchi couldn't remember what it was to sleep for a whole night. As a boy he had slumbered like a stone, or so his mama always said, a sleep so deep nothing could wake him. When he came to Florence the sounds of the city at night were different from the small Tuscan village where he had grown up, but Strocchi still found little difficulty in sleeping until dawn. After Tomasia came into his life he had slept less, but that was because of their hunger for each other. His sound sleep returned when Tomasia was with child.

But Strocchi doubted he had known two hours of sleep side by side with Tomasia since Bianca was born. She was a beautiful bambina, six months old now. Leaving her tore a hole in his heart each morning, but coming home at night filled his heart again. Strocchi loved everything about his daughter. But she did not, could not – would not – sleep through the night. Was that unusual? Strocchi had been an only child himself and knew little about infants. In the months leading to Bianca's birth he had known so much fear. The prospect of becoming a father was what it must be like to stand before the sea, waiting for the tide to come in.

Now all he knew was exhaustion.

How could a soul be so tired, so weary? Tomasia tended to Bianca most nights, but Strocchi did what he could to help. He hummed the lullabies Mama had long ago sung to him, rocking Bianca in his arms until she drifted back to sleep. Yet no sooner was she nestled in her cot than she would wake again, often as Strocchi was returning to bed.

How did other parents cope? How did they keep going?

If nights were bad, the days were worse. He would stumble to the Podestà, struggling to stay awake while Bindi complained about whatever was vexing him that morning. The segretario seemed even more disagreeable now Strocchi was close to becoming an officer. As a constable he had been spared much of Bindi's wrath. Not anymore.

Once Bindi's tempests had finally blown themselves out, Strocchi faced long hours of patrols and questions and lies. Then he staggered back to the narrow rented room in the city's western quarter. A single smile from Bianca could lift his mood when he got home, but the restlessness of her nights made Strocchi weary to his bones.

Tomasia finished feeding Bianca and put her down in the cot

before coming back to bed. Strocchi rolled over, nuzzling himself into her back and buttocks, sharing his warmth with her. Even when he was this exhausted his cazzo still twitched at Tomasia's closeness, enjoying her presence. She reached back to slap him away. 'Not now, Carlo. It's too hot.'

Summer had come early this year, and the nights were already sweltering. He didn't blame Tomasia; the instinct was more reflex than lust. It had taken them a while to find a way back together after the birth, and their mutual weariness did not help. But being close to Tomasia always comforted Strocchi, soothing away his cares as sleep wrapped itself—

'Is it here?'

Strocchi jolted awake. Someone was shouting outside. But it was still dark, which meant it was still curfew. Only those with authorization were permitted on the streets at night, and few had that other than the Otto's night patrols. No, please don't let it be—

Before Strocchi could finish his silent prayer, heavy feet were stamping up the stairs. A fist beat at the door. 'Strocchi, you there?' someone called from the landing.

That woke Bianca. She was crying by the time Strocchi got up. He lifted her from the cot and handed Tomasia the baby before stalking to the door, muttering dark curses all the way. Strocchi opened the door to see which fools had come calling. It was Benedetto, a fellow constable banished to night patrols by Bindi, along with another idiota whose name Strocchi couldn't recall. Manuffi, perhaps, or Maruffi? It didn't matter.

'What do you want?' Strocchi kept his voice a terse whisper, the sound of Bianca's cries behind him a dagger in his ears.

'There's a fire,' Benedetto replied, 'at Piazza della Signoria.'

'Why wake my family and probably everyone in the street to announce that?'

The other constable – Manuffi, that was his name – attempted an ingratiating smile. 'The segretario always says if we see something on night patrol, something that won't wait until sunrise, we should find an officer and tell them.'

'I'm not an officer,' Strocchi said. 'Not yet.'

'But we knew where you live.' Manuffi pointed at Benedetto. 'Well, he did.'

'What kind of fire?' Strocchi stepped out onto the landing, closing the door behind him. With luck, whatever had happened would be some foolhardy prank by drunks lurching home long after curfew. But the grim edge to Benedetto's features said otherwise, as did the heavy pall of woodsmoke seeping from the constables' tunics.

'A cart, set ablaze in the piazza,' Benedetto said. 'There was a gibbet nailed to it.'

'A gibbet?' Strocchi wasn't sure he had heard right.

'Like a gallows,' Manuffi added, 'for hanging someone.'

'I know what a gibbet is,' Strocchi hissed. There was more than woodsmoke clinging to the pair; another odour tainted them: roasted meat. Strocchi's belly rebelled at what that meant but he still had to ask. 'Was there a body on the gibbet?'

Benedetto nodded, his eyes cast down.

'Santo Spirito,' Strocchi said, making the sign of the cross. Who would burn a body in this way, and in such a place? What madman would choose to— No. There would be time for questions later. 'Is the cart still burning?'

'Yes,' Manuffi replied. 'At least, it was.'

'Who did you leave there?'

'Leave there?'

'Is one of the other patrols at the piazza?' Neither of the pair responded. Strocchi shook his head. The fools had not realized one of them should remain with the cart while the other came to fetch him. Such stupidity was little surprise from Manuffi, but Benedetto should have known better. 'Return to the piazza, both of you. Nobody else is allowed near the cart, understand me? Nobody. I will be there as quick as I can. Go.' Still the pair remained where they were. 'Go!'

Strocchi went back into his home as the constables thundered downstairs, the faint smell of sour milk comforting after the stench that had clung to Benedetto and Manuffi. Tomasia was sitting up in bed, nursing Bianca. 'I washed your hose and tunic. They're hanging over the chair, should be dry by now in this heat.' Strocchi nodded his thanks, already pulling off his nightshirt. 'How long will you be?' she asked.

'I don't know. Hours, if what they said is true.'

Tomasia grimaced. 'I heard.'

'The whole building probably heard.' Strocchi pulled on his hose, shivering despite the warmth in the air. 'Burning a body in Piazza della Signoria? It's madness. The whole city will know about this within hours.'

'That's probably why the piazza was chosen. Whoever did this, they want everyone to know. They want the attention.'

After shrugging on his tunic, Strocchi leaned over the bed to kiss Tomasia and Bianca. 'I'll be back when I can.' He strode from the room. There was nothing to fault in Tomasia's reasoning. But it asked a more troubling question: if burning a body in the piazza was a stratagemma to get attention, what would those responsible do next?

Chapter Two

Cassandra opened both shutters in the signore's bedchamber, letting the first glimmers of dawn into the vacant room. She wasn't expecting Ruggerio to return to his country villa before the end of June but airing the room was part of her daily chores as housekeeper. Besides, it was an excuse to linger by the window and gaze out at the Tuscan countryside. She never tired of this view, the vines and olive groves. Tall cypresses lined the dirt track down to the village of San Jacopo al Girone, treetops swaying in the early morning breeze.

Two figures trudging up the hill caught Cassandra's gaze. One appeared familiar, though it was difficult to be certain at this distance. She had seen too many summers and her eyesight was not so strong as before. More and more she caught herself squinting, or needing two lanterns at night to illuminate her needlework. But she recognized the man on the left as the pair got closer. They must be coming to the villa, there was nothing else this far up the hillside, but why?

Cassandra descended the sturdy wooden stairs to the villa's lower level, her simple skirt dancing around her calves. She strode along the hall to the front door, continuing outside to the courtyard. The sound of insetti filled the air already, though the sun was still clearing the hills. Another scorching day lay ahead, parching any soil that lacked irrigation. Fortunately, the estate was blessed with its own spring. This was one of the reasons the villa had been built here. Another was the view. When Ruggerio was in residence during the summer, he saw anyone coming up the hill long before they reached his country home.

Cassandra waited in the shade by the door for the visitors to arrive. When they did both men were breathless, sweat soaking their clothes and dust clotting their hose. She had been right about the one on the left: Cesare Aldo. He had settled in the area the previous summer, introducing himself as an officer of the Otto de Guardia e Bali, Florence's main criminal court. When Cassandra had asked why an officer had been sent out into the dominion, he'd simply smiled and changed the subject.

That proved typical of his behaviour in the months that followed. Aldo kept to himself most of the time, renting a hut on the edge of the village. He made little effort to become part of life around San Jacopo al Girone, as if he expected to return to the city soon. Cassandra understood that instinct, having herself come to the estate from Florence the previous year. She would never be fully accepted by those born and raised here. But she still made an effort to be involved with things when she could. Remaining an outsider was a lonely way to live.

A year in the countryside had darkened Aldo's skin, making the silver strands in his hair more evident. He remained lean of face and long of limb, clad in a simple tunic and hose. His leather boots were uncommon among the farmers he lived beside down in the village, but made sense for a man whose jurisdiction covered a considerable distance.

Aldo was breathing hard when he reached the courtyard; the other man seemed close to collapse. Both appeared tired and stiff, as if they had been awake long before dawn. The man with Aldo was pale and sunburnt at the same time. He was missing an arm, and his hose were torn and stained. Yet he also wore a rich doublet of black embroidered silk and brown leather boots that befitted a richer man. Cassandra took a better look at those boots.

She had noticed a pair of the signore's best boots were missing the previous night. Now she knew where they had gone. Cassandra peered at Aldo's companion. Yes, it was the same man who came to the villa the day before the boots disappeared. He had claimed to be buying and selling old clothes. Most living in the dominion could not afford new tunics, dresses or hose. Those who could not weave garments themselves bought old clothes from itinerant hawkers. But Cassandra had doubted the visitor's tale and sent him away.

'You've seen this man before,' Aldo said.

Cassandra told the story of the missing boots. 'He must have come back after dark and taken them from inside the kitchen door.'

'Lippo here is a common thief, from Florence. He also stole a capon from here, along with a barrel of wine, two more capons and half a sack of millet from other estates in recent days,' Aldo replied. 'What about this doublet he's wearing?'

Cassandra shook her head. 'No, I know every garment in the signore's wardrobe. He has plenty of silks, but never wears anything in black. Says it is not his colour.'

The thief spat on the courtyard dirt. 'Sounds like a peacock to me.'

That earned a slap to the ear from Aldo. 'Take the boots off.'

'But you said we're walking to the city,' the thief protested. 'That's miles from here. What am I supposed to wear on my feet?'

'Should have thought of that before you stole those. Now get them off.'

Cassandra exchanged a smile with Aldo while the muttering thief removed the boots. 'It'll be another hot day,' she said. 'Are you sure you wish to walk to Florence? You could borrow one of the horses in the signore's stable. Vincenzo says they need to be ridden.'

Aldo smiled. 'That would be easier. And some rope, if you have any.'

Lippo looked back and forth between them. 'What do you mean, one of the horses?'

Strocchi strode towards Piazza della Signoria as dawn coloured the sky, softening the dark to a mottled bruise of blue and black. He smelled the fire before reaching the square: burning wood, meat and oil. They were the aromas of summer feasts from his childhood, those rare occasions when a pig was cooked for the whole village to enjoy. Strocchi's mouth salivated at the memory, but his belly rebelled. Knowing where these fresh scents were coming from soured the recollection.

Benedetto and Manuffi were standing by the cart, greasy black smoke still billowing from it. Behind them loomed the stern black shadow of the Palazzo della Signoria, where Florence's senate gathered to argue and vote. Burning the cart and body here was an obscene gesture against those who made the laws by which people lived. There could be no hiding this, though Bindi and other men of importance would probably do their best to conceal what had occurred.

The cart was smaller than Strocchi had expected. One person could have pushed it into the piazza, though the extra weight of the gibbet and body would have made that hard work. The wooden base and sides of the cart were still smouldering, but the gibbet had fallen forward, along with its occupant. Then there was the stench . . . The closer Strocchi got, the worse it became. He took care not to be caught in the foul smoke coming from the cart.

Covering his mouth and nose to block the stench, Strocchi approached the other constables. 'Have you seen anyone else in the piazza?'

Benedetto shook his head. 'The gibbet fell as we returned. Nothing else has changed.'

Strocchi studied the buildings overlooking the piazza. There were no lights at the windows, but it seemed certain citizens would be watching. Was whoever did this among them? 'What about the body? What did you see when you first got here?'

'It was burning,' Manuffi said.

No wonder he was on night patrols. 'Besides that?'

'It was a man,' Benedetto replied. 'He'd been bound to the gibbet. His clothes were on fire but there were not many of them – an undershirt, maybe hose. I didn't see a tunic. Hard to tell with all the smoke and flames, but his head looked bloody.'

'As if he'd been tortured?' Strocchi asked.

Benedetto shrugged. 'He had no hair, but there seemed to be cuts on his scalp as if someone had shaved the head in a hurry. He still had his beard and moustache.'

Strocchi nodded. 'Did you recognize the man on the gibbet?'

Benedetto shook his head, as did Manuffi.

Someone called out, and two men came running towards the cart. Strocchi recognized them as another pair of constables on night patrol. Overhead the sky was brightening, dawn not far away. Benedetto and Manuffi talked to the others while Strocchi walked a slow circle around the cart, studying it for evidence.

There were no markings on the wooden sides, nothing to suggest who owned it. The fire was dying. Either the gibbet collapsing had flattened the flames, or whoever built the fire had not done a good job. Strocchi's belly growled. It was hard to ignore the aroma of roasted meat. Charred limbs had come away from the torso in the fire, or when the gibbet fell. Yet inside the cart the burning was clustered around where the gibbet had been fixed. Whoever did this had wanted to burn the body, not the cart. It was a funeral pyre, set ablaze in Florence's most public piazza.

'What do we do now?' Benedetto asked.

Strocchi ignored the question. Something was nagging at him. There must be more to this than burning a corpse; it was all too elaborate . . . Strocchi stopped himself. He had no proof it was a corpse that had been set aflame. What if the man tied to the gibbet had been alive when the fire was lit? That would make this murder.

No, not merely murder – an execution.

On rare occasions Piazza della Signoria was used for public executions, especially when those ruling the city wanted everyone to witness it. Strocchi had never seen such a killing himself, but long-serving constables at the Podestà shared grisly tales when they were too drunk to know better.

'Strocchi, what do we do?' Benedetto asked again.

They couldn't leave the cart where it stood. Better to move the smouldering mess to a place where it could be examined in private; a stable or empty courtyard. There was nowhere close enough to take the cart except . . . Strocchi winced. It was a solution, but the consequences would not be enjoyable. 'The Podestà,' he announced. 'We push it there.'

Benedetto laughed, glancing at the other constables. 'That's a jest, isn't it?'

'I wish it was,' Strocchi replied. 'We can't leave this mess here, and we haven't got anywhere else to take it. Curfew will end soon; we have to move this from the piazza.'

'But the segretario . . .'

'Shifting the cart is what matters. We can worry about Bindi later.' Strocchi soon had the other constables pulling the still-smoking cart north towards the Podestà. He paused, taking one last look around. Dozens, if not hundreds, of windows overlooked the piazza, so going door to door for potential witnesses was impractical. Moving the cart out of sight would delay the whispers about what had happened here, but sooner or later word would spread. People used coin to buy food and clothes, but gossip was Florence's most popular currency.

Aldo left Cassandra keeping watch over Lippo. Should the thief be foolish enough to flee he would not get far, especially once Aldo was atop a horse. The stable stood across the wide courtyard from the villa; close enough to be convenient but not in a place where it would impede the view from the upper level of Ruggerio's country retreat. Inside, the stable was clean and well kept, a door on the far side open to welcome morning breezes.

A lean, muscular man was tending to one of the horses, brushing its mane with care, whispering to the beast. He wore a simple tunic and hose with a leather apron to protect them. The stable hand gently eased one of the horse's legs upward, raising the hoof. He pulled a metal tool from a pouch on his apron, using it to free a stone caught in the hoof.

Aldo cleared his throat. 'One moment,' the stable hand said, finishing his task and giving the horse a pat. 'Yes?' He had a fierce face, a stark contrast to his gentle manner with the beast. The stable hand had seen at least thirty summers, if not more, but it was often difficult to judge the age of those who worked in the country, the sun adding many lines to their skin. Aldo could not recall seeing the stable hand down in the village.

'You're Vincenzo?' Aldo asked, getting a nod in return. He introduced himself, and his work for the Otto. 'Cassandra suggested

I borrow one of the signore's horses for a trip to Florence. I would probably have it back here tomorrow.'

Vincenzo studied Aldo. 'How fast will you be riding?'

'Not at all.'

The stable hand rubbed a hand across his stubble. 'Take that one.' Vincenzo nodded at the horse he had been tending. 'But treat her well. Saddles are on the wall.'

'I will.' Aldo grimaced. 'I also need some rope.'

Vincenzo's brow furrowed. 'Rope?'

'For my prisoner. He's a thief I'm taking back to the city.'

'Good. Best place for his kind.'

Massimo Bindi had a bounce in his step as he waddled towards the Podestà. Being segretario for the most powerful criminal court in Florence was all too often a task without thanks. When the Otto ably fulfilled its remit of enforcing the laws of the city, that work went unnoticed. Any praise went to the magistrates, the eight men who passed judgement over those brought before the court. The fact that those magistrates were replaced every few months, as was the Florentine custom for such courts, went ignored. The segretario was the one true constant within the Otto, the lone individual who ensured justice was both done and seen to be done . . . That truth was forgotten, or unappreciated.

But if anything went awry with the workings of the Otto, should the rule of law be under threat, or the dispensing of justice prove in some manner unsatisfactory, then it was always the segretario who suffered such accusations and recriminations. Magistrates could not be found wanting because their role was transitory. When the time came to cast blame, the segretario was the Otto incarnate.

Yet for once, just once, praise had fallen upon the person most deserving.

Bindi smiled to himself, savouring the last few days and their outcome. The Otto had dealt with a disciple of the notorious, long-dead Dominican Girolamo Savonarola. The monk had risen to prominence when Bindi was a young boy, but the segretario could still recall how the power of the monk's oratory had held sway over many in Florence. Those who followed Savonarola were initially dismissed as Piagnoni – whiners, weepers and grumblers. But they had claimed that derisive name as a badge of honour.

Soon half the city was crowding into the cathedral to hear Savonarola speak, believing his promises that if they lived a purer life Florence would become a new Jerusalem, a true city of God. The monk sent thousands of young men and boys whom he called his Fanciulli out into the streets as emissaries and messengers. Clad in white to symbolize their purity, the Fanciulli gathered alms for the poor and confronted those who gambled, profaned or committed other sins. Bindi had been of an age to join the Fanciulli but open displays of religious piety were not for him, even as a young man. He believed faith should be a private matter, not an act of public performance.

Savonarola's hold over the city culminated in a bonfire of the vanities. The Fanciulli went door to door demanding citizens surrender possessions the monk deemed sinful: masks and mirrors, cosmetics, wigs and perfume, musical instruments, books and paintings seen as heretical. A great pyramid of confiscated items was built in the Piazza della Signoria and set aflame while the Fanciulli sang hymns. But Savonarola overstepped himself and was soon excommunicated by the Pope. Within months the monk was executed by the city.

Savonarola had been dead for decades, yet his prophecies – that

Florence could become a God-fearing republic if its people cast out the Medici – still found favour with some. Not long after Cosimo de' Medici became the city's leader, he promulgated a ban on confraternities, the religious groups that did charitable works in God's name. The duke believed some of them were masks for anti-Medici factions. Most confraternities complied with the duke's will, but a few fervent followers of Savonarola's teachings still refused to be silenced. One such individual, a notary called Cristoforo da Soci, had prophesied that Florence would be freed from Medici control by the middle of May. He announced this would be preceded by famine, fire, plague and a bloody slaughter. He urged all to pray, to confess their sins, and to spread his prophecy further if they wished to save the city.

Bindi smirked as he approached the Podestà. Unfortunately, da Soci had shared his vision with a man called Guidotti, who promptly brought it to the Otto. When the segretario reported this to Cosimo, the duke ordered da Soci's immediate arrest. The notary was interrogated by torture, which Bindi personally supervised. Examination continued until the predicted day of deliverance passed without significant incident. There was a drought across the dominion, but no plague, fire, famine or slaughter. The prophecy was discredited.

Cosimo wished to avoid giving renewed life to Savonarola's legacy, and Bindi was proud of the solution he proposed to the duke: have da Soci be judged a madman by the Otto, suitable only for the scorn and ridicule of other citizens. The notary was convicted and sentenced to three years in Le Stinche, condemned to serve that time in the pazzeria, the prison's ward for lunatics. Should he survive – not true of all those held at Le Stinche, and even less so of those within the pazzeria – da Soci would be released and exiled from Florence.

The segretario had also suggested one last indignity as a warning to others: da Soci was sentenced to cerca maggiore, a punishment that saw him paraded through the streets atop an ass to suffer insults and physical abuse from watching crowds. He was whipped and birched along the way while wearing a mitred hat that bore humiliating inscriptions. His shame was abject and complete.

The entire matter had been a triumph for the Otto and, in particular, for its most esteemed segretario. That was what the duke had called Bindi in front of others the previous day: most esteemed. It was all Bindi could do to keep himself from laughing as he neared the Podestà. All those years of bowing to men who deemed themselves better than him, all the petty humiliations and indignities he had suffered in the service of the Otto and the city. All of it was worth suffering to hear such praise, to have that blessed moment.

The segretario was still smiling as he waddled into the Podestà, enjoying the chill that seemed to settle on all who entered the home of the Otto. In winter and autumn that stark cold was liable to whiten the fingers and toes until they were numb, but in spring it was a welcome escape from the sweltering streets. Come summer the Podestà might be one of the few places in Florence where afternoons were bearable. No man of sense and means stayed in the city during July and August, not unless they took pleasure from wallowing in their own sweat. It was not yet June and already the city was roasting beneath the remorseless sun.

Bindi paused in the short corridor between the main gates and the inner courtyard to dab a cloth in the folds between his chins. Walking had been unwise. He should have called his carriage for the short journey from home. But after such a triumph the previous day it seemed a shame not to—

He stopped. What was that stench, and from where was it coming?

Bindi flared his nostrils, taking in more of the fetid odour. Woodsmoke, yes, but there was something else. Something far less pleasant. Burnt meat that had remained too long on the fire and then been left in the sun to rot. The foul aroma was coming from the courtyard. It was coming from inside the Podestà!

Clamping the damp cloth over his nose and mouth, the segretario stamped towards the courtyard. Some fool was going to pay for whatever was— Bindi stopped, staring at what was choking the air in the courtyard, not certain he could believe the truth of his own eyes.

The smouldering remains of a wooden handcart stood next to the central well, greasy black smoke wafting upwards. The wheels and base of the cart were intact, but its sides appeared to have burned away. A charred mass lurked in the belly of the cart, with a wooden post toppled across it. Constables Benedetto and Manuffi stood close by, both doing their best to avoid the segretario's gaze.

Bindi snorted. They would not ignore him for long.

'Who did this?' he demanded.

Neither man replied.

'Well?' he bellowed, the word echoing around the courtyard's stone walls. Bindi knew that would bring curious eyes to the windows on the two levels above. Good. Let them be reminded of his authority. Let them know who commanded all those working in the service of the Otto. 'Speak, damn you!'

Benedetto responded first, still staring at the stones beneath his boots. 'We don't know, segretario.'

'Who is this "we"?'

The young constable frowned. He had shown some promise when joining the Otto, but that had proved as fleeting as his wits. A tendency to lay the fault for his mistakes with others and a bitter, surly streak were frailties that did not endear themselves to anyone.

Bindi doubted Benedetto would ever progress beyond a constable, and this hesitancy was not changing that doubt. 'I don't understand . . .'

The segretario sighed. 'Who brought that' – he jabbed a finger at the smoking remains of the cart – 'into my courtyard?'

'We did,' Manuffi replied, stepping forward. The other constable appeared to have less guile than a loaf of stale bread, and none of the wit. 'Strocchi told us to, sir.'

'Did he?'

Manuffi nodded, and Benedetto joined him in that. Eager to shift the blame, as usual.

'Why?' Bindi asked. It was a sensible question, but not one either man seemed able to answer. 'Very well. Where is Constable Strocchi?'

'He just left for Oltrarno,' Manuffi said. 'Something about fetching a doctor. Don't know why – the poor soul in that cart is dead as can be, if you ask me.'

'Indeed.' The segretario edged nearer the smouldering cart, but the body atop looked no better than a roasting pig that had fallen into the fire and been left to burn. A gust of wind blew smoke from the corpse into Bindi's face, forcing the aroma of cooked meat into his nostrils. He gagged, remembering the meal he had gorged on after returning from the duke's praise. That had been roast pork too . . . Bindi staggered back, clamping a hand over his mouth. 'Fetch water,' he said. 'Throw it over that mess.'

'But the fire's out,' Manuffi replied.

'It will stop the smoke,' Bindi snapped. 'Now do as I say!' He stamped to the wide stone staircase that led up to the court's administrative uffici. 'And when Strocchi returns, have him report to me immediately. Someone will answer for this indignity.'

Chapter Three

*A*ldo should have been within sight of the city's eastern gate. It was five miles at most from San Jacopo al Girone to Florence, and he was astride a well-kept horse. Even at walking pace the animal would have reached Porta la Croce by now but for the prisoner stumbling along behind it, tethered to the saddle by a generous length of rope. Lippo had complained while the rope was looped round his chest and remaining arm several times to bind him, but that was nothing compared to his incessant whining now.

'Can't we stop?' the prisoner asked. 'My feet aren't used to this punishment.'

'Should have thought of that before stealing those boots,' Aldo said.

'Look,' Lippo went on. 'The ends of my hose are worn through.'

Aldo didn't reply. It only prompted his captive to talk further. Not that Lippo needed encouragement. He had complained and questioned and cajoled all the way.

'You still haven't told me why you're working in the dominion.'

Again, Aldo kept his own counsel.

'Officers of the court stay in the city. Only constables, cowards and the corrupt get kicked out into the countryside.' Lippo left a long silence to linger, perhaps hoping that might provoke a response. Aldo had no difficulty ignoring such a strategia, having used it himself on the guilty and weak of will. 'So, which one are you?' Lippo asked.

Aldo pressed his heels into the horse a little, prompting it to increase pace.

'What are you doing?' Lippo wailed. 'I can't keep up!'

The horse trotted onwards.

'Please,' Lippo called, sounding short of breath. 'Please, I'm sorry!'

Aldo eased his pressure against the horse's sides, and it slowed to a walk again. That stopped the questions for a while, but his prisoner was soon bemoaning unjust punishments and court officers abusing their power.

'Enough,' Aldo muttered, pulling the horse to an abrupt halt. There were many things he missed about not living in Florence. The city had been his home as a boy and returning after too many years away as a soldier had made clear how much it stirred his heart. But dealing with men like Lippo was a stark reminder of the lies and self-interest that ran through Florence with a strength that rivalled the Arno in full flood. Aldo untied the rope and swung one leg over the saddle, sliding down to the ground. Retrieving the stiletto from his left boot, Aldo pointed it at Lippo. The prisoner stopped short, fear evident in his features.

'What are you going to do with that?'

'I'm giving you a choice. You can continue walking behind the horse all the way to Florence, but you'll be doing it with fresh bruises. Or you can shut your babbling mouth and ride behind me on the back of the horse until we reach the city gate. Well?'

Lippo frowned. 'Is your question a trap?'

Aldo gripped his stiletto tighter. 'Walk or ride? Which is it?'

'Ride,' Lippo replied. 'Don't think I could walk much further.' He lifted one foot, his hose hanging in tatters from the dirty, tender sole. 'See?'

'Give me one of your feet, I'll lift you up.'

'Thank you.' Lippo shuffled to stand alongside the horse. 'But . . . aren't you going to untie me first? How will I ride behind you with my arm still bound?'

'Easily.' Aldo made a stirrup of his hands. Lippo put one foot into the cupped palms. 'Get ready,' Aldo said, crouching a little before hoisting Lippo up and across to the horse's back behind the saddle – belly first. That forced the wind from the prisoner, leaving him no air for protesting. Aldo looped the rope over Lippo and the end swung back beneath the horse. A quick knot to the saddle strap tied the prisoner down, face-first.

Aldo strolled round the horse to look at Lippo. He was crimson, panting and puffing, still struggling for breath. 'Comfortable?' Unable to speak, Lippo spat instead but missed his target. 'Good.' Aldo climbed back atop the horse and snapped the reins, urging it into a canter. He could feel Lippo bouncing behind him, each jolt bringing another curse.

Strocchi paused outside the open door. The last time he had come to Dr Orvieto's home in the Jewish commune, a young man had died when Strocchi pursued him. It was a sad end and not one of Strocchi's making, but he still carried a measure of guilt for it. Confession had soothed some of it away but returning here brought back those nagging doubts. There was another reason for hesitating, but Strocchi didn't want to think about that now.

Duties for the Otto often took him across the Arno to the city's southern quarter, but few gave him reason to visit via dei Giudei. Most of the Jews in Florence lived in humble homes along this dirt road, little more than a narrow alley leading away from the river. Moneylending or working with textiles were the usual trades for Jews, but it had become popular for wealthy merchants to have Jewish physicians tend their family's illnesses.

Aldo had found a different use for Dr Orvieto, employing his skills and knowledge as a physician to assess how and when a body was killed. Several times those talents had helped the Otto solve crimes that might otherwise have proven beyond the court. Strocchi was uncertain if Orvieto would be able or willing to assist with what remained of the corpse burned inside the cart, but it could not hinder the investigation to ask. Better to use all the tools to hand, Strocchi's papa had often said, than fail for want of trying.

A young woman emerged from the doorway, carrying a small pot of what looked like salve. There was something familiar about her face . . .

'May I help you?' she asked.

'I've come to see Dr Orvieto,' Strocchi replied.

'He's seeing a patient, but they are nearly done. You can go in.'

'Grazie.' He stood aside to let her pass, but could not resist asking a question. 'Excuse me, but have we met before?'

She paused, her brow furrowing. 'Perhaps. My name is Rebecca Levi.' The young woman held up the pot. 'I must deliver this to someone. Good day.' She strolled away, whistling a cheerful tune. It was only when she was out of sight that Strocchi recalled their previous encounter. Aldo had investigated the murder of Rebecca's father two winters past, and Strocchi had met her briefly when the killer was revealed. She seemed much happier now. Strocchi was grateful she did not remember the circumstances of their last meeting.

He stepped inside the doctor's home, removing his cap. Light spilled from a room at the end of the corridor. It was Orvieto's home, but he saw patients here too. 'Hello?'

'Keep coming,' a male voice called. 'I'm at the back.'

Strocchi did as he was told, venturing along the dim corridor. At the other end he found Orvieto in an examining room lined by shelves and cabinets laden with bottles and jars, exotic names etched into each of them. A wooden table occupied much of the room's centre, plain chairs positioned around it. The doctor was tending to a young girl sitting on one of the chairs, her knees scraped and bloody. A concerned woman wearing a simple brown dress, a shawl covering her hair, glared at Strocchi. She whispered in words he did not recognize. Hebrew, perhaps? The language had a kind of music when she spoke.

'I'm sorry,' Strocchi said. 'I can come back.'

Orvieto looked up from where he was kneeling by the girl. Like other men of his faith the doctor wore a skullcap, in his case atop brown hair streaked by silver. Orvieto's fulsome beard had autumn shades of red and brown, while his eyes were a warm hazel with no hint of fear or anger in his gaze. 'Please, wait. I'm almost done here.' He murmured reassurance to the mother and her girl while cleaning the wounds. 'She fell while playing,' the doctor explained to Strocchi. 'But these things heal soon enough.'

The constable noted how good Orvieto was with the child. She must be seven or eight, with a friendly face that resembled her mother's in all but attitude. The girl carried no suspicion in her yet, no reason to fear the unknown. Strocchi hoped his Bianca would know that same happiness growing up. Being the parent of an infant seemed a battle between exhaustion, worry and wishing. He did not doubt the years to come would be harder still. May my child know happiness, he prayed every night. Let her know peace. He did not doubt the Jewish mother felt the same about her daughter, though she followed a different faith.

Orvieto finished his work and ushered the pair out before

returning to wash his hands in a bowl. 'Constable . . . Strocchi, isn't it? You came here once, with Cesare.'

'With Aldo, that's right.'

The doctor reached for a cloth. 'How can I help?'

Strocchi explained what had been found in the Piazza della Signoria. 'I know it is asking a lot, but could you come to the Podestà and examine the remains? There is not much to see, and what is left will not be pleasant. But we need to know how this poor soul died if we are to find who killed him.' When Orvieto did not reply at once, Strocchi found himself babbling on. 'I know that Aldo – Cesare – considered you a man of insight before he left the city. If you could help us . . .'

Orvieto smiled. 'Of course. I would be happy to assist. Patients are fewer as summer approaches, so long as disease does not take hold of the city. Should I come now?'

'Yes, thank you.'

The doctor removed his apron, resting it on the back of a chair. 'You look tired, constable. Have you been having trouble sleeping?'

'I have a little daughter, Bianca. When she does not sleep, neither do we.'

Orvieto nodded. 'Has this been a problem for long?'

'Since she was born, in November.'

'That makes her about six months old.' The doctor went to a small chest atop a nearby bench and pulled out a short piece of paper rolled into a narrow cylinder, twisted shut at both ends. 'Are you feeding her anything besides mother's milk yet?'

'Tomasia is trying the bambina with small pieces of fruit and vegetables.'

'A good idea, your daughter is probably ready for that. Now, there is powder in this paper. Sprinkle a few grains of it on some soft fruit near her last feed of the day. That will help Bianca sleep a little more, and then you will not be quite so exhausted.'

Strocchi took the powder, slipping it inside his tunic. 'Thank you.'

The doctor wrote a brisk message on a scrap of paper and folded that in two before placing it by a candlestick on the table. 'A note for my new student,' Orvieto said. 'She's making a delivery for me.'

'I met her on the doorstep,' Strocchi said. 'Rebecca?'

Orvieto nodded. 'I was reluctant to apprentice her, but I am not getting any younger and people along this street will need a physician when I stop. The other Jewish doctors spend most of their time tending wealthy merchants across the river. The pay is certainly better, but our people still require a healer. Now, shall we go see these remains? I have limited experience with burnt bodies but may be able to offer you some small assistance.'

Bindi struggled up the stone staircase inside Palazzo Medici. Each morning he was required as segretario of the Otto to report on cases coming before the court, any changes in the number of those incarcerated at Le Stinche, and the state of any current investigations. Florence's previous leader had paid little attention to such reports. Before his death Alessandro de' Medici had preferred lounging in an ornate gold chair while his cousin Lorenzino whispered snide remarks, rather than giving any heed to Bindi.

The new duke could not be more different. Cosimo was not yet nineteen but – at least to Bindi's eyes – showed an attention to detail that his predecessor had sorely lacked. Within months of being elected leader of the city, Cosimo had crushed an army raised by rebellious exiles in the countryside, executing or imprisoning the ringleaders. His offer to wed Alessandro's widow – the illegitimate daughter of the Holy Roman Emperor, no less – had been rejected, but Charles V did agree that Cosimo could officially be called Duke of Florence. That pleased Cosimo's mother, the formidable Maria Salviati, who had devoted herself to preparing him for leadership. Once that was achieved, she had stepped back into the shadows, content to see the new duke rule. There were rumours about her health, whisperings that she was far from well these days. But Bindi gave such gossip little heed.

Meanwhile, the loudest voices in the city's Senate, men who believed they could manipulate the young Medici as they might a puppet, had learned the strength of Cosimo's resolve. Francesco Guicciardini soon retired to his country villa to write, while others of his standing had died or been diminished. In place of such men a new Florence was emerging, one built on bureaucracy and careful administration. This was an approach Bindi appreciated, one that took power from those who served their own needs and placed it in the hands of those who put the city first. The segretario had seen Florence suffer from fools and folly, siege and savagery. Now, at long last, it seemed she might be nearing a period of stability. If that proved true, nothing would make him happier.

The prospect of upsetting that careful equilibrium did not please Bindi. But he could not hide what had happened in Piazza della Signoria. The duke had spies secreted across the city, keeping him apprised of anything that might imperil Florence or his leadership. Better to bring ill news to Cosimo at the earliest opportunity and assuage whatever anger that provoked. A reed bending with the wind rarely broke in Bindi's experience, while the branch that could not bend would be torn asunder when a storm came. He had to hope Cosimo was not in a mood for storms and tempests this morning.

Francesco Campana was waiting by the double doors to the

duke's private ufficio, clad in the traditional black gown of an administrator. Reserved in his manner and plain of face, Campana was private segretario to the duke. The fact that Campana had kept his position within the palazzo after Cosimo's election said much about his skills and importance.

'You're late,' Campana said, a rebuke in his quiet words.

'There was an – incident overnight. One requiring my attention at the Podestà.'

'The fire in Piazza della Signoria?'

As Bindi feared, word had already reached Palazzo Medici. 'Yes.'

'Very well.' Campana ushered Bindi into the ufficio. The elaborate carved table and golden throne favoured by Alessandro were long gone, replaced by a plain chair and simple table. Cosimo was sitting next to the table, its surface covered in reports and other documents. This was now a place of work, not a room for frivolity. Campana went to the duke's side, whispering in one ear. Cosimo looked up, beckoning Bindi closer.

'What do we know about this person who was burned in the piazza?' the duke asked.

Bindi fought an urge to sigh. A few hours before, he had been the Otto's most esteemed segretario. That glorious moment was gone; now he was the bearer of ill news. 'Very little,' Bindi said. 'Nothing, in fact, beyond a report that the body may have been stripped to its underclothes and the scalp shaved before being set ablaze.' Strocchi had not returned to the Podestà by the time Bindi was due to make his report to the duke, forcing the segretario to question Benedetto and Manuffi further for the little they knew.

'Was there anything to indicate why this was done?'

'Not that my men have yet uncovered. It is perhaps an idle killing, or some petty vendetta enacted in the piazza, but I suspect something else is at work here.' Bindi relayed how the burnt cart, gibbet and body had been moved to the Podestà for private examination.

Campana cleared his throat. 'Your Grace, may I . . . ?' Cosimo gave a brisk gesture of assent. 'You said this man was stripped of outer clothes and shaved?'

'One of the constables who found the burning body believes so,' Bindi said.

Cosimo frowned. 'Is that significant?'

'In the past,' Campana replied, 'when a priest or friar was executed for sinning, they were first stripped of outer clothes and their scalps shaved. It was called "degradation".'

'You're suggesting this victim may have been a man of faith.'

'Perhaps.'

Something was scratching at Bindi's reason, clawing at him for attention. He had witnessed what Campana described, many years ago . . . 'Tell me, what is today's date?'

'The date?' Cosimo responded.

'Yes,' Bindi said. He should know it without asking, but the knowledge had abandoned him momentarily. 'What is it?'

'May the twenty-third in the year of Our Lord fifteen thirty-eight,' Campana said.

Bindi grimaced. Then this was no idle killing, and no petty vendetta. Whoever was responsible for burning that man in the piazza was making a statement for all to see.

'Why does that . . .?' Campana's words trailed away. 'Of course.'

Cosimo glared at his counsellor. 'What? What does today's date signify?'

Bindi answered for Campana. 'On this precise date Girolamo Savonarola and two other Dominican monks were brought out from the Palazzo della Signoria. Each man was degraded before being hung in the centre of the piazza. Their bodies were burned while still on the gibbet to ensure there was nothing left but ash.' Bindi had been among the thousands who witnessed Savonarola's end. Women wept and wailed as the monk burned. Afterwards the ashes were taken on a cart to the Arno and tipped into the river so no fragments were left that could be claimed as relics of the martyred.

'The execution took place in 1498,' Campana added. 'Forty years ago today.'

Cosimo sank back in his chair. 'That cannot be happenstance. Using the same means, the same method, in the same place . . . This was intentional. But who would do such a thing?' The young duke rubbed a hand across the thin brown beard he was growing. 'Could it be retaliation by followers of Savonarola for what the Otto did to da Soci?'

'Perhaps,' Bindi conceded. 'But to undertake such an elaborate killing in the centre of Florence . . . it seems an extreme response.'

'Indeed, but that should still be investigated,' Cosimo said. 'Better to be certain of the facts than rely on mere opinion. If it was not followers of Savonarola, who else might do this?'

'Whoever they are, the men of the Otto will find them,' the segretario replied, 'you can be certain of that.' Bindi chose his words carefully to avoid making the pledge his own personal promise. Should the officers and constables fall short, better it be a collective failure than one on which his own reputation depended.

'Make sure they do,' the duke said. 'And tell them to make haste. Hanging and burning a man in front of the Palazzo della Signoria is a calculated attack in the heart of our city. But such an act on this date . . . Whoever is responsible wants people to link this killing to Savonarola's execution, perhaps even to his prophecies that Florence would one day become a republic again.

Word will be spread by fair means or foul, of that we can be certain. When it does, men like da Soci may be the least of our troubles.' Cosimo returned to his papers.

Realizing he was dismissed, Bindi bowed as low as his rotund belly allowed before departing. In the past he would have given this matter to Aldo, an irksome officer with a skill for solving mysteries that defied the wit of others. But the fool had chosen to leave the city, volunteering to bolster the Otto's law enforcement in the dominion.

Someone else would have to take his place for this investigation.

Aldo climbed from the saddle as his borrowed horse approached Porta la Croce. The city wall stretched away from the east gate in either direction, south towards the Arno and north towards the hills. Aldo untethered Lippo and pulled him down off the horse. 'You bastardo,' Lippo spat. 'That nearly killed me.'

'You're still alive,' Aldo replied. He walked the horse and captive through the gate, giving his name to the guards. After stabling the horse near the city wall, Aldo marched Lippo south past the convent of Le Murate before turning west. It was not far to Le Stinche or the Podestà, but Lippo did all he could to delay their arrival. He stopped by the stone statue of a lion guarding the main entrance to the church of Santa Croce, legs crumpling beneath him.

'Please, I can't go any further,' Lippo whined. 'Coming all that way strapped across the horse's back ... I'll be black and blue tomorrow. Let me rest a minute here. Please.'

Aldo retreated to the side of the church, getting out of the relentless sun. Not yet June and already the days were uncomfortably hot. He had forgotten how hot it could be in the city, all the stone reflecting the warmth until walking during the day was akin to being inside an oven. Movement across the street caught Aldo's eye. A maid was closing shutters on the middle level of a once-grand residence, no doubt to block out the worst of the day's heat. Aldo did not recognize her, yet Palazzo Fioravanti was all too familiar. He had spent his first twelve years there, brought up as a member of the famiglia despite being born illegitimate. But he was cast out before his father's body was cold, exiled by a step-mother who resented him. No, resented wasn't strong enough. Lucrezia Fioravanti hated him: who he was, what he was, and whom he loved. He had long vowed not to step inside the palazzo again until she was dead, but made the mistake of breaking that promise a year ago. Lucrezia despised him still. If anything, her venom was stronger than ever. The vicious old strega clung to life with a tenacity Aldo might admire in another person. But not her.

'Enough,' he said, returning to Lippo and pulling the prisoner to his feet. 'You have a choice to make. I can take you to Le Stinche and let the inmates welcome you back. Or we can go on to the Podestà, where you can rot in a cell till the court gets to your case. Stay long enough, you might be one of those released to mark the feast day of St John the Baptist.'

'That isn't until the end of June,' Lippo protested.

Aldo shrugged. 'What's it to be?'

The thief studied him. 'Is there another option?'

The snare was set. Time to see if the quarry would take the bait . . .

'Perhaps,' Aldo said. 'I might let you go—'

'That sounds promising,' Lippo cut in.

'—if you say why you were watching Ruggerio's villa. Here. Now.'

The thief frowned. 'Whose villa?'

'Don't bother pretending. We both know that is Ruggerio's

country home. You weren't there to steal some boots and a capon, otherwise you would have left once you had them. There was another reason why you introduced yourself to Cassandra: you were studying the building. Looking for ways in and out, seeing if any other servants were in the villa besides the housekeeper. Now, are you going to tell me the truth?'

Lippo shook his head, features a picture of puzzlement. 'I don't know what you're—'

'Enough lying,' Aldo sighed. 'Either you were planning to rob that villa, or assessing it as a target for somebody else. Ruggerio wouldn't leave anything of value in his country home when he isn't there. That suggests you were studying the villa for someone else. Who?'

The thief put his single hand over his heart. 'God be my judge, I have no notion of what you are talking about. Truthfully, you have this wrong.'

Aldo glared at Lippo. 'Rotting in a cell at the Podestà it is. Move.' He shoved the thief out into Piazza Santa Croce, the blazing midday sunshine baking the expansive square.

'But you said you'd let me go,' the thief complained.

'If you explained why you were watching the villa.' Another push kept Lippo moving forwards. The piazza was emptying, people going home to escape the worst of the day's heat.

'I did tell you!'

'You lied, as usual.'

'That's not fair—'

'You lie more often than the politicians in the Senate,' Aldo said.

'I resent being compared to politicians,' Lippo retorted. 'I have some honour.'

'What, honour amongst thieves? Only a fool believes that. A

smart thief, one who cares more for his own skin than those paying him to take risks, would make a deal.'

Lippo slowed as they reached the far side of the piazza. 'If I give you names – if I have any names to give – you'll let me go, here in the city?'

'I would have done, if you told me when I asked. But that was then. Now we're going to the Podestà.' He grabbed Lippo by the arm and marched him away from the piazza.

'I can still give you names,' Lippo offered.

'Feel free. But you'll be spending tonight in a cell. Consider it a punishment for keeping me up all night watching for you at the villa.'

'I didn't know you were there. I wouldn't have taken the job if I'd—' The thief stopped but the words had already escaped his mouth.

'So you were working for someone else,' Aldo said. It had been a suspicion before, one that fitted the facts but lacked supporting evidence. Now he had the start of a confession.

Chapter Four

When Strocchi escorted Dr Orvieto into the Podestà the smouldering cart was missing from the courtyard, only a few charred pieces of wood remaining by the well. But black wheel marks led them to a large storage room beneath the courtyard's internal staircase. Strocchi paused at the heavy wooden door. 'Have you seen burnt bodies before?'

Orvieto grimaced. 'Once, many years ago. A husband driven mad by grief set himself on fire. It was . . .' The doctor shook his head. 'Open the door. Let us see what is inside.'

Strocchi turned a sturdy metal key in the lock and pulled at the latch. Greasy smoke billowed out, forcing him back several paces. Santo Spirito, the stench! Wood and metal and meat, all cooked together, as if the storage room was some unholy oven belching its foul fumes into the world. Strocchi turned away, gasping for air not tainted by what was inside.

Orvieto clasped a sleeve over his nose and mouth. 'I'll need a lantern to make a full examination. Probably two.' Strocchi went to fetch them, grateful to escape the aroma of cooking flesh. When he returned, the doctor was inside, studying the grisly remains of the man and cart. 'Thank you,' Orvieto said. 'Now, what do we have here?' Strocchi watched as long as he could but the acrid stench inside was too much, making him cough and cough . . . 'You don't have to stay with me,' Orvieto murmured. 'Why don't you wait in the courtyard? But please, don't close the door on your way out.'

Strocchi stumbled from the dank chamber, still coughing. It was as if one of those burnt fingers was in his mouth, charred skin stretching down into his throat, rasping. He sank to the ground, a thin stream of bile bursting from him.

'Carlo? Carlo, are you all right?'

Strocchi twisted to see a figure hurrying towards him, concern on that familiar face: Aldo. 'It will pass,' Strocchi gasped between spasms, struggling to keep hold of what was left inside him. He held up a hand to stop the officer coming any closer.

Aldo did as he was bid. 'Very well.'

Strocchi wiped a hand across his mouth, wishing for water to wash away – no, best not think about that. He got to one knee, easing himself upwards while studying Aldo. The officer's tunic and hose were dusty. Living in the dominion had coloured his inquisitive features, sun and time etching the wrinkles round his eyes deeper. 'Why are you here?'

Aldo tilted his head towards a forlorn figure across the courtyard, rope bound tight around the man's chest and single arm. 'Caught Lippo stealing from a villa above San Jacopo al Girone. Seems he was studying the residence for someone else.' Aldo sniffed the air, his eyes following the cart tracks into the nearby storeroom. 'And you?'

'There was a murder.' Strocchi gave as few details as he could, not wanting to invite any involvement. But Aldo couldn't help himself.

'Doubtful that whoever did it pushed the cart far,' he said. 'They would have risked being heard or meeting one of the night patrols. Those responsible probably used a nearby stable to store the cart and build the gibbet, away from curious eyes but still close to the square. Has anyone searched the alleys near Piazza della Signoria?'

Strocchi cursed under his breath. 'Not yet.'

Aldo rubbed a hand across his greying stubble. 'If you need—'

'No,' Strocchi cut in. He forced a smile. 'You have your own investigation to pursue.'

The officer nodded. 'Indeed.'

'Cesare?' Dr Orvieto emerged from the storeroom, a smile spreading across his face. 'I thought that was your voice. What are you doing back in the city?'

'Business for the Otto,' Aldo replied. 'I take it you're helping Carlo.'

'Yes,' the doctor said. 'Would you like to see? This is quite fascinating.'

Strocchi cleared his throat, glaring at Aldo.

The officer shook his head at Orvieto. 'Sorry, no. I have other matters that need my attention.' He nodded to Strocchi. 'Best of luck with your investigation.' Aldo turned away, marching towards the forlorn figure bound with rope.

The doctor turned to Strocchi. 'Are you recovered?'

'Yes. It was the smell, I couldn't—'

'Of course.' Orvieto gestured to the storage room. 'Shall I show you what I've—'

'Where is Strocchi?' a voice bellowed across the courtyard.

There was no mistaking who was shouting, nor the anger in his words. Bindi was unhappy and when he was unhappy, others suffered too.

'I had best discover what the segretario wants,' Strocchi told Orvieto. 'I'll return as soon as I can. Please, continue with your examination.'

* * *

Bindi waited until he was behind his imposing table and lowering himself into the sturdy, tall-backed chair before replying to the knock at his door. 'Who is it?'

'Strocchi,' the constable replied.

'Enter,' Bindi commanded. He watched Strocchi come in, dutifully closing the door behind him. Little more than a year ago, the constable had seemed a good son of the Tuscan countryside but too callow and trusting to succeed in the service of the Otto. While Strocchi remained youthful of face, his attitude had hardened. He now carried the suspicion necessary to enforce laws and intimidate criminals. Someone or something had betrayed his trusting nature, Bindi supposed. The segretario did not care who or how or why, but the scarring made Strocchi a better weapon for the court.

'I have good news,' Bindi said, enjoying the confusion this caused in Strocchi's face. 'You are being promoted from constable to officer. It is unusual in one so young, but the Podestà has been short of officers and you have shown – potential.'

Strocchi did not reply, remaining as still as a statue.

'Well? Have you nothing to say?' Bindi asked.

'Forgive me, segretario,' the new officer replied, shaking his head. 'I was not . . . I thought . . . Thank you, sir. Thank you.'

'You may not be so grateful when I have finished,' the segretario continued. 'This killing in the Piazza della Signoria, I am putting you in charge of the investigation. You will be responsible for finding whoever committed such a foul murder in our city. Duke Cosimo already knows what happened and is expecting swift justice. Understand?'

Strocchi's features paled as he nodded. Yes, he understood. If the culprits were found soon enough, all credit for that would go to the Otto – and to its most esteemed segretario. Should Strocchi fail, he would be the one to shoulder the blame.

Bindi gave a brief summary of what he had discussed with the Duke and Campana, the significance of the day's date. Strocchi had seen twenty-two summers at most. Even if he were a native son of Florence, Strocchi was too young to know much about Savonarola's execution forty years earlier. 'You should also determine whether followers of Savonarola are involved in this. I have my doubts, but the duke wants those who believe in Savonarola's teachings to be investigated.'

Strocchi nodded again.

'Any questions?'

'No, sir.'

'Very well,' Bindi concluded. 'You may go.' The new officer stumbled away, wiping both hands on the sides of his hose as he departed. Bindi waited until Strocchi was at the door before calling out. 'One more thing.' Strocchi paused. 'Find a place away from the Podestà where that burned body can be kept, at least until his name is known. I don't want it in my building a moment longer. And make sure you are back here well before curfew to give me a full briefing so I can report your progress to His Grace the next morning. You will do that every evening until this matter is settled. The duke is not a patient man, nor am I. Bear that in mind as you hunt those responsible for this abhorrent crime.'

There was much Aldo missed about Florence, so much of the city that his new life in the dominion could never replace. But being at the beckoning of the bloated, self-important Bindi was not among those losses and regrets. He certainly did not envy anyone the task of satisfying the whims of the segretario.

When Strocchi had trudged up the wide stone staircase to the

Otto's administrative area, Aldo crossed the courtyard to the storage area where he had seen Saul. The doctor was still inside, examining the burnt remains of a corpse. The aroma reminded Aldo of the capon Lippo had been roasting so ineptly the previous night.

'Cesare,' Saul said, a smile warming his kind face despite the grisly task in front of him. 'Have you come to see for yourself?'

'Yes, but don't tell Strocchi. He won't appreciate you letting me in here.' Aldo slipped inside the storage area to study what was left of the charred body.

'I didn't expect to see you for another month,' Saul said.

'Nor I you.' Aldo reached across the cart to clasp the doctor's hands. Murder had first brought them together, and now another killing had done so again. They both preferred the company of men, something that was a sin to most and a crime to others. Yet Aldo had been drawn to Saul, and the doctor to him. They could not live together, not while Aldo was an officer of the court nor while Saul tended to his people's needs. Aldo transferring out into the dominion had kept them even further apart, but when they were able to meet . . .

A gruff voice shouted in the courtyard, and Saul withdrew his hands. 'Will I see you later?' the doctor asked. 'Or do you have to leave the city before curfew?'

'All being well you'll see me tonight,' Aldo said. 'I must go before Strocchi returns.' He leaned over the cart to kiss Saul before hurrying out of the storage room. Striding from the Podestà he turned south in the early afternoon sun, heading towards Piazza della Signoria. What had happened wasn't his case to investigate, but Aldo still wanted to see for himself. It couldn't hurt to visit some of the stables close to the piazza, could it?

* * *

Strocchi stumbled down the stone staircase to the Podestà courtyard, still struggling to grasp what had happened. He was an officer now, no longer a lowly constable. The promotion he had craved for more than a year was his at last. So why did it taste so bitter, as if served in a cup brimming with hemlock? The segretario's delight was part of it, so pleased was he to pass on the burden of finding the killer. Yet Bindi offered little guidance and nobody to help with the task. Strocchi had little experience in such matters, and even less in leading other men. Some of the other constables would be happy about him becoming an officer, but many would resent it. The chances of solving the murder seemed slender.

Seeing Aldo had shaken him too. The officer had departed the previous summer, announcing he wished to enforce the laws of the Otto outside the city walls. In truth it was Strocchi who had driven Aldo away after discovering what the officer was capable of, what kind of man he was. The few times they had met since had been as awkward as earlier. Strocchi had considered Aldo a mentor until discovering the truth of him. Now conscience and guilt were a swollen river between them, without a bridge either man could or would cross.

The urge to find Aldo was strong, to seek his counsel on how to discover who had killed the man burned in the cart. But Strocchi could not bring himself to do so. He might be guilty of pride, but there were worse sins and Aldo was guilty of too many of them.

Strocchi returned to the storage room, clasping a hand across his nose and mouth before going inside. Orvieto was rolling the charred corpse over atop the cart so the body was lying on its back. The doctor had removed what was left of the victim's clothes, revealing the roasted torso and limbs. 'What was done to this poor soul . . .' Orvieto said. 'I've never seen such brutality. It is possible he was still alive when the cart was set ablaze.'

'The men who found him said he was hanged from the gibbet.'

'He was tied to the gibbet,' the doctor agreed, 'but it was not a hanging.' He pointed to the burnt skin around the corpse's neck. 'If there had been a rope taut round his neck, the burns on the skin here would be less severe. The flames would have to burn away the rope before they could reach the neck behind it.'

Orvieto held a lantern above the body to better illuminate it. Strocchi leaned closer to peer at the neck. He could see no difference in the damage done by the fire.

'This is supposition on my part, but I think the gibbet was . . . for show,' Orvieto continued. 'It held him upright while he burned, but nothing more. Whoever did this wanted it to look as if the victim was hanged and then set on fire. But no, this was not a hanging.'

'He could have been killed before all of this,' Strocchi said, looking at the cart.

'True,' the doctor agreed. 'But have a look in the mouth and below the nose.' He opened the dead man's mouth so Strocchi could see inside. It was blackened, the tongue like a flap of cooked meat. Two channels below the nostrils ran into the victim's moustache. 'I'm no expert, but it appears he breathed in smoke and heat. To do that . . .'

'He must still have been alive when the fire was lit,' Strocchi concluded. Why would a murderer go to such elaborate lengths? Bindi had said the killing could be linked to the execution of Savonarola forty years ago. The doctor's examination seemed to confirm that. The gibbet, setting the victim ablaze . . . It was all a stratagemma to make this barbaric murder appear like the killing of the Dominican monk. 'What else can you tell me?'

'Not much – the fire burnt away most of the signs I would seek, and it seems someone later threw water over what was left in the cart, probably to douse any remaining flames. But I can say the victim had seen more than fifty summers, judging by his greying hair and the sag of his belly. He had eaten well, and I found no callouses on his hands. More likely a merchant than a worker.' Orvieto paused. 'You mentioned a possibility that this man's scalp was shaved not long before the fire.' Orvieto pointed to angry red lines on the head. 'These scrapes and cuts confirm it. The shaving was quick and awkward, the hair removed with a dull blade. I doubt the victim shaved himself. He would have struggled to reach the back of his own scalp. No, this was done by another hand, and in haste.'

Strocchi nodded. It was all useful, but added little to what he knew and did even less to help name the dead man. The reason why this man was chosen to die in such an obscene way remained elusive. Was he picked at random, or did his death signify something else beyond echoing the execution of Savonarola? 'Anything else?'

'Yes,' Orvieto said. 'He has green eyes. I haven't seen that often, so it should make discovering his name easier. Now, help me roll him over.'

Strocchi had no wish to get any nearer to the victim but refused to be afraid of a dead body. The first touch was shocking. He let go, stepping back to make the sign of the cross. 'Sorry,' Strocchi whispered. 'I hadn't expected the body to be . . .'

'Still warm.' The doctor nodded. 'The fire roasted his skin and flesh. I'm not sure I'll be eating meat for some time. Take a firm grip and roll him towards me.' Strocchi did as he was told, breathing through his mouth to keep the stench from his nostrils. Orvieto pointed to two thick bruises on the back of the victim's skull.

'He was struck with something heavy, probably a cudgel, to silence him.'

'Could that have happened when the body and gibbet fell into the cart?'

'Corpses don't often get new bruises, because the blood stops moving,' Orvieto replied, 'but bruises made before death can become more apparent after death. You can roll him back again, constable.'

Strocchi lowered the body. 'Actually, I've just been made an officer.'

'Mazel tov! Cesare often says you will make an outstanding officer of the court,' the doctor said. 'But . . . you don't seem that pleased by your promotion.'

'Nothing is as simple as you might hope,' Strocchi agreed. 'Not in this city.'

You approach the heavy wooden doors of the palazzo, weapons in your grasp. A hammer, a handful of sturdy nails, and a scroll of thick paper. You glance around but nobody is watching, nobody paying attention. The sun has reached its highest point, the searing heat driving indoors all those who might notice you. Your cloak is wool, too much for such a warm day, sweat soaking beneath your arms. But the shadow of its hood helps hide your face. Better you are not seen, not yet.

You stop at the door, hands trembling as they unfurl the scroll. You press it flat against the wood, a nail between two fingers. You hammer it through the paper and into the door, fixing one corner there. Another nail, and the top corners are in place. Your hand slides down, unrolling the lower half of the paper. Two more nails, and it is done.

You step back to admire the words, the bold declaration they make:

FRATE
SAVONAROLA
LIVES!

Chapter Five

*A*ldo spent two fruitless hours in the many alleyways that joined Piazza della Signoria, knocking at doors and stable entrances. It had seemed simple when he suggested this task to Strocchi, but the truth was more complicated. As the city's largest public square, the piazza was joined by numerous streets and alleys. Aldo started in those near the imposing Palazzo della Signoria, grateful for the shade in narrow passageways between buildings. But most people had retreated to their homes, escaping the heat. That meant few replies.

Despairing of his efforts, Aldo was ready to admit it was a lost cause when he heard a door opening behind him. A burly man was emerging from a stable, a sack under one arm, muttering and cursing to himself. 'Something wrong?' Aldo asked.

'Yes, but I shouldn't be surprised,' the man replied. He was sweating through his dull green tunic, brown curls plastered across his pate. 'Rented out my stable to some stranger for two weeks. Said he wanted to keep his horse near the piazza. Don't know what he's been doing, but no horse has been in there.'

'Can I see?'

The man's eyes narrowed. 'Why do you care?'

Aldo introduced himself as an officer of the Otto, not mentioning his jurisdiction was now outside the city walls. 'If the person who rented your stable broke the law, you might be helping us to bring them before the court. There could even be a reward.'

That changed the owner's attitude. He announced himself as Pietro Martegli, landlord and faithful citizen of Florence. Aldo had little interest in Martegli's lengthy complaints about finding trustworthy people to rent his stable but nodded along while the landlord reopened the doors. 'When did this tenant rent your stable?'

'A week ago. Paid both weeks in advance.'

'Did he give a name? Could you describe him to the court, if necessary?'

Martegli shook his head. 'Never met him. He sent a messenger with a letter and coin. Before you ask, no, I don't have the letter with me. Think I burnt it.' He pulled open the doors, revealing what was inside.

Aldo was not surprised Martegli had difficulty renting his stable. The cramped space did not deserve the name, and any horse kept here would be the worse for it. The ceiling was low, the floor was rough dirt without hay and there was no obvious source of water. The only light came in through the doorway where they were standing.

But there was evidence here.

Someone had left a scattering of thick nails in the dirt alongside a hammer. Rope coiled against a wall, its end fraying where someone had used a knife to cut it. Crimson spots in the dirt caught Aldo's gaze. He moved inside, knees creaking as he crouched to study the red circles. Blood. Not much, but it could easily have come from the victim. Looking back at the entrance, Aldo could see wheel marks in the dirt leading outside. Yes, this was where the cart had been, where the victim was tied to the cart. This was where it began.

'Did you find anything else in here?' Aldo asked.

'No,' Martegli replied, shaking his head. But the response was too quick, too certain. The landlord had been clutching a sack when he'd first emerged from the stable.

Aldo stood up. 'What are you holding behind your back?'

Martegli licked his lips. 'Nothing.'

'Show me.'

The landlord lingered in the doorway, looking left and right as if contemplating an escape. Aldo marched to Martegli, twisting him round to reveal the sack grasped in a clammy fist. Aldo tore it free, emptying the contents onto the dirt: a richly embroidered silk tunic, a velvet cap with sparkling plumage sewn into the fabric, and a purse full of coin.

'I-I-I wasn't stealing it,' the landlord stammered. 'I was going to take it to the Podestà.' He made the sign of the cross. 'As God is my witness.'

Aldo slapped Martegli's hands aside. 'Why is it the worst hypocrites always invoke the Almighty when you catch them thieving and fornicating?' He picked up the tunic, stepping into the scorching afternoon sunshine to better examine it. The garment was made of finest blue silk with exquisite stitching, while the pattern embroidered across the tunic was distinctive. Palle! Aldo knew only one merchant who sold silk with this pattern: Girolamo Ruggerio. The emblem was that of the Company of Santa Maria, a confraternity that had once had considerable influence with the Church. Ruggerio had been a leading figure in the confraternity for years, using its charitable endeavours as a shield for his own ends.

Aldo dismissed Martegli, confiscating the pouch of coin as a fine for the attempted theft. Once the grumbling landlord had departed, Aldo took a last look around the stable. There was no sign of the hair shaved from the victim's scalp, but it had probably been burned with everything else in the cart. The blade used for the shaving was gone too, presumably taken by the killer. Aldo shut the stable door and set off west at a brisk march, despite the heat.

Having seen the corpse, Aldo knew it wasn't that of Ruggerio. The silk merchant prided himself on being thin and certainly never wore a moustache or beard. But whoever had died in the piazza did so after being stripped of clothes bearing the emblem of the Company of Santa Maria. That meant the victim must be among Ruggerio's brethren. This should make it easy to determine who had been murdered, but Ruggerio never gave away anything without gaining a greater benefit for himself. Fortunately, Aldo had a morsel he could trade, something more valuable to Ruggerio than silk, coin or other worldly goods: information.

Strocchi wasted valuable time seeking somewhere willing to accept the burned body, at least temporarily. Eventually he persuaded the nuns at Santa Maria Nuovo to take the remains into the care of their ospedale. Strocchi rented a fresh cart for removing the body from the Podestà. Once that was done, he reluctantly prepared for a visit to Le Stinche. Few people went to the prison willingly, but Strocchi knew it was the simplest way to determine whether the murder was linked to da Soci's incarceration.

He was about to leave the Podestà when a constable burst into the courtyard, shouting to anyone who would listen that Savonarola was alive. It took a while to get any sense from the man, a pot-bellied newcomer called Macci. By then the segretario had waddled downstairs to see who was causing so much noise.

Macci said he had stepped in to stop a violent brawl between two men. One insisted he had seen an official proclamation announcing Savonarola was alive. A much older man was adamant he had witnessed the Dominican monk's execution long ago, so it was impossible for Savonarola to be alive. Macci found the proclamation nearby, at a palazzo close to the Arno. People were gathered around the entrance, arguing about a piece of paper nailed to the doors.

'I can only read a little,' Macci admitted, 'but I have enough letters to understand the words "Savonarola lives!" He looked at the segretario. 'Please, sir, tell us . . . is it true?'

'Don't be a fool,' Bindi snorted. 'That madman was publicly executed, and half the city witnessed it. Savonarola is no more alive than I am capable of swimming to Rome.'

'But it was written on the proclamation,' Macci insisted. 'It must be true . . .'

Bindi dismissed the constable before taking Strocchi to one side. 'Go to this palazzo, see if what that fool says is true. Tear down the proclamation and bring it back here.'

Strocchi took three constables with him, running all the way. They dashed across the sun-baked expanse of Piazza della Signoria before pressing on towards the river. It didn't take long to locate the palazzo Macci had described, not with so many people shouting and arguing outside the entrance. When he saw the mob clustered by the palazzo doors Strocchi was grateful to have brought so many constables. One man on his own would have no chance dealing with all these people; even four were going to struggle.

The crowd was a collision of different people, some on the way back to work after their afternoon break, others returning home from the mercato. Many were red in the face from shouting, the heat or both. A few prayed out loud as the rest jostled to see what was on the palazzo doors. Strocchi shoved through the throng, using his hands and elbows to push aside those who would not move. When finally he reached the front, Strocchi found an old woman kneeling on the stone steps, dressed in the black of a widow. She was flanked by two more grey-haired women, all kneeling in prayer, tears streaming down their deeply lined faces.

Macci had been right, there was a notice nailed to the palazzo doors. At first sight it appeared to be a city proclamation, but Strocchi knew no official would permit such a notice to be posted in public. He read the text, shaking his head in disbelief.

FRATE SAVONAROLA LIVES!

Forty years ago today, the Senate put to death the preacher and prophet Girolamo Savonarola. He was a good brother of the Dominican faith, a loyal servant to God and the ordinary people of Florence. His excommunication by the Church in Rome was an attack on our city, while his execution by hanging and fire in the Piazza della Signoria was an act of murder by men desperate to destroy the truth of his teachings.

But the spirit of Savonarola lives! Earlier today one of those who betrayed him was executed in Piazza della Signoria by the same methods used to kill our beloved frate. Others will soon suffer as that traitor did, their sins made manifest, their punishment long overdue. Pray for our city, and you shall bear witness as this prophecy comes true.

FRATE SAVONAROLA LIVES!

This was no official proclamation yet it seemed to convince those around the palazzo doors, as if their reason was a stone tumbling down a hill. In Strocchi's experience, few working people in the city could read much more than their own name. Most of those gathered probably could not grasp what was nailed to the palazzo doors. Someone must have announced what the largest words on it said and that was all people needed to hear. He had to put a stop to this madness . . . but how?

'Out of the way, people want to see!' Strocchi twisted round to find a big-nosed man with the dusty hands of a stone worker jabbing a finger at him. 'Yes, you! Out of the way!'

'I am an officer of the Otto di Guardia e Balia,' Strocchi announced, his voice loud enough for everyone to hear. 'Go about your business, or else the constables behind you will start making arrests.' Some twisted round to face the constables, but most ignored his warning.

'Why should we believe you're an officer?' the stone worker demanded. Sweat was soaking his work clothes, sticking hair to his sun-bronzed forehead.

Strocchi realized he didn't have any proof of his promotion. Instead, he tore the paper from the palazzo door, crumpling it in his hands. 'This is not an official proclamation. Frate Girolamo Savonarola is not alive. He was executed forty years ago, as it says here.'

'No, that says Savonarola lives!' someone shouted.

'He died in 1498. That is a fact.'

Still questions persisted. 'How do you know? Were you there?'

'No,' Strocchi had to admit. He was far too young; that was obvious to all.

'I was there,' one of the women praying on the stone steps said. She struggled up from her knees, helped by the stone worker. 'I saw what those monsters did to our frate, our blessed prophet. They took away his holy robes, leaving him in his underclothes. They shaved his head in front of everyone to humiliate him!'

That brought an angry murmur from the crowd. Strocchi knew they were growing sourer by the moment, but the woman's words had his attention. The killer had been recreating what happened to Savonarola in every possible detail. They must have seen the monk's execution, or been told about it by someone present that day . . .

'They did the same to two other Dominicans,' the old woman went on, 'shaming them in front of the whole city.' She shook her head. 'Those jackals hung all three from a gibbet like common criminals. They set fire to men of God, burning them for everyone to see.' She wiped tears from her eyes. 'This city has been crushed beneath the boots of the Medici and their kind ever since! But our frate is returning . . . He will save us all!'

Some voices called out in agreement, but others shouted against the old woman. 'Savonarola was a monster,' one cried out.

'He was our saviour!' another replied.

Strocchi had seen and heard enough. 'This is your last warning,' he bellowed. 'Go about your business or spend tonight in Le Stinche!' That got their attention. Some retreated from the palazzo. The name of Le Stinche put fear in the hearts of Florentines. The prison was notorious for its unforgiving conditions. Strocchi nodded to the constables at the back of the crowd. All three men chose a target, loudly announcing those arrested would go to prison.

For a moment it seemed Strocchi's stratagemma would not succeed, tempers raised by the hot afternoon sun refusing to be soothed. But the prospect of Le Stinche was enough to sway those stopped by curiosity rather than religious fervour. Soon the gathering was broken, workers returning to jobs and others to their homes. The immediate threat was passing, like a cloud across the sun. But Strocchi feared there would be more moments like this, judging by the words on the proclamation: *Others will soon suffer as that traitor did . . .*

Strocchi eased his sweat-soaked grip on the torn paper, let his shoulders straighten as the throng melted away in the sticky afternoon sun. Soon only the three old women remained, each glaring at Strocchi. 'It does not matter what you say,' the widow whispered. 'We know the truth. The frate's prophecies will come to pass. This city will be freed.'

She shuffled away, the others close behind. Strocchi waited until only he and the constables remained before examining the false proclamation again. It was written in black ink aside from a few words in bloody red: *LIVES*, *Florence*, *fire*, *traitor* and *true*.

Strocchi suspected there were two intended audiences for the document: the common people of Florence who worked hard and prayed harder; and those who led the city through the Senate, the guilds and the courts. The first group would be filled with hope or fear by the words inked so carefully on the paper, believing they signalled a return to the days when one man's sermons shook the city to its core. The second audience would be suspicious, wondering who was responsible for the warning and what it meant.

Two things seemed certain. Whoever had written the false proclamation was involved with the murder in Piazza della Signoria. They knew too many details to simply be repeating the gossip of others. And whoever was responsible for that murder was promising to strike again. One killing would become two or more unless they were stopped.

Strocchi joined the constables on the dirt road in front of the palazzo steps, twisting round to study the grand building. It was the home of a wealthy merchant, judging by the quality of stone-work. The windows became smaller and more elegant on each of the three successive levels, while a famiglia crest was fixed above the main doors. Not being a native son of Florence, Strocchi was still learning the names behind each crest. 'Does anyone know who lives here?' he asked the others.

'This is Palazzo Dovizi,' one replied. 'Belongs to the silk merchant Sandro Dovizi.'

It wasn't a name Strocchi knew. That meant Dovizi had neither served the court as a magistrate nor had reason to stand before it as witness or accused. Of course, few wealthy merchants did, coin buying them out of any such trouble. So why had the doors of Palazzo Dovizi been chosen for the false proclamation?

An answer nagged at Strocchi, but he didn't give it voice, not yet. 'You can return to the Podestà or your other duties,' he said. 'I shall talk to Signor Dovizi.' Once the constables were gone Strocchi knocked at the palazzo doors. He got no reply but did not expect one. If anybody was within, the noise of the crowd would have been frightening, even terrifying. Strocchi tried the smaller door by the main entrance – it was not bolted. He slipped inside, not knowing what he might find within.

Chapter Six

The interior of Palazzo Dovizi was even grander than the outside, with an impressive marble floor and beautiful statues in each corner of the entrance area. Beyond that, an internal courtyard was filled with exotic trees and plants, while windows around the two levels above looked down on any visitors. Strocchi called out, announcing himself as an officer of the Otto. The words sounded strange from his mouth, as if he was pretending to be a person of importance. But a servant appeared from an archway, a nervous man with thinning hair and clasping hands. He was not much older than Strocchi yet was stooped over in the browbeaten way of someone who spent their life bowing. 'How may I help you?'

'This is the home of Signor Sandro Dovizi?'

The servant nodded.

'May I speak with him?'

'I'm sorry, no. The signore is not here. Perhaps you could return later?'

'Where can I find Signor Dovizi?' Many merchants conducted business from the street level of their palazzo, but Strocchi saw no signs of that here. Not today, at least.

'I . . .' The servant hesitated, wringing his hands in a hapless manner.

'Well?'

'I do not know,' the man admitted.

'Your signore is not here, yet you do not know where he is.'

Again, a hesitation. 'That is correct.'

'What about his family? Do any of them know where he might be?'

Sadness crept into the servant's face. 'He does not have a family. His wife died in childbirth, as did their son. Our master has lived alone ever since.'

'I'm sorry to hear that.' Strocchi suspected what answer his next question would bring but had to ask. 'When did you see Signor Dovizi last? Yesterday?' That got a nod. 'Near to curfew?' Another nod. 'So, he left the palazzo not long before curfew, and never returned.' A third nod. Strocchi glanced around the entrance area. In his experience those with the coin to afford such a home were not always known for their humility. 'Can you tell me if your signore has a painting of himself? A portrait perhaps, or his likeness as part of a fresco?'

The servant ushered Strocchi through an archway to the foot of a stone staircase that led up to the next level. A large portrait hung opposite the stairs so that anyone coming down would be watched by the piercing eyes depicted in the painting.

'When was this completed?'

'Not long after I came to work here as a boy, twenty years ago.'

The man in the painting had seen at least thirty summers. No doubt the artist had flattered his subject – only a fool paints an ugly portrait of the person paying them – but the similarities to the charred body were still apparent. It was the piercing green eyes that settled the matter. Strocchi knew why the proclamation had been nailed to the doors of this palazzo.

Sandro Dovizi was the man murdered in Piazza della Signoria.

* * *

Girolamo Ruggerio believed few things were as profitable and enjoyable as a secret. True, he had made his fortune as a silk merchant, importing the finest of materials and employing the best workers to transform these into exquisite cloths and garments. But it was discovering the secrets of his rivals that enabled Ruggerio to steal away their best suppliers and their most skilled staff. It was the secrets of his enemies that gave Ruggerio the power to destroy them or bend them to his will. If banking and trade were the lifeblood of Florence, then secrets were the city's most prized currency – and in those he was richer than any man alive.

It brought a warm smile to Ruggerio's thin lips when a servant came with news that Cesare Aldo was in the courtyard, seeking an audience. Ruggerio doubted Aldo had phrased it so – the Otto officer thought far too much of himself to use such obsequious words – but the meaning was the same. He never came to the palazzo without a question to ask or an accusation to make. Aldo had proven useful in the past, but unlike other men he had avoided becoming indebted to Ruggerio. Aldo kept himself at arm's length. It suggested the officer had secrets of his own to keep, but thus far they remained elusive.

Ruggerio had been bemused – and yes, perhaps even a little saddened – when Aldo departed the city a year earlier. What reason could there be for such an abrupt decision? The laws of Florence extended beyond the city walls but enforcing those laws in the dominion seemed a waste of Aldo's talents. Ruggerio knew there must be another reason but none of his usual sources were able to provide answers. None of the women at the bordello where Aldo had lived south of the river would say, no matter how much coin they were offered. Ruggerio's men inside the Podestà could provide nothing beyond the official explanation that Aldo had been granted a transfer by that fool Bindi. Aldo still returned to the city on occasion, but the cause of his departure remained unknown.

Now the answer was waiting in the courtyard, if Aldo could be persuaded to reveal it. Ruggerio nodded to his waiting maggiordomo, Alberti. 'Very well. Show my visitor to the . . . crimson room. I will be with him presently.' Once the servant had gone, Ruggerio strode to his dressing chamber. Making Aldo wait was an obvious ploy, but it would do him good to stand in an empty room. Besides, Ruggerio wanted to look his most imperious for their meeting, and that meant changing. The purple silk robe, trimmed with gold and richly embroidered. That would be perfect.

It was some time before Ruggerio swept into the crimson room. His maggiordomo had put a single ornate chair in the centre, but there was no seat for Aldo. Instead, he was leaning against one of the red walls that gave the chamber its name, a dirty sack by his dusty boots. The room was ripe with the odours of horse and woodsmoke, both coming from Aldo.

Aldo straightened up and gave the briefest of bows. 'Signor.'

Ruggerio gracefully lowered himself into the chair, returning the bow with an even briefer nod. 'To what do I owe this unexpected visit? I understood you were banished to the dominion, enforcing the law in the Tuscan countryside.'

Other men would have bristled at such a comment, striven to defend their reputation; Aldo simply ignored it. 'Are you still a founding member in the Company of Santa Maria?'

Now it was Ruggerio's turn to ignore a provocation. 'I believe Duke Cosimo has promulgated a law against such confraternities.'

'But you were one of the founders, yes?' Aldo persisted.

Ruggerio gave a nod of assent, uncertain where this was heading.

'No doubt you've heard about what occurred in Piazza della Signoria?'

'Of course,' Ruggerio agreed. He had received three separate reports of the bizarre killing, two from his men at the Podestà and the third from a member of the Senate. Nobody seemed certain who had been hanged and burned in the square, but Ruggerio expected to know before the day's end. His sources could be relied on for such secrets.

Aldo retrieved his sack from the floor, reaching inside it to pull out a bundle of blue cloth. He came closer, brandishing the garment. 'Recognize this?'

Ruggerio did. It was his finest cerulean blue silk, the emblem of the Company of Santa Maria. Only the five founders had the right to wear this particular emblem. Ruggerio leaned forward, wanting to be certain. 'Where did you find that?'

'It was stripped from the man who was murdered last night,' Aldo said. 'His clothes were taken from him, and his head shaved, before he was tied to a gibbet and set aflame.'

Ruggerio sank back in his chair. Benozzo Scarlatti had retired to the countryside a year ago, so it could not be him. That left Luca Uccello, Roberto Ghiberti and Sandro Dovizi. 'Who was it who died?'

Aldo pushed the cloth back into the sack. 'That's what I came to ask you.'

Ruggerio noticed the officer studying him. 'But why are you the one doing the asking? Does the Otto not have officers inside the city capable of investigating this? Or have you been summoned back by that fool Bindi to do his bidding once more?'

'I came to the city on another matter,' Aldo replied. 'One that also involves you.'

'Yes?'

'More accurately, it involves your villa in the hills above San Jacopo al Girone. I caught a thief who stole some boots and a capon from your country retreat.'

Ruggerio smirked. 'If you were expecting a reward for doing your job . . .'

'The theft was a pretext,' Aldo said. 'I believe this man was spying on your villa. Assessing how easy it would be to get inside, what defences it has. I have yet to discover who sent him . . . but I will.'

Any amusement Ruggerio had taken from Aldo's presence vanished. If what he said was true . . . But Aldo offered nothing further. That suggested he was crafting conclusions from mere surmise, or his words were a feint to force a reaction. 'Do you have any proof of this?'

Aldo did not reply.

'Then I have nothing further to say.' Ruggerio rose from his chair, pulling the purple silk robe close around him. 'My maggior-domo will escort you out, in case you have forgotten the way. It is some time since you were here last.'

Aldo gave the slightest of bows in return. 'Signor.'

Ruggerio stalked from the crimson room, not caring to hide his anger. He had hoped to enjoy jousting with Aldo again. Instead, the officer had presented two morsels of most unwelcome news. Ruggerio wasn't sure which perturbed him more: that one of the five founders had been murdered, or that his villa had been a target for prying eyes.

Neither trespass could go unpunished.

The afternoon was fading as Strocchi returned to the Podestà, the first cool breezes of evening replacing the day's heat. Though it would not be curfew for hours yet, the sun was starting its lazy descent. Terracotta rooftops and the bold curve of the Duomo were still basking in the sunlight, but many narrow streets and alleys were now in shadow. That did not stop ripe aromas of waste filling the air, yet for once Strocchi inhaled them gratefully. They kept away the stench of searing flesh that had haunted his nostrils all day.

Santo Spirito, had it only been that morning when he first saw the burning cart and its unholy contents? He was tired to his very bones, thanks to baby Bianca and being dragged from bed to witness that murderous fire, but Bindi was still expecting a report. Strocchi trudged up the stone staircase to the Podestà's administration level, shivering all the way. No matter the season, the courtyard always seemed to chill his bones unless the sun was directly overhead. Having to face the segretario's wrath was adding to that coldness.

Strocchi knocked at Bindi's door. The segretario always made those outside his ufficio wait for permission to enter, a tiresome ploy to prove his authority. Once summoned within, Strocchi presented the false proclamation, smoothing the crumpled paper on Bindi's table so he could read it. Strocchi gave a brief account of what had happened outside Palazzo Dovizi, and what he learned inside the residence.

'So now we know the dead man's name – Sandro Dovizi,' Bindi said, leaning back in his tall chair. 'But why was he chosen for such a public killing?'

Strocchi pointed to the crumpled paper. 'This describes Dovizi as one of those who betrayed Savonarola. But the victim can't have been much more than fifteen when the monk was executed. I'm uncertain how young Dovizi could have betrayed the preacher.'

The segretario scowled. 'You were not alive when Savonarola was tormenting the city. His sermons had half of Florence bowing before him, and the other half fearing what he would do next. Dovizi must have been one of his Fanciulli.' Bindi explained how the monk sent thousands of boys and young men into streets and homes, demanding people surrender their vanities. 'Those boys were supposed to be servants of God, dressed in white to show their purity while ridding the city of unholy objects. But many tales were whispered of excesses, violence . . . and worse.'

That did not surprise Strocchi. In Florence the Church seemed close to being corrupted by its own wealth and influence, indulging excesses that should have brought nothing but shame. Strocchi recalled the bullying he had faced as a boy. Putting absolute power into anyone's hands was asking for trouble, let alone young men already full of their own importance.

'You think whoever killed Dovizi believes he betrayed the ideals of Savonarola?'

'Perhaps,' Bindi said. 'But there is a more pressing problem.' He clutched the false proclamation in one of his chubby hands. 'This suggests others will suffer as Dovizi did. That means more killings.'

Strocchi nodded. 'There is a third problem, sir. The document was seen by quite a crowd. Most didn't fully understand it. Some believed it was an official notice announcing Savonarola is alive, as Macci did earlier.'

The segretario snorted. 'Never underestimate how easy it is to dupe those who lack wit, imagination or both.'

Strocchi fought the urge to argue. Yes, many Florentines were simple people unable to read, yet they were good souls with faith in the teachings of the Church. It didn't mean they deserved to be sneered at or mocked by Bindi. But arguing with the segretario would do no good. 'Nonetheless, word of what they saw will be spreading across the city,' Strocchi said. 'Soon others will believe.'

'Forty years that monk has been dead and still he haunts us.' Bindi sighed. 'Have you questioned da Soci about Dovizi's murder?'

'Not yet,' Strocchi admitted.

'Why not? You've had a day to investigate this yet you seem to have achieved nothing.' The segretario scowled. 'I will tell His Grace about all of this when I make my report tomorrow. Your task is to find and stop those responsible for Dovizi's murder before any more proclamations are posted, and before there are any more murders.'

'Yes, sir.' Strocchi retreated from the ufficio, shaking his head. How was he supposed to hunt down the killer or killers with no witnesses and almost no evidence? There were so many different potential pathways the investigation could take, all of them demanding immediate attention. Perhaps he should have sent men door to door inside the buildings overlooking Piazza della Signoria earlier, in case someone had witnessed the murder. Aldo's suggestion of searching the stables close to Piazza della Signoria in case one of them was used by the killer also had merit. And now Bindi was insisting that da Soci be questioned in case the imprisoned follower of Savonarola had some involvement . . .

It was overwhelming.

Aldo had time to spare before visiting Saul at home. The good doctor preferred Aldo to arrive after curfew, when fewer eyes would be watching. Two men together was against the law of the city and against the faith of those living in via dei Giudei. Some of Saul's neighbours might ignore what happened in his home after dark, valuing his skill and kindness as a doctor over other things. But there were many who wouldn't hesitate to denounce both men. Punishments for sodomy were brutal. When the Otto needed to make an example of someone, they were hung outside the Podestà and their bodies set ablaze. For an officer of the court, the sentence would certainly be execution, with Saul probably hanged alongside him.

Aldo could not – would not – allow that to happen.

He wandered Santa Maria Novella, the city's western quarter. Time in Florence was all too rare these days and most of his trips were for court business. Having an hour or two to enjoy the city without obligation was a luxury. But that pleasure was stifled by his meeting with Ruggerio. The silk merchant had appeared truly surprised to learn the man murdered in Piazza della Signoria was from the Company of Santa Maria. Ruggerio knew the dead man, that much was certain, but it seemed the silk merchant was not responsible for this killing.

Ruggerio's reaction to his countryside villa being watched was less illuminating. Aldo cursed himself. Why blurt that out? He had given away a secret and got nothing in return. Palle! A year outside Florence had dulled his edge when dealing with courtly intrigues and political machinations.

Stopping in the middle of a piazza, Aldo let the last of the late afternoon sun warm his skin. Enough. He had blundered, but there was nothing to be done about it now. Better to find something or someone that might raise his spirits. Aldo realized he was not far from where Strocchi lived with Tomasia and their baby. Strocchi should still be busy on court business. There was time to pay a visit before he got home.

Aldo strode south towards the narrow street where they lived. He and Strocchi had been close once, Aldo recognizing potential in a young constable eager to learn. But Strocchi also had an unbending morality. He'd grown up in the Tuscan countryside where there was a clear divide between right and wrong, and the teachings of the Church were beyond question. Florence was another world. Here, beauty and brutality mixed with politics and patronage. In this city those craving power or seeking to retain it believed the end always justified whatever actions were necessary for their desired outcome. Here, what was preached and what was practised were often two very different things.

When Strocchi had discovered what Aldo was willing to do, how far Aldo would go to protect himself and others . . . it had sundered their friendship, though it might have been repaired in time. It was Strocchi learning what kind of man Aldo was, who he loved, how he loved – that was something Strocchi seemed unable to forgive. Bending or breaking the laws of the city he might understand, in the right circumstances. Breaking the laws of God was too much. He had given Aldo an ultimatum: one of them must leave the Otto or depart the city. Strocchi was newly married at the time with a child on the way, so Aldo decided he was the one who should go. A year or two in the Tuscan countryside, there were worse places to be. And it got him away from the pettiness of Bindi. Leaving Saul had not been so easy, but time apart made their reunions more enjoyable – and less dangerous.

Aldo found the narrow building where Strocchi lived and climbed the wooden stairs to its middle level. An infant was wailing behind the door, its sobs almost drowning the sound of a woman's gentle, soothing voice. Aldo knocked twice, paused, and twice again. Tomasia opened the door, a crying baby on one hip. Her hair was pulled back in a severe bun and exhaustion had left dark smudges under both eyes, but she was still the handsome woman Aldo had met when they were inmates of Le Stinche. They had protected each other inside the prison and stayed in touch since, even after Strocchi had given his ultimatum.

'You're back,' she said, smiling at Aldo.

Chapter Seven

'I'm only in the city for one night,' Aldo replied and stepped inside. 'Delivering a prisoner to the Podestà.' Aldo closed the door behind him, putting the sack of clothes beside it. Strocchi rented the middle level of the building – a single, narrow room divided in two by a curtain. It was humble but clean with a kitchen at the front, a bed and cot visible behind the curtain. Aldo held out both hands for the tear-stained baby. 'May I?'

'Please,' Tomasia replied. 'She's been crying for an hour, no matter what I do.'

Aldo lifted Bianca from her mother's arms. The baby was six months old, with curls of brown hair and piercing eyes. Tomasia had chosen not to swaddle Bianca, so the baby was able to tug at Aldo's chin as he nestled her in his arms. She seemed to forget whatever had been troubling her, sobs becoming gurgles of delight as he whispered nonsense at her.

Tomasia groaned. 'I don't know how you do that. If Carlo picks her up, she cries and cries. Most of the time I can get her back to sleep or find a way to soothe her, but not today. You take her for a moment and she's all smiles.'

Discovering an affinity for babies had surprised Aldo too. But he'd always enjoyed playing with his half-sister Teresa when she was an infant. Her mother Lucrezia had wanted nothing to do with children, content for wet nurses and maids to look after them. As a boy Aldo often snuck into the nursery to visit Teresa. He only shared a father with her, but they still had a bond. That infuriated Lucrezia more, of course.

'Your baby likes my stubble,' Aldo said. 'And maybe the sound of my voice.'

Tomasia sank into a simple wooden chair. 'I don't know how she can still be awake. She hardly slept last night. When finally we got her settled, the night patrol came banging at our door, demanding that Carlo go with them.'

'There was a murder in Piazza della Signoria.'

She nodded. 'I heard about it when I went to the mercato. Some people claimed it must be a secret execution. Others thought it was something to do with the monk Savonarola.'

Aldo poked his tongue out at Bianca, making her laugh. 'I'm surprised you know his name. I hadn't been born when he was terrifying half the city with his sermons, and you're a lot younger than me.'

'Mama used to rant about him. According to her, Savonarola was the best and worst thing that ever happened to the city. She said Florence was a more God-fearing place when he was preaching, but others used fear of his name to terrify people.'

Aldo nodded. His own papa had also held strong views about the Dominican monk.

'Besides,' Tomasia went on, 'the court has been dealing with someone obsessed by Savonarola.' She told Aldo how da Soci had been convicted and paraded through the streets for people to abuse as a false prophet, before being locked away in Le Stinche.

That a man was murdered the same way Savonarola had been executed only a few days after a pro-Savonarola prophet was publicly shamed could be coincidence, but Aldo did not believe in coincidences. Yet it was not his case to investigate.

'How long until Strocchi – Carlo – gets home?' he asked.

Tomasia looked at the fading afternoon light outside the shutters. 'A while yet.'

'And how is he?' She didn't reply. 'I saw him at the Podestà; he seemed angry.'

Tomasia frowned. 'You're right. He has been angry, and that isn't him.'

'Working directly with Bindi isn't easy.'

'I've heard.' She grimaced. 'Frequently. But Carlo's anger starts elsewhere. He misses working with someone he can trust at the Podestà, someone he can go to for advice or counsel. Most of all I think he's frustrated with himself, but he doesn't understand why. I've been doing what I can to make him see sense, but Carlo has a stubborn side.'

'Once he fixes on something, it is hard for him to let go,' Aldo agreed.

'When he found out what kind of man you are . . .' Tomasia shook her head. 'In some ways he is still the boy who grew up in the countryside. The idea that people could love in ways other than what he was taught in church . . . He may understand, in time, but it goes against so much of what he believes – and that troubles him.' Her eyelids were drooping.

'Why don't you get some sleep? I can look after the bambina.'

'You sure?'

Aldo nodded. 'I'll be gone before Carlo comes home.'

Tomasia stood. 'Thank you.' She kissed Bianca on her curls and Aldo on the cheek before retreating behind the curtain. Cradling the baby in one arm, Aldo took the wooden chair to the shutters overlooking the street.

He lowered himself carefully before settling Bianca in his arms. 'Would you like to hear a story?' he murmured.

Strocchi trudged towards his home, the narrow space between buildings in shadow as sunset grew nearer. Then the bells would chime across Florence, announcing the end of the day and the beginning of curfew. Each city gate would be shut and locked for the night, while the streets would be forbidden to all but those few authorized to be outside during darkness.

He hoped none of the night patrols would find any more burning bodies. Bindi had announced Strocchi's first task as an officer was hunting down the killer of Sandro Dovizi. That meant any murders after curfew would drag Strocchi from his bed to investigate.

He stumbled up the stairs to his home, muttering a silent prayer. Dear God, please help Bianca sleep tonight. But his prayer was forgotten when he opened the door. Aldo was slumped in a chair by the window, gently snoring, baby Bianca asleep in his arms.

'What are you doing here?' Strocchi demanded. He stamped across the room, not caring how loud his boots were on the wooden floor. 'Answer me!' Bianca woke at the same time as Aldo and was immediately crying. Strocchi lifted her away from Aldo and she cried even harder, little hands curling into fists as her face reddened. 'Well?'

Aldo struggled to his feet, rubbing sleep from his eyes. 'I'm sorry – I didn't mean to still be here when you— I'm sorry.'

Strocchi did his best to soothe Bianca, without success. 'Where's Tomasia?'

'She needed to rest,' Aldo replied. 'I offered to look after the bambina . . .'

'Don't call my daughter that,' Strocchi hissed. 'She's not your child.'

'I never said she—'

'You still haven't told me why you're here.'

'You haven't given me a chance,' Aldo replied, his voice remaining gentle, quiet. 'And shouting at me is only upsetting Bianca more.'

'How dare you—'

'Enough!' Tomasia pushed aside the curtain, stalking towards them. She took Bianca from Strocchi, wiping tears off the baby's round cheeks. 'Carlo, what's got into you? Aldo was kind enough to stay while I slept, that's all. You're the one upsetting Bianca, not him.'

Strocchi knew she was right, but that only made things worse. 'It was—'

'You didn't expect to see me here,' Aldo said.

Strocchi nodded, not trusting himself to say any more.

'I have visited Tomasia three times before today,' Aldo volunteered. 'Once before she had Bianca and twice after. I do not live in Florence, but I still care about people in this city.'

Tomasia had got Bianca to stop crying, nuzzling the baby into her chest. 'And I didn't tell you about his visits because I wanted to avoid something like this happening.'

Strocchi stayed silent. Yes, Tomasia had kept this from him, but he had responded like a fool, proving her fears correct with his bluster and accusations.

'I should go,' Aldo said, moving to pick up a sack by the door. Strocchi hadn't noticed it when he came in; Aldo must have brought it with him.

Tomasia was glaring at Strocchi. He knew what that meant: make this better. 'I'll see you to the street,' he said, following Aldo out and down the stairs. Neither spoke until they were in the alley. Strocchi could see Tomasia above, watching through the shutters.

'Carlo, I'm sorry—'

Strocchi held up a hand. 'No. It's . . . This is my fault. You were the one giving Tomasia a chance to rest. Thank you.' He rubbed a hand across his weary face. 'Having a baby, it's wonderful but . . . I never knew it would be so . . .'

'Exhausting?'

'Yes.'

Aldo nodded. 'Tomasia told me about da Soci, his public humiliation. This new killing, do you think . . .?'

'I don't know,' Strocchi admitted. 'One so soon after the other makes the murder seem like a response, especially after the false proclamation was—' He stopped, but the words had tumbled out so Strocchi told Aldo about what had been put on display.

'You still need to question da Soci,' Aldo said, 'if only to make certain he isn't linked to this murder. Have you a name for the victim yet?'

'This is not your murder to solve,' Strocchi said, struggling not to raise his voice. 'I am leading this investigation. The segretario promoted me to officer today.'

'Congratulations,' Aldo replied, a smile lighting up his tired features. 'Well done, Carlo, I always knew you would be an officer.'

'Thank you.' Strocchi glanced at the shutters, Tomasia was gone. 'Now, I need to—'

'Your victim was a member of the Company of Santa Maria,' Aldo cut in. He held open the sack in his grasp. 'I found his clothes earlier, the ones removed by his killer.'

Anger twisted inside Strocchi. 'You did what?'

'They were in the stable where the victim was beaten and shaved and tied to that cart. I was right, it was in an alley west of the piazza, opposite the Signoria tower. The dead man's clothes were still there, the killer left them behind.' Aldo pulled a tunic out of the sack. 'See this embroidery? That's the emblem of the Company of Santa Maria. I showed Ruggerio, one of the confraternity's founders, and he confirmed it.'

Being made to look a fool by Aldo was the last thing Strocchi needed. 'Have you told anyone at the Podestà what you found?'

'No. I hoped Ruggerio might be able to name the dead man for you.'

'I already know who the victim was. Now Ruggerio does too, assuming he wasn't responsible for the murder.' Strocchi knew from bitter experience that the silk merchant would not hesitate to have someone killed if they were a danger, though Ruggerio never got his own hands bloody. He paid others for that.

Aldo shook his head. 'Ruggerio's surprise was real when he saw this tunic. He—'

'Enough!' Strocchi snatched the tunic and sack from Aldo. 'You have done enough, more than enough. Taking evidence and showing it to a potential suspect. Coming into my home when I'm not here . . .' He stepped back, not wanting to be close to Aldo. 'Stop trying to help me. Just . . . stop.'

Aldo did not reply. He stared down at the dirt road between them before giving a brief nod and striding away. Strocchi waited until he could no longer hear the receding boots. Pushing the tunic back inside the sack, he went upstairs to his family.

Ruggerio did not often know fear. Born into a comfortable life, he had transformed the famiglia fabric business into one of the city's most exclusive and expensive suppliers of silk. That had required a flair with numbers, a talent for finding those with the skill and creativity, and a ruthlessness few other men possessed. By rights his brother should have taken charge as first-born son, but Angelo was persuaded to step aside for a healthy share of the profits. He drank himself to a stupor most days, so it was little surprise when too much good wine and a tumble from the top floor of Palazzo Ruggerio put an abrupt end to him. Angelo had never possessed a head for business, and certainly not for heights. Besides, it saved sharing profits.

Rising through the ranks of the silk weavers' and merchants' guild, Ruggerio had soon become an influential voice within the Arte della Seta. It helped that he had no interest in being leader, letting others hold positions of apparent power. There was far more advantage in guiding those burdened by leadership and, when necessary, encouraging those who wished to replace them. Men who do not wear the crown never need worry about losing it.

It was the Company of Santa Maria where Ruggerio preferred being in charge. It was his right, after all, as one of the confraternity's founders. Most such brotherhoods sought to venerate their chosen saint through charitable good works. The confraternity Ruggerio helped found was similar in many ways. Its brethren made significant donations to the Church and other institutions. Membership also brought other privileges. Brethren could call on one another at any time, in any way.

Ruggerio had shaped the confraternity in his image, assisted by the other founders. The five of them had grown to hate one another, and yet remained together. They were not relatives. None shared famiglia, even by marriage. Indeed, none had ever been blessed with children who survived infancy. Ruggerio possessed no interest in women but the others – Scarlatti, Uccello, Ghiberti and Dovizi – did their best to sire heirs. For whatever reason, no offspring lived long enough to succeed them. A younger company member once called it the curse of the five founders. He was expelled, but the seed of doubt was planted.

It was that fool Scarlatti who claimed the curse was their punishment for past sins. The five had all been members of the Fanciulli, acolytes of Savonarola, caught up in the fervour of his sermons. Ruggerio was no true believer but he had recognized the way power was flowing towards the monk, much as the Arno flowed through the city. Better to be swept along with that power than be swept away by it. The five were bound together by what they did in the monk's name. After Savonarola's execution they made a pact to protect each other, no matter what. That led to creating the Company of Santa Maria. If one should fall, the rest knew they would soon suffer the same fate. If one turned on the others, he knew they would destroy him.

Ruggerio had known fear when Scarlatti announced he was retiring to his villa in the hills above San Jacopo al Girone. That threatened to dissolve the pact, set the five against one another. Ruggerio had little cause to worry about Scarlatti, long the weakest among them, lacking the others' will or venom. His estate was no more than an hour's gentle ride from Florence, standing within sight of Ruggerio's own villa. Scarlatti did not have the palle to be a threat, but his departure widened the gaps between the others. Ruggerio had watched and waited, expecting an attack from one of those who remained: Uccello, Ghiberti or Dovizi.

Now Dovizi had been murdered.

There was good reason to fear.

Dovizi was strongest of them all, in body and spirit. He had long been a rival within the Arte della Seta, the guild of silk weavers and merchants. If any of the five were to launch a strike against the others, Ruggerio always believed Dovizi the most likely. That he had been the first one killed, and in such a grotesque manner . . . The person responsible was sending a clear message: none were safe. Uccello or Ghiberti might have paid others to kill

Dovizi, as he would have done. Now they would be watching to see how the surviving founders responded. But Ruggerio had one advantage.

He knew someone had sent a thief to spy on his villa.

Aldo had arrested the thief at San Jacopo al Girone on the same night that Dovizi was being burned in the heart of Florence. That must be significant, part of a larger stratagemma. Whoever killed Dovizi was putting pieces in place, making ready for what was to come. Ruggerio doubted his villa was the only one being studied, either by the thief Aldo had arrested or by others.

To learn who was responsible, Ruggerio needed to reach inside the Podestà. He called for his maggiordomo. The path ahead was clear, the next steps must be enacted with speed and sleight of hand. That would not be cheap, but the truths he sought were worth every coin.

Chapter Eight

*A*ldo missed many things about Florence – but Zoppo's tavern was not one of them. It was a disreputable hovel at the best of times, and there were not many of those. Most days the place reeked of despair and decay, mould and merda, vomit and vermin. But if the stench that filled the tavern was appalling, the wine Zoppo served was worse. Discharges collected from the suppurating pores of plague victims would make for a better bevanda than the poison available at Zoppo's bar. It was no mistake that the tavern was hidden away in a dark and narrow alleyway, a sore festering in a forgotten crevice.

So it made no sense at all that the tavern was busy when Aldo went there on his way to Saul's home. What had brought about such an unlikely event?

Aldo fought his way in through the door, shoving aside two drunks arguing about the size of their respective noses. Normally they were the sole occupants of the tavern, usually found slumped at the bar. Both noses were equally large, but one had the benefit of a bulbous and unsightly wart on the end. Aldo didn't bother adjudicating their dispute, despite being invited to do so by the pugnacious pair. He pushed his way further into the tavern, struggling to believe the evidence of his eyes. Every table was full, each and every seat occupied. The women who usually worked in the bordello above had come down to mingle with the drinkers, happy to service several of them where they stood, sat or lay.

Aldo had seen such debauchery before, but it was usually when men at arms got paid in a new town after surviving a battle, or when Florentines indulged their vices at Carnival, those precious few days before the long weeks of abstinence that came with Lent. But this was May, not February, and none of the men in this tavern were soldiers.

'What are you doing here?' a familiar voice bellowed above the babble of grunting drunkards and orgiastic groans. 'Thought you'd retired to the countryside!' Zoppo emerged from behind a couple rutting atop a rickety table, the tavern keeper stumping towards Aldo on one leg and a wooden crutch. The usual leer was smeared across Zoppo's pox-scarred features.

'I've been enforcing the will of the Otto in the dominion,' Aldo replied. He gestured at the chaotic crowd around them. 'When did this place get so busy?'

'Started about noon,' Zoppo shouted, 'and hasn't stopped since. Seems there's a rumour going around that Savonarola has returned from the dead, and he plans to ban drinking, gambling and whoring. This lot want to have their fun while they still can before it gets outlawed. Been the last days of Gomorrah in here for hours.'

'Savonarola's been dead for forty years,' Aldo yelled back.

Zoppo shrugged. 'You know what this city's like. Once a rumour takes hold, it's all people want to believe.' He looked around the room. 'At this rate I'll have to put buckets in the latrina to refill my wine barrels.'

Aldo shuddered. 'I need information, and I don't want to be shouting it in here!'

Zoppo jerked a thumb at the back door behind the bar. Aldo followed him outside to an alleyway so narrow there wasn't room to turn round. They had to stand with their backs against opposite walls, Zoppo on one side of the door and Aldo on the other. At least the noise from the tavern was reduced to a dull roar out here.

'What do you need to know?' Zoppo asked.

'Who hired your brother to spy on merchants' villas in the countryside?'

'Spying? My brother?' The crippled tavern keeper did his best to appear innocent, but it was a feeble effort. The permanent leer on his face didn't make it any more convincing.

'Don't waste my time with denials and evasions,' Aldo warned.

'Honestly, I don't know what—'

Aldo swung a forearm up under Zoppo's chin, pinning him to the stone wall, before pressing hard against his throat. 'I said don't waste my time.'

Zoppo gurgled, weakly clawing at the arm that was choking him. Flecks of spittle dribbled from his lips as he struggled for breath, desperation and fear in his eyes.

'Ready to tell me the truth?' Aldo asked.

Zoppo nodded – not easy in the circumstances.

Aldo leaned back, pulling his arm away. Zoppo folded forwards, coughing and choking, fingers grasping at the collar of his grubby, sweat-stained tunic. Aldo gave the tavern keeper a few moments to recover before pulling him upright again. 'Well?'

'Lippo came to me . . . not long after he was released from Le Stinche,' Zoppo replied, his voice a rasp of pain. 'He was in the merda, as usual. Fool tried to steal the purse of an Otto magistrate.'

'I know what Lippo did. What I need to know is how you tried to help.'

Zoppo shrugged. 'Told him get out of the city for a while. Try life in the countryside. Easier pickings for a one-armed thief.'

'Only if they're competent,' Aldo said. 'What else?'

'I'd heard about a job. Somebody wanted a thief with a good eye to visit some villas owned by rich merchants, see how well secured they were.'

'Does this somebody have a name?'

Zoppo shook his head. Aldo sighed, raising his arm back towards the tavern keeper's throat. 'I'm telling the truth this time. Honest!'

Aldo glared at Zoppo but, for once, the liar appeared to mean what he said. 'If this mysterious person didn't have a name, how could they ask you to find a good thief?'

'It was all done by messengers. I never met whoever hired Lippo.'

'But you can remember which villas he had to visit, yes?'

'All of them were up in the hills, east of the city. One was just outside Fiesole, another was close to Settignano, and the third was –'

'In the hills overlooking San Jacopo al Girone,' Aldo said.

Zoppo frowned. 'How did you – oh. That's where you arrested Lippo.'

'He stole a capon and a pair of good boots while he was there.'

'Like the fool he is.'

'Lippo stole them from the villa of Girolamo Ruggerio,' Aldo added.

Zoppo rolled his eyes. 'I swear, my brother has a death wish. If that bastardo Ruggiero had a family, he'd have his own children murdered to make a point, if he had any.'

'What can you tell me about the first two villas?'

'Only the directions for finding them, and I can't remember all of those. You'd be better asking my idiota of a brother.' The tavern keeper shared what he recalled, but was lacking key details. There were plenty of villas around Fiesole. It was the retreat of choice for rich merchants of Florence: close to the city, but high enough up in the hills to offer privacy, refreshing breezes during summer, and cheap land to build on. Zoppo was right – the easiest source of answers was in a cell at the Podestà.

Aldo contemplated returning there but curfew was close, and he couldn't be bothered wasting more time on Lippo tonight. Let the thief curdle in a cell until dawn and see what he had to say come morning. Besides, Saul would be waiting by now, and his welcome was far more inviting than an hour in the snivelling company of Lippo and his lies.

'Very well,' Aldo said, pulling open the tavern door.

'What about some payment?' Zoppo asked.

'Why? You've told me nothing I didn't know or hadn't guessed for myself.' A roar of laughter burst from the tavern. 'Besides, you're making far more coin from the drunks inside than I could give you. Don't be greedy, Zoppo. It doesn't suit you.'

When Ruggerio was not staying in his country villa, Cassandra went to the loggia on the upper level to watch the sunset. The signore rarely spent more than July and August at the villa, meaning she was the only permanent staff member living inside the villa the rest of the year. Ruggerio did make occasional visits at other times but, like most rich Florentines, largely used his estate as an escape from the city during the summer months.

That meant Cassandra could treat the villa as her own home for much of the time, despite being merely its housekeeper. There were others who lived elsewhere on the estate, such as Vincenzo in the stable across the courtyard, and workers and peasants in barns and huts scattered further down the hill. Two women came up from San Jacopo al Girone to help with cleaning when Ruggerio was away, but they returned to the village each afternoon.

Cassandra was alone once more by the time cool breezes were rippling the nearby cypress trees, heralding the end of the day. Many of the estate workers and peasant farmers had gone down to the village church where Father Ognissanti was saying a special Mass to pray for rain. The rest had returned to their barns and huts. Cassandra poured herself a cup of wine and climbed the stairs to the loggia. Ruggerio often took his meals on the covered terrace in summer, though he rarely paid much attention to the magnificent vista it offered.

The signore's indifference was typical of someone used to their own wealth. So far as Cassandra could tell, Ruggerio took for granted that so much he could see from the loggia belonged to him. The view was the best on the estate. Here Cassandra could watch the Arno glistening in the last glimmers of sunlight as the river made its patient journey westward towards Florence. The city was but a few hours' walk from San Jacopo al Girone, yet, with its churches and palazzi with their terracotta roofs overshadowed by the mighty Duomo, it seemed a world away.

From here the city shimmered in a distant haze of heat, as if it were more a dream than the home of tens of thousands of people. Cassandra had lived most of her life in the city before she first worked for the signore at his palazzo three summers ago. But the noise and the stench and the press of people around her became harder to tolerate as she got older, her body growing weary of such burdens. When the previous housekeeper at Ruggerio's country estate died in a fall, Cassandra had surprised the signore by asking for the job. To her delight he had agreed, moving her from the city a week later.

Getting used to life at the villa had not been easy. The work was no harder than she had known in the city, though there was more for her to do and less help. The challenge came from the villagers of San Jacopo al Girone, who'd expected one of their own to be housekeeper, as had happened before. That disappointment brought resentment and mutterings when Cassandra walked down the hill twice a week to attend Mass. But she eased her way into the villagers' favour, persuading Ruggerio to increase the wages of those working on the estate, and buying more from the locals instead of bringing things from the city. Cassandra knew she would always remain an outsider, but that did not matter.

Other things were more important.

From the loggia Cassandra could see villas built on the hills between the city and where she stood. All were owned by wealthy merchants, some of them acquaintances of Ruggerio. The signore often hosted visitors at his villa during July and August, but none could be called friends. Most were business associates, members of the same guild as him.

As his housekeeper, Cassandra could not help but hear their conversations as she served meals and brought drinks. She found it curious that the other four founders of his confraternity never came to visit, even though two of them owned villas not far from here. Signor Scarlatti had retired to his country estate the previous summer, and that was on the next hillside west of Ruggerio's villa. Yet neither man chose to make the brief journey between their two homes, and the signore never mentioned Scarlatti's name. Cassandra had only learned how close Scarlatti was from idle village gossip.

She put a hand to her forehead, shielding her eyes from the sun setting in the west behind Florence. A cloud of smoke was rising from the next hillside. Fires were common in the dominion, and woodsmoke a frequent scent on the wind. White or pale smoke was the sign of a planned fire, often the burning of old, fallen wood in a field or on a hillside. So long as the flames did not spread, all was well. But black smoke was the sign of an unplanned blaze, of things burning that were not intended for the fire.

The cloud billowing upwards was greasy black, a dark stain against the sky.

It was coming from Signor Scarlatti's villa.

Chapter Nine

❧

Friday, May 24th 1538

Aldo woke before dawn, as always. It was a habit formed while riding with the condottiere Giovanni dalle Bande Nere as a man at arms: rising before the sun gave a better chance of surviving the day. It also gave Aldo the chance to slip away from Saul's home before any of his neighbours in the Jewish commune were awake. Much as Aldo would love to linger in bed with Saul, the need to keep their secret was more important.

Aldo got up, retrieving his tunic and hose from the corner where they'd been flung. Both garments were ripe with the smell of sweat, smoke and horse. He should have washed them the previous night, the warmth of Saul's bedroom would have dried them by now. But lust and longing had come first, as often was the case when he and Saul were together. The nights they shared a bed were too few to waste time on laundry.

After emptying his bladder Aldo gave himself a brisk wash from a bowl of water. He pulled the hose back on before slipping the tunic over his head. Boots, where were his boots? A memory of them sliding under the bed arose, along with a twitch in his hose at recalling what had come next. Aldo bent over by the bed to reclaim his dusty boots from the floor.

'Leaving already?' Saul asked, rolling over to face him.

'I lose interest easily,' Aldo replied, pulling on a boot.

'Not according to that bulge in your hose.'

Aldo smacked Saul's hand away. 'Unless you plan to keep me in here all day—'

'Sounds tempting . . .'

'I should be leaving.' The other boot surrendered to Aldo's foot. He leaned over to kiss Saul, savouring the taste of him.

'When will I see you next?'

'I'm not sure,' Aldo admitted. Arresting Lippo had been a reason to come to Florence, but such opportunities were infrequent. 'You should visit San Jacopo al Girone. Leave your student in charge here. You did say she needs to start meeting patients unsupervised.'

Saul had upset some in the Jewish commune by taking on a woman as his student, even if Rebecca Levi was already familiar to most of them. Born and raised in via dei Giudei, she'd left Florence after her father's death to stay with cousins in Bologna. But Rebecca had returned a few months later, asking Saul if she could study medicine with him, learning by apprenticeship. Female doctors were uncommon but not unknown among Jews.

'I'm not sure people are ready for Rebecca to be their doctor yet, even if only for a day or two,' Saul said. 'Besides, a Jewish doctor arriving in a small village would certainly be noticed, especially if he stayed the night with an officer of the court.'

Aldo surrendered to Saul's reason. It was a disagreement they had whenever Aldo came to Florence. Both wanted to be together, but the laws of God and man said otherwise. Saul would not abandon his patients, and Aldo had made a promise to Strocchi. Until something significant changed, their time apart would remain greater than the nights spent together. Aldo glanced at the shutters across Saul's window; it was getting light outside.

The urge to stay tugged at him, but he had to go before it was too late.

You approach the heavy wooden door to the monastery of San Marco with hammer, nails, and paper in hand. The bell tolling for the end of curfew still rings in the air. There is nobody in the piazza behind you to see, but you move with swift resolve, face hidden by the hood of your cloak. You press the paper against the wood, hammering nails into it top and bottom.

You have six more scrolls to put up across the city. Doing so at Palazzo Medici proved impossible, not with guards standing sentry outside the duke's residence day and night. But there are other places more important to the people of Florence. The doors of the archbishop's residence. The entrance of the Palazzo della Signoria. A column at the Mercato Vecchio. Places where good, humble people gather to talk and argue and make decisions.

Places where they could see the words on each scroll:

SAVONAROLA LIVES!

Strocchi woke in a way he had not known for six months. Instead of opening his eyes already overcome with exhaustion, he was . . . rested. Yes, it was only one night's sleep but after so long surviving with so little, the relief was like a downpour of rain after months of drought. His prayers had been answered at long last, and it was magnificent. This was more than being rested; this was a blessing.

That little Bianca had slept most of the night was thanks in no small part to Dr Orvieto's powders. So exhausted was Strocchi the previous night, he had forgotten the remedy from the Jewish physician until the twist of paper fell out of his tunic when he was preparing for bed. Eager to wash away the day's grime and frustration, Strocchi had pulled off his clothes and flung them to one side. The twist of paper came free, sliding across the floor.

Tomasia was hesitant about giving the powders to Bianca, but Strocchi reassured her. Orvieto was a good man and a very good doctor, beloved by the Jewish commune. He would never do anything to hurt their daughter. Nonetheless, Tomasia insisted she and Strocchi taste the remedy first, to be sure it was safe. When that caused them no harm, Tomasia added a few grains to Bianca's food. The effect was . . . remarkable. Their little girl was soon falling asleep on her mother's lap. Tomasia lay Bianca down in the cot and she slept for several hours without stirring once. Tomasia woke Bianca for a night feed and the bambina went straight back to sleep again. No crying, no wailing, nothing but blessed sleep.

Strocchi offered up a silent prayer of thanks as he dressed. One good night's sleep would not solve all his problems, but it brought strength to tackle the challenges ahead. The first was finding those responsible for Dovizi's murder.

'You're thinking about the case.' Tomasia was watching him from the bed, Bianca still asleep in the cot. 'You always chew your bottom lip when you think.'

Strocchi smiled while pulling on fresh hose. Tomasia had a mind as sharp as knives, able to make connections he sometimes struggled to see. 'I know who was murdered, how he died and where. But I have no witnesses, and no evidence that leads towards a killer.'

'Do you know why this man was killed?' Tomasia asked, sitting up to check on the bambina. Strocchi told her about the false proclamation, and how it linked the murder to Savonarola. 'That doesn't help much,' she said. 'Is it saying Dovizi was a traitor to Savonarola himself, or to the monk's ideals?'

Strocchi didn't have an answer. 'The way Dovizi was killed, the false proclamation . . . For all I know the accusation that he betrayed Savonarola – however he did that – could simply be a strategia to hide the true motives of those responsible.'

'Then pursue other questions, things you can be certain about, and perhaps the answer to why he was killed will emerge.' Tomasia arched an eyebrow. 'If I was Aldo, what would I want to know next?'

'Please, I had enough of him—'

'The sort of man Aldo is doesn't make him any less of an investigator. If anything, I'd say it makes him better than most. He understands those who live outside the law. That gives him insights you might not have.' Tomasia smiled. 'So, what would Aldo want to know next about Dovizi?'

Strocchi paused while pulling on his boots. 'Who benefits from the murder, that's what Aldo would ask. Who gains from Dovizi being killed?'

'It's as good a place to start as any,' Tomasia agreed.

She was right. Again. Strocchi climbed on the bed to kiss her. 'You look like a man who's rested,' she murmured, her hands sliding around Strocchi to pull him closer. 'Do you have to leave right now, or can you stay a little longer?'

Aldo strode north across Ponte Vecchio, grateful to be crossing the bridge before the butcher stalls and fish sellers were open for business. The early morning air was still fresh and crisp, but another scorching day seemed certain. Soon flies would be settling everywhere as the heat grew stifling and sticky, the sun a relentless presence overhead. The bridge would stink of guts and spilled blood as servants and wives sought fresh fish for Friday. Better to be as far from Ponte Vecchio as possible before that.

Leaving the bridge Aldo continued north, avoiding the turn east that would take him across Piazza della Signoria. He had seen enough of the square yesterday and carried no wish to walk across a dead man's place of execution. The murder of Dovizi had been precisely that, an execution designed to get the attention of Florentines . . .

But it was not Aldo's case to investigate. Strocchi had made that all too clear.

After passing several impressive palazzi Aldo went east, striding along dirt roads to reach the Podestà. The main gates were already open, two guards gossiping outside when they should have been standing sentry. Talk of Savonarola's supposed return had led drinkers to Zoppo's tavern the previous night; perhaps the same rumours had now reached the Podestà. But when Aldo approached the guards, the two men were ashen of face, shaking their heads.

'What's wrong?' he asked. 'What's happened?'

'A death,' one guard replied. 'In the cells . . .'

Aldo sprinted inside, a cold fist clenching within. Not Lippo, it mustn't be—

But the open cell door on the far side of the courtyard would not be denied. That was where Lippo had been secured. Now a handful of constables were standing around, staring into a cell as dark as a tomb. One of the men looked familiar.

'Benedetto,' Aldo called out. 'What's happened?'

The constable scowled. 'Stupid bastardo killed himself. He's not the one who will have to clean up his mess afterwards.'

Aldo fought the urge to slap Benedetto. A man was dead, and all the surly young constable could do was complain. 'Fetch a lantern.'

'Why should I—?'

'Fetch it,' Aldo hissed, not hiding the threat behind his words.

Benedetto scuttled away. Aldo glared at the others. 'Who found the body?' A hand went up. 'Name?'

'I don't know,' the constable replied. He was heavy of build and had a face lacking in guile. 'Never seen him before.'

'Not his name. Your name!'

'Oh. It's ... Manuffi.' He attempted a smile. Hapless and hopeless, it seemed.

'How did you find him?' Aldo pressed, wanting all the facts he could gather before going inside the cell. 'Well?'

'I was on night patrol with Benedetto,' Manuffi said. 'We got back as curfew ended. One of the guards asked us to check the cells, see if anyone needed water.' There was a half-empty wooden pail by his feet, a ladle inside it.

'And?'

'I opened the door, and the prisoner was dead. Hanged himself.' The constable made the sign of the cross. 'Our priest always said people who end their own lives burn in damnation. I don't care how bad life gets, I still wouldn't do what the prisoner did . . .'

Benedetto returned at last with a lantern, already lit. Aldo took it, sending the guards and other constables away but ordering Manuffi and Benedetto to stay.

The inside of the cell was all stone – walls, floor and ceiling. A straw mattress lay beside one wall, while the stench of human waste wafted from a hole in the centre of the cell. There was no window, no place for light to come in. Once the door was shut it would be dark as night in here. Aside from obscenities clawed into the stones, the only decoration Aldo could see was a single metal hook hammered into the mortar of one wall, above head height.

That was where Lippo had hanged himself.

Aldo moved closer, studying the dead prisoner. Lippo had

removed his hose to make a noose. He must have tied one end to the hook, put the noose round his neck and let himself drop. The dangling body reminded Aldo of a discarded child's toy, broken and unwanted.

He put a hand to Lippo's face. Cold, so probably dead for several hours.

Why had the thief killed himself? It made no sense. A single night in the Podestà cells was unpleasant, even frightening, but for most men it wouldn't be enough to drive them to end their lives. Lippo had been fearful of a return to Le Stinche, but Aldo had meant it when he'd offered to free the thief in exchange for information. No, this made no sense . . .

Aldo stepped back. A man in possession of both his arms could have done this easily, but Lippo only had one. Making the noose would have been difficult. Tying it to the hook even more so, especially in the dark, with only one hand to make the knot. Even then, the drop should not have been enough to break Lippo's neck. Aldo held the lantern close to the dead man's head. The neck was broken, twisted at an unnatural angle. That took force, and plenty of it. Far more than Lippo could have achieved by dropping himself.

Somebody did this to him.

They put the noose around Lippo's neck, tied the other end to the hook and then pulled the prisoner down with all their might. That would have broken his neck.

Aldo lifted Lippo's hand into the light of the lantern. Three nails were broken, his fingers bruised and bloody. He had fought back. His lips were bruised too. Something had been shoved into Lippo's mouth to keep him quiet, otherwise his cries would have alerted the few guards working in the Podestà after curfew. Unless it was guards who did this. Extra-judicial justice was sometimes administered in the cells, but only by order of the city and always with a priest present to give the last rites. That was never done after dark, and nobody but officers of the court and night patrols came or went from the building after curfew. So it was one of them – no, it probably needed two men – who had done this.

It was murder, committed by members of the court's own staff.

Aldo stalked from the cell, slamming the lantern down on the stones outside. 'Who was on guard duty last night?' he demanded.

'I-I'm not sure,' Manuffi stammered.

Aldo ignored him, jabbing a finger at Benedetto. 'Who was it? Tell me!'

'Nesi, I think,' the constable replied. 'Paoli and Ughi. Maybe Bocci?'

'Where are they?'

'Gone,' Manuffi said. 'They left when curfew was lifted.'

'Were they here when the body was found?'

The constable shrugged. 'Maybe?'

Aldo was struggling to contain his anger. 'Has Bindi arrived yet?'

Benedetto answered that. 'The segretario usually goes to Palazzo Medici first to deliver his morning report to the duke before coming to the Podestà.'

Aldo nodded. He had a choice to make: wait for Bindi, or confront the person responsible for what had happened to Lippo. The thief had been murdered inside a cell, his death made to look like a suicide. If one or more of the night guards had done this, it wasn't their idea. Judging by the body, whoever killed Lippo had been trying to get something from him – and Aldo already knew what that was. The death could have been accidental, but the outcome was still the same: a life ended and for no good reason.

Aldo knew in his palle who was to blame. Someone who never got blood on his own delicate hands, a man who used others as his weapons.

Ruggerio stared out of a window on the middle level of his palazzo, listening to the report from his maggiordomo, Alberti. The man had been a faithful servant all his adult life, rising from the role of messenger to lead the palazzo staff. More than that, Ruggerio had shaped Alberti to follow orders without question or qualm. Should someone require an inducement to act on Ruggerio's behalf, Alberti knew the precise frailties to exploit without being told. If punishment was necessary to protect Ruggerio's interests or his reputation, Alberti knew how much pain would be required and who was best chosen to administer it.

It was an unwelcome surprise to hear Alberti admitting error.

'Regretfully, signore, I have failed you in this matter. My preferred men within the Podestà were not on duty last night, so I had to employ the services of those less . . . skilled.'

Ruggerio fluttered a hand to dismiss any further apologies. They were of no interest.

'The thief was unable or unwilling to name those who had him spy on your villa,' Alberti continued, 'despite suffering considerable pain. That suggests he did not know his employers. He was a minor pickpocket, a man without loyalties or prospects. He had no reason to withhold anything. Even when close to death the thief denied such knowledge.'

Ruggerio sighed. Alberti was reliable to a fault in most circumstances. This lapse was . . . disappointing. 'Will your preferred men be on duty tonight?'

'Yes, signore. But that will not change the outcome.'

This explained why the maggiordomo had begun with an apology. 'The thief is dead?'

'Yes. The men pressed him too far and . . .'

Ruggerio let the admission of failure linger in the air. Beyond his window the city was stirring into life. Traders pushed carts laden with fruit and vegetables. Shopkeepers were opening their doors, hanging displays of wares outside to lure customers. Above the city was an unbroken expanse of pure azzurro, not a cloud in sight. It promised to be another day of Florence baking beneath the sun's relentless glare.

'The men did their best to make it seem like the thief took his own life,' Alberti said.

Ruggerio snorted at the chances of this convincing Aldo. He was too clever to believe such a ruse, and he would know who was responsible. But he must not be allowed to prove it. 'Those at the Podestà who failed, have you made suitable arrangements?'

'Yes, signore. My preferred men are meeting with them now.'

Ruggerio did not need to hear any more. He left the window, shedding his blue silk robe on the cool wooden floor as he returned to bed. 'Very well. I can expect a visit from Aldo before the morning is over. Have one of the kitchen staff bring me a selection of fruits. Send the pretty one, with the curls.'

'Raphael.'

'Yes, him. I need some amusement before the tempest arrives.'

Alberti retrieved the discarded robe, placing it carefully across the back of a chair. He bowed low before withdrawing. Ruggerio slipped into bed. It was regrettable the thief had died before revealing who sent him to study the villa. Ruggerio had his suspicions, but confirmation would have been useful. The killing was clumsy, inviting Aldo's wrath and potentially that of the Otto, but it did serve one purpose.

Now the thief could tell no one else what he knew.

Chapter Ten

Bindi waited in the duke's ufficio, head lowered in respect. Cosimo was listening while Campana whispered in his ear, the ducal segretario making sharp gestures with one hand. Bindi strained to hear what was passing between them, but the words eluded him. Whatever the topic, anger was settling into Cosimo's young features. That was not good.

Eventually the duke gave a curt nod and Campana stepped back. 'Well?' Cosimo asked Bindi.

'It seems the man killed in Palazzo della Signoria was Sandro Dovizi, a silk merchant. The evidence suggests he was once one of the Fanciulli, young men Savonarola sent to—'

'Yes, yes,' the duke cut in. 'I know who the Fanciulli were, and what they did.' He glanced at Campana. 'The name Dovizi sounds familiar. Did it not come up when we were drafting the law to forbid confraternities?'

Campana's brow furrowed. 'Yes . . . Yes, I believe it did. Dovizi is, or was, among the five founders of the Company of Santa Maria. We had a man inside that confraternity. He did not report any evidence of anti-Medici or pro-Savonarola activity within its membership or their activities. But if Dovizi was one of the Fanciulli when the monk held sway over the city, it is possible that the confraternity's other founders also held pro-Savonarola views.'

Bindi had dealt with them before, mostly when Girolamo Ruggerio had used his influence to interfere with or hamper investigations by the Otto. If Ruggerio was involved in Dovizi's killing, this matter had become even more incendiary . . . The segretario realized Cosimo was waiting for him. 'Forgive me, Your Grace, could you repeat that?'

'What is the matter with you?' the duke asked. 'Yesterday you did not know what the date was. Now you seem unable to answer simple questions. I asked what you knew about these false declarations that have appeared across the city, announcing Savonarola lives?'

Bindi frowned. He still had the document Strocchi had brought back from Palazzo Dovizi, yet the duke spoke as if there were others. 'Sorry, Your Grace, I don't—'

'Someone is putting them up in prominent places,' Campana cut in. 'Outside the monastery of San Marco. On the door to the archbishop's residence, even at the entrance of the Palazzo della Signoria.' He moved the letters atop Cosimo's table, revealing five proclamations, each like the document Bindi had locked away at the Podestà. But when Campana gave one to Bindi to read, he saw there were differences. The heading and first paragraph were the same, but the second block contained new threats:

The spirit of Savonarola lives! Those who betrayed him will suffer as our beloved frate suffered. Their punishment is long overdue. They must burn for their sins, as will all those who stand against the true teachings of Savonarola. Pray for our city and pray for your souls. Pray for forgiveness and you will know God's mercy. Pray for Florence and you shall bear witness as the frate's prophecies come true.

'My men confiscated a similar document yesterday, one that had been nailed to the doors of Palazzo Dovizi,' Bindi said. 'It claimed he was killed for betraying Savonarola. There was also a threat that others would soon suffer as Dovizi did.'

'You believe these false proclamations and the murder are linked,' Cosimo said.

'Yes, but my men are still—'

'Spare me your excuses,' the duke said, his lips whitening with anger. 'When this was a simple matter, the murder of one man, it was of limited consequence. But the more I hear of the circumstances surrounding that murder, the more significant it becomes. Someone is using this to sow doubt and discord across the city. There are people in Florence who still believe in Savonarola. The longer this continues, the more dangerous it becomes for our city. Do you understand?'

Bindi nodded. He also understood what Cosimo wasn't saying: that the young duke's brief reign over Florence was at risk if pro-Savonarola sentiment took hold again. The monk might be long dead, but there were plenty inside the city who would use a new surge in religious fervour as a weapon for their ambitions to topple Cosimo and all the Medici.

'Find who is doing this and bring them to justice,' the duke continued. 'Otherwise, I shall be forced to appoint a new segretario, someone capable of fulfilling their duties.'

Bindi took a step back, staggered by the sudden shift. Two days before he had been Cosimo's most esteemed segretario. Now the duke was threatening to replace him. 'The men of the Otto will find those responsible,' Bindi said, bowing as low as his rotund belly would allow, beads of hot sweat dripping down into his eyes.

'See that you do,' Cosimo replied.

A wave of his hand dismissed the segretario.

Bindi retreated from the ufficio, bowing again on his way out. But the duke did not acknowledge him.

Aldo stalked into the palazzo, pushing aside a servant and stopping only when he reached the internal courtyard. 'Ruggerio!' he bellowed, his voice bouncing around the walls. 'Ruggerio!' Aldo knew this was a mistake. Goading the silk merchant was as foolish as putting a hand in a basket of angry serpents, but he didn't care. For too long he had tolerated Ruggerio's meddling and interference. For too long he had been willing to accommodate Ruggerio, exchanging what was right for what was expedient. But any reward from making a contract with a diavolo was never worth the price, and Lippo had paid for that folly.

Ruggerio appeared at one of the windows overlooking the palazzo courtyard, pushing open the shutter to smirk at Aldo. 'My dear Cesare, is that you? What a delightful surprise.'

'Spare me your lies,' Aldo snapped. 'Why did you do it?'

Ruggerio feigned ignorance. 'Do what, may I ask?'

'Why have your men murder him?'

The silk merchant abandoned his pretence. 'If you're going to make such baseless accusations against me, I would have you do so to my face rather than shouting them from below. Come up to the parlour. My maggiordomo Alberti will escort you.'

Ruggerio withdrew, but Aldo wasn't willing to wait. He stormed up the main palazzo stairs to the middle level. The merchant's manservant appeared from a side door to usher Aldo into the same parlour as the previous day. This time Ruggerio was already present, perched in a high-backed chair like a prince or archbishop receiving a guest.

'Now, you were saying . . . ?'

'Why have Lippo murdered?' Aldo demanded. 'He was no threat to you.'

Ruggerio frowned. 'Lippo? That name isn't familiar. In fact, I can honestly say that I have never met anyone with the rather unfortunate name of Lippo.'

'He was killed last night in a cell at the Podestà.'

'Then I'm afraid your journey was wasted. I stayed here all night, with a guest. My servants could have confirmed that, if you'd bothered to ask them.'

Aldo was struggling to contain his anger, and the smug smile on Ruggerio's thin lips was making it worse. 'I never said you killed him. But I know you had him murdered.'

'Really? And what proof do you have for your assertion?'

'I—'

'Have you arrested whoever killed this poor soul while he was in the Otto's custody?'

'Not yet—'

'Have you a witness or some correspondence that confirms your accusation?'

'We are still—'

'Do you have anything whatsoever that links myself or my staff to this death?'

Aldo didn't trust himself to reply.

Ruggerio sighed and shrugged. 'In that case I'm not sure why you have come here. My dear Cesare . . . You don't mind if I call you that, do you?'

Aldo stayed silent.

'I'll take that as a no,' Ruggerio beamed, rising from his throne. 'My dear Cesare, you really must learn to control that temper. I thought you were better than this, but perhaps too many long months in the dominion have coarsened you, dulled your instincts.' He strolled over to a window, looking out at the city beyond. 'The man I knew would not have come to my palazzo, shouting accusations like some common country constable.'

'Nonetheless—' Aldo began.

'No, no, no.' Ruggerio cut him off. 'That won't do, it won't do at all. You have lost any element of surprise you might have brought here. You have flung words at me as if they were weapons but without any force of proof behind them so they cannot wound. You have made mistake after mistake since you came back to the city yesterday and this is yet another blunder on your part. Truly, I once thought of you as admirable, a man with whom I could enjoy the intrigues and intricacies of life here in Florence. But you have become an idiota, it seems, incapable of even amusing me. How . . . regrettable.'

Far worse than Ruggerio's scorn was the truth behind his words, and Aldo knew it. He had been a fool yesterday, and had made a fool of himself again today. It was his fault Lippo was dead. Others had killed the thief, either by accident or intention. But Aldo knew it was his visit to Ruggerio the previous day that had tied the noose around Lippo's neck.

'I could suggest you shouldn't blame yourself for what has happened,' Ruggerio said, glancing over a shoulder to smile at Aldo, 'but we both know that would be incorrect. You brought that thief to the city, you brought his presence to the attention of those who might wish to do him harm. What happened next was regrettable, yes, but accidents do occur – even inside the Podestà.'

Aldo was unable to swallow any more of this condescension. He stalked from the parlour, pursued by the taunting voice of

Ruggerio. 'What was it you said to me last year, Cesare? Consequences catch up with us all one day. Perhaps today is that day for you!'

It was a miracle the blaze had not spread from Signor Scarlatti's villa. The building was still on fire even though a full night and most of a morning had passed since Cassandra had first seen clouds of black smoke billowing into the air. But hard work and vigilance had kept the flames in place. If there had been strong winds all the surrounding hillsides would now be burning, the peasants' huts and farm buildings with them.

Cassandra made the sign of the cross. God had been with them during the night.

On seeing the smoke, she had cried out to Vincenzo in the stable block, sending him to find any workers still on the estate. Most were at the special Mass down in the village or had returned to their homes, but a few came running. Thanks to her vantage point in the loggia Cassandra had grasped the true danger of the fire. If it spread to fields and grasses parched by a month of drought, it would put everyone's home at risk.

Cassandra had Vincenzo run down to the village to tell those at the special Mass about the fire. She sent the fastest among the estate workers to help anyone already fighting the fire at the Scarlatti villa – the quicker assistance arrived, the better the chance of stopping the blaze. Fortunately, there were pathways between the estates, otherwise everyone would have had to run down to San Jacopo al Girone and back up the next hill.

Once the first workers had gone, Cassandra took a few minutes to organize those who remained. Stopping the fire would need water, and buckets to move it from the well on the Scarlatti estate.

She could see the fire already had a firm hold on the villa, large flames leaping towards the twilight sky. They would be fighting it for hours and fighting their own exhaustion while they did so. Cassandra had the women prepare food they could carry to those battling the blaze. Once everyone had a task, she ran across the hillside, weaving between the olive trees and grapevines, her path illuminated by the flames ahead.

By the time she reached Scarlatti's villa the building was lost, tongues of orange and yellow and red licking through shutters and consuming what was left of the roof. That heat . . . It had been hotter than the worst day of summer. People were hurling buckets of water at the fire, but Cassandra could see it was a wasted effort. 'Forget the villa!' she shouted at them. 'Save the other buildings! Save your homes!'

Soon lines were formed from the estate well to those dwellings most in danger from the fire. Buckets of water passed hand to hand in one direction, empty pails going the other way. Cassandra found Scarlatti's estate manager, Trigari. He was a jolly figure most days, content to let others strain and sweat while he tended vines. But the burning villa seemed to transfix him, like someone in the Bible turned to stone by the vengeful will of God.

'Where is Signor Scarlatti?' Cassandra had asked. 'Was he at home tonight? Is he still inside the villa?' Trigari did not reply, dancing flames reflected in his staring eyes.

Cassandra saw her counterpart at the Scarlatti estate, a plain-faced housekeeper called Federica. 'Have you seen the signore? Did he make it out?'

Federica shook her head, grim-faced. 'I pray he has, but none of the servants were inside when the fire started. We had all gone down to the village for Mass.' That explained why it had taken so long for the fire to be noticed. The parish priest Father Ognissanti had been saying a Mass for rain to break the drought.

At that moment the burning villa gave an almighty groan and its roof fell inward, hurling clouds of sparks and embers into the night air. A beam must have given way . . .

All of that was hours ago. Everyone had battled through the night and long past dawn to keep the flames restricted to the villa. Scarlatti's residence was still aflame, but the worst of the danger seemed to have passed. Cassandra certainly hoped that was true. The villagers and estate workers were spent, most slumped on dry dirt, faces streaked with soot and sweat.

She heard a gasp behind her and turned to see Ognissanti approaching. The priest clutched a bible to his chest in one hand, the other making the sign of the cross. 'How was it this fire did not get any further?' he asked Cassandra.

'The Lord must have heard our prayers last night.'

Strocchi headed east across the city, carrying the sack of clothes he had taken from Aldo the previous night. It was early enough for the tall buildings on either side to shield him from the sun, yet he was already perspiring. Drought was a problem for those out in the dominion, especially farmers struggling to grow their crops, but soon it would affect the city as well. If late May was this hot, what would Florence be like by July, by August? Perhaps he could persuade Tomasia to take Bianca to his mama's home in the countryside, to give them an escape from the sweltering months ahead. Duties for the Otto would stop him going, but there was no reason they should have to suffer alongside him. The humid summer nights would be unbearable for the poor bambina. If Bianca was suffering, he and Tomasia would suffer too.

He stopped at Piazza della Signora and, thanks to Aldo's description, soon located the stable where Dovizi had been tied to that cart. But there was nothing more to be found there, no fresh evidence. Strocchi continued east until he came within sight of Le Stinche. The forbidding stone prison glowered at anyone who approached. Many citizens crossed the narrow road to avoid passing in front of its entrance. Built like a fortress, the few windows in the thick stone walls were high up with bars across them to stop the curious looking in or prisoners getting out. Little else announced the building's purpose – but everyone knew. Most inmates were there due to unpaid debts, so being a prisoner in Le Stinche was a mark of shame. Few emerged unchanged. Tomasia certainly avoided talking about the months she had spent inside the prison for her late brother's losses.

Strocchi would rather go anywhere else, but da Soci was inside the prison. He had no choice but to try to discover if the notary had had any part in Dovizi's murder. Strocchi paused at the low doorway, studying the two words carved into a stone plaque above the entrance: *Opertet Misereri*. Strocchi had seen little evidence of mercy during his few visits inside these walls. He hammered at the door and was soon admitted.

Protocol required officers of the Otto to seek permission to question an inmate, so Strocchi was shown into the ufficio of the prison's formidable commander. Captain Duro lurked behind a plain wooden table. He had a shaven head, a grizzled face and the surly manner to match. 'What's in the sack?' Duro asked.

'A dead man's clothes,' Strocchi replied, holding it open for the captain. Duro glanced at the silk tunic, grunting his disinterest.

'You want to see who?'

'Cristoforo da Soci,' Strocchi said. 'He was brought here a few days ago, sentenced to three years for conspiring against the city.

The court directed he serve that time in the prison ward for lunatics.'

Duro picked at a piece of meat caught in his teeth. 'Doubt you'll get much from him,' the captain said. 'Being locked in with the lunatics breaks a man fast. But you're welcome to try.' He nodded to the guard by the ufficio door, who opened it. The audience was at an end.

Strocchi didn't move. 'Has da Soci had any visitors?'

'No. And he's not received or sent any letters.' Duro did not bother hiding his impatience. 'Anything else?'

'Yes, I need one of your men to bring da Soci out into the prison courtyard. He's more likely to give me answers in the open air.'

Duro scowled before sucking breath in between his teeth. 'Very well. But make it quick. Disruption to the daily routine is a disruption to all inside my prison.'

Strocchi was escorted to the internal courtyard and told to wait. He found a bench against a wall in the morning sunshine, hoping the warmth might stop his shivering. If summer had come early to Florence, inside the prison was closer to autumn. Stone walls loomed on all four sides, a watchtower above the main entrance. Strocchi could hear distant screams and cries of bleak pain from the few doorways leading deeper into the prison. A small tabernacolo on the wall opposite offered a place for inmates to worship, though no one seemed to notice it. Instead, a handful of haggard prisoners shuffled round the courtyard in a slow circle, their faces empty of hope. But they were as playful as a courtesan flirting for business in a church compared to the prisoner brought from the pazzeria.

Cristoforo da Soci had been a notary before coming to the attention of the Otto. If not for his belief in Savonarola and a willingness to spread prophecies about the monk, da Soci would probably have lived a life without incident or accident, a minor functionary in the life of the city. The man who had stood accused was earnest, bewildered at being brought before the city's most feared criminal court, yet confident that the truth would deliver him. That man was now gone, replaced by a broken husk.

The prisoner stumbled across the courtyard to Strocchi, a guard following. When he reached the bench, da Soci crumpled onto it, as if will alone was all that had been holding him up. Strocchi gestured for the guard to leave; da Soci was no threat to anyone anymore. His skin was pale, so drained of life it was almost grey. There were bruises on both his arms, disappearing beneath his torn tunic. Purple and yellow also blossomed across his face where dried blood and scratches marked both cheeks. Strocchi did not know what age da Soci had been when he stood trial – close to sixty, perhaps – but a few days in Le Stinche had added years. A stench of stale piss and worse rose from his stained clothes.

'Have you come to release me?' da Soci asked, hope lightening his eyes a little.

'No,' Strocchi replied. 'I need to ask you about Sandro Dovizi.'

'Who?' There was no hesitation in the response, no sign of recognition in the face.

'Signor Sandro Dovizi. He was murdered yesterday. His killer accused Dovizi of betraying Savonarola.'

'Sorry, I've never heard of Signor Dovizi before. I am sorry for his death.'

Strocchi pulled the dead man's tunic from the sack, showing it to da Soci. 'Do you recognize this?' The prisoner shook his head. Strocchi believed da Soci. He was making no attempt to deceive and there was no guile in him, just as there had been none when da Soci stood before the Otto. 'Do you believe there were men in this city who betrayed Savonarola?'

'Betrayed the frate?'

'Yes.'

'I don't understand,' da Soci said. 'Why are you asking me this? The frate has been dead forty years. His beliefs live on in the hearts of good men, but that is all . . .'

Strocchi signalled to the guard, telling him to return the prisoner to the lunatic ward. There was no reason to ask any further questions, not when da Soci knew nothing of what had happened to Dovizi. It was clear the murder following so close to da Soci's imprisonment was happenstance, after all.

Someone else was responsible for the murder in Piazza della Signoria.

Chapter Eleven

After leaving Ruggerio's palazzo Aldo did not return immediately to the Podestà. That would not be wise. He was too angry, most of all with himself, for letting frustration and guilt get the better of reason. Far safer to go somewhere he could find peace and quiet. He marched south to the Arno before turning east, stalking beside the river until his pace began to slow.

Ruggerio's mocking words had cut to the bone; it hurt how accurate his comments were. There was no proof that Ruggerio was responsible for the death of Lippo at the Podestà. As for blundering into the palazzo making wild accusations . . . that had achieved nothing. Lippo was still dead, and now the silk merchant was on his guard. Ruggerio was probably drafting a letter of complaint to the Otto as a way of twisting the knife.

Better to go back to the Podestà, and find out more about the guards on duty the previous night. Aldo knew Ruggerio would not have been so foolish as to employ them himself, but the men who killed Lippo might still name their paymaster. That could prove a link between them and the merchant, assuming Ruggerio hadn't already broken the chain. He possessed a ruthlessness that would make a diavolo blush.

Aldo strode north. The quickest path to the Podestà was across Piazza della Signoria. The square would be busy but there was little time to waste. Aldo emerged from an alleyway into the piazza and regretted his choice at once. A crowd had gathered where Savonarola had died forty years ago and where Dovizi had been murdered less than forty hours ago. Aldo was turning away when he heard them chanting: 'Savonarola lives! Savonarola lives!'

The contrast with the drinkers crowded into Zoppo's tavern the previous night was stark. Those had been typical Florentine workers, people of simple pleasures who feared a return to the days when religious fervour turned the city into a fortress of piety and prayer. This mob forming in the piazza was cut from other cloth. These were people of fervent faith and righteous indignation, believers of absolute certainty and merciless condemnation. Zoppo's drinkers were satisfied with more wine. Those shouting at the Palazzo della Signoria would never be satisfied because the new Jerusalem promised by Savonarola could never be attained. He was long dead, but the men and women in the piazza were convinced he lived.

Fools, all of them.

Aldo went round the edge of the piazza, avoiding the throng. The crowd was growing larger and louder, but those with jurisdiction here in Florence could attempt to bring this rabble to order. It was not his fight, and for that Aldo was grateful. As he approached the Podestà a familiar figure was waiting outside the stone citadel, leaning on a crutch in the scorching sunshine. It was a shock to meet Zoppo away from his tavern, so much so that Aldo did not recognize the cripple at first.

'Is it true?' Zoppo asked. He jerked his head at the men standing sentry outside the Podestà. 'They wouldn't let me in, but I heard my brother is dead.'

'Let me talk to the guards, see if—'

'Is it true?' Zoppo demanded, trembling with anger.

Aldo stepped back. He'd never seen the tavern keeper so furious, but Zoppo deserved an honest answer. 'Yes. Lippo's body was found in a cell not long after dawn.'

'How? How did he die?'

'It looked like he hanged himself—'

'What? That's a cartload of merda. Lippo was too much of a coward for that.'

'I told you what it looked like,' Aldo went on. 'I think he was killed.'

'Who would want him dead?'

Leading Zoppo away from the gates, Aldo explained what he believed had happened: the failed torture, Lippo's death, the attempt to make it seem as if the prisoner had taken his life. 'I suspect one or more of the overnight guards did this, acting for someone else. Someone who wanted to know what Lippo was doing in the countryside.'

Zoppo stopped, his brow furrowing. 'You're saying Ruggerio found out what my brother was doing and had him killed for it?'

'I can't prove that, not yet.'

'And you never will. I told you, that bastardo would have his own children murdered to save his skin, if he had any. Whoever killed my brother is probably dead by now too.'

Aldo feared Zoppo was right. Ruggerio had been too calm earlier, no sign of fear in his face when confronted about Lippo's death. Yes, the Podestà would likely be short two men when the night guards came on duty at curfew.

'But how did Ruggerio find out about Lippo, what he'd done?' Zoppo jabbed a finger into Aldo's chest. 'How did Ruggerio know where my brother was?'

'I . . .' Aldo couldn't finish his sentence, but it didn't matter.

'You told him,' Zoppo hissed. 'Why would you do that?'

'It was . . . a mistake.'

The tavern keeper laughed, but the sound was bitter and angry. 'A mistake? Yes, it was. You make a mistake, and my brother pays for it – with his life!' Zoppo flung a fist at Aldo, but he swayed out of its way and the cripple went sprawling. Aldo reached down to help but Zoppo slapped the hand away. 'Get off me, you piece of merda!'

The guards outside the Podestà moved to intervene but Aldo waved them back. Zoppo retrieved his crutch and clambered back upright. He glared at Aldo. 'Don't you ever come back to my tavern. You're as dead to me as my brother is now.'

Zoppo lurched away on his one leg, leaving Aldo alone in the street.

Strocchi headed for Palazzo Dovizi, intent on learning more about its owner. Returning to the grand residence was a different experience from the previous afternoon. The warmth of the day was becoming oppressive already, but there were no angry citizens clustered outside this time. A few people peered at the palazzo while hurrying by, whispering to those alongside them. It seemed Dovizi's death was common knowledge.

Strocchi took in the wealth that had been spent building the palazzo. It was bounded on all four sides by streets and alleys, occupying the entire plot of land between them. The finest stone had been used to construct the walls, while decorations carved around the windows became progressively finer the higher the eye rose. The palazzo had three levels, as was the way with the homes of wealthy merchants: a ground floor given over to business, the middle to family, and the upper level to servants.

When Strocchi first came to the city he could not understand why the bedchambers of servants were on the highest level of a palazzo. Did that not mean they had the best views across the city? Perhaps; although where there were such vistas to be appreciated, the owners often had a loggia built so they could savour these sights for themselves. The cost of living on a palazzo's upper level was paid in the summer months, when those rooms became sweltering ovens. Sleeping in a puddle of sweat was neither a pleasure nor a privilege.

Nonetheless it was clear from Dovizi's home that he had been a man of considerable wealth, even among the merchants of Florence. Aside from inheritance, few acquired such riches without making enemies. That meant discovering whether any of the victim's most fierce rivals might have chosen to rid themselves of Dovizi. His murder was extreme, even obscene. But that could have been a stratagemma, a feint to draw away the eyes of the Otto towards other suspects. Strocchi sighed. The further he progressed with this investigation, the more complicated it became. Like a serpent attempting to swallow large prey, there always seemed to be more to take in. But it was too late to stop now. Better to keep going and see where that led.

Strocchi approached the palazzo doors. Nails still protruded from the wood; nobody had thought to pull them out. The main entrance was closed, the large double doors shut and bolted from within – a sure sign of troubles. No merchant shut his doors to business during daylight, except to attend church or because of a family tragedy. But the smaller door to one side for servants remained ajar, so Strocchi slipped through that.

The interior of Palazzo Dovizi still had its impressive marble floor and exotic plants, but the difference in mood from the day before was stark. Strocchi could hear weeping in a distant room, hushed whispers, voices full of fear and worry even if the words were not clear. In other circumstances an assistant would be ready to welcome any visitor before ushering them to the merchant's showroom. But Dovizi was dead, his business at a standstill.

A servant appeared, the same nervous man who had answered questions the previous day. His face fell at seeing Strocchi. 'We were wondering when you would return. Before you came here yesterday, we did not know . . .' The servant crossed himself.

Strocchi offered sympathies for what had happened before asking the servant's name.

'Zitelle. I am – was – the signore's maggiordomo,' he replied, his pride blossoming for a moment. Zitelle could not have seen more than twenty-five summers, but that thinning hair and stooped stance made him appear closer to forty.

'Can you tell me about Signor Dovizi? What kind of man was he?'

'A good man. A wise man,' Zitelle replied.

'Did he have many enemies?'

'No, of course not.' The servant seemed affronted. 'Why would he?'

'I understood your signore was a successful silk merchant—'

'Very successful,' Zitelle volunteered.

'A very successful silk merchant,' Strocchi agreed. 'But that is a fiercely competitive trade. He must have rivals, yes? Men who would wish to best him in that business?'

'I'm sure he did . . . but none that could better him. Signor Dovizi was among the finest of men. He would never rejoice in the failures of others.' The servant's face showed a fervour Strocchi had seen the previous day in the old women praying for Savonarola outside. Zitelle believed in Dovizi's goodness much as those widows did the monk's teachings. There would be little of use coming from the mouth of this servant; like the widows, he was too blinded by devotion to a dead man.

'To run such a successful business, Signor Dovizi must have had help,' Strocchi said. 'Are any of his assistants in the palazzo today?'

'Yes, young Orbatello. I believe he is in the showroom.' Zitelle led Strocchi through the exotic trees and plants of the internal courtyard to a pair of doors painted a vibrant azzurro, adorned with gold leaf. The servant tapped at the doors with chaste modesty.

'Who is it?' a terse male voice called from within. 'I asked not to be disturbed.'

Strocchi announced himself as an officer of the Otto.

'You'd best come in.'

Zitelle bowed before withdrawing, leaving Strocchi to open the doors for himself. When he did, a powerful aroma billowed out, a heady mixture of woodlands and menthol, herbs and spices that made Strocchi's nose tingle and his eyes water. That distinctive, almost overpowering scent could only be one thing: camphor. Cloth merchants used it to keep moths away from their precious fabrics. Strocchi studied the showroom. Yes, there were metal bowls suspended from the ceiling above Dovizi's stock.

The room was an array of vibrant colours: azzurro and cinnabar, cerulean and topaz, every hue Strocchi had ever seen in nature and more besides. Bolt upon bolt of silks were piled high around the chamber, some rolled out as displays across tables while others stood ready to be shown. Moving among them was a man with a harassed expression. Zitelle had called him young Orbatello, but the assistant appeared closer to thirty than twenty – perhaps it was the name Dovizi had called him. Orbatello had raven black hair swept back from intense features and a sharp nose. He wore a crimson silk tunic, far grander than most assistants.

The wave of camphor overwhelmed Strocchi, making him cough.

'Don't worry, it will pass,' Orbatello said, gesturing at the bowls suspended in the air. 'The signore is – was – very protective of his silks. He insisted I refill the salt and camphor every day. I must have done so this morning without even questioning it.'

Strocchi's coughing eased, the scent lessening with the doors open. 'Why are you here? Signor Dovizi is dead.'

'I've nowhere else to go,' the assistant replied. 'This room and the silks here have been my life for fifteen years. With the signore gone . . .' He held up a small, leather-bound journal. 'I'm making an inventory of his stock, in case any of our rivals wish to buy them. I believe it's what the signore would have wanted.'

'Are there no relatives to inherit the business?'

Orbatello shook his head. 'Signor Dovizi was the last of his line. He has – had – no other famiglia and was never blessed with children himself. No doubt his rivals will be here soon to make derisory offers for his best silks before the signore can even be buried.'

'Perhaps one of them will also offer you a job,' Strocchi said.

'Perhaps, but not as their closest assistant. I will have to take whatever position they offer me, no matter how demeaning, and prove my worth all over again.'

Orbatello made no effort to hide his frustration and bitterness, but it was loosening his tongue, so Strocchi did not begrudge the sour mood. 'Who were Signor Dovizi's main rivals? Who stands to benefit from his loss?'

'All of them,' Orbatello replied. 'We have the finest fabrics in Florence, despite what others might claim. Those jackals in the Arte della Seta will be fighting amongst themselves for his customers.'

'You don't sound fond of the silk guild.'

'With good reason,' the assistant replied, scowling.

'Is there any particular member who clashed with Signor Dovizi?'

'Oh, yes,' Orbatello said. 'They had known each other for more than forty years, were supposed to be brethren. They even founded a confraternity together, along with three others. But there was no love lost between any of them.'

Strocchi suspected he already knew whom the assistant was talking about but still had to be certain. 'And what is the name of your signore's main rival?'

'Girolamo Ruggerio. If anyone will gain from the signore's death, it is that bastardo.'

Strocchi had first encountered Ruggerio two winters ago, not long after becoming a constable. The merchant had ordered the murder of a young man who might have disclosed a secret about Ruggerio. When the investigation got too close, Ruggerio had two of his own guards confess to the killing. He was a sly man who used others as weapons and savoured making fools of his enemies. Strocchi had hoped to avoid meeting with Ruggerio, but it seemed that could not be escaped.

Orbatello's gaze slid to the sack in Strocchi's grasp. A silk sleeve was hanging from it. 'May I see that?' the assistant asked. Strocchi emptied the sack onto a chair. Orbatello picked up the tunic, holding it aloft. 'I know this garment. It belonged to the signore, though he didn't wear it often. I haven't seen him in it for at least a year. Where did you find this?'

'Signor Dovizi wore it to meet whoever killed him.'

Orbatello shook his head. 'That makes no sense, no sense at all.' He pointed to the emblem embroidered in the silk. 'That is the symbol of the Company of Santa Maria, the confraternity he helped found. You'll find similar garments upstairs in the signore's clothes. This version . . . only the five founders are permitted to use it. But the confraternity has not met for months. There was no reason for the signore to be wearing this.'

Strocchi added this to the list of unanswered questions arising from the murder. 'You said Dovizi and Ruggerio are two of the confraternity's founders. Who are the others?'

'Benozzo Scarlatti, Roberto Ghiberti and Luca Uccello. The five of them used to meet here in the palazzo, but I haven't seen them all together for several years.'

Strocchi pressed the assistant for more, but Orbatello had nothing else to share. He was too concerned with his own prospects. Without famiglia to claim Dovizi's inheritance, it seemed certain the business would be consumed by his rivals. Once that happened the palazzo was likely to be sold or stand empty. Strocchi thanked the assistant for his help before leaving the showroom. It was a blessing to escape the camphor-laden air.

On his way out Strocchi encountered Zitelle lurking near the palazzo entrance. 'What will happen to us?' the servant asked. 'Signor Dovizi kept a full staff of servants. Where will we go, what will all of us do now he's . . .' The words faltered in Zitelle's mouth, as if he was still unable to admit what had happened to Dovizi out loud.

'I do not know,' Strocchi admitted. 'But if your signore is – was – the man you believed him to be, it seems likely he would have anticipated this day.'

Zitelle flinched. 'He knew that someone planned to kill him?'

'No, that's not . . . Signor Dovizi would have made a will for his estate. If you can find that document, it should reveal what he intended after he was . . . gone. For all of you.'

The servant managed a weak smile. 'Yes, the signore was a thoughtful, thorough man. He would not have left anything to chance. I will search among his papers.'

Strocchi could stay and look through the papers himself. There might be documents pointing to who was responsible for Dovizi's death. But it could take hours, even days – and Bindi would not wait that long for answers. Zitelle was used to his signore's handwriting, he was far more likely to recognize any important papers. 'If you find the will, bring it to me at the Podestà. The court may be able to help you and the other servants get justice.' That was less than honest – the Otto had no jurisdiction in such matters – but it offered some comfort to the maggiordomo and should keep him searching.

Zitelle nodded, opening the door so Strocchi could leave. 'Thank you, thank you.'

Strocchi stepped out of the Podestà into roasting sunshine. A year ago, bending the truth like that would never have occurred to him. Now it was an approach he was willing to consider in pursuit of justice. Perhaps, slowly, he was becoming a true Florentine.

Ruggerio sat alone in his sala, picking at the platters of food spread out in front of him. A fish pie flavoured with oranges competed with spiced veal, roasted peacock tongues and a selection of salads. Most households would not serve meat on a Friday, but Ruggerio had little interest in Church rituals. As if the Almighty cared whether meat was eaten on one day but not the next. Such dogma was fit only for the foolish and the faithful.

He had called for the feast after Aldo's departure, eager to enjoy his triumph over the troublesome officer. But by the time the food was ready Ruggerio's appetite had gone. Much as he savoured tormenting Aldo, the failure to discover who had paid that one-armed thief to spy on the villa above San Jacopo al Girone was gnawing at Ruggerio. Someone wanted to know the strengths and weaknesses of his country estate – why? What did they hope to gain from such knowledge? Despite the early summer drought parching the city, he had no plans to visit his villa for at least another month. Or had they sent the thief knowing Lippo was incompetent enough to be discovered? Was it one stratagemma hidden within another, a feint designed to make him believe the villa was unsafe as a sanctuary? Did those responsible want him to stay in the city instead, driven mad by heat?

Dovizi's murder, the intrusion at the villa, both events coming so close together . . . This could not be happenstance. For months now – no, more than a year – Ruggerio had sensed a gathering threat, like the first aroma of burning as sparks catch hold of tinder. It started with his sister, and the Convent of Santa Maria Magdalena. For years his confraternity had used the convent as a place to store holy relics, while the five founders kept certain documents relating to their quintet nestled among the bits of bone supposed to come from saints and saviours. Locking those documents away kept them safe from outsiders – and stopped any of the five using what was hidden in the papers against their fellow founders.

The previous spring Ruggerio had clashed with his sister, the convent abbess. He wished to reclaim the documents, but she refused, insisting all five founders must be present when the papers were taken from the convent. Attempts to secure them by other means were no more successful, to Ruggerio's frustration. Keeping himself distant from certain actions was usually a wise strategia, but it meant entrusting important tasks to others. That did not always bring the desired outcome. The failed efforts led to the convent being dissolved, and the confraternity's papers disappeared during the dissolution.

The missing documents could bring ruin on any of the five founders. That was the true reason why the coward Scarlatti had announced his retirement to the countryside. Rather than spend his final years in Le Stinche, Scarlatti had fled to cower in his hillside villa. The others stayed in Florence, but the law promulgated against confraternities by the new duke meant none of them had been in each other's company since Scarlatti had fled from the city.

That had suited Ruggerio . . . until now. There was no escaping the truth any longer. One of the founders was attacking the others. Scarlatti could not be responsible, he was too busy hiding in his country villa, praying for redemption. That left only Uccello and Ghiberti. Both had the palle; to determine which man it was, Ruggerio knew he had to look them both in the eyes.

He clapped his hands and Alberti appeared from a side door. 'Signore?'

'I need you to take a message to two old friends. Make sure you deliver my words to them yourself and return with their replies as fast as you can. Is that clear?'

The maggiordomo bowed in acknowledgement.

'Tell them this: come to my palazzo now. All our lives depend upon it.'

Chapter Twelve

Bindi festered in his ufficio after returning from Palazzo Medici. Hearing a prisoner had died in the cells during the night only worsened his mood, as did the unwanted correspondence delivered by messenger soon after that. But it was the injustice of what had occurred at Palazzo Medici that was the largest stone in Bindi's shoe. A day ago, Cosimo had seemed satisfied with a promise that the Otto would find those responsible for Dovizi's murder.

Now that young upstart was threatening to appoint a new segretario to the court, all because someone was posting false declarations that Savonarola was alive! What could a humble functionary do against such folly? Nothing. In truth there was nothing to do except ensure the duke's orders were carried out. But that didn't mean others shouldn't suffer. That didn't mean others shouldn't know the same overwhelming sense of humiliation.

And Bindi knew just the man who should suffer first.

He left orders with guards outside the Podestà that if Aldo returned, the officer must report immediately to the segretario's ufficio. When Bindi heard the knock at his door, he made Aldo remain outside before allowing him in. Aldo seemed much the same as he had been before leaving the city. Where other men felt obliged to fill a silence with words, Aldo stood quiet and still in front of the table. Eventually Bindi tired of waiting.

'I'm told you have claimed our night guards killed a prisoner in his cell.'

'I do not know who murdered Lippo,' Aldo replied, 'but his death was a crime.'

'Those who found the body said it was suicide, and plainly so.'

'Then they are fools or cowards, unwilling to accuse one of their fellow guards.'

'The prisoner hanged himself—'

'Lippo only had one arm,' Aldo cut in. 'He could not have done this.'

Bindi sat back in his chair. 'You dare to interrupt me?'

Aldo stopped himself replying. Bindi enjoyed the anger in Aldo's face, arching an eyebrow at the way both fists were clenching and unclenching at his sides. Finally, Bindi gave a gracious nod, indicating he would allow the officer to speak. 'Forgive me, segretario,' Aldo said. 'I brought the prisoner to the Podestà yesterday, intending to question him today. He was killed before I could do that.'

'This explains your frustration but does not excuse it. And as for these accusations . . . Do you have any proof? Any evidence that Lippo was murdered by one of our own men?'

'As I said, Lippo could not have done this to himself.'

'The correct answer is no. You have no evidence.'

'I believed he was tortured for information. His fingers were bruised and bloody. Three of his nails were broken. That shows he fought back against whoever did this. It must have been at least two men. His lips were bruised as well, suggesting someone gagged him.'

'Why would these supposed attackers gag the prisoner if they were torturing him for information?' Bindi snorted at that. 'He couldn't speak with a gag in his mouth, could be?'

'The gag was for when Lippo was being hanged, so he couldn't cry out for help.'

The segretario tired of this nonsense. 'I'm sorry, but I do not accept a word of this. Any cuts or bruises or broken nails were suffered while he hanged himself. As you say, he only had one arm, so it's little surprise he found ending his life such a difficult task.'

'But segretario—'

'Enough!' Bindi snapped, losing control of his temper for a moment. 'Enough,' he repeated, making his words quieter. 'There is another matter we must discuss.' Aldo did not speak, so Bindi brandished the letter he had received. 'This came to the Podestà, marked for my attention. It seems claiming the Otto's own guards are guilty of murder isn't enough folly for one day. You have been out in the city, accusing a prominent citizen and leading guild member of commissioning this murder. Is that correct?'

'I had good reason to—'

'Is that correct?' Bindi demanded, rising from his chair. He'd had a bellyful of this insolent, self-righteous officer. It was time Aldo understood who was in charge. 'Well?'

'I believed Girolamo Ruggerio was—'

'No!' Bindi slammed a fist down on his table. 'I do not need to hear any more about your beliefs or your justifications. I do not know why you chose to accuse Signor Ruggerio in his own palazzo, nor what you hoped to achieve by such madness. But it is evident you have become a liability to this court and its position within the city.'

Aldo glared at the segretario. 'I do not represent the Otto in Florence. My jurisdiction is outside the city walls in the dominion.'

'Precisely. And that is where you shall remain until you are summoned back. I hereby demote you to constable. You have until curfew tonight to leave the city. If you do not, you will be arrested, convicted and summarily banished.' Bindi sank back down into his high-backed chair. 'Need I say anything more?'

Aldo shook his head.

'Then you may leave.' Bindi dismissed the constable with a wave of his hand. He waited until Aldo had stalked to the ufficio door before speaking again. 'One last thing . . .'

Aldo stopped but did not look back.

Bindi smiled. 'Do enjoy the countryside. I suspect you will be there quite a while.'

Aldo marched from the Podestà and headed east, seething at Bindi's intervention. That the segretario sided with Ruggerio and his accusations was little surprise. Bindi would always give way when someone of significance or influence applied pressure or threatened his position. The man was as servile as he was craven. In the past it had been possible to stiffen Bindi's resolve by persuading him to defend the Otto and its men from attack. Doing so ensured the authority of the court – and, naturally, that of Bindi himself – remained sacrosanct. Such a tactic could not be presented to the segretario directly; for that to be adopted he had to believe it was his own initiative.

But something had changed during the months Aldo had spent outside Florence. Bindi seemed less willing to hear reason. And it was likely Cosimo was putting pressure on the Otto to find those feeding the flames of pro-Savonarola fervour taking hold of the city. The duke was young, but advisors such as Campana would have been whispering to him about what had happened to the Medici last time religious mania swept Florence. Cosimo had been leader little more than a year, and officially recognized as duke for even less. Aldo knew the young leader a little, having encountered him several times in the days before Cosimo was chosen to succeed his cousin. Cosimo would use every tool to hand to avoid the same ignominy as that which had befallen his Medici predecessors.

Aldo strode past Le Stinche, ignoring the prison. There was no use blaming Cosimo or even Bindi for all that had gone wrong in the past day and night. It was his own fault that Bindi was unwilling to see sense about Lippo's murder. Perhaps the taunts of Ruggerio had stung so much because the barbs were sharpened with the truth. All those months in the dominion . . . He had lost his ability to persuade and his talent for seeing danger before it struck. Aside from a night spent with Saul, this trip to Florence had been disastrous. Angering Strocchi, being humiliated not once but twice by Ruggerio, the killing of Lippo, losing Zoppo as an informant . . . Even a happy hour visiting Tomasia and little Bianca had turned sour, driving Strocchi further away from him. Now he was effectively being banished to the countryside and demoted to constable. Palle!

In truth Aldo cared little about that last indignity. Officer or constable, it made little difference. But the pleasure the demotion had given Bindi made Aldo's anger as hot as the sun overhead. A man was dead, killed in the Podestà cells, yet the segretario was more interested in petty victories and demeaning those whom he could bully without fear.

Aldo found the stable where he had left the horse borrowed from Ruggerio's estate. The beast was well rested and ready for the ride home. Returning to San Jacopo al Girone would certainly be quicker without Lippo to slow his progress.

That was what Aldo regretted most. It was his fault Lippo had died, regardless of whether the cause was murder or an accidental killing. The thief would probably still be alive if he had been questioned the previous night. And he would certainly still be breathing if Ruggerio had never been told about Lippo studying the merchant's country villa. Each step had been ill chosen, all of them leading to one place. Nothing Aldo could say or do would reverse this. He had not tortured or killed Lippo, but the outcome was still the same. All that remained for Lippo was a pauper's grave, and the bitter anger of his brother.

Aldo walked the borrowed horse through Porta la Croce before climbing into the saddle outside the eastern gate. He rode away from the city, not looking back. Florence was behind him now, and would remain so for some time to come.

Ruggerio stood by the windows of his salone, watching the street below. He wanted to see how Uccello and Ghiberti arrived, so he could judge their attitudes to being summoned. Alberti had reported on how both men responded to the invitation. Uccello arched an eyebrow before grandly nodding his assent, dismissing the maggiordomo with a flutter of his fingers. Ghiberti had cursed and stamped around his ufficio, demanding more detail. When none was forthcoming, Ghiberti gruffly agreed to come when he was able.

The responses were typical of both men.

Ruggerio had known each since before their palle dropped. The five founders had grown up within a few streets of each other in the western quarter. They'd played dice together behind the nearest church while their families were inside praying. But for being the same age and living close together, Ruggerio doubted they would have been friends, let alone bonded for life.

Savonarola was responsible for that.

It was Dovizi who'd suggested they join the Fanciulli when the monk's grip on the city was taking hold. Aside from the gullible Scarlatti, none of them was fervent in their faith. The Church was part of life, yet that was true of everyone. But Dovizi had heard how the Fanciulli were being encouraged to gather donations from the people of Florence. Ruggerio was the first to agree. His only hesitation had been a prick of envy at not having seen for himself the opportunity to fill their pouches with coin while being seen to do good deeds. No longer would the five of them be called troublemakers; now they would be servants of God.

It was the perfect mask for them to wear. When else could youths yet to see sixteen summers knock at doors and demand those within surrender coin or valuable possessions? As Savonarola's influence on the city grew, fewer people were willing to challenge the Fanciulli. The five of them proved so successful that Savonarola himself sent a summons to have them brought to his monastery at San Marco. Ever the coward, Scarlatti all but pissed himself as they waited, so convinced was he that the monk knew their secret: for every coin they added to the Church's coffers, the five were hiding away more for themselves.

Savonarola cut an unimpressive figure when they were brought before him. Thin of face, with a prominent hooked nose and bulging eyes, he was an ugly man. But there was no denying the power of the monk's speech when talking. For a few moments even Ruggerio was swept along, nodding and crying out 'Amen' in response to Savonarola's words. When the monk was finished, the five of them were handed a written document he had signed, granting them full authority to continue his works. They would be warriors against sin and depravity. From that day, no citizen would deny them. They could do as they wanted . . .

A grand carriage rolled to a halt on the street outside, its woodwork adorned with crimson and gold leaf, pulled by four white horses with plaited manes and embroidered leather harnesses. This must be Uccello, ever the peacock. He had never shown interest in sharing a bed with other men, yet Uccello craved being centre of attention in a way that had long left Ruggerio wondering. Uccello always wore the finest clothes, the softest wools, the most delicate silk and damask. Amid the conservative membership of the Arte del Cambio, Uccello was the exception. Most bankers preferred sober clothes to reflect their serious approach to such work, but Uccello revelled in upsetting that. Even his servants were dressed as if ready to be summoned by the Holy Roman Emperor at any moment, their tunics and hose far more extravagant than those worn by many in the Senate.

One of his servants opened the carriage door, offering a hand to Uccello as he stepped down to the street. He slapped the assistance away, his face curdling with distaste. Yes, still the peacock. He remained slender, seemingly little changed in the past forty years – at least from a distance. Uccello looked up and, seeing Ruggerio watching, gave a grand bow before sauntering into the palazzo. Behind him the carriage departed, the horses leaving a pile of dung. 'Typical!' a rasping voice shouted from further along the street.

Ruggerio saw Ghiberti stamping towards the palazzo, a servant in plain garb hurrying to keep up with him. The wool merchant did not believe in wasting time or coin on such luxuries as a carriage. On the few occasions he left his palazzo, Ghiberti stalked everywhere. The man had been spoiling for a fight his entire life. That belligerence made him a fearsome figure in the Arte della Lana, the guild for wool merchants and manufacturers. Those who broke a deal with Ghiberti lived to regret such folly, their reputations never recovering, their workshops standing empty or facing closure. Ghiberti suffered no fools.

He stopped by the horse dung, glowering at the fresh merda. He was a barrel of a man, fat and sinew fighting for supremacy. His clothes were plain, his attitude as abrasive as his voice. 'Typical!' Ghiberti spat again before stalking inside the palazzo without looking up. He never looked up. Ghiberti's focus was on the next step in front of him, nothing more. What he lacked in imagination the wool merchant more than replaced with anger.

Ruggerio turned as Alberti entered the salone. 'Your visitors are here, signore.'

'Have them wait in the parlour while I change, then bring them through.'

The maggiordomo bowed and withdrew.

Ruggerio allowed himself a small shiver of anticipation.

One of the men waiting downstairs planned to kill him. But which one?

Strocchi was having no success finding the Company of Santa Maria's surviving founders, let alone questioning them. First, he had to discover where each of them lived. That might be a simple task for a native son of Florence, but not so for someone born and raised in a small Tuscan village. Strocchi knew from bitter experience where to find Palazzo Ruggerio, but he had not met the others. It was a suggestion once made by Aldo that solved this problem. He had advised Strocchi it was important to nurture useful sources to succeed as an officer.

Informants must be willing to share what they knew about the city – for the right coin, naturally – and provide answers that might otherwise prove elusive. Strocchi had recognized the wisdom in those words. He also realized it would be foolish to wait until he was made an officer to cultivate such sources. Better to have them ready when promotion came, available to help if required. He had sought out those with access to places beyond easy reach of the Otto. Some Strocchi encountered arresting them; others he met during investigations. Many lived in less reputable parts of Florence, while some moved among the upper ranks of society, giving them knowledge of its courtly intrigues.

To find the residences of the confraternity's surviving founders, Strocchi turned to a swarthy fruit seller called Bacci. He made his own deliveries, which took him in and out of wealthy households north of the Arno. Tomasia met Bacci while she was still working at the mercato, before the bambina came, and suggested the fruit seller might make a good source. Her instincts, as ever, were correct. Twice Bacci had provided information that helped locate suspects in different matters before the Otto. He was a gruff bear of a man, but a fondness for gambling meant Bacci was always in need of extra coin.

Strocchi went to the fruit seller's stall and soon had addresses for the residences of Uccello, Scarlatti and Ghiberti. 'But don't bother going to Palazzo Scarlatti,' Bacci said. 'That fool fled to his country villa last summer, hasn't been back to Florence since. Scared of his own shadow, that one. My over-ripe figs have more backbone.'

'Do you know why he left the city?'

Bacci leaned closer, his breath so heavy with garlic it made Strocchi's eyes water. 'The cook there said the old fool was frightened for his life. Kept muttering about retribution. Scarlatti paid for special services to be said for his soul. Even tried to buy a papal indulgence.'

'What about the others, Uccello and Ghiberti?'

The fruit seller told Strocchi where their palazzi were, but knew little else about either man. 'They don't buy anything from me.'

Strocchi thanked Bacci with coin before leaving the mercato. But a second challenge soon emerged: knowing where the men resided didn't mean they would be there. Strocchi went to Palazzo Uccello first as it was closer. But Uccello was not at home, and his servants were not sure when he would return. They refused to say where their signore had gone, only admitting that he had left after receiving an urgent message.

Marching through scorching streets to Palazzo Ghiberti proved equally frustrating, especially during the hottest part of the day. Ghiberti's residence was not far from the Arno and only two streets west of where Dovizi had lived. The main doors were closed, but the servants' entrance round one side of the building remained open. However, Ghiberti was not home, and his servants could not – or would not – say when he was expected back.

'When did he leave?' Strocchi demanded, wiping sweat from his brow.

'Not long ago,' Ghiberti's maggiordomo said. 'He received—'

'An urgent message?' Strocchi cut in.

The servant frowned. 'Yes, how did you know?'

'Was this message conveyed in person, or by letter?'

'In person, by the maggiordomo of—'

'Girolamo Ruggerio,' Strocchi cut in.

'Oh. So you know him?'

'Unfortunately, yes.'

Chapter Thirteen

*R*uggerio smiled through the necessary pleasantries. Better to let Uccello and Ghiberti empty themselves of talk before asking the question he had summoned them both to answer. As ever it was Uccello who spoke most, like a bird that had seen the sun and felt obliged to sing its heart out. Ghiberti was still the same taciturn, scowling figure he had always been, sour of mood, quick to anger, but equally fierce in his loyalty. While Uccello twittered on with gossip about this merchant and that servant girl, Ghiberti remained silent, studying the other founders. Where Uccello was flighty and coloured, Ghiberti was a clenched fist.

Ruggerio knew them better than to judge by the faces they presented to the world.

Either one could be responsible for Dovizi's murder.

Alberti entered with wine and tasty morsels. The maggiordomo placed the tray on an ornate golden table specially brought into the room before the meeting, along with three matching chairs, each one the same distance from the others.

'Signori,' Alberti announced when everything was ready. Once they were all seated – Uccello to Ruggerio's left, Ghiberti to his right – the maggiordomo poured each man a goblet of wine before retreating, closing the doors on his way out. The servants who had accompanied both guests to the palazzo were occupied elsewhere.

There was nobody to overhear.

'Dovizi is dead,' Ruggerio began. 'Murdered. Tied to a gibbet in a handcart, pushed into Piazza della Signoria two nights ago, and set ablaze. My sources tell me he was burned alive, as Savonarola was in that same place, forty years ago.'

'I heard,' Uccello said, flapping a hand at his face as if he was a young woman discovering what young men did with their cazzi. 'It's shocking. Beyond belief!'

'Spare us the performance,' Ghiberti rasped. 'You're not among your bankers and their wives now. We've all known each other too long to indulge in such strategia.'

'For once I have to agree,' Ruggerio said. 'Let us talk plain and true here.'

'Plain I can do,' Ghiberti replied. 'You might find truth harder to speak, Girolamo.'

Ruggerio forced a smile. 'Nonetheless, I shall try.'

Uccello took a sip of his wine. 'And I shall do my best to match you both.'

'Good.' Ruggerio licked his lips. 'So, tell me . . . which of you killed Dovizi?'

'What?' Ghiberti shot upwards, chair falling to the floor behind him. 'You dare accuse me of murdering one of my closest friends?'

'I must agree,' Uccello sniffed. 'Poor Sandro has been dead for all of two days, yet you invite us here to insult us with this . . . this . . . accusation.'

Ruggerio raised his hands as if surrendering to their anger and outrage. He was doing nothing of the sort, but the responses of both men told him what he wished to know. 'Forgive me, but the evidence that one of us was responsible is quite compelling.'

'What evidence?' Ghiberti demanded, still on his feet.

'Sit and I will explain,' Ruggerio said. 'Please, Roberto, sit.'

Ghiberti did as he was bid, righting the fallen chair and lowering himself into it once more, grumbling throughout. He folded both arms across his chest. 'Well?'

Ruggerio detailed his belief about what had happened, based on Aldo's accusations and facts divulged by men working within the Podestà. Dovizi had been lured to a stable close to Piazza della Signoria. He went there alone not long before curfew, wearing his silk tunic embroidered with the emblem of the five founders. Then he was murdered.

'That does not prove either of us were responsible for Dovizi's death,' Uccello said.

'Not alone, but it asks incriminating questions of us,' Ghiberti replied. He glowered at Ruggerio. 'Of all of us. How do we know you were not the one who had Sandro killed?'

'You don't,' Ruggerio admitted. 'I was with a friend all that night, yet I could easily have hired someone else to murder Dovizi, so that disproves nothing. But, as you say, the killing asks questions of us all. Why was Dovizi wearing his founder's emblem tunic? There was no reason to unless whoever summoned him to the piazza requested it.'

'I don't understand,' Uccello said. 'Why would they do such a thing?'

'I prefer not to speculate about his killer's motives.' Ghiberti scowled. 'You know about the proclamation that was nailed to the doors of Sandro's palazzo yesterday?'

Ruggerio nodded, but Uccello appeared none the wiser. Ghiberti explained how the proclamation accused Dovizi of betraying Savonarola as the reason for his murder. 'It promised others would soon suffer as Sandro did. Others guilty of the same sins.'

'Whoever did this was telling the rest of us we could expect the same,' Ruggerio said.

Uccello frowned. 'Yes, I understand that. But why accuse us of killing Sandro? If this is about what happened when we were part of the Fanciulli, we are all as guilty as him.'

'Precisely,' Ruggerio agreed. 'That is what has bound us together all these years. We know if one of us should fall, all would perish alongside him. But the document that would have ensured our mutual destruction went missing last year when the Convent of Santa Maria Magdalena was dissolved. I will admit seeking to obtain it myself—'

'You did what?' Ghiberti snarled, meaty fists clenching on his chest.

'—but I was unsuccessful,' Ruggerio continued. 'For a time, I was certain Sandro had the document. Now I believe he was lured to his death by the promise of obtaining that document. Lured by one of you two.'

'Why us?' Uccello asked, his nose up in the air. 'Why not Scarlatti?'

Ghiberti snorted with derision. 'Don't be ridiculous. As if Benozzo has the courage to attempt such a stratagemma! No, it had to be one of us.'

Uccello continued protesting his innocence. 'Why not somebody else? Anyone could have got hold of that document when the convent was being dissolved.'

A knock at the door prevented Ruggerio answering. 'Forgive me. I gave Alberti strict orders we were not to be disturbed, unless the circumstances were exceptional.' He had given the maggiordomo no such instructions, but the lie came as naturally to him as breathing. Ruggerio went to the door, where Alberti was waiting close by.

'Forgive me, signore, but an officer of the Otto is here to see you.'

'If Aldo has returned, send the fool away. He is no longer amusing or welcome.'

'No sir, it is another officer,' Alberti replied. 'A much younger man, who wishes to question you and your guests about what happened to Signor Dovizi.'

Black smoke rose from the hills as Aldo approached San Jacopo al Girone. He was riding east alongside the Arno where the dirt track was easiest, smoothed by centuries of travellers headed in the opposite direction towards Florence. To Aldo's left the ground rose steeply into hills overlooking the valley. Up there, merchants had their country villas and rich estates; below, people struggled to make a living on land leased from merchants, surrendering half their crops in payment. It was a divide almost as old as the hills, known as mezzadria. Most farmers made enough to survive in a good year, but never enough to buy land. As it was in Florence, so it was in the dominion: the rich got richer from the sweat of the poor.

Aldo had lived in the countryside long enough to know black smoke meant an unplanned fire. He was still half a mile from San Jacopo al Girone, so the blaze could not be on Ruggerio's estate. Each hillside from here all the way back to Fiesole was home to another grand villa, but who lived here? Aldo slowed his borrowed horse to a halt as he drew level with the smoke on the hillside. Scarlatti, that was it. Benozzo Scarlatti. The merchant had retired to his villa in the Tuscan countryside the previous summer, around the time Aldo had first come to this area. He knew little about Scarlatti, save one important fact: long ago Scarlatti and three others had helped Ruggerio found the Company of Santa Maria.

If the smoke was coming from Scarlatti's estate, that was worth investigating.

Aldo dismounted, tying the horse to a tree by the track where there was grass and shade from the blazing sun. Satisfied the beast was secure, he set off up the hill. It was no coincidence that Scarlatti and Ruggerio had their villas so close together. The estate of another confraternity founder, Roberto Ghiberti, was also nearby, while Sandro Dovizi and Luca Uccello had owned land east of Florence in the past. Aldo had discovered all this while investigating the Company of Santa Maria the previous year.

His interest had been sparked by repeated attempts to steal documents about the five founders stored at the Convent of Santa Maria Magdalena. A man had been killed in the convent during the final, failed attempt, before the convent was dissolved. But when Aldo sought to see the documents for himself, nobody was able to find them. The papers had disappeared, and even the convent's former abbess did not know who had them.

It was no coincidence that Aldo had proposed the lands east of Florence as his jurisdiction. There were several areas in need of experienced men to enforce the law, so the segretario had given Aldo free choice. Bindi probably expected him to go west or north, as they offered more lucrative opportunities to earn rewards by capturing banditi and arresting fugitives. Aldo explained that his choice was a recognition that he was getting older, not so able when it came to pursuing law breakers. There was little east of the city aside from the estates of merchants, and those were rarely troubled by crimes worse than petty theft. Bindi had accepted the lie without question.

Aldo chose the small village of San Jacopo al Girone beside the Arno as his new home. He'd expected there would be more trouble involving the Company of Santa Maria's founders, so establishing himself close to country estates owned by three of them made strategic sense. But little of note had happened. The previous summer became autumn, autumn turned to winter, and still nothing. Now, finally, the certainty Aldo had known in his palle was proving true. Dovizi was dead, burned alive in the city. A substantial fire at Scarlatti's country estate no more than a day later might be happenstance . . . but Aldo doubted that.

Passing the peasant huts and farm buildings that dotted the hillside, Aldo could see that none of them had been touched by fire. Black smoke was still billowing into the clear azzurro sky further up the slope, but the source was hidden behind tall cypress trees. It was only as Aldo passed the final barn that he saw what had been burning: Scarlatti's own villa. There was not much left beyond blackened walls and choking clouds of smoke. Nobody could have survived that, yet other buildings nearby were untouched bar soot stains on their walls.

Aldo could see woodwork still burning inside the villa. Most of the smoke and stench was rising into the sky, but occasional gusts of wind blew it in the faces of those nearby. Aldo put a hand across his nose to shield it from the acrid stench. The heat was fierce, worse than the hottest day of summer. It would be days before anyone could risk going inside what remained. Aldo glanced at those around him. Their features were darkened by soot, lines down through the blackness where sweat or tears had run. Among them was one he knew from her trips to San Jacopo al Girone. The housekeeper at Ruggerio's estate stood watching the fire burn. Her top and skirt were grubby from smoke and ash, her features stained with soot like the others. But where they all appeared exhausted, their shoulders slumped and weary, she remained upright. 'Cassandra?'

She frowned at hearing her name before recognition took hold. 'Aldo. You're back.'

He found it difficult to know Cassandra's age but she must be close to fifty. Lines were gathering around her eyes and across her neck. Aldo was no judge of female beauty, his eyes always sought the bodies of men, but Cassandra had a striking face. A strong nose swept down from her brows in a way Aldo had seen on plates from Greece. But it was her eyes that always took his attention. Cassandra had the look of a woman with resolve, someone who knew their mind and was not afraid to speak it.

Aldo gestured at what remained of the villa. 'How long has it been burning?'

'Since dusk last night,' she replied. 'Signor Scarlatti's home was lost before the moon was in the sky. Everyone here has been fighting to stop the fire spreading.'

'Looks like they succeeded.' Aldo studied those around him. Some were standing, but most had collapsed on the dirt or were leaning against walls. He recognized many of their weary faces from the village, or from the few times he'd attended Mass. Most Sundays he found a reason to be elsewhere but in a place like San Jacopo al Girone everyone was expected in church, even outsiders. It was a matter of trust. 'Was anyone caught in the fire?'

'Nobody is quite certain, but it seems only one soul was lost – Signor Scarlatti.' She explained how the servants and estate workers had been down in the village at a special Mass to pray for rain. 'The housekeeper can't stop weeping. Federica says Scarlatti had a habit of falling asleep while reading by candlelight. She told him not to but . . . he did not listen.'

Aldo had met Scarlatti, not long after settling in San Jacopo al Girone. The merchant had been a rotund man, bloated by food and wealth. Yet there was a watchfulness in his eyes, and he startled easily, as if afraid of his own shadow. His death sounded as though it had been a simple accident. If that was true, Scarlatti probably choked on smoke from the fire rather than burning alive like Dovizi. But this death coming so soon after his fellow founder

. . . The blaze could have been deliberate, an act of murder. Had Scarlatti also suffered an ordeal by fire and been found wanting by the flames?

The answers would have to wait until it was safe to enter the burning villa. The eyes of another studying Scarlatti's body could be helpful – assuming there was enough left to examine. 'Have you sent news of this to Signor Ruggerio in Florence?' Aldo asked.

Cassandra shook her head. 'Stopping the fire's spread was all that mattered last night. But I shall have to let him know. He got drunk once and told me how he was close with Signor Scarlatti long ago. Ruggerio will need to be informed of this tragedy.'

'When you do, I may have a message or two that will need carrying to Florence. I could bring them to you later?' Bindi needed notifying about the fire, though Aldo doubted correspondence from him would receive any attention from the segretario.

'Of course,' she replied. 'And you can return that horse you borrowed.'

Aldo smiled. 'I'll bring it up before nightfall.'

Strocchi was not surprised to be kept waiting by Ruggerio. Past encounters had made it apparent the silk merchant rejoiced in teasing and tormenting others, delighting in courtly intrigues. Bindi seemed to believe that making visitors wait outside his ufficio at the Podestà demonstrated his authority, but the segretario was a mere novice in such tactics when compared with Ruggerio. At least an hour had passed since Strocchi had arrived but still there was no sight of his host. Strocchi was determined to stay. The trio he needed to question were within these walls; it made no sense to go elsewhere.

Strolling around the palazzo's internal courtyard, he could hear raised voices from above, all of them male. The words were not loud enough to be distinct, but their anger was apparent. Ruggerio, Uccello and Ghiberti had helped found a confraternity long ago, but it sounded as if the three men were no longer on good terms. Fear could be the fuel for this argument, but was it fear of outsiders targeting the founders or were the founders turning on each other? Any answers required an audience with the three men, and that meant waiting.

Finally, Ruggerio's maggiordomo returned, a sneer of disdain across his features as he approached. 'The signore will see you now. Follow me.' The servant led Strocchi up to the middle level, ushering him into a large room decorated in crimson. The three founders were standing round an ornate golden table, all facing him, Ruggerio in the middle.

The man on Ruggerio's left was dressed in the finest silks, clothes of such richness they rivalled even those of his host. He was thin, his nose in the air, one eyebrow arched. Strocchi recognized the prominently embroidered famiglia emblem, a bird with its wings outstretched in triumph – this must be Luca Uccello. As a banker his ruthless reputation was second only to the Medici, yet his appearance was quite the opposite, near that of a buffone. Looking one way, acting another . . . He was a man fond of confounding expectations, a wearer of masks. Getting the truth from him would not be easy.

The figure on Ruggerio's right could not have been more different: plain of clothes, bristling with anger, a clenched fist of a man. He must be Roberto Ghiberti. Strocchi had heard whispers about violent outbursts, staff left bruised in body and spirit, rivals surrendering deals to him. But none ever dared lodge a complaint against Ghiberti. Much as they feared him, they feared his downfall even more. Ghiberti would make sure he did not suffer alone, or so the rumours said. How much of that was legend? Again, discovering the truth would take longer than Strocchi had time to spare. But he could see what brought these three men together; they were all distinct from one another yet cut from a similar cloth. Trusting a word that came from their mouths would be folly.

Strocchi bowed to the trio. 'Signori, thank you for seeing me.'

Ruggerio feigned a smile. 'My guests were just leaving, Constable . . .?'

Having announced himself to the maggiordomo as an officer of the Otto, Strocchi knew his rank must have been communicated to Ruggerio. Experience had taught Strocchi it was wiser to ignore such jibes, better to get whatever answers he could in the time these men allowed him. That would not be long with the three of them already standing.

'I came to offer my condolences on the death of your fellow founder, Sandro Dovizi,' Strocchi said, dipping his head as if in respect for their loss.

'Death?' Ghiberti spat the word, making it sound more an accusation than a question. 'He was murdered, plain and simple. Isn't your court supposed to prevent such things?'

'The Otto does what it can to enforce the laws of Florence,' Ruggerio said in a soothing tone to Ghiberti before sweeping his steely gaze back to Strocchi. 'I imagine you have more to offer us than condolences, yes?'

Strocchi nodded. 'Like all law-abiding organizations, the Company of Santa Maria has been inactive since the duke promulgated his law last year. Yet Signor Dovizi was wearing his confraternity founder's tunic on the night of his murder. The reason for that remains to be found, but it prompted a question: where were the other four founders that night?' Strocchi smiled at the haughty figure on Ruggerio's left. 'Signor Uccello, perhaps I could ask you to answer first?'

Ruggerio and Ghiberti also turned to Uccello.

'Well, I can't immediately recall,' he said, flapping a hand in the air.

'It was long after the bells had rung for curfew,' Strocchi continued, 'when all good men and women are in their homes, observing the city's laws.'

'Yes, of course,' Uccello replied, forcing a smile. 'Then I was at home. I'm sure if you ask my servants, they can provide ample testimony of that fact for you.'

'As any good servant would,' Ruggerio purred.

'Was anyone else with you?' Strocchi asked, keeping his voice light, as if enquiring whether Uccello wanted another cup of wine. 'Your wife? Your children?'

'No,' the banker said, his expression darkening. 'I have not been blessed with children, and I have no wife.' He gestured at the others. 'What about these two? Why don't you ask them where they were the night Sandro was murdered?'

Ghiberti grunted. 'I was home. Alone. My staff will confirm that.'

Strocchi smiled his thanks. 'And Signor Ruggerio?'

The silk merchant beamed. 'It seems I was the only one among us fortunate to have somebody sharing my bed that night. But I doubt they would be willing to say so to the Otto.'

'And why is that?'

'The person in question is married.' Ruggerio knitted his fingers together in front of his bony chest, all trace of amusement draining from his face. 'My maggiordomo and half a dozen others who work here in the palazzo will testify I never left that night. And as for the fourth surviving founder of our confraternity, Signor

Scarlatti retired to his country estate last summer. To the best of my knowledge, he has not returned to the city since. If he had, I believe it would be noted by the guards at the gates.'

Strocchi nodded. Ruggerio's knowledge of such matters was correct. 'May I ask, where is Signor Scarlatti's estate?'

'Up in the hills east of the city, past Settignano,' Ghiberti replied. 'His estate stands between mine and that of Signor Ruggerio here, not far from San Jacopo al Girone.'

'Grazie mille,' Strocchi said, 'this has been most helpful. I have only one question to ask, and then I shall leave the three of you together to conclude your . . . discussion.' He let that linger in the air, so the trio knew he had overheard their raised voices. 'Proclamations have been posted around the city that accuse Signor Dovizi of betraying the Dominican monk Savonarola, citing it as the reason for his murder. If that is true, it suggests the killer knew Dovizi when he was a young man, was perhaps even a fellow member of the Fanciulli. Should any of you recall an individual from that time who might carry a grudge against Signor Dovizi, please send a messenger to the Podestà with the name of that person.'

The three men offered their polite agreement, and Strocchi departed once their empty words were said. The meeting had gone much as he expected. These men were too sly, too adept in the ways of Florence to blunder into giving a confession. The powerful were rarely convicted for their crimes, and the few foolish enough to come before the Otto could always buy their freedom from the court. The cost to their reputation, that was another matter.

He had expected little from them and received it in abundance, but his words were not intended to prompt meaningful replies. Instead, he sought to plant a seed of doubt. The trio must already suspect one another of killing Dovizi. Let them know the Otto was pursuing the same path and it might persuade one among them to denounce the person responsible. A faint hope, but mighty trees grew from small seeds. Perhaps it would be the same here.

Strocchi strolled down marble steps to the palazzo entrance, letting a quiet smile play on his lips as he passed the maggiordomo. Let Ruggerio's servant report that to his signore.

Chapter Fourteen

$\mathscr{A}$ldo went back down the hill to the Arno. His borrowed horse was waiting by the track in the late afternoon shade where he had left it, evidence of how few banditi were east of Florence. Leave a saddled horse unguarded beside most roads out of the city and it would soon be stolen. But thefts were rare around San Jacopo al Girone. People living in or near the village all knew each other. Most lived their whole lives within a mile of where they were born.

Visitors to this area were unusual, aside from occasional itinerant tradesmen such as coopers and those who sold old clothes. That was one of the reasons why it had been so easy to find and arrest Lippo. He drew attention to himself by being an outsider and having only one arm made him even more memorable. He was unable to pass unnoticed in the dominion, let alone to survive for long in the countryside. It made enforcing the law here much easier.

Aldo untied the horse and walked it towards San Jacopo al Girone. Riding into the village on one of Ruggerio's horses – let alone one with a saddle bearing his famiglia crest – would draw unwanted attention. There was already enough gossip about an officer renting an empty hut at the edge of the village. It was years since a representative of the Otto had been stationed nearby, let alone an officer. Rumours had swirled, speculating on why Aldo was there. After a year people were finally becoming used to his presence. He would never be one of them, but at least the villagers no longer stared when he went past.

His hut stood apart from the other houses, facing back towards Florence. Aldo stopped there, tying the horse to a tree behind the one-room residence. He went inside, coughing at the dust kicked up by opening the door. After a night in Saul's bed in Florence, Aldo could see how shabby the hut was. It had a cupboard, table and single chair – but precious else to recommend it. Why would Saul want to come and stay here? There was not even a proper bed, merely a lumpy mattress resting against a wall. Most of Aldo's things were still back in the city, locked in his room upstairs at the bordello run by Signora Robustelli.

Aldo sniffed at his clothes. They stank of horse and sweat, not a surprise after wearing them three days in succession. He took a ceramic jug down to the river, fetching fresh water back to the hut. Once inside he shed both boots and peeled off his tunic and hose. A brisk scrub removed the worst of his stench. He pulled on clean clothes before plunging what he had worn into the water. Better to wash away the grime of the last few days, make a fresh start.

Lippo was dead, nothing would bring him back. The murder of Dovizi, that was for Strocchi to solve. But the fire at Scarlatti's villa . . . Perhaps it was simply an accident, an old man falling asleep with a lit candle by his bed. Evening breezes could have blown a cloth or paper into the flame. Once the fire took hold, it would spread fast. Yes, it could be ill chance that burned down the house and claimed its owner's life. But for this to happen so soon after Dovizi was murdered . . . That was too much to accept.

It must be investigated.

* * *

You wait and you watch. You see a young man departing the palazzo, though you do not know his face. He cannot be much older than twenty, certainly not yet twenty-five, yet he has a certainty about him. A man of purpose, it seems. You will yourself to know his face, in case you should see him again or your ways should cross. Anyone who associates with the owner of this palazzo is not to be trusted.

You wait. You watch.

You are patient.

Soon an ornate carriage rolls past and stops in front of the palazzo. It has four white horses with braided manes and embroidered leather harnesses. You know the carriage well.

Two men emerge from the palazzo, their servants following.

One man, stocky and powerful, stamps away with a single servant hurrying after him.

The other, tall and graceful, sees you. He smiles and nods before stepping into his carriage. The remaining servants divide themselves. Some climb on the back of the carriage as it rolls away, others hurry along behind, avoiding the dung dropped by the four horses.

You glance up at the palazzo windows. A single figure stands at one, staring out.

You watch. You wait.

You are patient.

Strocchi strode back to the Podestà, sweltering in his tunic and hose even though the hottest part of the day had passed, and evening was approaching. The stone buildings on either side seemed to have swallowed the sun's heat and were now breathing it back out again so that walking between them was like being in a kitchen as meat was roasting. Strocchi pulled at his tunic, wishing for a cool breeze to ease the stifling closeness.

So long as he kept moving, it was almost bearable. But once he stopped . . .

The prospect of reporting to Bindi was equally unpleasant. Aside from confirming that da Soci knew nothing about Dovizi's murder, there was little else to share. Why the dead man had been wearing his founder's tunic remained unknown. The name or names of those responsible for luring him to the stable was still a mystery. Even the source of the false declarations about Savonarola remained elusive, an unseen hand twisting the mood of the people with paper and ink. None of that would satisfy Bindi.

Strocchi struggled to find some morsels that demonstrated his day's work had not been in vain, but so far, his successes were limited to eliminating potential killers rather than identifying them. Dovizi had no famiglia to benefit from his death. The silk merchant's rivals would enjoy having one less competitor, a fact that made his fellow founder Ruggerio a fair suspect. But accusing such an influential and important merchant without evidence as solid as stone walls was folly. The segretario would never risk his position in such a way.

Besides, Aldo had been certain Ruggerio was not responsible for Dovizi's murder. There was much Strocchi could neither understand nor accept about Aldo, but his instincts in such cases were usually reliable. What about the other founders? If Scarlatti was still outside the city – confirming that would have to wait until the next morning – it left Ghiberti and Uccello as possible suspects. But direct questions had provoked no false answers from either man, nothing to support a denunzia. The founders were bound up in this somehow, the proclamation nailed to Dovizi's door made that clear. But there were too many questions and too few answers to know why.

There was another possibility, one Strocchi did not wish to consider yet: that the founders had nothing to do with Dovizi's murder. The killing could be the result of some personal vendetta. Perhaps Orbatello had reason to see his employer dead – if so, the assistant hid it well. Perhaps Dovizi was guilty of an affair with another man's wife or daughter or sister. Perhaps the murderer's target was random, and Dovizi had been lured to the stable and killed by someone obsessed with returning Florence to the days of Savonarola. That explained part of the proclamation, but not all of it.

Strocchi saw a lonely figure lurking outside the Podestà gates as he approached the stone fortress. The man appeared out of place, uneasy in such surroundings. He was facing away from Strocchi, yet the stoop of his shoulders was familiar . . . It was Zitelle, the servant from Palazzo Dovizi. Strocchi called to him and Zitelle twisted round, clutching a document in his hands as if it were a sharpened blade. 'You must read this,' he said, proffering it.

'Your signore's will?' Strocchi asked, accepting the document. He turned the paper over in his hands. A black wax seal was still fixed across the join; it had not been opened.

'It may be, but I cannot be certain,' Zitelle replied, wringing his hands.

Six words were written on the document's reverse: *Open this if I should die.*

'I found it in the signore's papers,' Zitelle continued. 'He kept them locked in a chest but entrusted me with a key before leaving the palazzo the night he—' The servant shook his head. 'I did not tell you about it before because I hoped the signore might still return.'

'I understand,' Strocchi said. 'May I open this?'

Zitelle glanced around, fear in his face, as if he expected Dovizi's murderer to appear from the shadows and attack them both. 'Out here?'

Strocchi smiled to reassure him. 'No, come inside. We'll open it there.' The servant peered up at the brutal silhouette of the Podestà, his fear all too apparent. Strocchi slipped an arm round those hunched shoulders, ushering Zitelle through the gates and along the stone corridor to the internal courtyard. Where the rest of the city was sweating and suffering, inside the Podestà was always cold. The servant shivered, either from worry or the sudden loss of warmth. Strocchi guided Zitelle to a bench before sliding a finger beneath the seal.

It opened with a sound that reminded Strocchi of his papa's last rasping breath.

'What does it say?' Zitelle asked as the single crisp sheet was unfolded.

Strocchi held up a hand for silence, his eyes adjusting to Dovizi's scrawl. The letter had been written in haste, words flowing together, making them difficult to read. It began:

By dawn tomorrow, I may hold in my hands the means of my deliverance. But if anyone bar myself is reading this letter, it means my quest was one of folly, and I have now paid for that foolishness with my life. Should that be the case, it may be a release in many respects, though I suppose this will depend upon the manner of my death.

I cannot abide pain, never have. So, if my end comes tonight, I pray it be quick.

Strocchi paused his reading. Dovizi's prayer had not been answered. To die by fire, burning alive in the flames, to breathe the scent of your own flesh cooking ... Strocchi pushed such thoughts aside, returning to the dead man's words. Let Dovizi reveal what he would.

Whoever you are, reading these words, you do not need to know why I have been killed. The details of my sins are for the confessional. God alone may forgive those, should he grant me such mercy. I do not crave your understanding, nor do I deserve your pity. What happened cannot be undone, and I shall be judged for that by my maker.

For more than a year I have known this night would come. When the messenger arrived with a missive inviting me to meet at a stable close to Palazzo della Signoria, I was not certain at first. But the demand that I wear my founder's tunic removed all doubt. I knew who was summoning me, and what bargain they were offering. It is a pact with a diavolo, but one I must accept. They have made it clear what will happen if I refuse.

I hereby bequeath my business and my estate to the Spedale degli Innocenti. I have always been proud that the Arte della Seta built and manages this orphanage for foundlings. My legacy means the wealth I have accumulated will serve the less fortunate of our city long after I am gone.

Strocchi shook his head. He had hoped for more from Dovizi's final letter.

'What's wrong?' Zitelle asked. 'Is this not the signore's will?'

'It is, but . . . Signor Dovizi wrote nothing about what should happen to his staff. The silk business and the palazzo have been willed to the foundlings' orphanage.'

'Oh,' the servant said, sinking back against the stone wall behind the bench.

Strocchi was about to hand the letter to Zitelle but then noticed a crease at the bottom of the single page, where the paper was bent over on itself. He unfolded it, revealing a final addition to the text. The hand was still that of Dovizi, matching what was above, but the words were ill-formed, as if the silk merchant had been trembling as he added them.

Should I perish tonight, there is one man I believe most likely to have arranged it. He will not kill me himself, as he has others who perform such bloody deeds. But I am sure that the person responsible for my death is one of my oldest friends:
*   Luca Uccello.*

Strocchi stared at the words, uncertain he had read them correctly. The peacock of a man who had sniffed and sneered at Ruggerio's palazzo? That was the person who paid for Dovizi to be burned alive in the Piazza della Signoria? Strocchi did not hold with the vice of gambling but, if he had, his wager would have been on Dovizi naming Ruggerio as killer. Rereading the last paragraph made no difference, the words stayed the same. Before leaving his palazzo for the last time, Dovizi had written a denunzia accusing Uccello of his murder.

If nothing else, that solved the problem of what to report to Bindi.

Cassandra heard Aldo before she saw him. The afternoon was fast giving way to evening, cool breezes coming up the valley, bringing the noise of Aldo's approach with the horse he had borrowed. She strolled to the courtyard in front of the villa, wiping both hands on her apron. He soon appeared round the corner, a scowl on his face, leading the horse rather than riding it. Both man and beast were sweating from their trek up the steep hill, but Aldo seemed the more tired. 'Returned, as promised,' he said. 'Where do you want it?'

'Vincenzo is waiting,' she replied. 'Once you're done there, come to the villa.' Cassandra went inside, pouring two cups of wine from one of the signore's better bottles. She wanted to know more about this officer, and a good drink loosened the tongue.

But Aldo came no further than the doorway, two letters in his hand. 'I brought these. They have instructions on the back, so the messenger knows where in the city to take them.'

'Good. Vincenzo is leaving at dawn; he should have them delivered by midday.' Cassandra took the letters, replacing them in Aldo's hand with wine. He stared at the cup.

'What's this for?'

'Drinking, usually.' Cassandra headed to the stairs. 'I want to show you something.' She went up, listening for how he responded. Aldo hesitated before following her. Once they were both upstairs, she showed him out onto the loggia. 'There,' she said, gesturing at the view. 'Wasn't this worth coming all the way up that hill?'

Aldo took in the valley below, the sun setting in the distance behind Florence. 'Yes, it was.' He admired the vista for a few moments before turning his back on it. 'Now, why did you really ask me up here? Did Ruggerio ask you to do this?'

Cassandra laughed out loud, surprised by the bitterness behind his questions. 'You must know the signore well to be so suspicious of him.'

'Let's say I have good reason to be cautious of anyone Ruggerio employs.'

She nodded. 'Having seen how he acts when he believes nobody is watching, that is probably wise. But I promise, you have nothing to fear from me. I may work for the signore, but I do not spy for him. My duties are those of a housekeeper, nothing more.'

Aldo arched an eyebrow. 'Is that so?'

'Ask me any question you wish,' Cassandra said, sinking into a chair. 'Please, sit.'

He lowered himself onto a bench, his back to the setting sun. 'Do you know what kind of man Ruggerio is?'

'You mean ruthless, venal and willing to have anyone stabbed in the back if they threaten him?' She sipped the wine. 'Or are you talking about who he invites to his bed?'

Aldo smiled for the first time since arriving. 'All of those things.'

'Then yes, I do know what kind of man he is. You can trust the signore, but only to do whatever benefits him. He believes himself to be clever, which is a common failing in men.'

'But not him?'

'Usually he is correct.'

Aldo lifted the wine to his nose before drinking. 'He certainly keeps a good cellar.'

'Made from his own grapes,' Cassandra said, pointing to the vineyards below them.

'What about you?' Aldo asked. 'Why work for such a man?'

'It suits me. He has no interest in women, and I have no interest in fighting off the attentions of men. I have the signore's protection while I live and work under his roof. He rewards loyalty well. And he only comes here two months a year. The rest of the time . . .'

Aldo twisted round to look at Ruggerio's estate as the setting sun painted fiery shades of yellow and orange across the sky. 'You have all of this to yourself.'

Cassandra emptied her cup. 'There are worse places for an unmarried woman.' She stood up, a little unsteady on her feet. 'Shall I fetch the bottle?'

'Let me,' Aldo offered, rising from the bench.

'It's on the kitchen table. Turn left at the bottom of the stairs.'

Cassandra smiled as Aldo left the loggia. He was some time returning, claiming to have needed to find and use the latrina. Cassandra suspected he had been making a brisk search of the lower level, but there was nothing incriminating to find down there. Ruggerio was too careful for such a mistake.

One bottle became two as twilight nestled across the valley, and Cassandra brought a platter of cheese, olives and cured meats up from the larder. She studied Aldo as he ate, the way he was with his food. The officer might have a gruff, even flinty manner but there was also a delicacy to him. No, delicacy was not the right word. He took care about what he did.

'You're watching me,' Aldo said, pouring her a fresh cup of wine.

'Forgive me,' Cassandra replied. 'Call it a servant's tendency. We wait and watch, doing our best to remain unseen and unnoticed while observing others.'

'So you can meet the needs of those you serve before they realize it?'

She smiled. 'You understand.'

'The work of an officer for the—' Aldo stopped, a rueful frown crossing his face.

'What's wrong?'

'It doesn't matter,' he said, but did not explain further. The scowl he had brought up the hill was gone, but something was itching at him. She did not ask. He would tell her in his own time, or not at all. 'My visit to the city did not go well,' Aldo eventually said.

Cassandra stayed silent.

He drank the last of his wine. 'Mistakes were made. Others paid the price of that.'

'Would you rather be in their place?'

'No, but—'

'But you bear the guilt of it.'

He nodded.

'Then that makes you better than some,' she said. 'Better than many I could name. They cause others harm and pay no price for that. They take what does not belong to them and show no remorse for their trespasses. I used to pray that all such men would face judgement for their sins, but I heard no answer to my prayers.'

'You're talking about Ruggerio?'

'And others like him. They are men without regret. I doubt most know the pain their actions have caused, and those who do recognize it do not care.'

Aldo drained his wine. 'If that's true, why keep working for a man such as Ruggerio?'

'I told you, there are worse places for someone like me.'

'You remind me of a woman I encountered last year,' Aldo said. 'She knew her own mind and was not afraid to speak it. Finding a place in the world took her many years.'

Cassandra leaned forward in her chair. 'And where was this place she found?'

'A convent.'

Cassandra laughed. 'Are you suggesting I become a nun?'

'Not at all.'

'Good, because I doubt the Lord would take me.'

'Then when the diavolo comes for you, we will both be in good company,' Aldo said, struggling to suppress a yawn. 'Forgive me,' he muttered, putting a hand over his mouth. 'Don't think I've slept more than three hours in the last two nights. But you must be tired too, you spent last night stopping the fire in Signor Scarlatti's villa spreading.'

Cassandra nodded. No sleep and too much wine were catching up with her.

'Do you think his housekeeper is right about a candle starting that?' Aldo asked.

'Of course. Why, do you think there could be another cause?'

Aldo stared across at the hillside where Scarlatti's villa had stood. Smoke was still rising from there, just visible against the deep blue sky as night fell. 'I can't be sure. But once it is safe to go inside, I intend to find out.'

Chapter Fifteen

❧

Monday, May 27th 1538

*B*indi waddled towards Palazzo Medici, his belly squirming, urging him to turn back. Despite three days of investigations by the Otto there was little of consequence to tell the duke, no significant progress in discovering who was responsible for Dovizi's murder. The search to find those behind the pro-Savonarola proclamations was proving equally fruitless. The documents were still being nailed to doors and stuck to stone columns across the city.

Stopping them was, if anything, even more urgent than catching Dovizi's killer. The proclamations were fuelling the fires of those still faithful to the dead monk's teachings. Each day saw new gatherings in piazze across Florence, people chanting the same phrase over and over: 'Savonarola lives! Savonarola lives!' Some of the fools seemed to believe their frate would rise from the dead, like the son of God on the third day. Others appeared quite certain Savonarola had already returned, that his execution forty years earlier had been an elaborate ruse by the Medici. Bindi suspected pro-republican factions in the city were adding their numbers to the crowds, encouraging others to join. But, again, there was no proof, nothing to support such suspicions. Nothing to show his effectiveness to the duke.

Three days had passed since Cosimo had threatened to appoint a new segretario to the Otto. Each morning of those three days Bindi went to the Palazzo Medici, doing his best to demonstrate that he and his men were doing all they could to stamp out this Savonarola fever before it engulfed the city. But with each new morning the duke's patience grew shorter, his frustration more evident. Bindi knew he did not have much longer, maybe two days to end this madness. If he could not . . . No. That would not, must not happen.

He would prevail. He would do his duty for Florence, no matter what.

It was still early as he approached the palazzo, but the morning was already hot and getting hotter. When the sun set the previous evening, it should have cooled the air. Instead, the segretario had sweltered through the night, struggling to sleep in a puddle of his own sweat. He got up early to wash away the worst of it but his trek to the ducal residence had soon undone that effort. Staying on the shaded side of the street seemed to make no difference. His robes were soaked with perspiration, not a gasp of breeze on the air to soothe him. Bindi mopped his brow with a cloth before swiping the sweaty folds between his chins. It would not do to appear before the duke like this. It would not do at all.

But he need not have bothered. When Bindi reached the palazzo, Cosimo's private segretario Campana was waiting by the internal courtyard. 'The duke does not wish to see you this morning,' he announced. 'You are to deliver your report to me, and I shall present a summary to His Grace. Unless you have found those responsible for these crimes?'

Bindi bit back the urge to demand his audience with the duke. Better to accept this fresh ignominy, to keep his own counsel. Short, simple answers were best. 'Not yet.'

'Then what do you have to report?'

'My men have been watching the three surviving founders of the Company of Santa Maria who still reside in the city, as His Grace commanded. There has been no change in the behaviour of Uccello, Ghiberti or Ruggerio. Each man continues to conduct business from their respective homes. They all attended Mass on Sunday, each at different churches.'

'What about these false proclamations? Have you any suspects for who is posting those across the city?' Campana demanded.

Not trusting himself to reply in a civil tone, Bindi shook his head.

'Then there's not much more to say, is there?' Campana stalked away. But Bindi refused to be dismissed in such a manner. He hurried after Campana.

'The Otto needs more resources to do what the duke asks of it,' Bindi said, keeping his voice low and quiet so nobody but Campana could hear. 'The Podestà was already short of men before he ordered us to watch Uccello, Ghiberti and Ruggerio. Two of my guards have been missing for days. Keeping watch on three men in different quarters of the city is occupying most of my constables and officers. Doing that while investigating whoever is putting up these false proclamations . . . It's impossible.'

Campana stopped at a staircase that led to the palazzo's upper levels. 'His Grace has more pressing problems,' Campana hissed at Bindi. 'There's a drought in the countryside that could devastate this year's harvest, leaving Florentines facing famine. Each day is hotter than the last, and it is driving people to madness. Yesterday, sermons at several churches urged people to pray for the frate's return as leader of the city. One preacher at San Marco openly called for the Medici to be overthrown before he was removed from the pulpit. There will be a rivolta within days unless an end is put to this. Do you understand?'

Bindi hadn't realized how fast events were unravelling.

Campana took two long, deep breaths before speaking again. 'I'll talk with His Grace, see if there is additional coin to hire new constables. Release any prisoners you have in the cells at the Podestà so the guards can act as constables instead. I shall suggest to Captain Duro at Le Stinche that he loan some of his men to the Otto for a few days. But for now, you must make best use of what resources you have. The duke needs your help, Bindi. Florence needs your help. Can you do that for your duke, for your city?'

Soon Bindi was striding from the palazzo, his exhaustion and despair banished by a renewed sense of purpose. Yes, he would do whatever he could. Serving the city was not merely his duty, it was his honour. The Otto would prove its worth, and the court's segretario would become the duke's most esteemed servant once again.

It was only when Bindi was halfway to the Podestà that his brisk pace slowed, an unpleasant truth insinuating its way into his mood like a raven pecking ripe grapes on a vine.

How was the Otto going to achieve this?

Three nights Aldo had been waiting. Three nights since returning from Florence, waiting for the smoking ruin of Scarlatti's villa to be safe enough to enter. Each morning he had marched up the hill, intent on getting inside the burned-out building. Each morning the heat and smoke still rising from it drove him back, keeping hidden whatever secrets might be lurking within. In truth he had limited expectation of finding much in the villa. The ferocity of those flames, the devastation they'd left behind, suggested there would be little left to uncover.

Yet two things still gave Aldo reason to hope. One was a large beam which had collapsed during the fire, bringing down part of the roof and upper level's ceiling. That might have cut off one or more rooms from the worst of the blaze. If so, there might be useful evidence inside those rooms. It was unlikely, but worth investigating. Scarlatti's household staff and estate workers seemed ready to accept his death as a regrettable accident, probably due to the signore falling asleep while reading by candlelight. Such a fire had happened once before. An evening breeze blew a cloth into the bedside candle, causing it to catch light. The housekeeper Federica had smelled smoke while passing the bedchamber and rushed in to stop the fire.

But she had not been at the villa the night it burned down, not when dusk fell. Like the other servants and estate workers, Federica was praying for rain at a special Mass in San Jacopo al Girone. That had been weighing heavily on her when Aldo had questioned her on Saturday. 'If a deluge had come when we all prayed, it would have saved the signore,' she said, eyes red from weeping, her face haggard with exhaustion and worry. 'If I had remained behind to look after the signore, he would still be alive.'

The second thing that gave Aldo hope emerged as he spoke with Federica and the other servants. All of them seemed sure Scarlatti had been in his bedchamber when they went down the hill for Mass, yet none recalled seeing him that afternoon. He had been absent for a few days before the fire, taking a rare trip away from the estate to visit an old friend in Fiesole. Yet nobody knew the name of this friend. Scarlatti had sent a letter to his estate manager Trigari, detailing plans to return late on Thursday afternoon – not long before the fire took hold of the villa. Trigari made sure Federica and the household staff prepared Scarlatti's bedchamber for his return, as he was likely to be tired from the journey, and food was left ready if he came home hungry. Then everyone departed for the special Mass.

Scarlatti's letter had burned with the rest of the villa, so Aldo could not compare the hand that had written it with other documents. But he was able to confirm one thing: nobody had seen Scarlatti come home. They had all simply assumed he was in his bedchamber when the fire started. How else could such a blaze have begun? Aldo had an answer for that but kept it to himself. He did not wish to raise false hope about Scarlatti not being inside the villa.

Not until there was proof.

Aldo strode up the hill to Ruggerio's villa, grateful for the long morning shadows still being cast by the hills. Another scorching day loomed ahead. The sooner he got inside the devastated villa, the better. Picking through charred ruins beneath a pitiless midday sun held no appeal. Getting in and out before the worst of the day's heat seemed the wiser choice.

Cassandra was already outside the front door as he approached, wiping both hands on her apron. 'How is it you are always waiting when I come up the hill?' Aldo asked.

'I see or hear you coming long before you get here,' she replied with a wry smile. 'Signor Ruggerio once told me that's why he built this far up the hill. Not for the view which every visitor admires when they stay here . . .'

'He wanted the strategic advantage this place offers,' Aldo said.

'And the slope above the villa is too steep for anyone to approach that way.'

'Ruggerio likes to see his enemies coming.'

'Exactly.' Cassandra put both hands on her hips. 'So, why are you here?'

'Is your stable hand Vincenzo back from Florence?'

'He returned yesterday but brought no replies for either of your letters. If he had, I would have sent them down to your hut.'

Aldo nodded. 'The court's segretario is unlikely to bother with any correspondence that I send him.' Aldo didn't mention the other person to whom he had written. Saul would come if he could, but that was asking a lot. Too much, it seemed. 'No, I had another reason for asking. I'm going inside the Scarlatti villa this morning to see what's left. I could have one of the estate workers there help me, but it is likely that I will find their signore's remains. If the fire consumed his body . . .'

'You don't want that to be their last memory of him,' Cassandra said.

'They have lost so much already.' Aldo didn't mention his other concern. One of Scarlatti's servants or workers might have had a hand in starting the fire. Better to keep them away from the villa until the blaze's cause was clear, keep any evidence undisturbed.

'Of course.' Cassandra called Vincenzo's name and the stable hand appeared, a leather apron over his tunic and hose, a hammer in one hand. 'Are you busy?'

'I was fixing broken boards the horses kicked. But that can wait.'

'Good. Aldo needs help at the Scarlatti villa, go with him.'

Vincenzo nodded, starting to untie his apron.

'No, keep that on,' Aldo said. 'This will not be clean work, better to have that to protect your clothes. I could do with an apron myself, if you have a spare.'

Strocchi crept down the stairs to avoid disturbing Tomasia or little Bianca. He had no wish to wake either of them, not now the bambina was sleeping better. Let them rest. Given a choice he would stay in bed too, but the night watch on Palazzo Uccello were waiting to be relieved and it was his turn. Once he reached the street Strocchi turned right, heading north. Uccello owned a grand residence a few streets north of San Lorenzo, near the church of San Barnaba.

Men from the Otto had been watching Uccello, Ruggerio and Ghiberti for two days and three nights at the behest of Bindi. Strocchi did his best to persuade the segretario there might be more efficient ways to know what the three confraternity founders were doing. He suggested devoting so much of the court's limited resources to such a strategia was unlikely to bring the desired results, but it was wasted effort. The order had come from Duke Cosimo himself, Bindi admitted, and there was nothing more to be said about the matter.

Strocchi chose to watch over Uccello, rather than the other two founders. Ruggerio was a dangerous man, and certainly capable of ordering the death of a rival, yet Strocchi did not believe Ruggerio responsible for the murder. There was no obvious, urgent reason why he would strike against his rival now, and not in such an obscene or public manner. Ruggerio favoured quick, quiet deaths that did not draw attention. His methods involved secrecy and subtlety. There was nothing subtle about the way Dovizi had been killed, quite the opposite.

Ghiberti was still something of a mystery to Strocchi, even after meeting him on Friday and hearing lengthy reports about Ghiberti's movements in the following days. Work, work, church and work were all that seemed to occupy his days. Ghiberti did not leave his palazzo during curfew and received no visitors except other merchants. No lovers came or went, no family, no relatives, nothing. There could be monks with more colourful or exciting lives, for all Strocchi knew. Ghiberti might look like the angriest man in Florence but that restless, bristling rage seemed devoted to his business and nothing else.

Uccello was another matter.

Most bankers were sober individuals, protective of the privacy surrounding their business and their lives. They dressed in dark, formal robes and did little to draw attention. But Uccello was quite the opposite, a man who appeared to crave being seen. Strocchi had already witnessed Uccello's colourful clothes first-hand while meeting the three founders. Two full days of observing the banker only added to the impression that Uccello was a peacock of a man. He had held a celebration at his palazzo on Saturday, with dozens of visitors arriving in wealthy carriages, all of them attended by numerous servants.

Other men might have chosen a display of mourning for their dead associate. Uccello showed no sadness, no shame, and no guilt. Even going to church on Sunday required a trip in Uccello's ornate carriage, despite the journey only being two streets from his grand palazzo. Everything about the man was a demonstration, a perform-ance. Strocchi suspected Uccello believed the murder was nothing to do with him, or there was no way the Otto could prove he was responsible for what had happened to Dovizi.

Either Uccello did not know about the letter Dovizi had left behind or he did not care. The accusation within it – that Uccello was the person responsible for Dovizi's death – had nothing else to support it, and no evidence to justify an arrest. But it persuaded Strocchi to volunteer to keep watch on Uccello, rather than Ghiberti or Ruggerio. Dovizi must have had good reason to suspect Uccello. The challenge was uncovering that reason.

Strocchi passed shopkeepers hanging wares outside their doors. Those selling fruit and vegetables were doing their best to make things look fresher by sprinkling water across sun-wizened leaves and wrinkled skins. It was early, the sun not yet visible above the narrow gaps between buildings, but the air was already ripe with piss and merda. Come the hottest part of the day, the stench of these streets would be unbearable.

When not keeping watch on Uccello, Strocchi had visited all his informants across the city. None of them could add to the little he knew. Nobody, not even Zoppo, knew who was behind the killing of Dovizi. The crippled tavern keeper had been reluctant to talk at first, believing Strocchi was asking questions on Aldo's behalf. But once Zoppo knew Aldo had returned to the dominion and he'd confirmed Strocchi was now an officer, the cripple was happier to talk – for the right coin, of course.

Zoppo did have one useful morsel, a vague description of the person nailing up false proclamations: a man, wearing a long woollen cloak with a hood hiding his face and hair. None of that would have been noticed but for the boots he was wearing, made of fine leather with tassels hanging below the cloak. It was not much, but still the first sighting of whoever was stoking the fervour of those calling for the return of Savonarola and his teachings.

'Watch out!' a gruff voice shouted at Strocchi. Hearing a clatter of hooves on the stones close behind, Strocchi lunged into a doorway on his left. Two horses pulling a cart laden with barrels charged close by, the sound almost deafening in the narrow street.

Strocchi bellowed at the driver to slow down and got an obscene finger gesture in return. It was his own fault, too busy obsessing on the investigation to hear the cart and horses coming, but that didn't make the driver any less reckless. Strocchi checked there were no others heading towards him before stepping back into the road.

When he reached the alleyway opposite Palazzo Uccello, the sun was already visible in the clear azzurro sky. Benedetto had spent curfew huddled in the shadows. His scowling face left little doubt how the constable felt about that. 'Where have you been?'

he demanded as Strocchi approached. 'I'm meant to be done by now.'

Strocchi ignored the complaint. 'Anything to report?'

Benedetto shrugged. 'Nobody went in, nobody came out. Not that I saw.'

'Then you can go—'

'Finally!' the constable muttered, stamping away.

'Then you can go back to the Podestà,' Strocchi said, 'and tell what you saw to the segretario. But I wouldn't take that attitude with you. Bindi won't appreciate it.'

Once Benedetto was out of sight, Strocchi found a place in the shade where he could watch the doors of Palazzo Uccello. It was bad enough having to spend the day out here, but it made no sense to do so in the full glare of the sun.

Aldo was sweating through his tunic by the time he persuaded Scarlatti's estate manager Trigari to find a ladder. Now the last embers of fire had died inside the burnt-out villa, it was clear that part of the upper level had survived the flames. As Aldo suspected, the fallen beam had created a barrier, shielding what was beyond it from the fire. Federica confirmed that Scarlatti's bedchamber was in the less affected part of the upper level.

'I don't understand,' the housekeeper said. 'How can that be, if the fire started there?'

'That's what I hope to discover,' Aldo replied.

The challenge was getting to what remained on the upper level. The villa's central staircase had collapsed during the blaze, and the stone steps up the back of the building only reached an empty doorway on the opposite side. It was Vincenzo who suggested using a ladder. 'Most estates have one for tending the upper branches of olive trees,' he explained, as if this was common knowledge. It might be for those who grew up in the countryside, but Aldo had been born and raised in Florence. Cultivating olives was not his concern.

The flames were gone but smoke was still rising from inside the ruined villa as Vincenzo put the borrowed ladder against the outer wall. The top rung did not quite reach the closed shutters outside Scarlatti's bedchamber, but it would do. 'Let me go first,' Vincenzo said, resting a strong hand on Aldo's arm. 'We don't know how safe it will be inside that room. If the floor should give way . . .'

'Better that I go myself,' Aldo replied, pulling on the leather apron over his tunic and hose. 'As you say, there might only be one chance to see what is in there. You hold the ladder steady. If it's safe for both of us, I'll call out.'

Vincenzo nodded, but his unhappiness was still evident.

Aldo gripped the ladder with both hands, ready to climb upwards, but stopped. He saw Federica watching and beckoned her over. 'What is it? What's wrong?' she asked.

'I can't recall what Signor Scarlatti looks like,' he admitted. 'I must have met him before he retired here, but I don't think I've seen him for at least a year. Can you tell me?'

The housekeeper nodded. 'The signore is a heavy man, fond of his food and drink. He prefers being cleanshaven, a beard makes his skin itch. His hair is more silver than brown these days, and he doesn't have much on top.' She paused. 'Do you need to know more?'

'That should be enough,' Aldo said, 'thank you. It's probably safer if you stay back.'

Federica retreated as a gust of wind swirled smoke around, making her cough.

Vincenzo put a foot against the base of the ladder to steady it. 'Ready?'

Aldo gave a quick nod and climbed upwards. The higher he got, the hotter the air became, as if the villa walls were the outside of an oven. The acrid stench made him cough. By the time Aldo neared the top rung sweat was running down into his eyes, forcing him to stop and wipe it away. The leather apron might be protecting his tunic, but it was only adding to his discomfort. He would not have long inside the bedchamber.

At the top of the ladder, he was able to open a shutter. Smoke and heat billowed out, forcing Aldo to arch back, threatening to send him toppling. The ladder shifted beneath him. 'Hold it steady!' he shouted down.

'I'm trying!' Vincenzo replied. One of Scarlatti's estate workers hurried to help. Between them the two men got the ladder back into position.

Aldo pulled the other shutter aside, making an opening into which he could climb. He stretched higher, gripping the frame with both hands and heaving himself upwards. The last part was awkward, Aldo half climbing and half falling through the gap. He tumbled forwards, collapsing to the bedchamber floor. Another smell assaulted his nostrils, so strong it overwhelmed the burning stench: ripe, full of decay and rot and worse. Aldo pressed both nose and mouth into an elbow to block out the smell, but he could hear insects in the air, flies and other creatures buzzing around.

He'd seen and heard enough to know one thing for certain.

There was a dead body in this room.

Chapter Sixteen

*L*ying on the floor beneath the window, Aldo let his eyes adjust to his surroundings. Outside the morning was bright, bathed in sunshine beneath a cloudless sky. But in here the only light came from the window, the rest of the room shrouded in darkness. Gradually he was able to make out shapes: fine furniture around the walls, a rug across the wooden floor, and a large bed against the opposite wall with small tables on either side. The beam that collapsed must have blocked the door, preventing the fire from getting in here. There was a shape atop the bed, beneath the covers, an unmoving figure. No, a corpse.

Aldo had doubted whether there would be a body in the bedchamber. Being believed dead would be an excellent way to avoid suspicion for Dovizi's murder. Scarlatti could easily escape justice if everyone was certain he had died sleeping in his own villa when it burned down. Setting fire to the building when none of his servants or estate workers were close by ensured none of them would be caught in the blaze. It was almost certain the flames would consume the villa, especially during the current drought, destroying any evidence that proved Scarlatti was not inside. The fact there was a body in Scarlatti's bed did not mean it was his corpse. What better way to persuade others than to leave a dead man to burn in here? The fallen beam that had cut the bedchamber off from the worst of the fire would have been impossible to predict.

Aldo peered at the bedside tables. There were candles on both, but no evidence the fire had started in this room. Even with the shutters open, the air in here was still thick with smoke and other scents, but it was obvious the fire had originated elsewhere in the villa. So much for the notion that Scarlatti had fallen asleep with a candle burning nearby. Something – or someone – else was responsible for the blaze that had destroyed this villa.

Voices were shouting outside, calling up from below. 'Aldo, are you all right? Can you hear us? Are you hurt? Do you need me to come up?'

He stood up, leaning out the window to reassure those waiting beneath the shutters. Federica was standing by Vincenzo at the ladder, other servants and workers clustered around. 'I'm fine,' Aldo said. 'Stay where you are for now. I'll let you know if it's safe to come up.' He retreated from view, turning round to approach the bed. The closer he got, the stronger the stench of decay became, a cloud of flies crawling across the sheet that covered the corpse. The size and shape of the body matched Federica's description of Scarlatti. Aldo pinched his nose shut, breathing through his mouth instead. He reached for the sheet, pulling it aside.

Palle! Aldo staggered back, repulsed by what was on the bed.

The corpse seemed to be Scarlatti, or what was left of him. Maggots writhed across the skin, a moving mass feasting on distended remains. They were eating away the flesh around the face, exposing the skull underneath. Flies rose into the air, swarming around Aldo, trying to get into his eyes and nose and mouth. He flung himself aside, lurching into a wall, flailing at the air to drive them back. His belly lurched. If he had eaten that morning, anything inside him would have come back up by now.

Eventually the flies settled back to their feast on the bed, leaving Aldo in peace. He studied what remained of the body, looking for signs to confirm if it was Scarlatti. The corpse was male and naked. The seething maggots and bloating brought by death made it difficult to be certain, but the dead man's hair matched what Federica had described. One of Scarlatti's servants or estate workers would need to identify him, but it seemed this was his body.

Aldo had seen more corpses than he could count: his own father, brothers in arms and enemies during battles, the bodies of those who had died or were murdered. He had added to that tally himself with different blades, including the stiletto in his left boot. He knew the face of death all too well, how it shifted and changed as days passed. Everyone believed Scarlatti had died on Thursday night, consumed by the fire. It was apparent now that the flames were not responsible for his death.

Could Scarlatti have been killed before Thursday?

It was possible. His absence before Thursday, an unusual trip away from the villa. The fact that nobody could recall seeing him return. What if Scarlatti had been persuaded to leave his home and was murdered elsewhere, just as Dovizi was lured from his palazzo to die? Could the same hand have been responsible for the deaths of both Dovizi and Scarlatti? Perhaps, but it was a long reach from the two founders dying so far apart in the same week to their killer being a single individual. There was no proof Scarlatti had been murdered, not yet. Aldo knew he lacked the skill to determine how many days had passed since death had claimed this corpse. He certainly did not have enough evidence to send a message making any such claims to Bindi.

More than ever, Aldo wished Saul was by his side, studying what was here. But he had another, more pressing problem to resolve.

How to get Scarlatti's body out of this room?

* * *

You find an excuse to leave the palazzo, tools hidden within your long woollen cloak. Once far enough away, you slip into a dark alley and pull on the cloak, lifting the hood up to hide your face. Soon there will be no need for such secrecy, but for now you must remain unknown.

You are patient.

You have waited this long.

You can stay in the shadows a while more.

You tuck the hammer, nails and papers under one arm as you leave the alley.

The doors of Santa Croce are first. You wait until Mass begins inside the church, knowing it will keep those within busy. You press one of the new proclamations against the wood with your palm, fingers holding a nail at the top of the paper. You hammer the metal in place, first at the top, then the bottom. Given the chance you would add more nails, but you can hear footsteps inside, hurrying towards the doors. It is time to leave.

You turn aside, slipping the hammer into the sleeve of your cloak. A guilty man flees, drawing attention to himself, so you stroll away. Behind you, voices are calling out. Some demand to know who nailed this new proclamation to the church doors, others are eager to read it. Those who believe in Savonarola crave more of his wisdom, his teachings.

People hurry past you, eagerness in their faces, all of them wanting to see what you have posted on the door today. Voices rise in the morning sun, becoming a chant of hope and anger: 'Savonarola lives! Savonarola lives! Savonarola lives!'

But then another voice calls out: 'You, over there! Stay where you are!'

You keep moving, hoping they mean someone else.

But the next voice removes all doubt.

'No, you, in the cloak – stop!'

Instead, you run.

* * *

Realizing there was no way to move Scarlatti's corpse without help, Aldo called for Vincenzo to climb up to the bedchamber. 'Wrap a cloth across your nose and mouth first,' he advised. While Vincenzo was doing that, Federica approached the ladder. 'You need to stay down there,' Aldo said, leaning out of the window. 'The fire has damaged this villa beyond repair. The walls could give way, or what's left of this level could collapse.'

'What about the signore?' she asked. 'Is he . . .?'

Aldo nodded. 'I'm sorry. There is a body in the bed that resembles Signor Scarlatti.'

Federica stared up, her mouth moving but making no sound, her eyes red yet dry. Perhaps she had cried too much to have any tears left. The housekeeper staggered back a step, then both legs crumpled beneath her. Other servants rushed to help, leaving the estate manager Trigari to hold the ladder. Vincenzo clambered up, his mouth and nose masked.

Aldo helped him inside the bedchamber. Vincenzo reeled at the writhing mess of maggots and corpse atop the bed. 'Mio Dio!' he gasped, making the sign of the cross.

'We can't leave him in here,' Aldo said, 'but moving Scarlatti will not be simple. I suggest we wrap the sheet beneath the body around it, and make knots at both ends.'

'I could fetch a rope,' Vincenzo suggested. 'No, we'll need two ropes. Tie one to each end of the knotted sheet. Use those to lower him out of the window and down to the ground.'

Aldo nodded. 'You get the rope, I'll stay here. While you're below, tell Trigari to move everyone else away. None of them need to see what has become of their signore.' Vincenzo was climbing down the ladder when Aldo heard a familiar voice calling.

'Cesare, are you here?'

Aldo leaned out between the shutters. A lone figure was

coming up the hill from the village, a satchel in one hand and his other adjusting the skullcap atop his head. He looked uncomfortable, no doubt sweltering beneath the morning sun.

'Saul, I'm up here!'

The doctor paused, shielding his eyes from the sun to peer at Aldo. A grateful smile appeared on Saul's face. 'You never said anything in your letter about hills!'

Aldo pointed at Federica on the ground beneath him. 'There's a woman down there who has just collapsed. Her name is Federica. See what you can do for her.'

Saul was tending to the housekeeper by the time Aldo climbed down, other servants and estate workers gathered round them in a circle. 'Please, she needs air,' Saul said, pressing a hand to Federica's forehead. 'And something to drink, too.' Water was brought by the time Saul and Aldo had moved her to sit leaning against a wall in the shade. 'Small sips,' Saul murmured. 'You have not been looking after yourself.'

'The fire,' she replied, gesturing at what was left of the villa.

'Of course.' One of the other women knelt beside Federica, taking the water from Saul. He stood, stretching his back and wiping sweat from his brow.

'You came,' Aldo said. He would have liked to hug Saul but not in front of all these people. 'When you didn't reply to my letter—'

Saul nodded. 'I was busy with a patient when the messenger arrived. He left before I could—' He pointed at Vincenzo, who came to Aldo, clutching lengths of rope. 'This is him.'

'Vincenzo works in the stables at the estate on the next hill,' Aldo said, pointing towards Ruggerio's villa. He had told Saul what the silk merchant was capable of, the blood that belonged on his hands.

'Ahh.' Saul glanced around. 'Your letter said there was a body to be examined?'

Aldo explained the difficulty in removing Scarlatti's corpse from the bedchamber. Trigari was nearby, listening to the conversation. He scowled at the skullcap on Saul's head.

'You sent for one of his kind? You mean to have him meddling with the signore's body?' the estate manager hissed. 'You may be an officer of the court in Florence, but that only goes so far out here in the dominion. We have our own ways here.'

Aldo chose not to mention the demotion. His authority was limited enough. 'I understand, but I need to be sure about the circumstances of Signor Scarlatti's death.'

'He died in the fire,' Trigari said.

'I found his body inside the villa, but the fire did not start in his bedchamber.'

The estate manager glared at Vincenzo. 'You've been up there. Is this true?' The stable hand nodded. 'Then how did the signore die?'

'Breathing in smoke is the likeliest cause,' Saul said. 'That is how most people die in burning buildings. The flames might reach them eventually, but smoke claims them first.'

'Dr Orvieto is one of the finest physicians in Florence,' Aldo announced, making sure all the servants and estate workers heard him. 'He assists the Otto, the most powerful criminal court in the city, with such matters. That is why I sent for him, to help us understand what has happened here. To make sense of this tragedy.'

Trigari folded his arms, still not satisfied. 'Even so . . .'

'I have a suggestion,' Saul said, smiling at those gathered around them. 'Let us send for your parish priest, ask him to come here. May I ask, what is his name?'

'Father Ognissanti,' Federica replied, getting up from the ground.

'Thank you.' Saul beamed at her. 'Let us send for Father Ognissanti. I shall seek his permission to examine your signore's remains. If Father Ognissanti agrees – and only if he is willing to be present while I work – I shall study Signor Scarlatti. That is all.' Saul looked at Trigari and the others, hands held out, palms upwards in supplication. 'May we do that?'

There was some grumbling from the estate manager but Saul's kindness to Federica seemed enough to convince her. She rallied the other servants, leaving Trigari little choice. He stamped down the hill himself to fetch the parish priest.

'Well done,' Aldo murmured into Saul's ear.

'It seemed the best solution,' he replied. The doctor looked up at the open shutters. 'Shall I climb in and see what other evidence I can find?'

'You do not wish to go in there,' Vincenzo warned, shaking his head. 'It is . . . bad.'

Aldo had to agree. 'Let us bring the body down. It's more than enough. Trust me.'

Bindi slumped in the sturdy, high-backed chair behind his table. It had been hours since his meeting with Campana at Palazzo Medici, yet the segretario was no closer to knowing what more the Otto could do to help the duke or the city. Having Podestà guards on patrol with constables would add to their numbers, but there was no sign of Captain Duro sending any of his men from Le Stinche to help. Tens of thousands lived inside the city walls. Finding whoever was behind this plot to revive the cult of Savonarola needed a thousand men, or more good fortune than Bindi possessed.

It was hopeless.

Another day, two at the most, and Cosimo would be asking Campana to appoint a new segretario for the Otto. Someone capable of succeeding where Bindi had failed. It took little effort to guess who might be chosen. The segretario for the Office of Decency was a man of notorious ambition, eager to volunteer his services when a better post became available. Bindi had heard whispers about another potential candidate, a rising star among the city's bureaucrats and administrators called Francesco Borghini, though the segretario was yet to encounter this young pretender. Borghini might be ready to advise the Otto within a few years, but not yet. Not if Bindi could find a way to stop that.

But how? How?

A timid knock at the ufficio door did nothing to relieve his humours. What fool was coming to disturb him now? They could expect the rasp of his temper and nothing more, not unless they had brought some useful means of deliverance for the Otto. After waiting the usual three breaths, Bindi bellowed for whoever was outside to enter. A pot-bellied constable stumbled in, closing the door behind him. Yes, this was the fool who had come running into the Podestà several days ago, claiming that diavolo of a monk was alive. No wonder he was so hesitant to come knocking when Bindi had left strict orders not to be disturbed. A newcomer to the Otto, Bindi knew that much, but he could not recall the man's name.

'What do you want, Constable . . .?'

'Macci,' the man replied, venturing closer. He was being careful to keep one hand out of view, held behind his back or hidden by his far side while closing the ufficio door.

'I repeat,' Bindi said, letting his exasperation show even more, 'what do you want? And don't make me ask a third time, or I shall not be responsible for the consequences.'

The constable swallowed hard, his fear all too apparent. 'We saw a man not long ago, nailing a proclamation to the front doors of Santa Croce. I called out and he ran. Manuffi and I, we pursued him for several streets, heading north-west towards the ospedale, but—'

'You lost him.'

Macci stared down at his boots. 'Yes, segretario.'

'What did this individual look like?'

'He was wearing a long cloak, one with a hood—'

'That concealed his face and hair.' Bindi sighed. 'Of course it did.' Typical. Even when fortune deigned to smile on his efforts, the fools doing his will were still incapable of grasping a victory when the opportunity arose before them.

'But we did see his boots, Manuffi and I.'

'His boots.'

Macci nodded, a smile spreading across his face.

'And are you going to tell me about these boots, or are they what you have clutched so tightly behind your back?' Bindi asked.

'Err, no,' the constable replied. 'I mean, yes, but . . . umm, no. Sir.'

'I see. Then you'd better describe these boots to me. I presume they were distinctive, otherwise you would not have noticed them, is that correct?'

Macci nodded again with the eagerness of an obedient but stupid hound.

'Well?' Bindi said. 'What did they look like?'

'Oh! Forgive me, segretario. They were fancy. Fine leather, from what we could see, with tassels and embroidery stitched into them. A rich man's boots, or those of a rich man's servant.'

'I see. Anything else?'

Macci's brow furrowed. 'Sir?'

'Did these boots have any other markings on them? Something

that might help the court find this fugitive that you and Manuffi allowed to escape?'

'I—' Macci shrugged.

'I'll take that as a no,' Bindi concluded.

'It was . . . those boots must have cost him plenty of coin, yet his cloak was patched and tattered. The two things didn't go together, if you see what I mean,' Macci said. 'Sir.'

Perhaps this constable wasn't quite the fool he first seemed. The segretario leaned forward in his chair. 'Anything else you observed about this troublemaker?'

'Sorry, no. But we went back and took this from the doors at Santa Croce.' Macci revealed what he had been keeping out of view: the latest proclamation. Bindi snapped his fingers for it and the constable laid the torn document on the table between them.

'You may go,' he told Macci, who retreated to the door. 'Relieve one of the other men on watch duty. The constable standing sentry outside Palazzo Ghiberti, for example.'

Once Macci was gone, Bindi read the new proclamation.

FRATE
SAVONAROLA
LIVES!

Forty years ago, your Senate put to death the preacher and prophet Girolamo Savonarola. He was a good brother of the Dominican faith, a loyal servant to God and to the ordinary people of Florence. His execution by hanging and fire in the Piazza della Signoria was an act of murder by men desperate to destroy the truth of his teachings.

But the spirit of Savonarola lives! The ordinary people of Florence are ready to once again proclaim the truth preached by our beloved frate. Today – Monday, May 27th, in the year of Our Lord 1538 – the spirit of Savonarola will rise once more. It shall strike against one of those who betrayed him, as all who stand against the true teachings must suffer.

Gather on the bridges of our city one hour before curfew and tonight you shall bear witness as this prophecy comes true. Stand above the waters of the Arno and see the suffering of those who would stop Florence becoming a new Jerusalem, a new city of God. Be there as the spirit of Savonarola leads us all to a better world, to a new tomorrow!

FRATE SAVONAROLA LIVES!

Bindi sank back in his chair. He should return to Palazzo Medici at once, taking this fresh outrage. Even if the duke would not grant him a meeting, it was vital that Campana be made aware of the threat contained within the proclamation. Cosimo's spies had probably delivered a copy of it to him already, but Bindi needed to be part of the decision about how to respond.

The Otto's remit included preventing significant crimes being committed within the city, though in practice the court devoted far more to finding those responsible and bringing them to justice. Rare was the occasion when a criminal announced his intentions, let alone provided the time and location for that crime.

But if this proclamation was to be believed it seemed murder would be committed in front of Savonarola's disciples before the end of the day. Bindi was certain that if this happened, he would be held personally responsible for it. After all, if the Otto could not prevent murder when it had been forewarned about the intended time and place, what use was the court or its segretario?

Chapter Seventeen

$\mathscr{R}$uggerio glared out through the shutters in his bedchamber. Men from the Otto had been watching his residence for three nights, waiting for him to emerge, ready to follow wherever he went. One of them was outside now, listlessly observing as servants came and went. Having sources in the Podestà meant that Ruggerio knew the dual purpose of this presence. The court was guarding the homes of himself, Ghiberti and Uccello in case there was a fresh attack against any of the surviving founders.

The surviving founders . . . Ruggerio sighed. It was not yet certain that Scarlatti had died when his country villa burned. Aldo had sent Bindi a letter about a fire at Scarlatti's estate, promising a further missive once the names of those who died in the blaze were confirmed. There was no mention if the fire was accidental or intentional, but coming so soon after Dovizi was burned alive . . . The timing seemed too close to be happenstance.

The housekeeper at Ruggerio's country villa had sent a similar letter. Cassandra was adept at keeping him informed of changes on and around his hillside estate, especially those involving the Tuscan retreats of allies and enemies. Ruggerio was not in the habit of trusting women. He had no interest in them, and most were of no help because they lacked the power to influence or alter important decisions.

His previous housekeepers had been able enough to do their

jobs, but Cassandra had shown she could do more. She effectively and efficiently managed the estate and those who worked on it, though custom required her title remain housekeeper. She chose not to fill her own pouch with his coin, an uncommon restraint in many servants. Best of all, Cassandra showed no interest in marriage or children, which suited Ruggerio well.

In her letter Cassandra noted Aldo's interest in the fire. Her implication was clear: Aldo was intent on uncovering whether the blaze at Scarlatti's estate had been a deliberate act. After being all but banished from the city – again, sources within the Podestà were most helpful – Aldo seemed determined to prove his value as an investigator. Not so much to convince that fool Bindi – Aldo's opinion of the segretario was all too evident – but to convince himself. Aldo had stumbled more than once during his recent visit to the city. Ruggerio surmised Aldo needed to prove himself, his skills, his insight. He needed to rediscover his purpose.

If Scarlatti was murdered, Aldo would find those responsible.

A newcomer approached the man watching Ruggerio's palazzo. They exchanged a few words before one left and the newcomer remained. A change, but the presence remained. Ruggerio knew the court was keeping watch on the trio for a second reason: to see if one of them was the killer. That meant whoever murdered Dovizi would find it harder to kill again while constables and officers from the court were outside. Yet safety was not assured. One bored constable would not stop a determined man with murder on his mind, especially if that killer was paid well enough. Such an arrow always found its target, sooner or later.

Worse still, the court representatives were dissuading others from visiting Ruggerio, especially those he would welcome to his table or his bedchamber. None of his favourites wanted to risk the questions that might arise if they stayed a night at his residence. At first this had been a nuisance, nothing more. But three nights without fresh company was fast becoming intolerable. Much as Ruggerio enjoyed toying with his servants, and he would sometimes use one for his own pleasure, there was little joy to be had in that. There was no wit in their conversation, no fresh secrets in their gossip, no hidden delights in their pillow whispers. For that he needed men not in his employ. He needed new entertainments.

He could depart his palazzo at any time during daylight, go wherever he wished. The court was doing nothing to prevent that. But Ruggerio saw no need to risk his life. Besides, staying within these walls had offered an opportunity to gather information from his many sources across the city. While officers and constables of the Otto were busy keeping watch outside the palazzi of Uccello and Ghiberti, the servants of both men came and went from those same residences without being challenged. Several had meetings with Ruggerio's maggiordomo where coin was exchanged for news. Alberti always returned from these private assignations with fresh intelligence that proved most illuminating.

Ghiberti had continued doing the things he always did, the way he always had. There had been a gathering of the Arte della Lana at his palazzo two days ago where senior members of the wool merchants and manufacturers' guild had argued about prices and supplies. Ghiberti had attended, his assistant revealed, making the usual forthright contribution to those discussions. Ruggerio smiled at such a polite description. Having known Ghiberti more than forty years, there was likely to have been far more shouting and banging on tables than the assistant indicated, along with far less delicacy to Ghiberti's words. He was not afraid to call a fool that to their face when in a good mood; when his humours were out of balance, he was prone to violence. Ghiberti was a dangerous man, but there was nothing subtle about him. Where Ruggerio preferred to keep his own hands clean, Ghiberti's instinct was always to attack or confront. He was a blunt weapon. Effective, but blunt.

If those responsible for Dovizi's death came for Ghiberti, they were not likely to leave unscathed. The wool merchant would succumb to no man easily, and he certainly would not die without a fight. That was beyond his understanding, and always had been.

Ruggerio found it hard to believe Ghiberti had sent others to kill Dovizi, let alone to have him murdered in such an outrageous manner. Ghiberti lacked the imagination for such a display, and he also lacked the motivation. The wool merchant certainly had no new quarrel with Dovizi that Ruggerio could discern. When the Convent of Santa Maria Magdalena had been dissolved the previous summer, Ghiberti appeared least concerned of all the founders that their precious documents were missing. Scarlatti had become so afraid that he'd fled to the countryside, but Ghiberti merely shrugged. Unless something dramatic happened to alter a person's attitudes or behaviour, most people did not change as they grew older – they simply became more so. To Ruggerio's eye that was particularly true of Ghiberti.

But Uccello . . . he was another matter altogether.

In the days since Dovizi's death Ruggerio had become increasingly convinced that Uccello might be the one behind these stratagemmi. The letter held at the Podestà in which Dovizi had accused Uccello was not part of that; Ruggerio had dismissed it as troublemaking typical of Dovizi, an attempt to smear Uccello. No, other factors were fuelling Ruggerio's conviction. The luring of Dovizi to that stable while he wore his founder's tunic, and the grotesque manner of his murder. And now this fire at Scarlatti's country villa, only hours after the death of Dovizi . . . There was a grandness to it. A sense of display. Someone was demanding attention, wanting to be sure everyone was watching.

What could be more Uccello than that?

His response when asked whether he or Ghiberti had killed Dovizi had been illuminating too. Ghiberti had leapt to his feet, outraged by the question. He responded as Ruggerio had expected, angry and aggrieved. But Uccello merely sniffed his disdain, calling the question an insult yet offering no other response. He displayed no outrage, no denial, and certainly no shock. It was almost as if Uccello had expected the accusation, as if he had been preparing himself for such an inquiry. Getting his answer ready for when the moment came.

Only a guilty man would do that.

Ruggerio called for Alberti, and his maggiordomo appeared within moments. 'It is possible that I may need to travel to my country estate sooner than I expected. Please commence preparations for a rapid relocation to the dominion, should I deem that necessary.'

'Of course, sir,' Alberti replied, bowing low.

'Keep these plans to yourself,' Ruggerio added. Just as Alberti had his sources within the households of Uccello and Ghiberti, it was likely that at least one of the other founders paid servants inside this palazzo for secrets and gossip. Such expenditures were a necessary price of life in the city. Better to be well informed and a little less rich than the alternative.

'Naturally,' Alberti said, retreating to the door.

'Oh, and one more thing,' Ruggerio added. 'Do we know the name of the constable lurking in the shadows outside, keeping watch on my movements?'

'He's called Manuffi.' The maggiordomo smiled. 'Not one of the Otto's sharpest minds, according to your sources within the Podestà.'

Ruggerio couldn't decide whether he should be insulted or gratified. 'Very well. Our friend across the street must be hungry and thirsty. Have the kitchen prepare a platter of good meats and cheeses for him. Send that across to Manuffi with my compliments, along with a bottle of decent wine. Make sure one of the prettier servant girls delivers it, won't you? I might wish to venture out later, once the heat of the day has passed, and that will be easier without a blundering fool from the Otto following me.'

Alberti smiled. 'As you wish.'

Strocchi was dry of mouth and empty of belly. He should have brought food or drink when he left home that morning but hadn't wished to disturb Tomasia or Bianca. It had seemed the right decision hours ago, but he was regretting it now. A constable should have come to relieve his watch outside Palazzo Uccello. The sun was now at its highest, wrapping a blanket of heat around those foolish enough to be sweltering outside at this time of day. The doorway Strocchi had chosen for his watch was no longer in shadow or shade, yet he was reluctant to move and draw attention. If someone wandered by on their way home with food or wine from the mercato, he could buy a little from them. But, aside from parishioners leaving Mass at the church of San Barnaba, few people passed Uccello's grand residence.

So Strocchi stood and sweated and waited.

He was becoming a little dizzy when Uccello's ornate carriage rolled into view, pulled by four white horses as usual. They trotted round to the main doors, stopping there a while. The driver climbed down to tend his horses, checking their embroidered leather harnesses, while another servant went inside. Eventually the servant returned, accompanied by two more, all in the gleaming livery favoured by their signore. Finally, Uccello himself appeared from the palazzo, dressed in a vibrant crimson tunic and black hose.

Each time Strocchi saw the banker he was wearing different clothes. There must be an entire room inside the palazzo set aside for housing them. Strocchi owned what he was wearing, one change of hose, and the clothes he kept aside for church.

Uccello strolled round the carriage, servants scuttling after him to open the door. Before getting in, Uccello turned and bowed to Strocchi, the gesture accompanied by a wide smirk. It was another performance, another show. 'I'm paying a visit to my friend Ghiberti,' Uccello called out. 'Shall I see you there as well?'

Strocchi ignored the jibe, refusing to give Uccello the satisfaction of a reply.

The banker climbed into his carriage and the horses trotted away, Uccello waving out of a window. Strocchi did not enjoy being mocked, but his orders from Bindi left no choice. He marched after the carriage as it rolled south, determined not to lose sight of his subject.

Uccello had spoken true about his destination. The carriage came to a halt outside Palazzo Ghiberti, not far from the Arno and only two streets west of where Dovizi had lived. Yet Uccello did not emerge from his carriage, instead sending one of his servants into the palazzo. Strocchi looked around and soon found the constable keeping watch on Ghiberti's home. It was Macci, the newcomer who had been so quick to believe that Savonarola was returned from the dead forty years after being executed. Macci was slumped in a doorway opposite the palazzo entrance, snoring in the sunshine.

Strocchi nudged the constable with a boot but got no response. He delivered a harder kick and Macci jerked awake, stumbling upright. 'What is it? What's happening?' he asked.

'I would ask you the same, but I doubt you have a notion,' Strocchi replied. 'Falling asleep while on watch can get you dismissed from the court.'

'I was only resting my eyes,' Macci protested.

'And snoring at the same time?' The constable muttered something beneath his breath that Strocchi couldn't quite hear. 'What did you see before deciding to rest your eyes?'

Macci shrugged. 'Merchants coming and going, a few servants, that's all.'

Noises behind Strocchi made him turn. The palazzo doors opened, Ghiberti emerging from within, Uccello's servant hurrying after. Strocchi moved to watch Ghiberti as he stalked to the carriage, glaring up at Uccello. 'Well?' Ghiberti demanded, a scowl across his face.

Uccello leaned out of the nearest window, smiling down at him. 'My dear Roberto, I wanted to see you, find out how you are bearing up in these most trying of times.'

Ghiberti folded both arms across his chest. 'If you've something important to tell me, come down here and say it to my face. Otherwise, I'll go back inside.'

'If you insist,' Uccello replied. He clapped his hands together and a servant hurried to open the carriage door, helping Uccello step down to the street. The two founders moved across to the palazzo doorway, getting away from the scorching sun. Strocchi edged closer, straining to hear what was being said, but both men had lowered their voices to a murmur.

Whatever was passing between them, it did not seem to satisfy Ghiberti. He became angrier and angrier, his meaty hands clenching into fists, the look in his eyes growing darker. Uccello remained smiling, his hands dancing in the air, making sweeping gestures. He patted Ghiberti on the shoulders, but this hand got slapped away. Uccello's smile faded. He leaned over Ghiberti, using his superior height to loom above the other founder.

'No!' Ghiberti snarled, stepping back from him. 'Go back to your palazzo and your parties. We'll soon see what becomes of that, what becomes of you.' The wool merchant spun round and stalked back inside his palazzo. Uccello remained quite still for a few moments before returning to his carriage, a broad smile restored to his features.

'What was that all about?' Macci whispered.

'I don't know,' Strocchi admitted, 'but those two are not what I'd call friends.'

Uccello paused at the door to his carriage, a waiting servant holding it open for him. Instead of getting in, the banker strolled towards Strocchi and Macci. 'I'm sorry you had to witness that unpleasantness,' he said. 'This is what happens to old acquaintances sometimes.'

'What did you suggest that Signor Ghiberti found so disagreeable?' Strocchi asked.

Uccello laughed. 'You are very amusing, officer . . .?'

'Carlo Strocchi.'

'I shall be returning to my palazzo now,' Uccello said. 'You are most welcome to ride with me, if you wish? It would be easier than running along behind me. More dignified, yes?'

Getting out of the sun would be a blessing, but Strocchi could not accept such an offer, not from such a prominent suspect. 'Thank you, but I must decline.'

'Very well.' Uccello went back to his carriage. 'Later I shall make my weekly visit to an old acquaintance across the Arno. Perhaps I will see you there,' he called over a shoulder.

'You may depend on it,' Strocchi replied.

Aldo was grateful to be in shade, away from what was left of the villa. The upper levels had collapsed not long after he and Vincenzo lowered Scarlatti's corpse from the bedchamber window. The two of them were climbing down the ladder when an almighty creaking and groaning filled the air. Aldo shouted at Vincenzo to jump clear. They both hit the ground as the upper level gave way, collapsing inwards. That threw out a cloud of ash and smoke, choking the air close by, but no one was hurt. A fortunate escape.

Father Ognissanti arrived as Saul and Vincenzo were moving Scarlatti's remains into an empty shed at the edge of the estate, away from any homes. Even wrapped inside two knotted sheets, the body gave off a powerful stench of rancid meat that repulsed all those close by. The sooner this corpse was laid to rest, the better. But Aldo was determined that Saul should examine Scarlatti first to determine how he had died.

The parish priest was reluctant to agree, his mood as sour as the smell coming from the corpse. Ognissanti had sweated through his clerical robes climbing up the hill from San Jacopo al Girone during the hottest part of the day. Aldo came close to losing his patience with the stubborn priest, arguing while the relentless sun overhead seared them both. It was Saul who interceded, his soothing words proposing an agreeable solution. Ognissanti would stay while Saul examined Scarlatti's remains to ensure their sanctity was not disturbed. After, the corpse would be interred in a crypt built nearby at Scarlatti's behest the previous year.

Aldo had taken off the apron borrowed from Vincenzo and was waiting in the shade when Cassandra arrived. She brought baskets of food and bottles of wine from Ruggerio's estate, giving them to Federica. 'Share these as you think best,' Cassandra said. 'It isn't much, but . . .' Scarlatti's housekeeper accepted, grateful tears on her sun-bronzed features.

Cassandra joined Aldo by the hut. 'Vincenzo told me what happened,' she said. Aldo had sent the stable hand back to Ruggerio's estate.

Aldo watched Federica dividing the food and wine between the servants. 'What will happen to them once Scarlatti is laid to rest? I'm told there is no family to inherit his estate.'

Cassandra shrugged. 'The farmers will stay on working the land until its ownership can be determined. But the servants . . .' She gestured at the smoking pile of stone and ashes where Scarlatti's villa had stood. 'They have nowhere to live or work now. Most have been sleeping in other buildings on the estate, but without the signore to pay them . . .'

Aldo nodded. A rich man's death could affect many.

Cassandra leaned closed, her voice a murmur. 'Vincenzo said the fire did not start in Scarlatti's bedchamber. Is that true?'

'That's how it seemed.'

'Then where?'

It was Aldo's turn to shrug. 'I doubt that will ever be known for certain. The fire took all the evidence. But for a collapsing beam, it would have taken Scarlatti too.'

Father Ognissanti emerged from the hut, a cloth clamped to his nose and mouth, sweat running down his forehead. He made the sign of the cross before stumbling away. Saul came out a few moments later grim-faced, all his usual warmth banished by what was inside. Aldo approached him but Saul shook his head. 'Not now, Cesare.' He went to the priest instead, putting a hand round Ognissanti's shoulders, whispering to him.

'Is that the doctor you brought from Florence?' Cassandra asked.

'Yes,' Aldo replied. 'His name is Saul Orvieto. He assists the court sometimes.'

'Will he be travelling back tonight?'

'Why do you ask? Are you in need of a physician?'

'No. But if he needs a bed, there are several empty at my signore's villa.'

'Would Ruggerio approve of you making such an offer?'

She smiled. 'I won't mention it if you don't.'

Aldo noticed Saul shaking hands with the priest. 'Let me see what Saul has to say. He may well take you up on the offer.' Ognissanti moved away to talk with his parishioners. Aldo waited until he got a nod from Saul before approaching the doctor. 'How are you?'

'Exhausted,' Saul replied, rolling his shoulders and stretching his neck. 'I never realized how hot it got in the dominion.' He glanced at the hut. 'And as for that poor man . . .'

'Can you tell me what killed him?'

'I think so,' Saul said. 'I'm certain that he did not burn to death.'

Aldo nodded. 'The fire started in another room, not his bedchamber.'

'No, you misunderstand.' Saul glanced at what was left of the villa. 'Signor Scarlatti died at least two days before any of this happened. I believe he was murdered.'

'You're sure?' Aldo kept his question quiet so Cassandra and others nearby would not overhear. Saul nodded. Aldo had no wish to look at Scarlatti's body again, but he needed to be certain. 'I know it is asking a lot, but can you bear to show me?'

Saul swallowed. 'Cover your mouth and nose,' he advised, leading Aldo to the shed. It was dark inside after so long on the sun-drenched hill, but Aldo's eyes soon adjusted. The corpse was lying atop a rough wooden bench, the sheets draped beneath Scarlatti stained by his rotting remains. Maggots had been brushed from the face and neck, exposing what was left of him. 'Nature is reclaiming this body,' Saul said. 'Doing what it will to all of us when our time comes. That's to be expected in this heat, several days after death.'

Aldo nodded, his eyes watering at the stench.

Saul gestured at the gap between Scarlatti's nose and mouth, what was left there. 'If smoke from the fire had killed him, there might be evidence of that here. But I cannot be certain; decay and the maggots have taken so much. The real proof is his neck.' Saul pointed to four small, distinct oval-shaped bruises on the skin, and a similar bruise further round the neck.

'Finger marks,' Aldo said. 'From a hand, gripping his throat.'

Saul nodded. 'His neck was broken. No fire did that.'

'You said he was killed at least two days before the blaze?'

'That is an estimate. The maggots, the amount this body has already decomposed . . .' Saul stepped back from the bench, shaking his head. 'I cannot be exact. I have encountered corpses before that lay undiscovered for six, seven days. They looked much as Scarlatti did when I first saw his remains. Even at the height of summer, this . . . It's too much for him to have been dead a few days. I would estimate he was killed six, perhaps seven days ago.'

Aldo had more questions, but Saul was unsteady on his feet and his eyelids were fluttering. Aldo led him outside, away from the sight and stench of Scarlatti's ripe corpse. Cassandra was waiting near the door. She helped Saul to a stone bench in the shade. He sank onto it, putting his head between his knees. 'I'm sorry,' he whispered.

'No, it's my fault,' Aldo said. 'I should have let you rest.'

Cassandra brought a cup of water from the estate well. 'Here, drink this.' She tended to Saul while Aldo stepped back, his head full of questions and speculation.

If Saul was right about Scarlatti having been murdered several days before the fire at the villa – and there was no reason to doubt his judgement – that changed everything.

Chapter Eighteen

*M*ost days, Bindi enjoyed making others wait for him. Whenever there was a knock at the door to his ufficio in the Podestà, the segretario left that person outside for longer than was necessary. Even when they were standing before his table, Bindi liked to shuffle court papers or keep himself occupied a while longer. Some might consider such behaviour petty, but to him it was essential. Doing so reinforced his authority, demonstrated who was in charge at the Podestà. It showed where true power resided.

To be on the other side of such treatment was . . . irksome. The segretario couldn't be sure how long he had been waiting in the courtyard at Palazzo Medici. One hour? No, longer than that. Two perhaps, or even three. Whatever the duration, remaining on this bench had become a matter of pride. He would not depart until he had met with the duke – or at least Campana. One of them would deign to grant him a meeting. Perhaps staying here so long was foolish and certainly it was stubborn, but there was a principle at stake. It was the duke who had ordered the Otto to use every available resource to find and stop those responsible for killing Dovizi and for inciting pro-Savonarola gatherings across the city.

The new proclamation Bindi was clutching was important information. It promised another murder before curfew. Bindi did not doubt the young Medici was already aware of this fresh threat, he had spies and informants across the city. But it was Bindi's duty to deliver a copy of the proclamation, to offer his counsel on how to respond, and to proffer whatever help the Otto could provide against this outrage.

Whether the duke would listen, whether he would even grant a meeting . . . that was beyond Bindi's control. At the Podestà he had authority. He was in charge, the true power of the Otto resting with him. But here he was a humble functionary, a minor administrator from a court that had failed in its duty to the city and the duke. No wonder Cosimo or, more likely, Campana had kept him waiting so long.

If Bindi had his way, constables and officers from the Otto would already be standing sentry on the bridges. Ideally the duke would call on militia to bolster those defences, but the city's men at arms had been at odds with Cosimo since he'd been chosen to lead Florence. The militia leader, Captain Vitelli, had been a frequent stone in the new duke's shoe. Bindi heard whispers of vicious disagreements between Vitelli and Cosimo. There were rumours that the captain was departing Florence or had already gone. Whatever the truth, it was doubtful the militia would be willing or ready for rapid deployment.

It was Campana who finally came into the courtyard, though he seemed surprised to discover anyone waiting there. 'Bindi, why are—?' the duke's private segretario said before realization crossed his face. 'I thought I sent word you should return to the Podestà. His Grace was occupied with other matters, he didn't have time to see you.'

Bindi rose from the bench, not bothering to conceal his wounded pride. 'Clearly.'

'What was it you wished to report?'

'You already know about the new proclamations telling citizens to gather at the Arno before curfew, yes?' Campana nodded, so Bindi went on. 'I came to offer whatever help the Otto and its men can give. Stationing officers and constables on the entrances to the bridges, arresting anyone who protests that, removing any other troublemakers.'

'Good, good, that will help,' Campana agreed. 'The duke's spies have been tearing down all the proclamations, but word is already spreading across the city.'

'Rumour and gossip have always been the favoured language of most Florentines,' Bindi said. 'Why not use that against whoever is fuelling this sedition? Have spies spread a new story that makes people stay away from the bridges.'

'Yes, that could work.' Campana used a hand to smooth down his brown beard. It was a habit Bindi had noticed before, a sure sign the duke's segretario was deep in thought. 'We could say these gatherings by the Arno are a trap to lure true believers of Savonarola out into the open so the Otto can arrest them. That may make some people more determined to be there, but most citizens fear spending a night at Le Stinche or in your cells at the Podestà.'

Bindi could see the benefits of such a strategia. This would bring the more poisonous elements out into the open, make the most ardent followers of Savonarola reveal themselves. But it was not without risk. How many of the frate's believers were within the city? Their numbers must be small. After all, forty years had passed since his execution.

'Very well,' Campana said, his voice full of decisiveness. 'Put your officers and constables on the approaches to the river at the appointed hour. I will have the duke's spies mingle with those on the bridges. If this self-appointed spirit appears, we will be ready for them. There must be no more murders in Savonarola's name.'

* * *

Aldo retreated to the shade to ponder the significance of Saul's findings while Cassandra tended to the doctor. The blaze in Scarlatti's villa had started on Thursday, not long before sunset – more than twelve hours after Dovizi was burned alive in Florence. That had made it seem as though Dovizi was killed first, with Scarlatti perishing in the fire later the same day. But Saul's assessment of the corpse made it apparent Scarlatti was murdered before Dovizi, several days before. Finding where the corpse was kept during those days might help uncover the killer. It must have been close to the villa, probably on Scarlatti's estate.

Why was the body hidden? Two answers occurred to Aldo, one the more obvious. The killer had been looking for a way to conceal their crime, and Father Ognissanti's special Mass had provided the perfect opportunity, taking servants and estate workers away from the villa. The killer had sent a letter to Scarlatti's estate manager, announcing the signore would return late on Thursday afternoon when everyone was down in the village. Once the servants and workers had departed, Scarlatti's body was brought to the villa and placed in his bed. Then the fire was started, with nobody left on the estate to stop it burning.

The plan almost succeeded. But the beam that fell from the ceiling kept the flames from Scarlatti's bedchamber, preventing the fire from destroying his corpse and the evidence of what was done to him. If Cassandra had not seen smoke rising from Scarlatti's villa, the flames might still have completed their task; instead, the corpse remained for Aldo to find. Was Scarlatti's murder the work of one person? Moving a dead man was not an easy task, Aldo knew that from experience. Getting the body upstairs to the bedchamber alone would have been challenging, but a strong man could probably have managed it.

Aldo chose not to ponder the reason a killer or killers murdered

Scarlatti, a retired merchant who presented no obvious threat to anyone – that could wait for now. There was still the second answer to the question of why the corpse was hidden. Keeping the remains out of sight could well have been a strategia to confuse those investigating the death of Scarlatti. He died before Dovizi, but the concealment of his body meant it was discovered second. That made the murder of Dovizi appear as the first attack in a larger campaign, especially if considered alongside the false proclamation on the doors to Dovizi's palazzo.

Had all gone as planned, the death of Scarlatti would probably have been dismissed as an accident. Indeed, any link between his death and Dovizi's murder in the city might not have been made at all, despite the two founders dying within hours of each another. Again, fortune had not favoured whoever was responsible for killing Scarlatti. But for Aldo's ill-starred trip to Florence, he might not have heard about Dovizi's murder for weeks or even months. By then, all evidence of what had happened to Scarlatti would have been long gone.

Another truth occurred to Aldo. Whoever killed Scarlatti could have hidden his body and travelled into Florence to murder Dovizi before returning to move Scarlatti's corpse. It was even possible the killer had crossed paths with Aldo on the dirt road between San Jacopo al Girone and Florence. But escorting the one-armed thief had taken all of Aldo's attention that day. He could not recall the faces of anyone else he'd met on that journey.

Aldo stopped, shaking his head. He was doing what he berated others for: leaping from one truth to another while assuming there must be a link between them. The deaths of Scarlatti and Dovizi were murders, yes, but there was no proof the same person was culpable of both killings. That the two victims were founders of the same confraternity and had died so close to one another could still be happenstance. He did not believe that, but nor could he dismiss the chance it was true – not without proof of the contrary.

'Cesare?' A hand touched Aldo on the shoulder. It was Saul, looking much better. 'I said your name, but you didn't hear me.'

'Sorry,' Aldo replied. 'I was thinking about what you found, what it means . . .'

Saul smiled. 'You get a look on your face when that happens.'

'I do?'

'Yes. I wouldn't call it excitement . . . joy is closer. You have a new puzzle to solve.'

Aldo smiled. 'The first task is finding where Scarlatti's body was kept before it was placed inside the villa. They needed somewhere close by, probably here on the estate, but also somewhere none of the servants or workers were likely to stumble on it.' He peered at the stables and farm buildings close to the villa. All were in daily use. Even if the corpse had been concealed from view inside one of them, the smell of a dead body would soon have become impossible to ignore. No, the body must have been hidden elsewhere . . .

Saul sighed. 'Well, I need to tell Father Ognissanti and the estate manager that they can take the signore to his last rest. The sooner those remains are in the ground, the better.'

'He's not being buried,' Aldo said. 'Trigari told me Scarlatti had a crypt built here on the estate . . .' Realization silenced his words. Aldo saw Trigari deep in conversation with the parish priest and hurried towards them. 'Forgive my interruption, but can you tell me where Signor Scarlatti's crypt stands? I've heard it is here on the estate.'

'It's up there,' Trigari replied, pointing towards the top of the hill. 'Why do you ask?'

You are preparing the carriage. It is hard work, more so in the late afternoon heat. You sweat in your uniform, especially the elegant leather boots the signore makes you wear. You pause as another servant comes to the courtyard, bringing word that the signore intends to leave the palazzo soon. You nod and reply that all will be ready.

You go to the stables where the horses are enjoying the cool of the shade. You check their water and feed, make sure they are ready and rested before bringing them outside, one by one. You fit their embroidered leather harnesses before fixing them to the carriage. Four white horses, all with plaited manes. You will see they are not hurt.

You bow your head when the signore's driver stalks into the courtyard, showing him the respect he demands but does not deserve. He mutters and curses, complaining about having to take the signore out again, though it should come as no surprise. You know this journey is a regular trip south from the palazzo, one the signore makes every week at the same time.

You see the driver sniff the air and worry clutches at you. Will he realize? Will he look inside the carriage? But his impatience pushes him onwards, and he demands you open the gates. You do as he asks, keeping your eyes down, your gaze hidden.

You do not want him to see what is in your heart.

You do not want him to know your plans.

But he does not look at you.

He does not care.

You allow yourself a small smile.

Your waiting is almost over, the moment is coming.

You watch as the driver climbs into his seat on the carriage before urging the four white horses forward. The carriage rolls after them and you follow, closing the gates after yourself. You doubt you will ever return to this palazzo, this place.

You know you may not survive what comes next.
You hurry to catch up with the carriage as it rolls away.

Strocchi was surprised to see Benedetto approaching him in the doorway opposite Palazzo Uccello. The scowling constable was on night patrol, what was he doing here? Benedetto grumbled about being pulled from bed to act as a messenger before eventually recounting the segretario's message. 'Bindi wants everyone standing sentry on the bridges.'

'Now?'

'Yes.'

'Why?' Strocchi asked.

Benedetto shrugged. 'How should I know?'

That attitude was the reason Benedetto had been banished to the night patrol. Working for the Otto had soured him, turning an enthusiastic young constable into someone who did the least they could. Everything was too much trouble for Benedetto, and he wasn't afraid to say so. Strocchi hoped never to become the same.

'You'll have to tell the segretario I can't leave here,' he said.

'Why not?'

'You didn't care about the reason for Bindi's message, why do you need mine?'

'Because Bindi will want to know. If I can't give a good reason, he'll blame me.'

It was a valid argument. 'Uccello will be leaving his palazzo again soon; he told me so. One man more or one man less on the bridges will make little difference.'

'You can't be sure of that,' Benedetto said.

Strocchi was about to disagree when Uccello's carriage appeared around the corner.

The carriage stops outside the main doors of the palazzo, the driver pulling the horses to a halt. You go to the side of the carriage, opening the door for the signore. The driver sniffs the air again, shouting at you about the smell. He wonders if it is oil or something else?

You admit spilling some inside the carriage while polishing the woodwork.

The driver snarls insults, calling you a fool, an idiota.

You do not reply, your eyes cast down.

You are patient. You wait.

The signore emerges from his palazzo, glancing in both directions. He waves to two men lurking in the shadows. The signore invites one of the men to join him for the journey, but gets no reply. Laughing, the signore approaches the carriage.

His face curdles as he reaches the door you hold open for him. You apologize for spilling a little oil inside the carriage, and point to the dry matting spread across the floor to protect his fine shoes. You suggest he take the smaller carriage. It is not so impressive, but will make the journey just as well. You wait, will he accept your suggestion? But you know this man, how much he values appearances, how it matters more than comfort.

Putting a cloth to his nose and mouth, the signore climbs inside.

He urges the driver to be quick. The carriage jolts away.

You clamber on the back as it passes.

You know what is to come.

You smile.

'Something must stink inside that carriage,' Benedetto said. 'Either that, or its wheels have rolled through the merda. Hot day like this, it bakes into the wood if you don't wash that off.'

The carriage jolted away, Uccello's browbeaten servant clambering on the back. Strocchi followed, Benedetto straggling along behind. They had no difficulty keeping sight of the carriage as it rolled through the city. Narrow streets forced the driver to take his time, while wider roads were choked by people going about their business now the hottest part of the day had passed. The carriage took a jagged path, but the general direction was clear.

'It seems Signore Uccello is heading south,' Strocchi observed, 'towards the river. Perhaps he means to visit someone south of the Arno?'

Benedetto snorted. 'He's going to find that difficult.'

'Why?'

'There were proclamations put up around the city this morning, telling people to go to the bridges an hour before curfew if they wanted to see a monk attack somebody.'

'A monk . . .' Strocchi stopped, grabbing Benedetto's arm. 'Savonarola?'

'Yes, that was his name.'

'Santo Spirito! Why didn't you say so?'

Benedetto shrugged. 'I didn't know it was important.'

Strocchi swore under his breath. If what the constable had said was true, it meant the killer was about to strike again.

Chapter Nineteen

Aldo was gasping by the time he found Scarlatti's crypt high above the burnt-out shell of the villa. He stopped in the shade to wipe sweat from his eyes, the air thick with the sounds of insetti. From here Aldo could see the whole estate, its farm buildings and the peasant huts scattered down the hillside. Ruggerio had only Cassandra and Vincenzo in residence most months, meaning other workers had to come up from their homes in the village. But Scarlatti had been living on his estate for a year and employed numerous workers, most of them living near his villa.

Tall cypress tress lined the dirt road down to San Jacopo al Girone, while grapevines and groves of olive trees hugged the curves and contours of the sloping ground either side of the track. Far below sprawled the rich expanse of the valley, the Arno glittering beneath the late afternoon sun. Finally, in the distance, Florence shimmered behind a haze of heat as if its terracotta-tiled roofs and the Duomo were little more than a dream, or a memory. No wonder Scarlatti had chosen this particular site as his final resting place – it was stunning. But the journey up here also stole the breath away.

By comparison his crypt was unremarkable: a simple stone structure built into the hillside, with a sturdy wooden door recessed in the entrance. Dragging the materials to build up here must have exhausted the stonemasons. It looked like the crypt had been here for months, even years. But there were fresh wheel marks in the long grass leading towards it, evidence that a handcart or something similar had come this way in recent days.

The crypt was not locked. Inside, Aldo found a small chamber dominated by a large slab of white marble, positioned atop other stones. He kept close to the walls, moving to the back so daylight spilling in from outside illuminated the interior. There were boot marks in the dirt and stone dust close to the slab – one set, perhaps two. Aldo edged closer to the slab, studying the marble. Unlike the rest of the crypt, there was no dust or dirt on it. Someone had cleaned the slab in the last few days, but there was still a ripe odour in the air: the stench of rot and decay. This was nowhere near as strong as it had been in Scarlatti's bedchamber, but the effect was much the same. Aldo retreated outside, his gut churning.

He found a nearby tree and sank down in its shade, leaning against the trunk. It seemed certain Scarlatti's corpse had been stored in the crypt. Nobody was going to visit there, not while it stood vacant, which left little chance that the body would be found. Yet the crypt was close enough to make the killer's task easier when the time came to move the body down to the villa. That explained the wheel marks in the grass. Had Scarlatti been murdered inside the crypt? Perhaps. But, if so, the killer had been careful to remove evidence of their crime.

The question Aldo set aside earlier came back to him. Why had Scarlatti been murdered? He had no family, nobody to inherit his estate. He had already retired, so his former rivals would gain no new benefit from having Scarlatti killed now. There could be another reason, another motive still to be discovered. More than a few rich merchants were predators, using their wealth to force others to their will. Aldo had heard no whispers about Scarlatti, but some secrets took years to emerge. On the rare occasions when such men were brought before the Otto, they usually bought their freedom. Better a fine than suffering injury to their reputation.

Out here in the dominion, justice was often delivered without judicial process. The Otto had limited influence beyond the walls of Florence, even when an officer or constable was living among local people. In small Tuscan towns and villages men from the Otto had to ask permission before attempting to arrest a suspect or fugitive. By the time permission was granted, the target had often fled. Aldo had not encountered such barriers yet, but they were likely to arise if his posting in the dominion became permanent. Judging by Bindi's anger at their last meeting, that was the direction in which the river was flowing.

Aldo got back to his feet, preparing to return down the hill. He could not ask Saul to join him in San Jacopo al Girone if the hostile response from Trigari was typical of attitudes towards Jews in the area. A difficult decision loomed ahead. Being an investigator for the Otto was what he did best. Was he willing to give that up for the hope of a new life with Saul?

Strocchi ran after the carriage. It had rolled several streets ahead while he was arguing with Benedetto. By the time Strocchi caught sight of the carriage, it was already approaching Ponte alla Carraia. The bridge was the most western crossing over the Arno within the city, linking the western quarter of Santa Maria Novella to the southern quarter. It was a simple, open span of stone, without the clutter of butcher shops and houses that stood atop Ponte Vecchio. Ordinarily carriages, carts and horses used Ponte alla Carraia to traverse the river with little to impede their journey, especially so late in the afternoon.

But this was no ordinary day.

A crowd was blocking the bridge, stopping anyone crossing the Arno there. Looking east, Strocchi could see mobs crowding the other bridges, stopping all movement across the river. Those blocking Ponte alla Carraia were a mix of men and women in their later years, citizens who had been alive when Savonarola held sway. None held weapons, and all appeared peaceful. Strocchi could see no obvious leaders amongst them, but the crowd members were united by their chanting. All repeated the same two words, again and again: 'Savonarola lives! Savonarola lives!'

Strocchi reached Uccello's carriage as it stopped short of Ponte alla Carraia, unable to go any further. The servant on the rear of the carriage was climbing down. 'Stay there,' Strocchi urged on his way by. 'I'm an officer of the Otto. Let me deal with this.'

Uccello opened a door to peer out. 'What's wrong? Why have we stopped?'

'Remain where you are, you'll be safer there,' Strocchi said.

'Tell me what's happening,' Uccello demanded.

'Some fools are blocking the bridge,' his surly driver replied. 'You want me to go east, signore, and find another way across?'

'It looks like all the bridges are blocked,' Strocchi said, 'but men are coming from the Podestà to put an end to this. Let me talk to these people, make them see sense.'

'Good luck with that,' the driver grunted.

'Do what you must,' Uccello sighed, closing the carriage door.

Strocchi strode to the bridge, looking for any faces he recognized in the crowd. It was possible Dovizi's killer was among them. Having urged believers of Savonarola to come and witness the frate's judgement, the person responsible would want to be close, to see their handiwork happening. But none of the faithful on the bridge were— No, there was someone Strocchi knew. The old woman who had been praying outside Dovizi's palazzo. She couldn't be responsible for this madness, could she?

Strocchi went to her, shouting to be heard amid all the chanting. 'Why are you here?'

'The frate summoned us,' she said.

'How?'

She held out a proclamation, its corners torn away. 'Men like you, those who do not believe in the frate, were tearing these down. But I got to this one first.'

Strocchi read the document in her trembling hands. It had been written by the same hand that had announced Dovizi's murder: *the spirit of Savonarola will rise once more . . . it shall strike against one of those who betrayed him . . . gather on the bridges of our city one hour before curfew and tonight you shall bear witness as this prophecy comes true . . .*

'Now is the time,' the old woman shouted. 'Now everyone shall see his return!'

The mob gathered around Strocchi, forcing him towards the eastern side of the bridge. He pushed back at them, fighting not to be crushed against the parapet, struggling to make sense of what was happening. Why had the killer brought all these people to the river? Surely their belief in Savonarola's return would be broken if the monk did not appear to them?

Unless . . .

This was not about Savonarola. This was about murder, an audacious murder, to be committed in front of all those gathered. If the killer made it seem as though Savonarola was responsible for what happened, the spark of belief that had been lit in these people could become a bonfire of religious fervour burning through the whole city . . .

* * *

You wait until the court officer is on the bridge before going to the four white horses in front of the carriage. There is no reason for them to suffer. You undo the harnesses, freeing the animals one by one. The driver shouts for you to stop as the first horse trots away. His words become curses as the second goes free. He clambers down from his seat as you release the third, and lumbers at you when the fourth escapes.

The driver is fat and slovenly, his hands curling into fists as he charges. You step to one side, leaving a leg behind to send him tumbling. He gets up and comes at you again, blood streaming from a cut on his chin. This time you smash the base of one hand up into his nose. His head snaps back and he crumples, collapsing in the dung left by the horses. You glance at the bridge, but the officer is still caught within the chanting crowd, unable to intervene. You are grateful he is the only officer near this bridge. It is less important, less regarded. The court has sent most of its men to Ponte Vecchio, as you had hoped.

The signore calls from inside the carriage but you ignore him. Instead, you retrieve two narrow lengths of wood from the back of the carriage, sliding one of them through the door handles on either side. Judging by his protests the signore does not understand what you are doing, not yet. As he shouts for help, you fetch an oil lantern stowed at the rear of the carriage. You light it, ignoring the pleading and abuse from inside the carriage. The signore is afraid, trembles and tremors in his voice now.

You open the door on one side. But when the signore tries to climb out, you push him back into his plush seat. You tell him he must pay for his sins. You suggest he look down, see the dry matting spread across the floor inside his carriage and the oil you have sprinkled beneath that. The mat is not to protect his fine shoes. It is there to burn . . . and so is he.

You smash the lantern on the carriage floor, forcing the signore further back.

You watch the fire take hold of the dry matting, the flames spreading.
You shut the door, shove the wood back through the handles.
There is no escape.
Not for him.
Not now.
You wait and listen.
He commands you to free him.
He pleads with you to open the doors.
He coughs and chokes and whimpers.
Now you can stride away.
Leaving him to burn.
He screams.
This is what he deserves.

Strocchi was still fighting to free himself from the mob when the crowd parted around him. He saw why as a white horse bolted onto the bridge, leather straps flapping round it. Strocchi threw himself to one side, narrowly escaping the horse's hooves as it charged by, followed by another. He glimpsed the embroidered leather on their harnesses. Those were Uccello's horses from his carriage, but why were they—

Then he smelled it. The acrid aroma of burning when there should not be any fire. No, no, not again. Strocchi scrambled to his feet, shoving the faithful out of his way, urging them to let him pass. But when he broke free from the mob, it was already too late.

Uccello's carriage was on fire.

Smoke billowed from inside, escaping through narrow gaps around the doors. Flames were spewing from the small opening in the woodwork behind the driver's seat. All four of the fine white horses were gone, freed or fled, Strocchi did not know which. Their driver was sprawled on the ground, blood cascading from a broken nose, eyes staring at the sky as if drunk. Uccello, where was Uccello?

Strocchi sprinted to the carriage, shouting for the other servant wherever he was to come and help. Someone had jammed wood through the door handles, wedging them shut. Strocchi pulled at it but his fingertips burned on the surface, forcing him back. The carriage doors were solid wood. They did not have leather curtains or open windows like some, meaning Strocchi could not see inside. Perhaps that was a mercy. He could hear screaming within the carriage, the noise of the fire overwhelming everything else. Heat blossomed from inside, as if the interior was an oven roasting meat on a Sunday afternoon.

The servant, where was the servant? Strocchi swung round, searching for the man who had been on the back of the carriage. What did he look like? Long brown hair swept back from a stern, bearded face. His grim features were at odds with the extravagant tunic and hose worn by Uccello's men. Strocchi spied the servant stalking away from the carriage, already some distance along the banks of the Arno. 'Where are you going?' Strocchi shouted.

The servant twisted round, an eerie smile on his lips. He made the sign of the cross before clasping both hands together as if in prayer. 'Savonarola lives!' he shouted.

'Savonarola lives!' all those on Ponte alla Carraia called back to him.

The servant pointed as flames burst through the carriage roof. 'See for yourself! Our frate's spirit strikes down one of those who betrayed him! Bear witness to his prophecy!'

'Savonarola lives!' the mob chanted again.

'A man is trapped in this carriage,' Strocchi bellowed. 'Will you not help me save him?' But the mob seemed transfixed by what was happening.

Did none of them care?

At that moment the door nearest Strocchi burst open, smoke and flames flying out. He stumbled back, pushed away by the heat. A figure tumbled from the carriage: Uccello.

He was on fire, his silk tunic and woollen hose burning; even his hair was aflame.

His mouth opened to scream, but no sound came out.

Santo Spirito! Strocchi made the sign of the cross.

Uccello lurched towards the bridge, every part of him ablaze.

The crowd melted back as he got closer.

'Out of his way!' Strocchi shouted.

Uccello reached the bridge parapet.

He clambered atop it, hands held out in supplication.

Then he fell, tumbling head-first into the Arno.

Strocchi sprinted to the riverbank.

But when he stared down . . .

There was nothing.

Uccello was gone.

Burned alive and swallowed by the water.

A lone voice cried out, breaking the silence: 'Savonarola lives!'

Strocchi twisted round to see who had spoken. The old woman from outside Dovizi's palazzo was kneeling on the bridge, hands clasped in prayer, tears on her cheeks. 'Savonarola lives,' she repeated. 'His spirit has struck down another traitor.'

Strocchi stalked to her. 'A man has died in front of your eyes, and that's what you say? Did you even know that man's name, who he was?'

She stared as if Strocchi was a fool to question her. 'Our frate would only strike down those who deserve it,' she said. 'It is the way of Our Lord.'

Strocchi shook his head, too disgusted by such murderous

sanctimony to reply. He glared at the others on the bridge. 'Do you all believe the same? Is this what you call being a true child of God, to savour the murder of a man you never knew?'

None of them spoke. Some glared back at him, unrepentant. Others could not meet Strocchi's gaze, shame colouring their cheeks. That was something, perhaps.

He shifted his gaze to the riverbank, certain that Uccello's servant was responsible for starting the fire. For the carriage to burn so fast, fuel must have been hidden inside it. The servant would also have been aware his signore made a weekly trip across the Arno to visit an acquaintance, that was why the frate's believers had been summoned here. By blocking all the bridges, they had created the opportunity to burn Uccello alive inside the carriage.

But the servant was gone. Uccello's killer had escaped.

You dare not return to the palazzo. That court officer knows where you live and work, knows your face. But it does not matter. Another of them is dead by your hand.

You can still hear Uccello's screams as you hurry away.

They may be only a memory, but the sound . . .

It is delicious.

You long for your cloak's hood to hide your face, but it will be curfew soon. The sun is already dipping towards the hills, and twilight is claiming the streets of Florence.

You cross Piazza della Signoria, passing by the other place of burning.

Only a few days in the past, yet a lifetime ago.

You continue west, towards the city gates.

Your work is not done.

You still have others to burn . . .

Chapter Twenty

*A*ldo led Saul to Ruggerio's villa as dusk approached. They would have been there sooner, but Saul insisted on helping take Scarlatti to his crypt. 'I see my patients to their final rest if I can,' Saul explained, 'even those I did not know in life.' The sun was sinking below the hills as Aldo guided Saul along the narrow dirt pathway, glimpses of ochre and pink in the sky. 'It gets dark so fast here,' Saul said.

'A good reason to keep moving,' Aldo replied, marching onwards. They reached the villa as night consumed the day, a lantern hanging outside the entrance helping guide them.

Cassandra was waiting in the doorway, a wry smile creasing her face. 'I wondered if you were still coming.'

'Grazie for having him here tonight.' Aldo rested a hand on Saul's shoulder. 'It's taken a year for villagers to stop staring at me. But having a Jewish doctor sleep in my hut . . .'

She nodded. 'All of us are outsiders to the people of San Jacopo al Girone. Even if we spend the rest of our lives here, we would still go to our graves as outsiders.' She stepped back to let them pass. Saul went in but Aldo remained in the courtyard. 'Not joining us?'

'The Otto still considers Ruggerio a potential suspect for Dovizi's murder,' Aldo said.

'And what do you suspect?' Cassandra asked.

'That the founders of the Company of Santa Maria are being killed, one by one. Who is doing this remains unknown.' Aldo hesitated. Whatever he told Cassandra would soon be communicated to Ruggerio. But that could also be useful. 'Scarlatti dying so soon after Dovizi would have been mere chance if the fire at the villa had been accidental. But Scarlatti being murdered before Dovizi was burned alive . . . That tells another story.'

'Scarlatti was murdered?' Cassandra looked at the doctor, who nodded agreement.

'Strangled,' Saul said. 'He died six or seven days ago.'

Aldo had been away from San Jacopo al Girone at the time, summoned east by claims about a dispute between two farmers that threatened to become bloody. Yet when he got there the argument proved to be a simple, if tiresome understanding. Looking back, Aldo could not help wondering if he had been called away to ensure his absence when Scarlatti was killed.

'Were there any strangers on the estate several days ago?' he asked Cassandra.

'Not that I remember . . .' she began. 'Your one-armed thief from the city came on Wednesday and stole the signore's best boots.'

Saul laughed. 'And you told me nothing happens out here, Cesare.'

'Anyone else?' Aldo persisted.

Cassandra frowned. 'An itinerant cooper came a day or two before. He asked if we had any barrels that needed mending, but there was no work for him here. He might have gone to Scarlatti's estate after leaving us.'

That sounded to Aldo like a potential suspect. 'What did this man look like?'

She shook her head. 'I never met him. He came while I was in the village. Vincenzo sent him away and told me about it later. That's why I didn't recall earlier, I suppose.'

Aldo could question the stable hand, but it was late. That could wait for the next morning, when he would be back for Saul. 'Any others?'

'No.' Cassandra peered at Aldo. 'Are you sure I can't tempt you to eat with us?'

'Thank you for the offer,' he replied. 'But it's been an exhausting day, and I have much to do in the morning.' Aldo nodded to Saul before turning away. Cassandra called to him, bringing the lantern from the entrance of the villa to Aldo.

'Take this to light your way down the hill,' she said. 'Bring it back when you can.'

Ruggerio sank back in his chair. It was as if he had been struck in the chest, the blow taking all the wind out of him, leaving him . . . He wasn't sure. He wasn't sure of anything anymore. 'Are you quite certain?' he asked. 'There can't have been some mistake?'

His maggiordomo frowned. 'I'm sorry, signore, there is no doubt.'

'Uccello is dead?'

Alberti nodded. 'He was retrieved downriver not long before curfew. The Arno is low due to the drought, so Signor Uccello's body caught on one of the weirs.'

Ruggerio reached for his wine, hand trembling as he lifted the cup from the table. The red was one of the finest from the vines on his estate but tasted sour on the tongue. He put the cup back down without looking and caught his plate, spilling wine across the table. Ruggerio jumped up, not wanting it to stain his silk robe.

The maggiordomo rushed forward, snatching at a cloth to stop the wine.

'Leave it,' Ruggerio said, but Alberti kept dabbing at the mess. 'Leave it!'

The servant retreated, the crimson-soaked cloth in his hands.

Ruggerio strode away from the meal. Uccello was dead. Murdered. Trapped inside his own carriage as its burned before throwing himself into the Arno to stop the flames. Drowned or taken by fire, it made little difference. But the way this was done, the cruelty of it . . .

'Will you be wanting anything else?' Alberti asked.

'No,' Ruggerio snapped. The maggiordomo withdrew, leaving Ruggerio alone to make sense of it all. First Dovizi, then Scarlatti, and now Uccello? Only two of the founding five remained, himself and Ghiberti. A bitter laugh escaped Ruggerio. He had been so certain Uccello was responsible for the killing of Dovizi. So certain that one among them must be responsible for the deaths of the others. Now he could see that was folly, built on decades of suspicion and mutual distrust between the five of them. All that had blinded him to the truth.

The founders were being hunted.

But this was no common vendetta, no argument between those with short tempers and angry words that escalated into bloodshed and retaliation.

Each man had died by fire.

Well, they were not going to burn him.

Ruggerio returned to the table, shoving the platters of food away. He called out, demanding the immediate presence of his maggiordomo. Alberti appeared within moments.

'Signore?'

'I leave Florence in the morning. Have the household prepare to travel.'

'Of course, sir. Where do you wish to go?'

The country estate was the obvious choice. It had a strategic advantage being so high in the hills above San Jacopo al Girone. There could be no surprise attacks. But . . . The fact that the one-armed thief had been sent to spy on the estate, to assess any potential weaknesses at the villa gave Ruggerio reason to doubt. Was the Tuscan countryside the safest place now? Would he be better going elsewhere? Perhaps a trip north to Bologna, even Venice? Or he could journey south towards Rome. He had acquaintances in other cities, those who would be happy to offer sanctuary in return for coin or favours.

But Ruggerio was reluctant to be in any man's debt.

No. He was ready to retreat from Florence but would not be driven from Tuscany.

'My villa. When curfew is lifted in the morning, send a rider ahead to let Cassandra know I am coming. I'm not sure how long I shall remain in the dominion. It could only be a few days, or I may be there for the whole summer.'

'I shall have the other servants pack accordingly,' Alberti replied. 'You can always send a messenger back here to fetch anything further you might need.'

'Very well,' Ruggerio said, dismissing the maggiordomo with a flick of one hand. But before Alberti could leave, one last thought occurred to him. 'Oh, and I need to send a letter tonight.'

'Signore, the bells for curfew will ring soon—'

'Tonight,' Ruggerio repeated. 'Take it yourself.'

Alberti bowed. 'To whom should this letter be delivered?'

'Roberto Ghiberti. I must warn him about the threat against us both. I doubt Ghiberti will take any heed, but he deserves to be told.' The maggiordomo bowed again before retreating from the room. Ruggerio sank back down into his chair.

Dovizi, Scarlatti, and now Uccello, all gone. He had known each man most of his life. To have them taken away, all within a few days . . . Yes, Ghiberti deserved to know. He was owed that much. Especially after what had happened, all those years ago.

Bindi was stamping down the stone stairs to the Podestà courtyard when the bells rang out announcing curfew. He had been waiting for Strocchi to give a report on events at the bridges, but the young officer never arrived. Whatever had taken place – early accounts brought back by several constables were too bizarre to be true – was no excuse for neglecting duties. Bindi had been quite clear that he required a full report on Strocchi's progress each evening. Anything less was unacceptable.

The segretario still had five steps below him when Strocchi burst into the courtyard, face smudged with soot and both tunic sleeves torn. 'You're late,' Bindi hissed.

'Forgive me, segretario,' Strocchi replied, gasping for breath. 'I was busy retrieving a body from the river and didn't notice how dark it was getting. When I heard the bells chiming, I ran all the way here.'

Bindi folded both arms across his chest. 'Well, then . . . Give me your report.'

The tale Strocchi told would have beggared belief had it not matched earlier accounts given by wide-eyed constables. Uccello had died, murdered when his carriage was set ablaze with him inside it. The banker had managed to get out, his body and clothes on fire, before tumbling into the Arno and drowning.

'And all of this happened while people were chanting for Savonarola on the bridges?'

'Yes,' Strocchi replied. 'It was . . . madness.'

'Did you see who started the fire?'

'One of his servants.'

The segretario noted Strocchi was alone. 'I take it this servant escaped you?'

'I was the only man from the Otto on the bridge,' Strocchi protested. 'Benedetto said you were sending constables and other officers, but none of them came until it was too late.'

Bindi did not reply. He had directed all his men to Ponte Vecchio, believing that was where the Savonarola believers would gather to cause trouble. It never occurred to him that an incident might happen on Ponte alla Carraia . . . but Strocchi did not need to know this.

'Can you describe this servant?' Bindi asked, getting a nod in return. 'Then be here when curfew ends in the morning to tell the others what he looks like. I shall inform the duke that he can expect this murderer to be captured before sunset tomorrow.'

'But how . . .'

The segretario stamped down the final steps. 'You would not make a liar of me, would you?' Strocchi shook his head. 'Very well. You have your orders. You may go.' Bindi waited until Strocchi was almost out of the courtyard before calling to him.

'One last thing . . .'

The officer stopped, shoulders slumping before he twisted back round. 'Yes, sir?'

'I want you to be clean and properly dressed next time you come into my Podestà. You are an officer of the court, a representative of the Otto. Citizens expect you to have a clean face and hands, not torn sleeves and blood on your hose.'

'The dirt is from the fire,' Strocchi replied, fists clenching by his side. 'The blood came from Uccello's driver, who was injured by the killer. My tunic tore while I was pulling the dead man's body out of the Arno. Sir.'

'Nonetheless, my point still stands. You will not disgrace this court.'

'Yes, sir,' Strocchi said. 'Thank you, sir. Will there be anything else, sir?'

'No,' the segretario announced. 'I've had quite enough for today. You may go.'

Aldo made his way down the hill from Ruggerio's estate, grateful for the borrowed lantern. In Florence there was usually enough light spilling from doorways and shutters for night patrols to find their way during curfew. But in the dominion, with the sickle moon waning to a slither in the sky, anyone outside after dark needed a lantern to see. Aldo could hear noises, the sounds of insetti and nocturnal creatures scuttling through the undergrowth nearby. It was reassuring, in a way. No matter what violence men did to each other, the rest of the world followed its own cycle.

A question Cassandra had asked was itching at him. Who did he suspect was behind the murders of Scarlatti and Dovizi? The only truthful answer would have been more questions. He certainly did not believe the spirit of Savonarola was behind these events. Was one person responsible for both killings? Perhaps. The proclamation nailed to the door of Dovizi's palazzo in Florence was an obvious strategia, an attempt to throw a stone into the river and stir up silt, clouding the clarity of those investigating the killings.

And something else was bothering him too: was there one murderer, or two? A single killer could have taken the lives of Scarlatti and Dovizi, though it would have required both good fortune and considerable planning. If the victims were slain by different men, that suggested the killers might be working to a common purpose. And whoever was committing these crimes could be acting on behalf of another. The fact that both victims were founders of the Company of Santa Maria prompted more questions. Was the person responsible one of the surviving founders? Or was it somebody nursing a vendetta against the founders?

Aldo was inclined to suspect the latter. Dovizi dying by fire and the attempted use of flame to destroy Scarlatti's body, it must mean something to whoever was behind these killings. A short stab with a blade could have ended either man's life far more easily, without the need for such elaborate efforts. No, these murders had the taste of ritual about them. The killer was using fire as their weapon for a reason. And why now? Dovizi and Scarlatti had been near the end of their lives. Why wait until this moment to murder them?

Reason suggested something stopped the killer from doing so sooner. Perhaps they had lacked the proof to know their targets. Perhaps the killer had been outside Florence, unable to enact their plans. Or perhaps the killer had promised not to pursue their revenge until now because . . . Aldo didn't know. Palle! Perhaps, perhaps, perhaps. So many possibilities, yet so few certainties. Only frustrations piled atop frustration.

Investigating matters without the Otto's resources or proximity was not making the answers any easier to uncover. For all he knew the killer could have struck again in the city. Ruggerio, Ghiberti or Uccello might already be dead. If so, it would probably be days before such news reached him. When he was still an officer, albeit one posted out in the dominion, the Otto sent occasional reports of significant crimes in the city, especially if the suspects had fled Florence seeking refuge in the countryside. Now he was a mere constable, there was less reason to share such reports. And after the way Bindi had dismissed him, it was unlikely the segretario would be sending messages or assistance to San Jacopo al Girone.

If Aldo was to find Scarlatti's killer, he would have to do it alone.

Chapter Twenty-one

❧

Tuesday, May 28th 1538

Strocchi could not sleep. Was it only a few days ago he had prayed for a single night of rest, for his bambina Bianca to slumber for more than a few minutes? Now she was quite happy in her cot, and he was the one awake. He wanted to sleep, he needed to sleep. But every time he closed his eyes, all he could see was Uccello leaping from that burning carriage, clothes and hair on fire . . . Lurching, staggering to the bridge . . . and then plunging down into the Arno, that hiss as the water consumed him . . .

When Strocchi did succeed in remembering something else – anything else – then the smell of what had happened at Ponte alla Carraia brought it back again. The stench had followed him home, clinging to his clothes. He shed them as soon as he got inside, telling Tomasia to get rid of them when she offered to mend the tears. Strocchi had rinsed away the blood and soot, but the aroma of burnt wood and roasted meat clung to him. He washed his hair and scrubbed his fingernails red raw. Still the scent invaded his nostrils.

Despairing of sleep, Strocchi went to the wooden chair by the shutters, staring out as the inky black of night slowly, too slowly, gave way to the murky blue of a new day. Would he never be rid of these memories, this stench? He had to believe the vividness of those moments would fade, the same way memories of his papa had faded. Strocchi could still recall papa's smile, the sound of his laughter, all rich and resonant. But the rest of him was becoming harder to summon back, wearing as thin as the skin of an onion. One day those memories would be gone, forever.

Strocchi clasped both hands together, lowering his head to whisper a few words. 'Our Lord in heaven, I do not ask much of you, and less for myself. I prayed Tomasia would become my wife, and she did. I prayed our child would be born safely, that both would be well, and they were. Lord, I must ask something of you now. I do my best to be a good man, to do as you wish and follow your teachings. I stumble and I fail, yet do all I can to please you. I know I do not suffer as Uccello did, and I promise I will find the man responsible for what happened. But I must ask you to take this pain from me.'

Bianca stirred in her cot, making little noises and snuffles before slipping back into sleep, her breathing returning to its steady ebb and flow. Strocchi waited before speaking again, keeping his whisper to a quietest murmur. The Almighty would still hear him.

'Lord, I know it is a lot to ask, but I cannot serve you if all I see and smell and taste and touch and hear is what I witnessed last night. Give me solace and I will worship you all my life. Lord, please hear my prayer. Amen.'

Strocchi heard Tomasia slip from their bed, padding across to him on the balls of her feet. She slipped both arms round his shoulders. 'Carlo, why didn't you wake me?'

'One of us needs to sleep.'

Tomasia kissed him on the neck. 'I can't smell fire on you,' she said. 'Not anymore.'

'But I can,' Strocchi replied.

'It will pass.'

'Do you promise?'

She took his face in both hands, turning it to look him in the eyes. 'I promise.' They kissed, her scent close and comforting. 'Now come back to bed,' Tomasia said, tugging at his hands, leading him away from the shutters where dawn was creeping in.

'I can't close my eyes,' Strocchi said.

'You don't have to. Just lie down with me. Just that.'

Cassandra put a platter of dried fruit on the kitchen table in front of Orvieto, along with olives, bread and wine. 'I don't usually eat early in the day,' he said, smiling at her. 'Is this what country life is like? I'm already round enough, I fear.' He patted his belly.

She shook her head. 'No, the signore only takes two meals a day when he is here, one in the afternoon and the other after dark. But you have a long walk back to the city. Eat what you wish now, and I can wrap more in a cloth for the journey.'

'You're too kind.'

Cassandra sat opposite, watching him eat. 'I didn't give you any meats. Signore Ruggerio once entertained a Jew at his table when I worked for him in the city, and orders went to the kitchen about what not to do . . .'

Orvieto nodded. 'There are some foods my beliefs preclude, but you have plenty here I will enjoy.' He poured a cup of wine and offered to do the same for her.

'No, thank you.' She set to work grinding herbs from the villa's walled garden in a mortar. 'May I ask a question?'

'Of course.'

'How is it that you know Aldo? I thought Jews in Florence always kept to themselves but the two of you seem very – close.'

Orvieto paused, wiping a drop of wine from his beard. 'It was murder that brought us together. A moneylender, stabbed in the Jewish commune. Cesare came to question me about the dead man and asked for my help in assessing the body. You can learn a lot about a person while standing over a corpse together. I have assisted him on matters for the Otto a few times since, and we've become friends.' The doctor cut a dried fig in half. 'Why do you ask?' he said, popping one piece in his mouth.

'The two of you working together is unusual. But Aldo is not a typical officer of the court. From what others say, the constable here before him was an indolent man, more interested in filling his pouch with coin than enforcing the law.'

Orvieto smiled. 'Cesare certainly does not seek to make his fortune, and cares little what others think of his conduct.' The doctor leaned forward. 'Don't tell anyone, but in Florence he lodges at a bordello.'

That made her laugh. 'An officer of the court, bedding down with . . .?'

'Sharing a home with them is what Cesare would call it.' Orvieto sipped more wine. 'He gets a room, and they have a man of the law present if visitors cause trouble.'

'A most convenient arrangement,' Cassandra agreed. She knew enough about men to see more than affection in Orvieto's eyes when he described Aldo. Having tidied up after the signore and his visitors, there was little that surprised her anymore. But the more she could discover about Aldo, the better. Ruggerio had a particular interest in the officer, and would reward whatever morsels she could provide.

The doctor pointed to the herbs she was crushing. 'May I ask what you're making?'

'It's a remedy for aching joints, from herbs grown behind the villa.'

Orvieto arched an eyebrow. 'Would you mind showing me the plants? I am always eager to find new solutions for old ailments.'

Cassandra smiled. 'I doubt they are anything you don't already know, but . . . yes, of course.' And it would give her an opportunity to ask more questions about Aldo.

Bindi did not expect to be shown into the duke's ufficio at Palazzo Medici. The segretario had been denied an audience with Cosimo for several days, though whether that was at his insistence or due to Campana's intervention remained unclear. Yet when Bindi arrived at the ducal residence not long after dawn he was ushered directly to the middle level. No long wait in the courtyard, no embarrassment at being forgotten. Campana was by the ufficio doors, but he did not prevent Bindi going inside. Campana whispered a hoarse warning. 'Be careful what you say. His Grace is short of temper this morning.'

Bindi nodded and went in, but Campana did not follow. This was to be a private audience. A cold dread clenched at Bindi.

Cosimo was at his table but staring towards a window rather than working. That was unlike him. The duke appeared tired, dark shadows under both eyes. Bindi stopped in front of Cosimo and waited. When the duke did not respond, the segretario coughed.

'Ahh, Bindi,' Cosimo said at last. 'Thank you for coming.'

'I serve at the pleasure of Your Grace.'

'Indeed. It's about that that I wished to speak with you . . .' The words faltered. He seemed unable to meet Bindi's gaze, as if ashamed of what needed to be said.

'Your Grace, may I say something first?'

Cosimo hesitated before giving a curt nod.

'I wish to apologize on behalf of the court. I told you the men of the Otto would find those responsible for the murder of Dovizi, and for posting false proclamations across the city. Until now, this has proven beyond the court's officers and constables.' Bindi paused. He had spoken these words to himself on the way here, uncertain there would be a chance to say them to Campana, let alone the duke. Now he had the opportunity, it was difficult to keep his voice from trembling. But perhaps that was no bad thing.

'You will be aware that another murder was committed last night. I am certain it was by the same killer. I must take responsibility for the court failing to prevent that, for failing in my duty to you and the city. I am segretario of the Otto and must often make difficult choices. So, I would understand if you wished to remove me from that post.'

Cosimo opened his mouth to reply but Bindi kept speaking.

'However, I will say this, Your Grace: the man responsible for these crimes – the murders, and the despicable proclamations that have stirred up such ill feeling among some citizens – is close to capture. Within the hour my men will have a full description of him, where he lives and works. He shall be captured or killed before curfew tonight.'

That got the duke's attention.

'I make this promise, Your Grace. If I fail, you will have my resignation tomorrow.'

Cosimo gave no immediate reply. Instead, he stared at the segretario with a gaze quite piercing from one so young. Finally, blessedly, the duke nodded his agreement. 'Very well. What assistance do you need to make this happen?'

Bindi held back a smile of triumph. He had gambled and won. There was still the matter of fulfilling his promise, but it had earned him another twelve hours.

That would have to be enough.

* * *

Aldo was sweating by the time he approached Ruggerio's villa. It was early, the sun still arcing up into the sky, yet already uncomfortably warm. Thankfully the dirt track was shaded by cypress trees most of the way, the air filled by the sounds of insetti. Another scorching day seemed certain, without a gasp of breeze for those working outside, tending the estate's grapevines and olive groves. Aldo cursed himself for not bringing a hat or cap.

For once Ruggerio's housekeeper was not waiting at the front door. He knocked but got no reply. Vincenzo emerged from the stable, wiping dirt from his hands. 'Cassandra told me to listen for you,' he said. 'She's in her walled garden behind the villa with that Jew.'

Aldo nodded, ignoring Vincenzo's dismissal of Saul. Such attitudes were common and arguing would change nothing for the better. Aldo followed a stone path to a walled enclosure behind the villa. Opening a wooden door there revealed a garden of herbs and vegetables, all growing in neatly tended rows and beds. Saul and Cassandra were on the far side, deep in discussion. The doctor tucked his wide-brimmed hat under one arm to wave at Aldo. 'Come and see,' Saul called. 'This is quite remarkable.'

Aldo strolled round to them while noting the numerous plants. The brassicas and some of the herbs he recognized, but many were unknown to him. Saul clutched a basket laden with leaves and flowers, beaming at his haul.

'Cassandra has ingredients for dozens of different remedies in this corner alone,' he enthused, pointing to one after another, reciting their names and uses. 'The difference it would make to my patients if I had a garden like this in Florence.'

Saul could have such a garden if he moved to the countryside but that was a conversation for another time. 'Perhaps you should ask Cassandra to have a little of her crop sent to you when it's ready? If there is any to spare.'

Saul's eyebrows shot up. 'I hadn't thought of that. Might it be possible . . .?'

Cassandra laughed. 'Of course! I had dreams of becoming a healer myself once. Our papa was an apothecary, and I used to watch him—' She stopped, her smile fading. 'That wasn't to be, but I still make some of the remedies he showed me.'

Cassandra reminded Aldo of Suor Giulia, a nun who was apothecary for sisters and novices at the Convent of Santa Maria Magdalena. Cassandra had some of the same sadness in her eyes, and the same enthusiasm for what she did.

'Saul, I have no wish to drag you away,' Aldo said, 'but you have a long journey. Better to leave now before the worst of the day's heat settles in.'

The doctor sighed. 'I do have patients waiting for me in Florence. Leaving them to my student for one day was acceptable, but she is still learning. Best that I get home.'

'You have a woman as your apprentice?' Cassandra asked as she led them out.

'Yes,' Saul replied. 'Rebecca has a gift for listening that I sometimes lack, and a capacity for knowledge. I hope she will replace me when I become too weary.'

Cassandra took the basket, sending him and Aldo round the side of the villa. She soon rejoined them at the front door with two small bundles and Saul's satchel. 'One of these has the flowers and leaves you picked. The other is food for your journey.'

'You're too kind,' Saul said, taking the gifts and his satchel.

'Send me a list of any plants you need for remedies,' Cassandra replied. 'Our stable hand often takes messages to Signor Ruggerio in the city. Vincenzo could easily add a few things to his saddle bag for you.'

'And he already knows where I live,' Saul added. 'He brought me your letter, Cesare.'

Aldo ushered the doctor away before Saul's friendly nature kept him talking all morning. They strolled down the dirt track towards San Jacopo al Girone, Saul chattering happily about how much he had enjoyed his brief visit. When finally he paused to appreciate the view back along the valley towards Florence, Aldo took the chance to ask a question.

'When do you think Rebecca will be ready?'

'To take my place?' Saul said. 'Four years, maybe five.'

'That long?'

'She's an apt pupil, but these things take time.'

Aldo nodded. The way Saul talked in the walled garden it had seemed . . . But no. He was not ready to leave Florence or his patients. Aldo did not blame Saul for that – it was his life's work. Were their places reversed, he would be the same. Perhaps if they had found each other years ago, in a different time or place . . . But that was an idle fantasia. They were who they were. There was no other life for them. Only this, only now.

'I will probably not be back in Florence for weeks, even months.'

Saul frowned. 'No?'

Aldo explained what had happened with Lippo, Ruggerio and Bindi. The demotion to constable, being all but banished from the city. Better to get it out at once, be honest with Saul. He deserved to know the truth, and what it could mean for them.

'Do you think the segretario will change his mind, in time?'

'Perhaps . . .' But Aldo doubted it. He had given Bindi every reason to punish him, if not enough for dismissal. A warm welcome at the Podestà was unlikely again, not unless Aldo could prove his worth. 'I would understand if you chose not to—'

Saul put a finger to Aldo's lips. 'Cesare, hush. We have been apart a year already. I am a patient man.' He leaned closer to whisper in Aldo's ear. 'I can wait if you can.'

Aldo resisted the urge to kiss Saul. In Florence, where almost everyone lived on top of one another, people often cared less about what their neighbours were doing. The countryside was not so crowded, yet someone was always watching.

Saul smiled at him. 'You have work to do, don't you?'

'Yes.'

'Then I shall go.' He glanced up at the clear azzurro sky. 'But you should wear a hat if you're going to be outside all day in this heat.'

'I know.' Aldo reached inside his tunic for two letters he had written, handing them to Saul. 'Can you take this to Bindi? It reports on what we uncovered about Scarlatti's murder. I doubt the segretario will pay much attention, but the court still deserves all the facts.'

Saul peered at the other letter. 'Your hand is even worse than mine. Who is this for?'

'Strocchi. He needs to know Dovizi's murder was not an isolated matter, that Scarlatti was slain several days before Dovizi. I suspect – no, I believe – that the Company of Santa Maria's founders are being hunted, either by an outsider, or from within their own number. Either way, the Otto should be keeping a close watch on the three surviving founders – Ghiberti, Uccello, and Ruggerio – assuming all of them are still alive.'

Saul slipped the letters in his satchel. 'I shall deliver these as soon as I reach Florence.'

Aldo rested a hand on Saul's chest. 'Thank you.' Then he went back up the hill. Better not to look back. Saul had risked enough coming to San Jacopo al Girone.

Chapter Twenty-two

Strocchi strode towards the Podestà, weary to his bones. He was meant to be there early, but Tomasia had refused to let him leave home without eating first. 'Carlo, you need food to get through the day,' she insisted. 'That tunic is hanging off you. Your mama will think I don't feed you, or that I can't cook.'

His belly had rebelled at the thought of eating, his head still filled with the sight and smell of Uccello on fire. But when Tomasia presented the cured meat, olives and cheese he had ignored the previous night, Strocchi was surprised to rediscover his hunger. He couldn't recall the last time he had eaten sitting down. Being an officer meant meals with his family were a rarity, not a nightly joy.

Preparing himself for Bindi's wrath, Strocchi ventured into the Podestà courtyard but the segretario was not there. 'Still at Palazzo Medici,' Manuffi said, a gentle smile warming his face. Manuffi might not be the sharpest stiletto, but he seemed to have a good heart. A dozen constables and guards clustered in small groups behind him. 'The segretario sent a message ordering those on duty to wait so you can tell us what this killer looks like.'

Strocchi realized all the men were looking at him.

Waiting for him to speak.

Santo Spirito!

He'd never had to talk to so many people at once, not when they were there to hear him speak. Shouting at Savonarola's believers on the bridge the previous night or trying to get the crowd outside Palazzo Dovizi to move on, that was different. Those were strangers. Most of the men gathered in the courtyard knew him by name. They were peering at him, expecting what . . . Wisdom? Strocchi was sure he had none to offer. No, just tell them what they needed to do their jobs. That was enough.

But he still had to be seen by all of them.

Strocchi went to the stone staircase leading up to the administration level, climbing several steps so he could see all of them at once. 'I—' His voice sounded strange, high as that of an excited girl. Strocchi cleared his throat, made himself speak slower, his voice lower. 'I need to tell you about the man we're hunting. We do not have his name yet, but he was a servant at Palazzo Uccello. Not long before curfew last night this man trapped Luca Uccello inside his carriage and set it on fire. This killer was probably also responsible for burning Sandro Dovizi alive in Piazza della Signoria. Most of you saw that body, what was left of it. You all know what this killer is capable of, how dangerous he is.'

Manuffi and the others nodded, a few making the sign of the cross.

'We are hunting a man with long brown hair which he keeps back from his face,' Strocchi went on. 'He had a stern look when I saw him, and a full brown beard. Last night he was wearing a fancy tunic, hose and leather boots with tassels, like all Uccello's servants do, but he may have changed clothes by now.' Manuffi raised his hand, drawing Strocchi's gaze. 'Yes?'

'Is it the same man who has been putting false proclamations up across the city?'

'He could well be.'

'Macci chased that man yesterday. He had a shabby wooden cloak with a hood.'

'Good, thank you—'

'The killer had the cloak on,' Manuffi added. 'Not Macci.'

That got a laugh from the others.

Strocchi smiled. 'Thank you, Manuffi. Yes, it is worth remembering this man has evaded all of us for days. That means he is good at avoiding the eye. He could well be wearing a cloak with a hood to hide his face. I know what I've told you is not much, but the segretario is at Palazzo Medici right now promising the duke that we will capture this man before curfew tonight. So, watch out for those who avoid your eye, who act as if they have something to hide. Most will not be the killer, but one of them could be, yes?' The guards and constables nodded. 'This man has promised to kill again. Be careful, and good hunting.' Strocchi nodded at them all, and the gathering broke apart. 'Manuffi, I need to ask you something.'

The constable joined Strocchi at the bottom of the stone steps. 'Yes?'

'Why don't you come with me today? One man alone, even an officer, is less impressive than two men representing the Otto.'

Manuffi nodded before worry furrowed his brow. 'Would I have to ask questions?'

'No,' Strocchi said, patting him on the arm. 'I'll do all the talking.'

You rise after a restless night on a hard wooden floor. The room stinks of piss and stale wine from the tavern below. There are no shutters, nothing to stop daylight flooding in, but it does not matter. Sleep is no companion for you now. Not after watching Uccello burn.

You have a change of clothes here. A plain tunic, hose and simple boots, nothing that will draw the eye. You know officers and constables will be searching for you.

You must not be caught.

You have tasks to do.

To succeed, you must change how you look.

The blade you always carry could be sharper, but the edge still cuts.

You grab a fistful of hair, sawing at it, casting aside what comes away.

Another fistful, and another, and another.

Your beard is next to go.

You have soap, a jug of water and a bowl.

You make a lather, rub it across your jaw and scalp.

The blade scrapes at your bristles, threatening to cut open your skin.

You dare not slip; you have tasks ahead.

It is slow work, painful work.

You remove all you can.

Some hair escapes the blade.

Your cloak and hood will hide the worst of it.

It does not matter. You do not need to satisfy others now.

The servant's clothes and boots you hide under a loose floorboard.

Someone will find them, but not today.

Not in time to stop you.

Justice will be done.

Aldo enjoyed the cool shade of the stables after marching back up to Ruggerio's estate. But getting useful answers from Vincenzo was not so simple. The stable hand spoke few words most days and today was no different. Yes, he did recall an itinerant cooper visiting before the fire at Scarlatti's villa. No, he had not paid the man much attention.

'We had no barrels in need of repair,' he said, as if that was an end to it.

'Which day was this?'

Vincenzo shrugged. 'The day before the fire? Two days? Three?' Another shrug.

'Well, what did this stranger look like?'

'Plain.'

'Plain?'

Vincenzo nodded.

'Was he as tall as I?'

'About the same.'

'Was he fat or thin? Strong or not?'

Vincenzo's brow furrowed. 'He was . . . plain.'

'Did he have a beard, or scars? What were his clothes like?'

'No beard. No scars. His clothes, they were—'

'Plain?' Aldo cut in.

Vincenzo nodded.

Aldo sighed. There were thieves in Florence who could learn from the stable hand's empty answers. 'Well, grazie for your time.' He strode to the door but stopped on the way out. 'Cassandra said this cooper might have gone to Scarlatti's estate after leaving here. Did he say where he was going next?'

Vincenzo shook his head.

'Did you see which way he went?'

The stable hand frowned again before replying, as if struggling to recall. 'No.'

Aldo stalked out into the scorching heat. He would have to question Scarlatti's estate manager and housekeeper to see if either could remember this stranger. It was not uncommon for itinerant coopers to move around the dominion, offering their skills to peasants and estates. Most farm workers did whatever jobs were needed, from making ropes to stonemasonry, blacksmithing to farrier. But making and repairing barrels was often easier left until a cooper came to the area.

If this outsider had visited Scarlatti's estate in the days before the fire, Trigari or Federica should remember him. Their memory could not be any worse than that of Vincenzo.

Strocchi found Palazzo Uccello in turmoil when he arrived with Manuffi, a stark contrast to the quiet desolation at Dovizi's residence a few days earlier. Then, the servants had hidden behind closed doors, as if shutting out the rest of the city would keep away the harsh reality of what had happened to their signore. But all the doors to Uccello's palazzo were wide open.

Bankers came and went through the smaller side door, their sober gowns and worried faces a testament to the concern caused by the murder of one of their own. If Uccello could die in such an outrageous way, and in full gaze of the city . . . There was much muttering and shaking of heads as the bankers entered and departed. Some carried away ledgers with LU etched into the leather bindings. Strocchi considered challenging how they were picking clean the bones of Uccello's business before his remains were even laid to rest. But this city lived and breathed through its banking and commerce. Few would question the ruthlessness of these men, and none would expect any different. Bankers were carrion eaters, feasting on the failures and folly of others. It was the Florentine way.

The main doors of Palazzo Uccello were surrounded by citizens. Those at the back of the throng peered past those ahead of them, curious to see what was worth so much attention. The rest of the crowd was red-faced from the rising heat and, it seemed, their own anger. Half a dozen men in the distinctive tunic, hose and boots of Uccello's servants stood sentry in front of the doors, arms interlinked as a barrier against the crowd. So far, it was working.

Strocchi studied the faces in the throng. It was unlikely Uccello's killer would be among them, but some men were drawn to the aftermath of their sins. Strocchi could not see the murderous servant, but there were other familiar faces. The stonemason from outside Dovizi's residence the morning he was burned alive. The old widow who had been on Ponte alla Carraia when Uccello died. Others alongside them seemed familiar. Having witnessed what had happened the previous evening, or having heard about it from the gossip of others, all looked eager for more. But Strocchi had heard of no new proclamations being posted, no fresh directions given to the frate's followers. So, they had come to the home of the latest victim.

Strocchi shook his head. What did they hope to find? These people could have good reasons for their anger. Perhaps they feared the world was changing too fast, leaving them behind. Perhaps they believed things were better in the past, when they had been young and life had seemed simpler, more certain. Was it that they craved a voice to lead them, one with strength and authority who told them what to believe and whom to hate? Was the faith of these lost souls so weak it could easily be bent to the will of others?

Strocchi prayed they would realize their righteous anger was being twisted into a weapon that benefitted others, not them. Their frate was long gone, his ashes silt on the bottom of the Arno. But as Strocchi's silent words were offered up, a fresh chant arose.

'Savonarola lives! Savonarola lives!'

'Didn't he die years ago?' Manuffi asked Strocchi.

'Yes.'

'So why are they saying he's alive?'

Strocchi shrugged. He didn't have an answer.

'Should we stop them, or move them away?'

'That would need more than the two of us. No, let's go inside and do what we came here to achieve.' Strocchi led Manuffi to the smaller side door the bankers had been using. A burly servant lurked inside, raising a hand to stop them.

'What business do you have here?' he demanded. Strocchi introduced himself as an officer of the Otto, investigating Uccello's murder. The servant stood aside to let them pass. 'The signore's maggiordomo is through there,' he said, pointing to the palazzo courtyard where a harassed, silver-haired man was arguing with two bankers over a ledger.

Strocchi marched to the courtyard, Manuffi close behind, announcing their reason for visiting and demanding the names of both bankers. After identifying themselves the bankers withdrew, scuttling away empty-handed. 'Thank you,' the maggiordomo said. 'Those vermin have been coming and going all morning, eager to steal the signore's clients.'

'Stealing?' Manuffi's shock was obvious. 'Should we pursue them?'

Strocchi stifled a bitter laugh. The constable was even more of an innocent than he looked. 'Regulating bankers is not within our jurisdiction,' Strocchi said.

'Consider yourselves fortunate the Otto only deals with murders and violence,' the maggiordomo added. 'The world of banking is far more cut-throat.' Leading both men upstairs to the middle level, the maggiordomo introduced himself as Eredi. He had worked for Uccello more than twenty summers.

Strocchi offered sympathies for the signore's death before asking about the two servants who had accompanied Uccello on his final journey.

'The driver, Nesi, has been here almost as long as I,' Eredi said. 'He drinks, curses, and treats the other servants like merda. But he is fiercely loyal to the signore. I cannot believe he had any prior knowledge of what happened last night.'

'Indeed,' Strocchi agreed. 'He was attacked by the other servant, the one who was riding on the rear of the carriage.'

'Marco.' Eredi frowned. 'It is strange. I had no reason to believe him capable of this. He joined the signore's service less than a year ago but gave us no cause for concern. Marco seemed a gentle soul. He cared for those horses as if they were his own.'

'Horses?' Manuffi asked.

'Four fine white horses pulled the signore's carriage,' Eredi replied.

'They were set free before the fire was started,' Strocchi added, remembering the two beasts that had charged across the bridge, almost trampling him beneath their hooves. 'What more can you tell us about Marco? Where did he sleep?'

'Most servants have beds on the top level of the palazzo, but Marco preferred to sleep above the stables. He said it was quieter, closer to the horses if they needed him.' Eredi shook his head. 'I have little to do with new servants. Most of my time is devoted to—' The words died away, sadness filling his face. 'Was devoted to the signore.' Eredi guided Strocchi and Manuffi into a grand parlour, the walls adorned with stunning frescoes and gold leaf. Having no family, it seemed Uccello had spent most of his coin on the palazzo. The maggiordomo sighed, glancing at his surroundings. 'Whatever shall become of all this?'

It might be wiser for Eredi to wonder what would become of him and the other servants, but Strocchi kept silent. Those worries would surface soon enough. 'Manuffi and I need to question Nesi about what happened. Has he recovered?'

'I believe so,' Eredi said. 'I will have one of the other servants take you to him.'

'We will also need to examine where Marco slept,' Strocchi added. The killer would have known he could not return here after murdering Uccello, so had probably left nothing behind – but they still needed to make certain. Everyone was fallible, anyone could make a mistake.

The maggiordomo clapped his hands to summon a younger servant. 'Take these men to Nesi, and then show them to Marco's bed above the stables.'

Strocchi and Manuffi followed the servant to the doorway. 'One last thing,' Strocchi said, pausing on his way out. 'How did Marco come to work here?'

'I'm not sure I understand your question,' Eredi replied.

'Did another servant suggest hiring Marco?' If so, that person might know more about the killer, more than Eredi was able to share.

'No, it was a recommendation by one of the signore's oldest friends.'

A shiver ran up Strocchi's back. 'Who?'

'Signor Ruggerio.'

Chapter Twenty-three

$\mathscr{R}$uggerio dressed for the journey to San Jacopo al Girone while Alberti confirmed all the necessary preparations had been or were being made. Yes, a rider left the city on a fast horse taking news to the estate that Ruggerio would arrive before nightfall. Yes, Ghiberti had been told to expect a visit from Ruggerio that morning – the maggiordomo took that message himself to be certain. And yes, four mercenaries were ready to protect Ruggerio on his journey, all carrying firearms.

Until this matter was ended, only those who could be trusted were to be allowed close. Alberti personally vouched for all the men, asserting he had known each at least five years. Ruggerio nodded, discarding one silk tunic after another as unsuitable for a long ride. 'What of the skies?' he asked. 'Is there any rain coming, or will this drought continue?'

'The day is dry and already hot,' Alberti replied. 'It seems likely to remain so.'

'Very well.' Ruggerio pursed his lips. 'Alberti, I wish you to stay here.'

The maggiordomo was unable to hide his dismay. 'Signore?'

'I am hopeful this – unpleasantness – will soon be ended. Once it is, I shall return to the city. There are many deals to be concluded before the worst of the summer heat is upon us, and I need someone here I can trust to send and receive messages.'

'Of course, signore, but could I not—'

'I am taking no servants with me,' Ruggerio went on. 'Cassandra has proven an able housekeeper; she can see to my immediate needs while I'm at the villa. That will suffice for a few days. If my time there must be extended, I will send for you.'

'Naturally, signore, yet I—'

'Are you questioning my judgement?'

'No, I would never—'

'Then the matter is closed.'

'Yes, signore. Please forgive me, I—'

Ruggerio dismissed the apology with a wave of his hand. 'That's all.'

The maggiordomo retreated, bowing at the waist before withdrawing from the bedchamber. Alberti was a loyal man, but sometimes seemed to believe he knew best. Reminding the maggiordomo of his place was necessary, ensuring he did not become complacent. That was more important than ever now.

Dovizi, Scarlatti and Uccello were dead.

Only two of the five remained.

Strocchi struggled to get much from Uccello's driver. Nesi was resting in bed on the top level of Palazzo Uccello, his face swollen, black bruises beneath both eyes. No, he had not known what Marco was planning. Yes, Nesi had smelled the oil spilled inside the signore's carriage, but he had not grasped what that meant – how could he? Marco had kept to himself, sleeping above the stables instead of with everyone else. He cared for the horses, but beyond that . . .

'Did you witness him talking to anyone from outside the palazzo?' Strocchi asked. 'Did he have any visitors, or receive any letters?'

Nesi shrugged, wincing in pain. 'Not that I saw.'

'Could Marco read or write?'

Nesi did not know. He'd never seen Marco with paper or ink. That was significant. It seemed certain Marco was responsible for posting the proclamations around the city, inciting those who still believed in the teachings of Savonarola. If Marco wrote the proclamations, it suggested he was responsible for all of this – a lot for one man, but possible. If Marco could neither read nor write, that meant somebody else had prepared those proclamations, that there was at least one other person helping, perhaps more. Marco might be the one killing, but somebody else could be guiding him.

Strocchi had sent Manuffi ahead to look around the stables. The constable was waiting outside when Strocchi reached them. 'Anything?'

Manuffi shook his head. 'An unmade bed, a change of hose and tunic.'

'Show me.'

The constable ushered Strocchi into the stables. The four white horses Marco had freed the previous night had been found and brought back to the palazzo. They appeared well kept, all the tools and stores in good order. Manuffi pointed to a wooden ladder leading to a space near the ceiling. 'He slept up there. Mind your head, there's not enough room to stand.'

Strocchi clambered up the ladder. It was much as Manuffi described, a simple platform with a mattress and some discarded clothes. No books, no ink, and no paper. Nothing to suggest what had been in the head or heart of Marco, or hint at what he might do next. Strocchi called down to Manuffi. 'Did you look under the mattress?'

'Meant to,' Manuffi said ruefully. 'Then I stood up.' He rubbed the back of his head.

Staying in a crouch, Strocchi lifted the mattress. A sheaf of papers was hidden underneath, black and red ink on each page. They were written by a familiar hand, matching the proclamations posted around the city. He searched further, but found no ink, no other papers. Whether Marco had written these remained unclear. Strocchi sifted through them, searching for answers. Most of the text matched what he'd seen before, claiming that Savonarola had been betrayed but his spirit was alive. No mention was made of specific targets until the final paragraph:

Gather outside Palazzo Medici one hour before curfew tonight and you shall bear witness as our beloved frate punishes the false leader of Florence. Stand in front of the home of this city's supposed duke and see him struck down by the spirit of Savonarola. Be there as our frate leads us all to a better world, to a new tomorrow.

Shocked by what he read, Strocchi stood straight up – and smashed his head into the ceiling. He sunk to one knee as white dots danced before his eyes.

'Are you all right?' Manuffi shouted.

'I will be,' Strocchi replied. He stayed still till he could read the proclamation without the words moving. But there was no denying the deadly intent on each page.

Marco planned to murder Cosimo de' Medici, the Duke of Florence.

Cassandra heard the rider coming up the hill, the laboured gasps of the horse, the sound of leather being used as a whip to force it onwards. She strode from the villa as the rider reached the courtyard, white foam falling from his horse's mouth.

'Vincenzo!' she called. 'Come and tend to this horse. Quick!'

The stable hand hurried out into the scorching sunshine, wiping both hands on his leather apron. He hurried forward, taking the reins as the rider dismounted. 'Message for Cassandra,' the rider said, pulling a sealed letter from the pouch strapped across his chest.

She snatched the letter from him. 'You galloped from the city without stopping?'

'Yes,' the messenger replied. 'The signore—'

Vincenzo struck the messenger hard in the face, sending him sprawling. The stable hand advanced on the messenger, fist clenched, ready to punch him again. 'Racing a horse in this heat is barbaric!'

'I'm sorry,' the messenger spluttered, scrambling backwards. 'I didn't think . . .'

Cassandra stepped between him and the stable hand. 'Vincenzo, can you help this poor animal?' He nodded, anger still twisting his face. 'Then please do so.'

Vincenzo led the exhausted beast away. Only when he and the horse were inside the cool of the stables did Cassandra open the letter. Her father had taught her to read and write long ago, useful skills for serving Ruggerio. 'There has been another murder in Florence. The signore is coming early this summer,' she said, reading down the page. 'Today, in fact.'

The messenger nodded. 'His maggiordomo believed Signor Ruggerio would depart the city by noon, if not sooner.'

'Coming by carriage or horse?'

'I . . . I don't know.'

She sighed. 'Very well. You had best start back.'

'But – how will I get there?'

Cassandra folded her arms. 'The horse you rode here cannot go another step, and Vincenzo will not loan you another. If you hope to reach Florence before the gates are locked at curfew, you'd best leave now.'

The messenger raised a hand to shield his eyes from the blazing sun. 'But it'll be the hottest part of the day soon. I'll roast if I walk back to Florence.'

'Think about that next time you ride a horse near to death.'

'Can I have some food or drink first? I'm parched and—'

'Go,' she said, in a voice of stone. 'Now.'

The messenger stumbled away, accompanied by the insistent sounds of insetti.

After marching along the sun-beaten dirt path between the two estates, Aldo was relieved to see Scarlatti's estate manager and housekeeper standing near the charred remains of the villa. The prospect of hunting for them in such oppressive heat was not inviting. But as Aldo got closer he saw Trigari shaking a fist at the sky.

A few moments in his company confirmed all was not well with the estate manager. Trigari's wits were sodden with wine, and Federica was more concerned with tending to him than answering Aldo's questions. Trigari had been a jolly figure before the fire. Now he was drowning his woes, refusing to surrender the wine in his grasp, no matter how Federica pleaded. Eventually he slumped against a wall, muttering and cursing his way towards sleep.

'How long has he been like this?' Aldo asked.

'Since we took the signore up to the crypt,' the housekeeper replied. 'Every time I get one bottle away from him, he finds another. Never knew he had so many hidden away.'

So Trigari's drinking was not new. 'Does he blame himself for Scarlatti's death?'

Federica scowled. 'No, this is self-pity. He knows whoever takes over the estate will soon dismiss him. Another man would have rid themselves of Trigari long ago, but the signore was too afraid.'

'Scarlatti was scared of Trigari?'

'No, you misunderstand,' Federica said. 'The signore was afraid of everything, and everyone.' She prised the half-empty bottle from Trigari's fingers, emptying it onto the dirt. 'Signor Scarlatti was always timid, a frightened mouse of a man. But he became much more so after he retired here from the city.'

'Do you know why?'

Federica glanced around, but the other servants and estate workers were elsewhere. Too embarrassed by Trigari's drinking, perhaps, or unwilling to help with him. 'Father Ognissanti came every week to hear confession. Afterwards, the signore would drink and weep into the night. I was the one who put him to bed . . .' Shame coloured her face. 'He kept saying punishment was coming. A divine reckoning, he called it, when he was making sense.'

Aldo remained silent. Better to let Federica reveal what she knew in her own time.

'Signor Scarlatti never told anyone what he had done,' the housekeeper said. 'What they had done. He kept talking about them, how he was one of them.'

The founders – Scarlatti must have meant the five of them.

'The signore said he hadn't meant to do it,' Federica went on. 'He was following the others . . . He wanted to be their friend, you see . . .' She gazed at Aldo, as if imploring him to understand. Trigari was making a grand display of his grief but that was self-pity. Federica was mourning a true loss. She had loved Scarlatti.

Aldo nodded his understanding.

'Many times,' she said, 'I could not follow what the signore was saying. He told me five of them had been doing the Lord's work, but if that was true, why was he so ashamed? He truly believed he was damned . . .' Federica shook her head, the words trailing away.

She was right. Judgement had come for Scarlatti and Dovizi, perhaps for more of the founders by now. But it was not God claiming them. What Federica had witnessed was helpful, but it wasn't enough. It wasn't proof.

The five men had been bound together for decades, yet something had driven Scarlatti to flee the city a year ago, soon after the founders' papers went missing. Aldo did not believe that was happenstance, but needed evidence. 'Did Scarlatti say why he was so afraid now?'

'Not in a way I ever understood,' she replied. 'He kept mumbling about something that had been stolen . . . I asked what, but he wouldn't say.' The housekeeper wiped her nose and eyes with a cloth. 'Signor Scarlatti didn't make sense when he was drinking.' She stared at Trigari snoring in the dirt. 'Much like this one.'

Aldo wanted to ask more, but Federica straightened her shoulders, her face hardening. 'What will happen to this estate?' she asked. 'The signore has no famiglia, no heirs. What will become of all those who work here if no one owns this land?'

'I do not know,' Aldo admitted.

'But you are an officer of the Otto . . .'

'Another court in Florence deals with such matters,' he replied, keeping his demotion to himself. 'I'm told an itinerant cooper visited the Ruggerio estate not long before the fire, but they had no work for him. Did he try here?'

'No.' Federica frowned. 'I had been hoping a cooper would come; we have barrels that need mending. I told all those in the village that if a cooper did pass through San Jacopo al Girone they should send him up the hill.' She gestured at the burned-out villa. 'Perhaps if our barrels had been mended, we might have been able to save this.'

'Nothing would have stopped that fire,' Aldo said. He nudged Trigari with a boot. 'Do you need help with this one?'

'No. He can sleep there for now.'

Aldo left the housekeeper staring at the charred husk that had been her home. It seemed strange that an itinerant cooper would go to Ruggerio's villa for work yet not try the large estate on the next hillside. Either the cooper had spied on the Ruggerio residence, as Lippo did, or Vincenzo was lying about a visitor coming to the villa. Whatever the truth, the stable hand had more questions to answer.

Ruggerio despaired of Ghiberti. The wool merchant was among the richest men in his guild yet he spent not one giulio more than was necessary on anything. Palazzo Ghiberti was an example of his tight-fisted ways. It had the three levels expected of a merchant's residence and enjoyed a fine location overlooking the Arno from the river's north bank. But the building was ugly as a pox-faced strega, made of brutal stone. It had none of the elegance a palazzo should possess, no hint of beauty.

Inside was little better: plain stone walls and columns, no marble on the floors, no frescoes or sculptures on show. The residence matched its owner. Ghiberti bothered with neither art nor artifice.

Servants bustled back and forth, ignoring Ruggerio as he waited in the palazzo courtyard. One had taken his name and hurried away upstairs, but never returned. Ruggerio stayed. He would see Ghiberti before leaving the city – he must.

Of all the founders, the wool merchant had always been the most direct among them, the most straightforward . . . the most honest. Ghiberti had kept their secret, assuring the others he would not betray what they had done. Their sin was a collective one, after all. Ruggerio had wondered many times what further secrets Ghiberti held close. What trespasses and crimes did he keep from the world? Every man had his transgressions, whether acted upon or not. Yet Ghiberti's truths remained hidden from his servants and assistants. Bribes had not been enough to unlock them, and threats proved no more revelatory.

'What do you want?' Ghiberti called from the main staircase, stamping down to the internal courtyard. His robes were plain, no thought given to colour or cut. Ghiberti would probably wear sack cloth if servants did not dress him.

'A pleasure to see you too,' Ruggerio replied, remaining still. He had waited long enough, let Ghiberti come to him.

'I got your message.' The wool merchant scowled, marching across the courtyard. 'Say what you will, and scuttle away to your country estate.'

Ruggerio swallowed his anger. Bluntness was often a useful quality in business, but it could also be needlessly rude. He should have expected nothing more from Ghiberti. 'Uccello is dead. Burned alive, like Dovizi. Murdered by one of his own servants.'

'And?'

Ruggerio stepped closer, lowering his voice so passing assistants would not hear. 'We are being hunted, the five of us. Now only you and I remain.'

Ghiberti shrugged. 'I have no intention of hiding in the country-side. If someone plans to burn me alive, they shall have to face me – here, inside my palazzo.'

'That is your final decision?'

'Hopefully not. But I refuse to be driven out of my home or my city by whoever killed Sandro, Benozzo and Luca. Run away if you wish, Girolamo. I am staying.'

Ruggerio shook his head. 'You were always the stubbornest among us.'

'That has served me well. I see no reason to change.'

'Even if it gets you murdered?'

Ghiberti pressed one meaty fist into the other, his knuckles cracking. 'They are welcome to try.'

'Then I hope to see you again when they have failed. Farewell, Roberto.' Ruggerio strode from the palazzo without looking back. Ghiberti had made his choice. So be it.

You are hungry. You venture out into the streets, cloak tight around you despite the searing heat, hood over your head. You will not be found, you will not be taken. Not until your work is complete.

You go to the nearest mercato, using what coin you have to buy food. You hear people talk, good and honest citizens of Florence. One phrase passes back and forth between them: 'Savonarola lives.' You smile and nod, letting them bring you into their quiet words, their hidden glances. 'Savonarola lives,' you reply.

They talk of the latest traitor to suffer the wrath of the beloved frate – a banker, some say, a pompous and proud man. You mention the name Uccello, and the others nod. One says they were on the bridge as the spirit of Savonarola set fire to Uccello. For a moment you fear this person will remember you but they are too busy basking in the attention of others.

Another joins the group, bringing word of a gathering outside the palazzo of the dead man. People are chanting the frate's name, unafraid of the Medici welp or his spies.

'Savonarola lives,' you say and the others nod again.

You thank them and stroll away, careful to take a new path away from the mercato in case anyone is watching you, following you. When you are certain there is nobody, you stop and gorge yourself on the food. You dare not go back inside Palazzo Uccello, but you can join those outside. A whisper in the ears of a few would soon spread. Those in the mercato prove the people are ripe and ready for a leader.

'Savonarola lives,' you whisper to yourself.

Soon the mighty Medici will tremble.

Chapter Twenty-four

*A*ldo was wilting beneath the scorching sun as he marched back towards Ruggerio's villa. A faint breeze was rippling the tops of the tall cypress trees on the horizon but it offered no relief for those labouring among the grapevines and olive groves on the hillside. At least they were dressed for this weather, with loose tunics and wide-brimmed hats to shield them from the sun. Further down the slope a farmer was burning a pile of fallen branches, woodsmoke drifting lazily upwards. Aldo didn't mind breathing that in. It was better than the stench of rotting corpse that seemed to linger in his nostrils.

A line of women were trudging up the dirt road from the village to Ruggerio's estate; seven, no, eight of them. Aldo had seen a pair coming and going from the villa most days. They cleaned and helped Cassandra with other mundane tasks. Why were so many of them coming up the hill at once? Realization stopped Aldo where he stood.

Ruggerio was coming.

The silk merchant must have sent word he was on his way, and Cassandra had summoned help from the village to prepare the villa. Ruggerio was not expected in San Jacopo al Girone until July, or late June at the earliest. To come now, and in haste . . .

He must be fleeing the city.

Aldo broke into a run, eager to reach the villa before the women from the village. When they arrived, Cassandra would be too busy to answer his questions.

For Ruggerio to leave Florence at such short notice must mean another of the five founders had been murdered. Having encountered both Ghiberti and Uccello in the past, Aldo suspected Uccello the more likely victim. Ghiberti was content to conduct his business without being noticed, but Uccello seemed to crave the gaze of others. The banker could not resist an opportunity to flaunt his wealth, to show everyone what he had accumulated. If wisdom suggested withdrawing from view, Uccello would insist on being seen in salons and on the streets of Florence. He was a far easier target than Ghiberti for a determined or cunning killer. And the person responsible for these murders was certainly cunning.

Aldo was gasping when he reached the villa. Hurrying anywhere on foot in this heat was folly, but running was dangerous. He stopped in shade cast by the stables, bending forwards with both hands on his thighs for support.

'Are you unwell?' Cassandra called from the villa entrance.

'Just – out of – breath,' Aldo replied.

The housekeeper brought a jug of water to the courtyard. Aldo poured most of it over his head and neck before drinking what remained. 'Grazie.'

'You're welcome,' she said. 'Why were you running?'

'Saw women . . . coming up . . . from the village.'

'And you wanted to get here first?'

Aldo nodded. 'When . . . does he arrive?'

Cassandra took back the empty jug. 'Signor Ruggerio will be here before sunset.'

'There's been . . . another murder – in Florence – hasn't there?'

She smiled. 'This is why the signore thinks so highly of you as an investigator.'

'Who – who was it?'

'Luca Uccello. Trapped in his carriage as it was set ablaze by Ponte alla Carraia, not long before curfew yesterday. He got out and flung himself into the Arno, but . . .'

Aldo straightened up. Now three of the founders were dead, fire involved in each murder. With Ruggerio coming to his country estate, the killer would follow, sooner or later. Unless . . . A stray notion crept into Aldo's dizziness. What if Ruggerio was behind the killings? That had seemed unlikely in Florence, but Ruggerio did try to have the founders' papers stolen from the convent before it was dissolved. Besides, Ruggerio had Lippo killed for spying on the country villa. That made no sense if Ruggerio was having the other founders murdered at his command . . . Aldo shook his head, the villa opposite him becoming a blur in the heat.

'You shouldn't be this pale,' Cassandra said. 'Come inside, sit down.'

'No, there isn't time,' Aldo insisted. If he caught the killer, Bindi would have to allow him back as an officer of the court. To do that he needed answers. 'Where's Vincenzo?'

'I sent him to help bring the signore's things here, but he should be back before nightfall. Why do you ask?'

Aldo told her about the stable hand's unhelpful description, and how nobody at Scarlatti's estate could recall such a cooper passing through San Jacopo al Girone.

'You think Vincenzo was lying?' Cassandra asked. 'Why would he do that?'

'That's what I need to ask him.' Aldo shared what he knew about Lippo being hired to study Ruggerio's estate. 'If Vincenzo was right about this cooper, it suggests they came looking for ways into the villa, points of vulnerability.'

'But why send two men to do the same job?'

It was a valid question. 'Perhaps they lost patience waiting for Lippo's report, or did not trust him to do the job well. Maybe events elsewhere forced them to move sooner than planned . . .' Aldo leaned back against the stables, his head spinning. The killing of Scarlatti, was that where the plan had gone awry? The retired merchant had been abducted, but his death did not fit with the others. Dovizi was tortured, suggesting the killer wanted information. Had they killed Scarlatti while questioning him? It explained why the body had been kept in the crypt for several days before being brought to the villa. But for the falling beam that stopped the fire, all proof of how Scarlatti had died would have been destroyed.

'Aldo? Aldo, are you listening to me?' Cassandra asked.

'My thoughts were . . . elsewhere,' he replied. 'What were you saying?'

'I asked if you wished to rest here. This heat has drained the life from you.'

Aldo wanted to decline but everything seemed to be whirling around him . . .

Ruggerio dismounted from his horse to lead it through Porta la Croce. Two of his men strode ahead, carrying arquebus firearms. The other two waited behind as he approached the city's eastern gate, both armed with a wheellock pistol. Alberti had accompanied them this far, but here the maggiordomo must turn back. That did not stop him making one last appeal.

'The cart will follow later today, signore, bringing your clothes, books and other things you require for the country. But, if I may ask again, are you certain I cannot—'

'My decision remains the same,' Ruggerio cut in. 'You will stay in Florence. I need someone I can trust to send reports of what is happening in the city, how the Otto's hunt for this killer is progressing. Consider that a mark of the esteem in which I hold you.'

'Yes, signore,' Alberti replied, bowing his head.

Ruggerio continued through the gate, leaving the maggiordomo behind. Only once outside the city wall did Ruggerio climb back atop his horse. He dug both heels into the beast and it trotted forward on the dirt road, heading east. One man went ahead of the horse while another followed to protect its flanks. The other two mercenaries fell in step on either side. Each man now clasped his weapon, ready to fire and held in view. The arquebuses looked especially impressive to Ruggerio's eye, though he was far from an expert. Hopefully their presence would dissuade potential attackers. Whoever was murdering the founders favoured flame as their weapon, and he had no wish to burn.

The sound of insetti became louder and more intrusive as Ruggerio rode away from the city wall. It always took him a few days in the country to become used to that insistent noise. As first, he would be irritated, made scratchy by the constant chirruping. In time, he stopped noticing and found it even lulled him to sleep at night. But now, with the relentless sun beating down on him, Ruggerio was sweaty and uncomfortable atop his horse.

He looked back over one shoulder at Florence, the Duomo's cupola becoming visible above the city wall the further away he rode. All being well, the threat to his life would be vanquished within days and he could return. Yet a cold shiver of doubt clenched inside him, despite the heat. All had not been well for far too long.

After returning to the Podestà from Palazzo Medici, Bindi had spent his morning ensuring every available officer, guard and constable was scouring the city for the servant who'd killed Uccello.

Satisfied all possible efforts were being made, and with the hottest part of the day engulfing the city, the segretario retreated to his office. Normally the court's headquarters was a haven when Florence sweltered, but even the Podestà was a clammy oven today.

Bindi had not been long behind his table when Strocchi burst in, ignoring a command to wait outside. The young officer insisted what he must say could not wait.

For once, he was correct.

'The killer's next target is Duke Cosimo?' Bindi asked, unsure if he had heard right.

Strocchi slapped a sheaf of false proclamations on the segretario's table. 'The proof is in the final paragraph,' he said. Bindi leaned forward to read the relevant section.

Gather outside Palazzo Medici one hour before curfew tonight and you shall bear witness as our beloved frate punishes the false leader of Florence. Stand in front of the home of this city's supposed duke and see him struck down by the spirit of Savonarola. Be there as our frate leads us all to a better world, to a new tomorrow.

'I found these beneath the killer's mattress at Palazzo Uccello,' Strocchi said. 'There is no date on them, so we can't be certain about when he plans to murder the duke . . .'

'But there is no doubting his intention,' Bindi said. 'Good work, Strocchi.'

The young officer blinked several times, his surprise evident. 'Grazie, sir.'

'I'm glad my decision to promote you is proving a wise choice.'

'I—' Words seem to fail Strocchi. He nodded instead.

Bindi tapped a finger to his lips. This development would have to be taken to the duke immediately. Alerting him to such imminent danger should help repair Cosimo's esteem for the Otto. Besides, if an attack was made against Cosimo and it emerged that the Otto had known but did not warn the duke, the consequences would be ruinous.

'Call back the men who are searching for the killer,' Bindi said.

'Sir?'

'It's a simple command. Call them back. Send messengers out into the city to find our men and summon them here. We'll need all of them to protect the duke.'

'But, surely he has his own guards . . .'

'Of course.'

'Then . . . why?'

Bindi sighed. 'I take back what I said about the wisdom of promoting you. This is Florence. Being seen to do the right thing is just as important, if not more so, than doing the right thing. The Otto helping to protect the duke is proof of this court's worth to him.'

'I understand that, segretario—' Strocchi replied.

'Good, perhaps there is hope for you yet.'

'—but abandoning our search for this killer, is that wise?'

'Do you believe you know better than I?'

'Of course not—'

'Then there is nothing further to say.'

'I beg to differ, sir,' Strocchi replied. 'One of the servants at Palazzo Uccello told me the killer, Marco, was hired on the recommendation of Signor Ruggerio.'

'You're suggesting Ruggerio sent this killer to work for Uccello? That Ruggerio is behind all of this?'

'It might explain why the victims have all been other founders of his confraternity.'

'But it doesn't explain this.' The segretario held up the new proclamation. 'Why would Ruggerio make the duke his next target? The silk merchant has never shown a hint of anti-Medici anger, of wanting to restore Florence to a republic. It makes no sense.'

Strocchi shrugged, the young fool actually shrugged. 'Perhaps that is a ruse to take our attention elsewhere. Ruggerio still deserves investigation.'

'No!' Bindi slapped a hand down on his table. 'Our priority must be protecting the duke. Once that is assured – and only when it has been assured – will you pursue other, less urgent matters. Is this clear?'

Strocchi did not reply, but his scowl was eloquent enough. A knock interrupted them. 'Who is it?' Bindi bellowed, still glaring at the presumptuous pup in front of him.

'Dr Saul Orvieto,' a male voice replied from outside the office.

'He's a Jewish physician,' Strocchi said. 'He helped with—'

'Did I ask you to speak?' Bindi snapped.

The young officer closed his mouth.

A prudent choice.

'Enter!'

The door opened and a bearded Jew came in, a satchel slung over one shoulder. 'Forgive my intrusion,' he said, approaching the segretario's table. 'My name is—'

'Orvieto,' Bindi cut in. 'What do you want, doctor?'

The Jew smiled. 'Nothing, sir. I am simply a messenger. Cesare Aldo asked me to bring this to you.' He pulled a letter from inside his satchel.

Bindi gestured at his table and the Jew placed the letter on it. 'And where was Aldo when he gave you that?' The troublesome merda better not have remained in Florence.

'Several miles east of the city, sir, at San Jacopo al Girone.'

'Very well, you may go.'

The Jew raised a finger. 'Actually, I have a second letter.' He pulled that from his satchel. 'This one is for Strocchi.' He handed it over.

'Anything else?' Bindi asked, not bothering to hide his impatience.

'No, segretario,' the Jew replied, bowing at the waist. 'Forgive me for my intrusion.'

'Take your leave.'

The Jew did as he was told, bowing again at the door before departing. Bindi opened a small chest atop his table, shoving the letter from Aldo inside.

'You're not going to read it?' Strocchi asked.

'The words of a demoted constable in the dominion are of no interest or value to me.'

'Aldo's been demoted?'

The segretario was losing what patience he had. 'I gave a simple order: call back all those men who are searching for the killer. I shall return to Palazzo Medici and inform the duke of this threat to his life. Go.'

You hear the crowd before you see Palazzo Uccello. They chant two words, over and over: 'Savonarola lives! Savonarola lives!'

You turn a corner and the chant becomes a roar, bouncing back and forth between buildings of stone. There must be a hundred people in front of the residence, men and women, even children among them. The citizens are angry, their faces red from the heat of the day, from demanding attention, from wanting to be heard, from wanting the impossible.

You look round.

You see a mob, craving a target.

You will give them one, though it means risk.

You make your way to the front, climbing atop a stone bench outside the palazzo.

'I saw a new proclamation!'

At first the chanting continues, but you shout the words again and some stop to listen.

'I saw a new proclamation,' you call out a third time. 'It says the spirit of Savonarola will come again today, as it did last night for the traitor who lived here.'

'Where?' someone cries out as more of the crowd listen.

'Outside Palazzo Medici, one hour before curfew tonight,' you reply. 'We will all bear witness as our beloved frate strikes down the false leader of Florence.'

'The duke!' another voice calls out. 'He means the Medici duke!'

'Savonarola is coming for Cosimo next,' a third voice shouts.

A roar rises up from the mob. 'Bring down the duke! Bring down the duke!'

'We should go to Palazzo Medici,' you shout, 'show them the strength of our belief!'

'Yes!' many roar back. 'Palazzo Medici! To Palazzo Medici!'

The crowd turns towards the duke's residence.

You step down from the bench, and become one with them, invisible. 'Savonarola lives,' they chant. 'Bring down the duke!'

Bindi waddled into Palazzo Medici, nodding at the two guards standing sentry outside the main entrance. The segretario stopped a passing servant in the courtyard and told them to find Campana. 'The life of the duke is at stake,' Bindi added. 'Should he fall, you do not wish it to be because you failed in your duties.'

Campana soon appeared, concern evident in his face. 'What is this about a threat to His Grace?'

Bindi produced the proclamation Strocchi had found. 'There were more of these waiting to be spread around the city, summoning people to watch the duke die. Similar messages were posted yesterday announcing Uccello's murder.'

'Madre di Dio,' Campana whispered as he read. 'The duke's spies have reported nothing about this. Come, he will want to hear from you directly.'

Bindi allowed himself the sin of pride while following Campana upstairs. For once the duke was less informed than the Otto. That should demonstrate the value of the court, and of its most humble segretario. Soon Bindi was standing before the duke's table while Cosimo read the new proclamation. The young Medici bristled at what it said.

'How seriously should I take this?' he asked. 'There are some inside the city and plenty beyond its walls who might delight in seeing me fall. But few have the courage to attack me directly, not while knowing they would likely perish in the attempt.'

'That is true, Your Grace,' Campana replied, 'but—'

'I was asking Bindi,' Cosimo cut in.

Crimson blossomed across Campana's face. It was quite delicious.

'Well, segretario?' the duke asked. 'What do you think?'

'Your Grace is, of course, correct in judging that most of your enemies and rivals are too cowardly to strike against you. But it only needs a single man with the means and the opportunity, especially if he is willing to sacrifice himself.'

Cosimo shifted in his seat. Bindi hastened his reply.

'This proclamation is similar to one posted yesterday, inviting Savonarola's followers to witness the murder of Uccello. Your Grace knows the killer made good on that promise. I believe this new proclamation should be viewed as a credible threat to your life.'

The duke nodded. 'It gives no indication when the attack will come.'

'One of my officers found the proclamations before they were posted. That has, at least, prevented—' There was a knock at the door, interrupting Bindi. Campana hurried to answer it, talking in hushed whispers with a servant behind the segretario. 'As I was saying, the intervention by one of my officers prevented the killer from—'

'Forgive me,' Campana said as he returned, 'but this cannot wait. Your Grace, a crowd of people is arriving outside the palazzo. This palazzo.'

'How many?' Cosimo asked.

'Fifty or more, but the number is growing in size. It seems they were gathered in front of Palazzo Uccello, but are coming here now. They are chanting two words, over and over: "Savonarola lives".'

The duke rose from his chair. 'So much for your man preventing this from happening,' he snapped at Bindi. Cosimo marched from the office, Campana and Bindi hurrying after. They strode through the palazzo to a salone that overlooked the main entrance on via Largo. The street below was choked with chanting citizens, more joining the throng below. 'And so much for waiting until an hour before curfew,' the duke added, scowling.

'I can have ducal guards break the crowd apart,' Campana said. 'Act now, and this mob will be driven away before it becomes too large.'

'But what is to prevent them from returning?' the duke asked. 'These are true believers, people of strong faith who are being manipulated by a killer for his malign purposes. All of this' – he gestured at the crowd outside – 'could well be a ruse. Whoever is responsible has fuelled the religious fervour and burning sense of injustice these citizens possess. Attack them and he wins. Even if you drive the people away, more will come, brought here by their righteous anger.' Cosimo looked up at the scorching sun in a cloudless azzurro sky. 'And this heat is only making matters worse.'

Bindi could only agree. The duke was young, but he had a wise head on his shoulders. His grasp of tactics was compelling, little surprise from the son of the great condottiere, Giovanni dalle Bande Nere. 'Your Grace, may I make a suggestion?'

'Yes, if it is brief.'

'Send your spies into the crowd. Have them try to reduce the size of this mob by persuading those swept up in the moment to leave. Station more guards at the palazzo entrances to ensure nobody can get in without your explicit permission. I already have the men of the Otto gathering at the Podestà, ready to help. They could block the roads leading here. Once the building is secure, all you need do is wait this madness out.'

The duke was staring outside but seemed to be listening, so Bindi pressed on.

'As you say, it is hot outside, far too hot for these people to stay where they are. Many will drift away if nothing more happens. When curfew comes and the spirit of Savonarola has failed to strike anyone down, the prophecy will be disproven.'

Cosimo nodded a little. 'Campana?'

'Withdrawing from view may be seen as weakness by some, proof you are hiding from your citizens,' the duke's private segretario replied. 'But Bindi's suggestion has the potential to take the heat out of this gathering.'

'That would require a rainstorm,' Cosimo said, 'and there's no sign of one coming.'

The duke's words stirred a recollection in Bindi, but he kept it to himself.

'Very well,' the duke said. 'We shall step back, let these people shout themselves hoarse in the sun. Campana, have your spies do what they can to persuade waverers. Bindi, send word to the Podestà. Your men will stop others joining those in front of the palazzo.'

'Your Grace, there are numerous streets and alleys that—'

'We shall watch and wait,' the duke cut in. 'Now do as I say.'

* * *

You move among the mob outside the duke's palazzo, punching a fist in the air and chanting with those around you: 'Savonarola lives! Savonarola lives!'

You sweat through your clothes, the sun overhead turning the street into an oven. The heavy woollen cloak you wear makes it worse, as does the hood hiding your head, but you dare not remove them. You can see guards gathering at the main entrance to the palazzo, staring out at the throng. You know men of the law must be searching for you, looking for you, expecting you to be here. They will have the proclamations from under your mattress, the proclamations you left behind. This mob is prophecy made flesh.

You turn your head one way, and then the other.

You look for the officer who saw you last night.

He knows your eyes, how tall you are.

He will be watching for you.

Searching for you.

You must elude him a while longer.

You still have work to do, a fire to light, a monster to destroy.

You see three men staring down from inside the palazzo.

You stab a finger at them.

'Look, the duke!'

Others stop their chanting, peering where you point.

'It's him, the false leader of Florence!' a man shouts beside you.

'Bring down the duke!' you shout, pointing at the palazzo.

'Bring down the duke!' others around you echo.

More take up the cry: 'Bring down the duke!'

You smile. The spirit of Savonarola is risen.

Strocchi was still gathering the Otto's men when a messenger ran into the Podestà courtyard. A dozen constables and guards had returned so far, most made surly by hours of scouring alleys and scorching streets without success. The others were supposedly still out searching but Strocchi suspected many had gone to a tavern, especially the likes of Benedetto, who had been summoned back in after their night patrols.

Giving in to such temptation was easy to understand, though Strocchi would have gone home rather than waste his time in a tavern. He had given too many hours to the court when he could have been with Tomasia and their little bambina. Bindi's casual mention of demoting Aldo had been a shock, too. Aldo often irritated the segretario, but what had he done to justify such a response?

The messenger's tunic was soaked with sweat. 'Strocchi?' he shouted. 'Which of you is Strocchi?' The red-faced youth was clutching a folded letter.

Strocchi took the document, giving the messenger coin for his trouble. Strocchi waited until the youth was gone before opening the letter. He recognized Bindi's scrawl, ink spattered across the page in haste. 'This is from the segretario,' Strocchi announced, loud enough for those around him to hear. 'We are to stand sentry on the roads and alleys that lead towards Palazzo Medici. We can permit those leaving the area to pass, but nobody may enter without written permission from the duke.'

There was muttering and grumbles from the men around him. Strocchi climbed atop a nearby bench so he could see all of them at once.

'I know you're tired and hot, so am I.' He held up the message. 'Now Bindi wants us to spend the afternoon arguing with citizens who want to get past. It won't be easy, but I have two suggestions that might help. First, work in pairs so you can support each other. If one needs to go for a piss, the other stays to stand sentry. Does that sound reasonable?'

He got a few nods from the men.

Manuffi raised his hand. 'What's the other suggestion?'

'The segretario doesn't say when we need to start,' Strocchi replied. 'I'm hungry and thirsty, and I'm sure you are too. Go get yourselves something to drink and eat, bring it back here. First one to return, I pay for their meal. Last one here pays for my meal. Reasonable?' The men seemed more enthusiastic about the chance to fill their bellies and satisfy their thirsts. Strocchi knew it was a risk letting them leave, some wouldn't come back. But those who did would be worthy of his trust, and he suspected that was going to be important.

Aldo woke in a bedchamber he did not recognize. The room was simple and elegant, a tapestry on one wall. It was the marble bust atop a column in one corner that removed any doubt. This must be Ruggerio's country villa. Only the silk merchant would have his own likeness watching over guests in a bedchamber.

Someone had laid a damp cloth across Aldo's temple. Cassandra, most likely. He recalled her pulling off his boots, guiding him towards the bed, and then . . . Nothing. It was his own fault for running outside in the heat of the day without a hat. His boots were by the bed but lifting the sheet revealed Cassandra had removed his clothes. They were not apparent in the room, but there was a silk robe draped over a chair.

Aldo sat up. The bedchamber tilted and blurred before settling again. He could hear distant female voices beyond the closed door – women from the village making the villa ready for Ruggerio. So much for questioning Cassandra before the women arrived. The bed beneath Aldo was soft and forgiving. He could still remember living in such surroundings, though it was many years since he had been banished from Palazzo Fioravanti. Little wonder Ruggerio did everything he could to retain this life, this comfort.

Before succumbing to the sun, an errant notion had occurred: could Ruggerio be responsible for the murders? Not personally, of course; the silk merchant never got his hands bloody, bruised or burnt. But could he be sending others to murder men who had once been his friends? Aldo had dismissed the possibility while in Florence, yet he knew Ruggerio was more than willing to see others killed if it protected his reputation. The brutal death of Lippo while a prisoner in the Podestà had reinforced that.

Ruggerio had made considerable efforts to secure the founders' private papers when they were being kept inside the Convent of Santa Maria Magdalena. Aldo was certain those papers had found their way to Ruggerio when the convent was dissolved. If so, this villa would be a wise place to keep them: outside the city, well removed from the view of others . . . And it explained why somebody had hired Lippo to spy on the villa. They needed to know how easy it would be to obtain the papers. Sending Lippo to visit more than one villa could easily have been a ruse to conceal the true target: Ruggerio's country residence.

Aldo shook his head. No, that was far too much speculation, too many presumptions, even for him. But he was inside Ruggerio's villa, without Cassandra watching. It would be ungrateful not to take such an opportunity to satisfy curiosity . . .

Swinging both legs out of the bed, Aldo reached for the silk robe. It proved tight across his shoulders, no doubt made to fit Ruggerio's narrow chest. Aldo rose, expecting his legs to buckle but they remained steady. The shutters were ajar, showing that the bedchamber was on the upper level. Aldo had searched the lower level when Cassandra had invited him in to see the view from the loggia. If Ruggerio kept an ufficio at the villa, it must be up here. The challenge was searching for it without being discovered.

Aldo ventured to the door. The voices beyond had faded, he could hear nobody else on this level. The door opened without noise, allowing him to peer out. Yes, the hallway was empty. He remained still, listening. Faint murmurs drifted up from below, but nothing more.

He slipped from the bedchamber, leaving the door ajar in case he had to hurry back.

Aldo crept along the hallway on the balls of his bare feet, peering in each room. Most were bedchambers or storage spaces. One doorway led out to the loggia. But close by that was a closed door . . . with a key in the lock! Aldo had not noticed it before, as a closed door drew little attention. But a closed door with a key in the lock was another matter.

He reached for the key, twisting it slowly—

'I'll be right back down,' Cassandra said, her words accompanied by footsteps on the staircase. Palle! Aldo froze, expecting to be caught at any moment. But another female voice called to Cassandra. Her footsteps stopped, then descended back to the lower level. 'What is it?' Cassandra said, her voice fading into the distance.

Aldo let his breath slip out between his lips. She would be back soon. Far more sensible to return to bed, forget about the locked room . . .

But all rewards required risk.

Cassandra was struggling to keep hold of her temper. She believed in order and preparation. Make plans for difficult tasks and they were easier to complete. Where others seemed to rely on good fortune and rushing around at the last moment to get things done, she preferred to be careful. Methodical. It might be less thrilling, but Cassandra still enjoyed a victory earned.

In many ways she was akin to the garden behind the villa. The ground had to be tended and prepared for the seasons to come if the herbs and flowers were to flourish. The pathways had to be kept clear, errant plants removed, the dead and dying foliage culled. Everything required nurturing, guiding, helping. It was a task for the patient, those willing to labour for years before knowing if their efforts would succeed. A great garden was the work of a lifetime, and must be able to withstand storms and droughts and winds and tempests and other interventions. And yet one bad day could still destroy everything.

Today was becoming such a day.

The previous summer the signor had sent word of his arrival a month ahead, giving her ample time to prepare everything. This summer? A few hours, at most. She had sent down to the village for women to help with hurried preparations, but two of the usual servants were unable to come due to illness and pregnancy. Their replacements did not seem to know one end of a mop from the other, forcing Cassandra to watch over everything they did. One in particular, Rafaella, was little more than a girl and required constant vigilance.

Then there was Aldo all but collapsing in her arms. Quite what the fool thought he was doing by rushing around in the hottest part of the day was beyond Cassandra's reason. Bringing a representative of the Otto inside the villa was a dangerous choice when Ruggerio could arrive at any time. The signor gave her the freedom to do as she saw best when he was absent, so long as his possessions and reputation suffered no harm. But once Ruggerio was present on the estate every guest, every meal, every detail required explicit approval. He would not respond well to having Aldo asleep in one of the bedchambers.

Cassandra had been as patient as she dared, leaving Aldo to recover while the women cleaned the villa's lower level. But each of the rooms above needed to be prepared, and that could not be completed while Aldo remained in bed. Cassandra was halfway up the stairs when Rafaella called for more help. But, finally, she seemed to be understanding.

'I am going to the upper level,' Cassandra announced so everyone could hear. 'Does anyone have a question they need to ask before I do that?'

The women from the village shook their heads.

'Is everyone quite certain?'

They all nodded.

'Rafaella?'

The girl shook her head, hiding a giggle behind one hand.

Cassandra smiled, despite her frustration. Rafaella was more hindrance than help, even if her heart was in the right place. It would be better if she did not come back, not while Ruggerio was in residence. His anger knew few boundaries when it was roused.

The room was dark, a few dust motes dancing in the thin slither of light that fell between the shutters. Letting his eyes adjust, Aldo could make out a table with a chair in front of it and another behind, documents in a neat pile beside a small chest. He sifted through the papers. Most were letters from the previous summer, along with reports about rivals in the silk weavers' and merchants' guild. Ruggerio never stopped plotting, it seemed, even while at his country estate. But there was no sign of the founders' documents.

Moving behind the table, Aldo found a smaller side table with various items atop it – blank paper, ink, wax, a blade for opening letters, and Ruggerio's personal seal. The small chest on the main table was locked with no key in it. Aldo knew he should leave . . . but resisting temptation had never been a strength. He slid the blade into the lock on the chest, twisting it sideways in the hope of forcing the mechanism. Aldo twisted harder . . .

. . . and the lock gave way with a loud thud.

He stopped, listening for footsteps. Nothing.

Aldo pulled the blade free, returning it to its home before opening the small chest. Inside were more papers. Aldo pulled those out, taking them to the shutter to read. The first few were more letters, but among them was a single sheet, different from the others. The paper was much older. The ink on it had faded, making the text hard to read.

One corner was missing, torn away.

Aldo recognized the document, though he had never seen most of it before. This was one of the papers that had gone missing when the convent was dissolved. He had found the torn corner under the corpse of Bernardo Galeri fourteen months before. Ruggerio had sent Galeri into the convent to steal the founders' papers. But Galeri had been unable to get what Ruggerio wanted, succeeding only in tearing a corner from one document. Galeri died before he could leave the convent, and it was his killing that led to the convent's dissolution. In the following upheaval, Ruggerio had obviously succeeded in procuring this document.

Aldo was opening the shutters for more light to read it when footsteps came striding along the hallway. Palle, he had lingered too long. Aldo returned to the table, putting the other papers back and closing the chest. There was no way to lock it again without a key. The footsteps kept getting closer until they stopped outside the door.

Chapter Twenty-six

Aldo dropped to the floor behind the table. It would not conceal his presence if anyone came in, but might be enough of a shield if they remained in the doorway. What if they locked the door while he was still inside? The prospect of getting out through the shutters and climbing down to the ground while wearing only a thin silk robe was not one Aldo savoured.

'Cassandra!' a distant voice called.

'Dio in paradiso,' Cassandra muttered on the other side of the door. She raised her voice to reply. 'What is it, Rafaella?'

'I can't find any wax for polishing these chairs.'

'The wax is where it always is,' Cassandra replied with exasperation, her footsteps striding away from the ufficio. 'I will come and show you. Again.'

Aldo folded the torn document in half, and half again before tucking it inside his robe to read later. Better to leave while he had the chance. Once Cassandra was stamping down the stairs, Aldo slipped out of the ufficio and locked the door again. He hurried back to the bedchamber, laying the borrowed robe back across the chair. Footsteps came up the stairs as he was getting into the bed.

'How are you?' Cassandra asked after tapping at the door.

'Better,' Aldo replied, sitting up as she came in. 'But embarrassed and foolish about what happened. Saul told me I should be wearing a hat in this heat.'

'Always listen to a doctor, especially a Jewish one,' Cassandra agreed. She pressed the back of her hand to Aldo's forehead. 'You are still very warm.'

'It will pass,' he replied. 'Thank you for letting me rest here. I would have come downstairs sooner, but I don't seem to have any clothes . . .'

'I washed them and put them outside to dry. They'll be ready by now.'

'How long was I asleep?'

'Quite some time. Signor Ruggerio will be here soon.'

Aldo nodded. 'Then I had better get dressed.'

Cassandra reached for the robe but Aldo remembered the folded document was still inside it. 'I prefer my own clothes,' he said.

'Of course.' She smiled. 'I'll get them for you.'

Once Cassandra had left the bedchamber Aldo grabbed the robe. The torn document fell on the floor, in plain view. As Aldo retrieved it, he noticed ink on the document's reverse, that text so faded it was impossible to read in meagre light. He stuffed the document into his boot for safekeeping. Twice, he had escaped discovery. There would not be a third time.

Strocchi positioned the Otto's men in pairs on the major roads leading to the front entrance of Palazzo Medici. Two stood sentry on via Largo north of the ducal residence, to stop anyone coming from Piazza San Marco – that was simple enough. The approaches from south, east and west were harder to protect, but he posted pairs on each road with the remaining men nearer the palazzo to challenge those who slipped by the outer ring.

The duke's own guards were blocking the palazzo's entrances. For now, their presence seemed to be keeping the mob outside.

Two chants filled the fetid afternoon air – 'Savonarola lives!' and 'Bring down the duke!' – but the crowd made no move to act on that. They reminded Strocchi of the citizens who had gathered on Ponte alla Carraia and the other bridges the previous evening to witness Uccello's murder. But the proclamations telling them to come here had not been posted around the city. So how did they know to come here . . .?

Marco. The killer must have been moving among Savonarola's believers, urging them to gather and see the spirit of their beloved frate strike down another traitor. That meant he could be in the crowd now, inciting them to revolt against the duke.

Strocchi studied the throng, struggling to see beyond the faces of those closest to him. But the street in front of Palazzo Medici was choked with angry, chanting people – more than a hundred of them. It was impossible to see all the faces, not at ground level. If he could get inside the duke's residence, look down on the mob from above . . .

'Can you see him?' Manuffi asked. He had stayed by Strocchi's side to help position the sentries. Manuffi was not the brightest of men, but he was popular with the guards and constables. They seemed to appreciate his lack of guile and ambition. Manuffi meant what he said and always believed the best of others. Strocchi had been the same not long ago, but working for the Otto had stripped away such innocence. It made him a better law enforcer, yet he still regretted the loss of who he used to be.

'No,' Strocchi admitted. 'If Marco is in this mob, he will be hiding his face.'

'But where else could he be?'

That was another quality of Manuffi that Strocchi appreciated, the ability to ask simple questions. Sometimes it was helpful to consider the obvious. Where would Marco go if not here? The day had been so hurried and Strocchi so tired, he'd had no time to consider the implications of other discoveries. The proclamations threatening the life of the duke had taken precedence, but something else from Palazzo Uccello had been itching at Strocchi, demanding attention. Marco was employed after being recommended by Ruggerio.

Why would Ruggerio risk his reputation – probably the thing about which he cared most – by vouching for a servant who proved to be a killer? Either the silk merchant had been unaware of Marco's murderous plans . . . or Ruggerio had placed Marco in Palazzo Uccello as a servant for that very purpose. Aldo had been so sure Ruggerio was not responsible for Dovizi being burned alive, that certainty was compelling. But Aldo had been wrong about other things in the past. Santo Spirito! What if Ruggerio was behind all of this?

'Manuffi, I need you to keep an eye on all our men,' Strocchi said. 'Can you do that?'

The constable nodded.

'Good.' Strocchi glanced at the relentless sun roasting all those foolish enough to be outside. 'Keep visiting each pair, make sure they take turns to get out of this heat.'

'I will.'

'Grazie.' Strocchi strode away, heading east.

'Where are you going?' Manuffi shouted, struggling to be heard above the chanting.

'Palazzo Ruggerio,' Strocchi called back. 'I'll be back as soon as I can!'

You watch him leaving, the same officer who was at Ponte alla Carraia. You cannot be certain, but you hear two words he shouts: 'Palazzo

Ruggerio'. You wonder why is he going there, what does he hope to find? Does he seek something that could stop you?

You do not know the answer, so you set that aside.

You look at those all around you.

Chanting.

Bellowing.

Punching fists in the air.

Their faces red from the sun and the heat.

Adding fuel to their frustration.

They will not leave here.

Not without seeing what they crave.

Another sign, another death.

'Savonarola lives!' they scream into the air.

Do they truly believe in a dead monk?

Many of those around you may have been alive in his time.

But some are too young for that.

'Bring down the duke!'

They have bloodlust in their faces.

They crave someone to blame.

Someone to hate.

'Bring down the duke!'

It will not be curfew for several hours.

You move to the edge of the mob, still chanting with those around you.

But you have something else to do.

This is not over, not yet.

Once he was dressed, Aldo went downstairs to the ground level of the villa. The shutters and doors were all open, warm afternoon breezes drifting through, bringing the scent of distant woodsmoke and the sounds of insetti. Cassandra almost collided with Aldo as she emerged from the kitchen, still talking to those inside. 'No, Rafaella, you need to—'

'Forgive me,' Aldo said, stepping out of her way.

The housekeeper frowned. 'Why should I? You've done nothing to forgive.'

'You have all of this to prepare. Looking after a foolish visitor can't have helped.'

'It was no trouble,' Cassandra insisted. 'Do you have every—?' A loud crash from the kitchen interrupted her. 'Rafaella, put those down before you break any more.' Cassandra shook her head, but still had a smile for Aldo.

'I will see you later,' he said, leaving her to deal with the young woman. Aldo strolled out of the villa to the courtyard, the torn document in his right boot rubbing against his ankle. He went to the stables but they stood empty, there was no sign of Vincenzo. If the stable hand was helping bring Ruggerio's things to the villa, it would probably be early evening before he returned. Even when travelling in haste, Ruggerio was too proud and too vain a man to be without a considerable collection of his clothes and most treasured possessions.

Aldo was leaving when something caught his eye. A small brazier stood by the far door, a few wisps of smoke curling upwards into the air. There had been a fire inside the metal cage earlier that day. He went closer but found little besides ashes and charred ends of wood. There was a scrap of paper on the ground close by, most of it blackened by the fire. Aldo crouched for a closer look, seeing the curl of letter – was that an S? He picked up the paper and it crumbled to ash in his fingers.

Putting a knee to the ground, he looked closer at the brazier. Something metal beneath the charred wood glinted. Aldo stood up and knocked the brazier over, stamping the embers as they fell out to prevent them starting a fresh fire. Yes, there it was, a small metal pot. Whatever had been inside was gone, taken by the flames, but black spots marked the outer surface, burnt into place: ink. It seemed Vincenzo had been eager to destroy papers and an inkpot. But why now? Aldo had his suspicions . . .

He sauntered down the dirt road towards San Jacopo al Girone, tall Cypress trees sheltering him from the sun. Once out of sight from the villa, he stopped and crouched to remove the torn document from his boot. Aldo sat down on the grass, his back against a tree trunk. Yes, this was definitely the same document that the founders had stored in the convent. The writing on one side matched what he'd found on that torn corner while investigating Galeri's murder. Now, at last, Aldo could read and understand the complete text:

By Order of Girolamo Savonarola, the holders of this document have the authority to search any and all homes for sinful objects. They shall be given every assistance and the full co-operation of anyone subjected to scrutiny by them. Refusing to permit the holders of this document into a residence will be an admission of guilt. Those without sin have nothing to hide and so have no reason to deny entry to the undersigned.

Below the text five names were written, each by a different hand:

Girolamo Ruggerio   *Benozzo Scarlatti*
Luca Uccello
Roberto Ghiberti   *Sandro Dovizi*

Finally, beneath their names, Savonarola had signed the document himself.

It was much as Aldo had expected. The monk must have written dozens of similar authorizations for his Fanciulli, sending young men out to confront and accuse the citizens of Florence. It was folly, placing power in the hands of those not old enough to know better.

Aldo recalled Scarlatti's drunken admissions to Federica about doing the Lord's work, how he'd only followed what the others did to be their friend. Scarlatti had believed himself damned for those sins. The five did things in Savonarola's name that had haunted Scarlatti for more than forty years, acts that no amount of confession or charity could undo. But what had the five done, and why was it leading to their murders now?

Aldo turned the document over. The writing on the reverse was so faded it was easy to miss. So faint were the markings, Aldo struggled to make out what was on the page. There was a date at the top of the document, but the day and month were missing. Aldo had not noticed any writing on the back of the torn corner he had found at the convent.

Only a year remained at the top of this document: 1498. All five founders had signed their names below the year, but in hands far less bold and certain than on the other side. Aldo held the document up in the sunlight, squinting to discern the text. Too many words and phrases were beyond him, but he could read enough to construct their meaning:

The five of us hereby . . . confess to our sins . . . and beg the forgiveness of . . .

We believed . . . the heretic monk . . . and led us . . . in his name.

On the night of . . . we went to . . . accusing those within . . . their daughter . . . but would not allow us . . .

We ... what we believed ... but it was a crime ... all of us ... on orders from the heretic ...

We plead for forgiveness ... immunity ... mercy on our souls ...

Much as Aldo stared, he could make out no more words with certainty. The other text might be lost, but the document's significance was clear. Not long before Savonarola's execution the five Fanciulli – Ruggerio, Scarlatti, Uccello, Ghiberti and Dovizi – stood accused of committing crimes against citizens of Florence. The youths had forced their way into the home of a famiglia. What happened there was missing, but it seemed to involve a daughter. Aldo could imagine the rest. To save themselves, the five struck a bargain with the authorities. They accused Savonarola of heresy, of ordering them to commit sins in his name. In return for evidence against the monk, the five escaped justice, while Savonarola burned.

No wonder Ruggerio and the others never wanted this document seen.

It proved the five were willing to betray their own beliefs to escape punishment. It made clear they could not be trusted. Worse still, it proved they were cowards, sacrificing and condemning Savonarola to save themselves.

Such a document would have destroyed the reputations of each man as they grew up. In Florence, reputation was among the most valuable commodities. It required years of nurturing and protection, yet would be swept away in moments by such an admission of guilt.

No wonder people had died for this document.

No wonder men had been murdered.

How had the five come to possess this document? It should have been kept in the city archives. One of them must have secured the poisonous piece of paper, by means legal or otherwise – probably the latter, knowing Ruggerio and his fellow founders. But that asked another question: why had the five men kept it? Why not destroy the document once it was in their possession? Aldo had pondered these questions before while investigating Galeri's murder. Back then he had not known the full significance of what was on this torn paper. But the same answer still seemed credible.

None of the five dared to use the document as a weapon because it would assure their own destruction, as well as that of their fellow founders. All were equally implicated by the text. Yet none of them trusted the others enough to put this weapon beyond use. So long as it was kept from view, it could harm none of them. It bound the five men together for decades, kept together by their crimes, by their sin.

But something had changed in the spring of the previous year. Convinced the convent was no longer a place of safekeeping, Ruggerio had made efforts to remove the document. That led to the convent's dissolution, and the document's disappearance, which drove a fearful Scarlatti out of Florence. Terrified of what would happen if the truth emerged, he retired to the dominion. Scarlatti had no idea the document was locked in a chest, less than a mile from where he slept . . . Less than a mile from where he would die.

Aldo folded the page back into a small square and returned it to his boot. The fact that Ruggerio had possessed the document for the past year shone a fresh light on these killings. The silk merchant had nothing to fear from the other founders, they could not harm him anymore. But he could choose to attack them without fear of repercussion. Was Ruggerio responsible for the murders? There was no way to be certain, not without looking him in the eyes and asking. Ruggerio would never confess, but his response might speak for him . . .

* * *

Strocchi approached Palazzo Ruggerio expecting to have his patience tested. Like Bindi, the silk merchant seemed to rejoice in playing games with visitors, making them wait at his whim. At least it would be cooler inside the merchant's grand residence than it would be sweltering on the street while heat-crazed citizens shouted at the sky. Yet when Strocchi arrived, Ruggerio's maggiordomo was wandering the palazzo courtyard, a man with seemingly little to do. That would not be the case if Ruggerio was present, which Alberti soon confirmed.

'He is riding to his country villa. He should arrive soon, if he is not there already.'

'Ruggerio has fled Florence?'

Alberti bristled. 'The signore has chosen to spend a few days at his estate – a perfectly understandable and quite sensible decision, in view of this intolerable heat. Summer arrives sooner and sooner with each passing year.'

Strocchi had no wish to discuss the weather. 'When will he be back?'

'The signore did not proffer a specific date for his return.'

'Meaning you don't know.'

'As I said, he left no date for his return.' Alberti's frustration at not having a better answer was all too apparent, but Strocchi still had one question to ask.

'The man who murdered Uccello was one of the banker's own servants.'

Alberti seemed to regain a little of his usual arrogance. 'That is common knowledge.'

'Less known is how the killer acquired his position among Uccello's staff,' Strocchi replied. 'I've been told he was employed on the recommendation of your signore.'

'Nonsense!' Alberti scowled. 'Whoever said that is a liar.'

'Are you denying Ruggerio recommended any servants to Uccello?'

'Of course. The signore never concerns himself with such matters. The hiring and dismissal of servants is beneath his notice.' The maggiordomo straightened his back, nose in the air. 'Perhaps this individual wrote a false recommendation, believing it would be taken on trust. But I am responsible for all matters involving servants within this palazzo. I have not recommended a servant to anyone else, and nor, to my knowledge, has the signore.'

'You're quite certain?'

'I'm certain about all matters concerning the signore.'

Strocchi smiled. 'Except when he might return from the countryside.'

That removed Alberti's superiority. 'I must ask you to leave. The signore is away from the city, but there is still much to be done.' He escorted Strocchi out into the sweltering late afternoon sun before slamming the palazzo doors.

Strocchi found Alberti's behaviour amusing, but his certainty that Ruggerio had not recommended Marco was compelling, even convincing. Yet the maggiordomo at Palazzo Uccello had been equally certain Ruggerio helped the killer get that position. The witnesses were in direct opposition, so both of them could not be correct. Their disagreement did not help to answer whether Ruggerio was responsible for the murders.

Not for the first time Strocchi wished he could seek Aldo's counsel. But the former officer was in the countryside— Of course! Aldo might not be in Florence, but his words were. Strocchi reached inside his tunic for the letter Dr Orvieto had brought. The paper was damp with sweat and difficult to open, but the writing was still legible. It read:

Carlo,

I hope you will not cast this aside, as Bindi probably shall with the letter I am sending him. You and I did not part on good terms, for which I apologize. Interfering in your case was a mistake, even if done with good intentions. I hope in time you will forgive me.

You should know that Dovizi's murder was not an isolated crime. Another founder of the Company of Santa Maria has been murdered out here in the dominion. The killer sought to make Benozzo Scarlatti's death appear accidental, his body consumed in a villa fire. But it is clear Scarlatti died several days before Dovizi was burned alive. The corpse was hidden to conceal when Scarlatti was killed. Thus his murderer could also be responsible for Dovizi's death – or there may be two killers, working together or independently.

There are too many questions that remain unanswered, but of this you can be certain: the founders of the Company of Santa Maria are being hunted, either by one of their own or by an outsider pursuing a vendetta against all five men. The way they are dying, the use of fire against them, suggests an element of ritual to the killings. By the time you read this more of the founders may be dead. If so, it confirms these suspicions.

I offer the following advice – do with it as you wish:

Ignore any new proclamations. Each one is a stratagemma intended to distract the duke and those investigating the murders. The spirit of a monk who died forty years ago is not responsible for these killings. It is the work of men, be it one man or more. You should keep a watch on the surviving founders. If any of them is behind this, he will be the last still alive. If someone else is hunting the founders, you know where the killer must strike next.

Lastly, Carlo, take care. The murderer has done his best not to hurt others so far, but as the circle closes he will become more desperate, take more risks to complete his work.

I would not wish to see you hurt, or Tomasia and Bianca left without you.

Cesare Aldo

Chapter Twenty-seven

*R*uggerio rode through San Jacopo al Girone, the village as dusty and dismal as ever. A few people emerged from their meagre homes to watch him pass, but most of their attention seemed to be on his four men and their weaponry. Ruggerio kept his head held high and his back straight, not bothering to acknowledge the villagers. Better to seem unaffected by the long journey from Florence. Better not to show any sign of age or weakness, though his body was sore and aching.

He would suffer for this in the morning. Most summers Ruggerio travelled to the villa by carriage. It was not comfortable, but better than hours atop a horse. His brisk decision to leave the city had not accounted for the fact that his carriage was still being repaired ahead of its usual journey at the end of June. And after what had happened to Uccello . . . Ruggerio was sure he would not be rushing to climb inside a carriage for quite some time.

Curse Ghiberti and his stubbornness. But for the time wasted attempting to make him see sense Ruggerio knew he would have arrived at the villa far earlier. Instead, he had ridden through the hottest hours of the day, forcing frequent stops to rest in the shade of a tree while the four mercenaries stood sentry around him. Now, finally, there remained only the trek up to reach the villa. Ruggerio's body ached to get off this horse.

He left the village behind, turning north onto the dirt track up the hill. But as he did so a lone figure stepped into Ruggerio's path, arms folded, a smirk on that face.

Cesare Aldo.

The last person Ruggerio wanted to meet right now.

The guard ahead of the horse stopped, aiming his pistol at Aldo. 'Step aside!'

'Of course,' Aldo replied, moving out of the way. 'I merely wish to welcome the signore back to San Jacopo al Girone. It's not often that such a significant individual graces this humble village with his presence.'

Ruggerio sighed. 'I come here every summer, as you well know.' He dug both heels into the horse, urging it forwards. The beast strolled on up the sloping track.

'I was referring to your significance in all these murders,' Aldo replied. He fell in step beside the horse, forcing the guard on Ruggerio's left to stay a few paces back.

'I had nothing to do with them.'

'With the murders . . . or with the victims? You knew all of them – Scarlatti, Dovizi, and now poor Uccello. You knew all of them very well indeed.'

Ruggerio pulled his horse to a halt again. 'I have no wish to hear whatever you wish to say, but know better than to believe you will desist. Speak, before I lose patience.'

'Grazie, signore.' Aldo gave a low, mocking bow. 'I had long wondered what bound the five founders of your confraternity together. Some of you were rivals, but most possessed no obvious connection. But now I know that your alliance was formed while all five of you were members of Savonarola's Fanciulli.'

Ruggerio dismissed this with a wave of his hand. 'That is a matter of no consequence. We were five among hundreds, even thousands, of young men in the Fanciulli.'

'But how many of those formed an alliance that bound them together for decades? Until these murders began, of course. Now only two of you are still alive . . .'

'Is there some point to your prattling?'

'I merely wished to congratulate you on escaping the attentions of this killer. I would have said you were wise to leave Florence, but that did not save Scarlatti.'

'Grazie for your fatuous wishes, and goodbye.' Ruggerio urged his horse forward.

This time Aldo did not follow, instead he called a few final words from where he stood. 'Consequences catch up to us all one day!'

Ruggerio snapped his reins, quickening the horse's pace. The four men around him broke into a run to keep up, but he did not care. They were mercenaries, being well paid to protect him at the cost of their own discomfort. Only when he was round a bend in the road and unable to be seen did Ruggerio slow the horse back to a gentle stroll.

There was something different about Aldo. He had been a pale shadow of himself at their last meeting in Florence, despite the country sun having darkened his face and hands. He'd blundered into the palazzo, making accusations without evidence, asking questions for which he did not seem to already know the answers. But this Aldo had a twinkle of mischief in his gaze, ready to slide a barbed aside into their exchanges. This Aldo knew more than he was saying. This was the Aldo of old, the man who had given Ruggerio such trouble.

It was almost a pleasure to see him restored.

Almost.

* * *

301

Bindi had remained at Palazzo Medici, rather than return to the Podestà. There seemed little value in going back to the Otto when the court was not sitting. Not when all of the court's available men had been ordered to stand sentry on the streets approaching the ducal residence. Besides, the prospect of attempting to leave was not enticing, not when it meant fighting through a mob of chanting men and women.

No. Discretion and common sense made good partners in most things, and this was no exception. Yet remaining at the palazzo was also far from satisfactory. Bindi had retreated to Campana's small ufficio. It was a cramped space, the air stifling even with both shutters wide open. Campana kept hurrying back and forth to the duke's adjoining ufficio, pallid face becoming ruddy, the air ripe with his body odour. Eventually, the duke went elsewhere in the palazzo, allowing Campana to collapse into the chair behind his plain wooden table. Bindi waited for his counterpart to recover a little before asking about the mob outside.

'Their number has grown no larger,' Campana said. 'We can thank your men for stopping any more of Savonarola's believers joining them.'

The segretario bowed his head a little, accepting the praise.

'Before, when we were with the duke looking down at the mob,' Campana went on, 'I noticed a change in your face. As if another notion had occurred to you.'

'Indeed?' Bindi kept his face impassive. Little escaped the duke's private segretario. No wonder Cosimo kept him close. Such perceptiveness was a valuable weapon.

'Yes. His Grace was talking about the heat making matters worse. He said it would take a rainstorm to put an end to this madness, but there was no sign of that coming. You looked as if you wished to say something, but held your tongue instead.'

Bindi nodded. 'It is true, an idea did come to me, but—'

'But what?'

'It is not without risk for the duke.'

'Everything His Grace does comes with risk, or a price to be paid. Share your notion. If it has as much merit as your other suggestions, we shall both take it before the duke. He and he alone will decide whether to pursue it.'

Bindi hesitated a moment. He had no wish to be thought a fool, but Campana was always discreet. 'Very well. When our city has faced great trials in the past – plague, war, flooding, pestilence, even droughts similar to this one – it has turned to the Church for help.'

'The Church is what brought about this madness,' Campana replied.

'The teachings and preaching of one monk led to the madness outside,' Bindi said, 'that and those damned proclamations. No, I was referring to another part of this city's faith. For centuries the people have believed the Madre di Dio protects Florence from harm. They pray to her for help and guidance. When the city most needs her, the people pray to her image – and she grants their wishes.'

'You're talking about Our Lady of Impruneta.'

Bindi nodded. 'My mama told me about seeing the painting carried into Florence to ward off plague. Other cities suffered terribly but ours did not – and many believe it was praying to the Impruneta that saved them and their families.'

Campana frowned. 'The Impruneta has never been under the control of the Medici, not in all the years I can recall.'

'And that makes it the ideal solution,' the segretario said, leaning forward in his chair. 'Processing the Impruneta through the city gives everyone a symbol to whom they can pray for rain, whether or not they favour His Grace. If relief does not come, it will be the Impruneta who did not hear people's prayers. If the Madonna does give us rain, it shall be Cosimo who was humble enough to let a procession carry the Impruneta through the city.'

The duke's advisor put a finger to his lips, eyes narrowing. 'Where is this painting now?'

Cassandra helped Ruggerio down from his horse in the villa courtyard. The signore looked tired, far more than he usually did after the journey from Florence. His tunic was soaked with sweat and his legs almost gave way when they touched the ground. She kept him upright, one hand under his right arm for support. 'Thank you,' he said, keeping his voice to a whisper so the four mercenaries accompanying him would not hear.

'I have prepared the bedchamber you prefer,' Cassandra said, 'the one near the loggia. And a meal awaits if you are hungry.'

Ruggerio nodded before pulling himself upright to address his men. 'You did well today, and will be richly rewarded for that. Now I need you to stand sentry outside this villa, day and night. You shall work in pairs, with one pair on duty while the other rests. Nobody enters or leaves this building without my explicit permission. Is that clear?' The men nodded. 'I leave it to the four of you to determine who takes the first watch.'

'I will make beds above the stable for those resting,' Cassandra volunteered.

Ruggerio looked around. 'Is there someone who can take my horse?'

'I sent Vincenzo to help with the cart bringing your things,' Cassandra said. 'Perhaps you passed him on the road from Florence?'

'Perhaps,' the signore agreed. But she knew he would not have noticed a servant, believing few were worthy of his attention. Ruggerio gestured to the mercenaries. 'One of you men, take my mount into the stable. Make sure it is fed and watered.' With that he headed towards the villa, limping a little as he crossed the courtyard.

'How was your journey?' Cassandra asked, following him in.

'Long. Painful,' he muttered. 'These bones were not made for bouncing atop a horse.' That Ruggerio had chosen to ride all the way rather than hire a carriage told Cassandra how hurried his departure had been. The glimmer of fear in his eyes confirmed it. In all previous encounters with the signore, his self-assurance – no, his arrogance – had been a cloak around his shoulders, protecting him from harm. Now he resembled what he was: a man in his autumn years, aware of his own mortality. Ruggerio was afraid.

Once they were inside, Cassandra guided the signore to a comfortable chair and presented him with a cup of wine. 'I poured this earlier, as you prefer.'

Ruggerio took a long, appreciative drink. 'From the year before last's harvest, yes?'

Even when in fear of his life, few things escaped him. 'Yes, signore.'

He took a smaller sip, his gaze fixed on her. Cassandra remained still, waiting for him to speak. 'I encountered Cesare Aldo on my way up the hill,' Ruggerio eventually said. 'He seemed full of his own importance, even more so than when he was an officer in Florence.'

Cassandra nodded. 'Aldo does enjoy displaying what authority he has.'

'Did he mention being demoted to constable?'

'No. He didn't.'

'That's not a surprise. Only a fool announces his own diminishing.'

Ruggerio sipped more wine. 'I knew he would be here, of course, but I expected him to be less . . . Aldo.'

Cassandra told the signore about events earlier that day: Aldo running between the estates, and collapsing from the heat. 'I let him rest in one of the guest bedchambers for a few hours this afternoon.' Ruggerio would learn of that sooner or later. Better he heard it from her at the earliest opportunity. 'I hope you do not mind, sir.'

The signore narrowed his eyes. 'I trust your judgement with such matters when I am not in residence,' Ruggerio said, but his tone promised there would be a price to pay. He rose from the chair. 'Well, shall we go to the loggia so I can look out over all of my domain?' It was what he always said upon arriving at the estate. The words seemed to amuse him.

She followed him up the stairs, remaining a respectful distance behind. He took more time than usual, but that was no surprise after a long journey atop an unfamiliar horse. When they reached the upper level Ruggerio paused, as if catching his breath. But Cassandra noted his gaze was not on the loggia, but a doorway close by. After a moment Ruggerio strode towards it, his exhaustion gone. He reached for the door but it did not open.

'Locked,' Ruggerio said.

'As always,' she replied, joining him by the door.

'Has it been unlocked today?'

'Once, when I went inside to clean. But I was alone, and none of the women from the village came in. They know better than to go where it is not allowed.' Ruggerio stared at her again. Another test. Even when the signore relied on another person, his reserve always remained. Ruggerio's trust only extended as far as his own shadow. 'Your message said a cart would be bringing your things. Is Alberti accompanying that?'

'No,' Ruggerio replied. 'I told him to remain in the city. I'm undecided how long I shall be staying. Better that he remain behind and watch over the palazzo in Florence for now. I can always summon him, if needed.'

Cassandra was grateful the signore had not brought his maggior-domo. Alberti was as irritating as an insetto bite, always insisting he knew best what Ruggerio wanted and needed. 'Very good, sir.' She followed him out to the loggia. The sun was dipping towards the hills, painting the sky in pinks and yellows, the first gentle evening breezes easing away the heat of the day. Yet it seemed to bring Ruggerio no joy. Instead, he stared across at Scarlatti's estate.

'Your last message said Aldo found proof that poor, timid Benozzo was killed days before the fire. It seems the blaze was an attempt to hide what happened to him?'

'Yes, signore. Aldo brought a Jewish physician from the city to examine Signor Scarlatti's body. He found the broken neck.'

'But Aldo has yet to discover who was responsible?'

'Correct, signore.'

Ruggerio frowned. 'Remarkable that nobody else died in the blaze.'

'Aldo seems to believe that was the killer's intention. They waited until all the servants were at a special service down in the village before starting the fire. I was still here, so I saw the fire and sent your estate workers to help fight it.'

'They seemed to have saved most of the buildings.'

'The villa was lost,' Cassandra replied, 'but the rest remain undamaged.'

Ruggerio nodded. 'Excellent news. Scarlatti's villa was always a blight on the landscape, disturbing my view back to the city. When all of this is over, I intend to buy that land. Owning it would give me both hillsides, doubling the expanse of my estate.'

He glanced at Cassandra. 'But not a word of that to anyone else.'

'Of course, signore.'

'Good.' He inhaled deeply, his hunched shoulders easing a little. 'Perhaps I will have something to eat. Bring a selection of whatever you have ready.'

'Do you wish to eat here on the loggia?'

'Yes.' Ruggerio smiled. 'I believe so.'

Cassandra bowed before retreating back inside to fetch his meal. The signore had known Scarlatti for decades yet he showed no sign of mourning for the dead man. It was as if Ruggerio had not a single bone of compassion in his body.

The worst of the heat had passed as Strocchi strode back towards Palazzo Medici. Afternoon was drifting towards evening, taller buildings casting long shadows as the sun made its slow, lazy descent. The street was crowded with people going home or rushing to reach the mercato before the final stalls closed for the day. The air was sweltering, thick with the stench of sweat and stale piss. Better that than burning flesh.

Strocchi dismissed the memory of Uccello burning alive. He concentrated on Aldo's letter instead, those closing sentences. How could Aldo be so certain the proclamations were a strategia? He had not been in the city for days, hadn't seen what happened to Uccello . . . Strocchi wanted to dismiss the advice as mistaken, Aldo unable to stop himself meddling, but some small part wondered if he was correct. Not about previous proclamations, but about the pages Marco had left beneath his mattress.

When he'd departed the palazzo for the last time, Marco must have known he would never be able to return – not if his plan to murder Uccello was successful. Yet the killer made no attempt to hide his face or conceal who he was. Had Marco left the papers behind so they would be discovered? The implied threat to Cosimo's life demanded an immediate and overwhelming response. The previous duke had ignored such a threat and paid for it in blood, so Cosimo would not make the same mistake. What better way to distract the Otto from hunting for Marco than by forcing the court to protect the duke?

Accept that and—

Strocchi collided with a man hurrying in the opposite direction, knocking both out of their stride. Strocchi staggered a little, turning to apologize for being so distracted. The other man glared back, the hood of his woollen cloak falling to reveal his face. He had no beard and most of his hair had been cut off, but Strocchi knew those intense eyes.

'Marco!'

The killer lashed out at Strocchi, sending him stumbling back into a nearby woman. Marco dashed away into the crowd. Recovering himself, Strocchi ran after him but the killer disappeared round a corner. By the time Strocchi reached it, Marco was gone.

Cursing, Strocchi returned to the stricken woman. She refused his help, spitting a stream of obscenities before stamping away towards Palazzo Medici. Strocchi stood in the street, watching her leave. Marco had been coming from the ducal residence. That suggested the killer had been in the mob outside the palazzo. The collision did make one thing certain: Marco was not at Palazzo Medici now. That suggested the duke was not his target . . .

If Marco was stalking the founders, only one remained in the city:

Roberto Ghiberti.

Strocchi twisted round to stare in the direction Marco had been hurrying. The street went south, towards the Arno. But an imposing residence at the far end blocked any view of the river. Strocchi had been there the previous day while keeping watch on Uccello.

This street led directly to Palazzo Ghiberti.

Strocchi started running.

Chapter Twenty-eight

Aldo waited in the shade of the tall cypress trees that lined the steep road to Ruggerio's villa. Evening breezes were caressing the branches, the sweltering air becoming less oppressive. The constant sounds of insetti were changing too, becoming less insistent, blending into other noises around them. Once the sun set, a welcome coolness would replace its heat. If the cart bearing Ruggerio's things was to arrive before nightfall, it would have to hurry.

Teasing Ruggerio had been a pleasure. It was too long since Aldo had enjoyed such an encounter, hinting at what he knew while keeping that secret close. It would nag and gnaw at Ruggerio, because he could not bear being ignorant. No, it was more that Ruggerio despised others knowing more about something that mattered to him. By the morning, Ruggerio would send a servant inviting Aldo up to the villa, perhaps even inviting him to a meal. The veil of civility masking the blade of questions.

Aldo worried a little that he had gone too far in his hints and taunts. Linking the five founders back to the Fanciulli, it risked sending Ruggerio to his ufficio to ensure the torn document was still safe. When he discovered the lock was broken, the document gone . . . It was not difficult to know how Ruggerio would react if word of what he and the other founders had done more than forty years ago became common knowledge in Florence.

There would be anger in the Senate, threats to expel Ruggerio from the guild. Some of his suppliers might withhold business, while sales of his silk would suffer. But it would be a summer storm to Ruggerio, a brief deluge at worst. The palle on that man were such that he would brazen it out, denying the truth written in faded ink. When the evidence was put in front of him, Ruggerio would argue it had been taken out of context, or that others had done much the same as him and his fellow Fanciulli when Savonarola was under attack.

If Ruggerio truly believed himself in peril, he would offer a humble apology, appear to throw himself on the mercy of others. There would be an announcement about how sorry he was for the anger his past actions had caused. A solemn speech before the Senate on how he had been a much younger man at the time, how he had learned from such follies. If necessary, Ruggerio would retreat from view so tempers could cool and fury fade. Perhaps some charitable works, with eager and well-paid friends whispering in the right ears about Ruggerio's generosity and his eagerness to help without anyone knowing.

Eventually the journey to redemption would be complete. Ruggerio's business would recover any lost revenue, his status within the guild would be restored, and those who had stood by him would be rewarded. If anything, his reputation for ruthlessness might be enhanced by revelations about his youthful actions. A man willing to betray someone so powerful as Savonarola . . . That was a man to be respected.

Or at least feared.

It was the Florentine way. Those with enough wealth or influence could endure what would destroy those less fortunate, those less privileged. The Medici were proof of that, if any was needed. More than once the family had been driven from power by rebellion and republicans, by assassins and insurrection. But like a plant that cannot be vanquished unless torn out by the roots, so it was with the Medici. Members of that bloodline always returned to restore themselves. The family's fate was inexorably intertwined with that of Florence.

Ruggerio did not have the power of the Medici, but those who turned against him inevitably suffered for it. And whoever dared bring the silk merchant's secret to light – they would suffer most of all. Ruggerio would make certain of that.

Aldo knew he must tread carefully from now on.

The sound of cart wheels scraping on dirt announced the approach of Ruggerio's possessions. Two horses were working hard to haul the heavily laden cart up from San Jacopo al Girone, accompanied by three men. One was a guard, armed with an arquebus. The other two were the cart driver, and an apprentice walking beside the horses. But there was no sign of Vincenzo, the stable hand from Ruggerio's villa.

Aldo fell in step with the cart, introducing himself before asking about Vincenzo.

'Never heard of him,' the driver replied, his voice that of a true Florentine. He jabbed a thumb at the cartload of trunks and crates behind him. 'The three of us brought this lot all the way from Palazzo Ruggerio. We saw a few travellers on the road, but no Vincenzo.'

Aldo thanked the driver for his time and let them roll ahead. Once the cart was out of sight, Aldo strolled back down the hill. There were several possible reasons why Vincenzo had not met the cart on its way from the city. The stable hand could have been attacked by banditi, though few bothered with the eastern road before June when wealthy merchants came from the city to enjoy their country estates. Cassandra might have lied about sending

Vincenzo to help with the cart, but Aldo had seen no duplicity in her words or deeds. Vincenzo could have chosen to leave Ruggerio's employ but, again, there was nothing to support that conclusion.

Or it was Vincenzo who had murdered Scarlatti.

Aldo stopped, letting that possibility glint and gem and whisper.

Vincenzo was familiar enough in the area to have gone to the dead man's estate without drawing attention. He had the strength to strangle Scarlatti, and to move the corpse unaided in a handcart. He had reason to lie about the supposed itinerant cooper, creating a suspect to divert attention. And it was Vincenzo who went back and forth to Florence, carrying messages. That gave him the opportunity to kill Dovizi and return to the estate.

But there had been another murder in the city while Vincenzo was out here in the dominion. That suggested two killers, one in Florence and Vincenzo in the countryside. Were they working together towards a common purpose? Yes, that made sense. Vincenzo's visits to Florence gave a chance to meet his counterpart, to plot and plan, to prepare for their attacks.

Now Vincenzo was gone, missing from Ruggerio's estate. Had he fled to escape capture? Or was he close by, watching and waiting for an opportunity to strike. If so, that target would not be easily killed, not while Ruggerio kept four mercenaries around him.

Vincenzo's disappearance signified something else.

The endgame was already being played.

The evening breeze strengthened, making Aldo shiver a little.

Ruggerio might be safe for now, but what of the other surviving founder? He was for somebody else to protect. Hopefully Strocchi had read the letter Saul had taken back to Florence, otherwise Ghiberti could soon be dead.

* * *

Strocchi was gasping by the time he reached Palazzo Ghiberti, exhausted from fighting his way through people on the street. As he rushed and pushed and shoved, Strocchi searched the faces of those around him, looking for Marco . . . but the killer was nowhere to be seen.

The main entrance to Palazzo Ghiberti was closing, the huge wooden doors being pushed shut from within. Strocchi pushed himself through the narrowing gap.

'Signor Ghiberti . . . is in danger!' he shouted, startling the guard who had been closing the doors. 'Didn't you . . . hear me? Signor Ghiberti is in danger. Go . . . fetch your master!'

The guard scuttled away, giving Strocchi a chance to catch his breath. Ghiberti's maggiordomo Uzzano soon appeared from an archway. He stopped, arching an eyebrow. 'You were here a few days ago.'

'My name is Carlo Strocchi and I am an officer of the Otto. I believe a murderer plans to attack Signor Ghiberti. When was the last time someone entered this building?'

'I'm sorry, but I don't—'

'When was the last time someone came in here?' Strocchi demanded, advancing on Uzzano. The maggiordomo stepped back, blinking in surprise.

'Nobody has,' he replied. 'Not since Ruggerio visited here earlier, full of warnings. That's why the signore told me to have a man standing sentry.' Uzzano glanced at the guard. 'No one has come here, have they?'

The guard shook his head.

Strocchi studied the palazzo interior. Ghiberti had been wise to hire a guard, but grand residences always had multiple entrances. 'Where do deliveries come into the building?'

'Large deliveries enter via the gates behind you,' Uzzano said.

'There's another door on the east side, leading out to a narrow alleyway . . .' He sniffed. 'But only servants use that.'

Strocchi almost laughed at the man's arrogance. 'It was a servant who murdered Luca Uccello! Where is this door? Show me!' Uzzano led the way across the internal courtyard. Strocchi followed, calling back at the guard to bolt the main entrance shut. 'Nobody gets in or out of this palazzo. Nobody!'

It had been Bindi's suggestion that he and Campana go to the small church where Our Lady of Impruneta was kept in the northern quarter, not far from Porta San Gallo. A request to have the revered painting carried through Florence was more likely to receive a sympathetic hearing, he argued, if the duke's own advisor asked in person, supported by the segretario of the Otto. This would demonstrate how important the Impruneta was to both men, how important it was to the whole city.

The cleric responsible for looking after the Impruneta did not agree. Monsignor Testardo had once been well regarded by the Archbishop of Florence but had fallen from favour the previous year for reasons Bindi had been unable to uncover. The segretario suspected it must be linked to the dissolution of the Convent of Santa Maria Magdalena. Testardo had led an ill-fated visitation there, with one of his men suffering grievous wounds while inside the convent. Unfortunately for the monsignor, that same man was a blood relative of one of the Archbishop's closest advisors. Now Testardo, who might once have aspired to becoming Archbishop, was spending his days being caretaker for a revered painting in a small church.

'This holy image is not a stratagemma for the duke to deploy at his whim,' the monsignor said, jabbing a finger at the painting.

'The Impruneta is brought forth in times of greatest hardship, when the people of this city need her most. Whatever troubles and difficulties His Grace may face, they do no merit moving the painting.'

'We do not ask on behalf of the duke,' Campana said, his voice hushed, respectful. 'We ask for the citizens of Florence. The Madonna of Santa Maria Impruneta has been carried through the streets to ward off plague, war, flooding, pestilence – and drought. You know how the city has suffered these past weeks from this intolerable heat. Out in the dominion crops are failing, and it is not yet June. Florence is already facing a drought. If the weather does not change, that could become a famine.'

The sour-faced monsignor glared, his mood unchanged. Bindi had not realized this cleric was so against the Medici. Something else had to be done, or all would be lost. 'Monsignor, may I have a word with you in private?'

Testardo regarded him with suspicion, but gave a curt nod. Bindi led the cleric away from Campana so that the duke's man could not hear their whispers.

'Processing the Impruneta through the city gives everyone a symbol to which they can pray for rain,' Bindi said, 'whether or not they favour His Grace. This holy painting has never been a tool of the Medici and their supporters, the Palleschi. Should rain not come, people will know it was not because the Impruneta did not hear their prayers. Instead, they will blame the duke and his kin. But if the Madonna does bless us with rain – and I pray that she shall take mercy on all of us sinners – everyone will know it was the Church that was responsible for her beneficence. The duke is ready to humble himself before the Impruneta. Grant permission, and His Grace shall be much in the Church's debt.'

Testardo removed his zucchetto to sweep a hand across his

greying hair. 'This church has been home to the Impruneta for more than a century, but suffers from a leaking roof and crumbling plaster. Other leaders of Florence have called upon the Madonna to protect our city, yet few have been eager to pay for repairs that would ensure the Impruneta remains safe and undiminished by weather or worse . . .'

Bindi nodded. 'I'm certain the young duke would wish to make amends for such past . . . omissions. Generously so.'

'Then, perhaps, the Madonna could be processed tomorrow,' the monsignor replied.

The segretario beamed. 'All of Florence thanks you,' he replied. Bindi was grateful that Campana would have the delicate task of explaining the cost for all of this to the duke.

Strocchi was relieved to see the side door of Palazzo Ghiberti closed. Uzzano opened it so Strocchi could look outside. A dark, narrow alley ran along the external wall of the palazzo. At the northern end was the street where citizens were hurrying by; at the southern end stood a tall stone wall. 'What's beyond that?'

'The Arno. Signor Ghiberti had it built to slow the waters when the river floods.' Uzzano was peering at the door he had opened, confusion in his eyes.

'What is it?' Strocchi asked.

'I was wondering why this door was closed. It's always open during the day . . .'

Santo Spirito! Strocchi pulled the side door shut again. 'Signor Ghiberti, where is he?'

'Why do you ask?'

'Because the man intent on killing him is already here! Tell me, where is Ghiberti?'

'On the middle level,' Uzzano stammered. 'In his office.'

'Where's that?' Strocchi demanded.

'Go up the main stairs and turn right . . . It's the third door on the left . . .'

Strocchi ran as fast as he could, hoping against hope he could get there before Marco. He had the advantage of knowing where Ghiberti was, but Marco was already inside the palazzo. How did the killer get past Ghiberti's servants? Perhaps he had pretended to be a messenger, bringing a letter – but that didn't matter now.

Reaching the main staircase Strocchi raced upwards, taking two steps at a time. 'Signor Ghiberti!' he shouted with what breath he had. 'Signor Ghiberti!' No reply. Strocchi got to the middle level and sprinted along the hallway, counting the doors on his left.

One . . . two . . . three . . .

His boots nearly went out from under him. The floor outside the door was covered with something slippery. Was that oil? Strocchi tried the door but it did not give way.

'Signor Ghiberti, are you in there?' Strocchi shouted, hammering both fists on the woodwork. 'Signor Ghiberti, can you hear me? Make a noise if you can!'

No voices from beyond the door, no sound. Nothing.

Strocchi stepped back. 'I'm coming in! If you're close by, get out of the way!' Still he heard no response.

After making the sign of the cross, Strocchi charged the door.

You are striding towards Palazzo Ghiberti when you collide with a man hurrying the other way, knocking the hood of your cloak back. You glare at him, and realize it is the officer from Ponte alla Carraia. His eyes widen, and he calls out your name.

You lash out, send him stumbling into a woman. Both fall and you sprint away, fast as you can. You glance back, the officer is getting up. You can't keep going south, this road leads straight to your next target, so you dive round a corner.

You find shadows behind an oil seller's stall and drop to one knee, pulling the hood back over your head. The officer rushes past. You slip out behind him, taking a sealed jug of oil from the stall, and go south once more.

The officer cannot know where you are going.

But he might still guess . . .

You hurry onwards.

You see a guard standing in the main entrance of Palazzo Ghiberti but know another way in from visits with Signor Uccello, a side door down a narrow alley. You slip inside, shutting the door behind you.

You move through the residence, nodding to servants as they pass.

Ghiberti's officious maggiordomo is coming down the main stairs as you approach them. You fear he will know your purpose . . . But a shout from above takes his attention. He calls back to the gruff voice on the middle level, promising to return soon. Uzzano mutters as he continues down the steps before disappearing through an archway.

You venture upwards, retrieving the knife hidden in your boot, using that to open the sealed jug from the oil stall. You sniff what is inside. Yes, this will burn well.

You creep along the middle level halfway, listening for the gruff voice – Ghiberti's voice. He is not beyond the first two doors you open. Did you mishear? But then his voice bellows again, calling for Uzzano. The signore must be in the next chamber.

The door is ajar as you approach it, inviting you inside.

Fear flutters in your belly.

Dovizi and Uccello put up little fight.

Ghiberti is another matter, a fierce man, an angry man.

He will not die so easily. It is why you chose the others first.

You have only one chance to do this—

'Signor Ghiberti . . . is in danger!'

A shout from below makes you stop.

You know that voice. It is the officer from the street.

'Didn't you hear me? Signor Ghiberti is in danger. Go . . . fetch your master! Go!'

You hear footsteps and hushed voices, angry exchanges.

'When was the last time someone came in here?' the officer demands.

More murmurs you struggle to hear. One of the voices sounds like Uzzano.

'It was a servant who murdered Luca Uccello! Where is this door? Show me!' Footsteps hurry across the courtyard. 'Nobody gets in or out of this palazzo. Nobody!'

The footsteps die away, the officer and Uzzano going elsewhere.

The side door, which is always open.

The door that you shut.

They will know you are here.

There is no time left, not now.

You pour the oil over your head and clothes.

Discard the jug, it is of no use now.

Ghiberti calls from beyond the door.

'Uzzano, is that you?'

Gripping the knife, you step inside.

Strocchi's shoulder smashed into the door, pain lancing through him as the lock gave way, the door swinging open. His momentum carried him inside, sent him stumbling into Ghiberti's office. The stench of piss filled the air, choking Strocchi. He clenched a hand across nose and mouth, searching his surroundings for Marco and Ghiberti.

The ufficio was plain, no rich tapestries or frescoes adorning these walls. A sturdy wooden table dominated the chamber, simple wooden chairs on either side of it. But the one behind the table was tipped over. Blood was spattered across the papers on top of the table. Not enough for a mortal wound, but enough to know there had been violence.

Marco must have been here, threatening Ghiberti. Had the wool merchant refused to co-operate? That would explain the blood, a blade being used to convince him. But there was no sign of either man in the ufficio now, and the door had been locked. Marco had taken Ghiberti out of the ufficio. But where did they go?

Strocchi whirled round, searching for another— there. A door, secreted into one wall. Had it not been left slightly ajar, he might never have seen it. Strocchi dashed to the door, pulling it open. Beyond was a hidden passage leading towards the front of the palazzo. He hurried along the murky corridor, boots slipping on drips underfoot. Another door appeared ahead, light visible around its edges, inviting him closer. Strocchi wished for a blade or a weapon, but had none.

He reached the door at the far end of the passage, pushing it open.

Santo Spirito . . .

Marco stood by two tall, open shutters, pressing the tip of a dagger up into Ghiberti's chin. A steady trickle of blood ran down the wool merchant's neck, staining his plain tunic crimson. Strocchi could see more blood on Ghiberti's hands, probably wounds from defending himself. The front of his hose was darkened by dampness. Ghiberti's skin was ashen, sweat dripping from his face. He looked terrified, and with good reason.

But Marco . . . Marco was glistening. The killer shone in the light streaming between the shutters, his skin and tunic soaked with oil. He was grinning, eyes wide with excitement. Marco clutched a lantern in his left hand, the wick burning inside it. 'Tell him,' the killer urged Ghiberti. 'Tell him what you are. Confess your sins, and I might let you live.'

'I don't know what you mean,' Ghiberti said, his hands trembling.

'Yes, you do.' Marco pressed the dagger upwards, forcing the merchant's head further back. 'Tell him what you and the others did, all those years ago. Why you deserve this.'

Still Ghiberti shook his head. 'Please, no . . .'

'Tell him!' Marco roared.

Ghiberti was weeping now, his brutish manner lost.

Strocchi had to stop this, but couldn't see how. The two men were across the room and out of reach. If he lunged at them Ghiberti would be dead in moments. But the crazed gleam in Marco's face, the vehemence in his eyes . . . Ghiberti was not leaving this room alive.

'Marco, listen to me,' Strocchi said, keeping his voice an unthreatening murmur. 'Whatever this man did, whatever crimes he and the others committed . . . I can see they face justice for that. I'm an officer of the Otto. I can bring Ghiberti before the court on charges.'

'Why should that be any different now?' Marco asked, still glaring at his captive.

Strocchi frowned. 'They were accused before?'

'Tell him,' Marco hissed at Ghiberti. 'Or die where you stand.'

The wool merchant whimpered, his chin trembling against the dagger's point. 'We didn't mean to hurt anyone . . . We were young . . . The power that Savonarola gave us, it went to our heads . . . we never meant it to happen . . .'

'Liar!' Marco swiped his blade sideways across Ghiberti's neck. The merchant clutched at his throat, blood spurting out between his fingers. He gurgled, choking.

'They all stood accused before the court,' Marco snarled, casting his dagger aside. 'But the five of them escaped punishment by blaming their sins on Savonarola. He was burned alive . . . and they were granted immunity. Not one of them could ever be tried for their crimes . . . for their sins.'

Strocchi held up both hands. 'You don't have to do this.'

Marco pulled Ghiberti close to him, embracing the wool merchant. 'It's the only way to avenge what they did.' He held the lantern's flame to his oil-soaked tunic so it caught light.

'No!' Strocchi cried out—

But it was too late.

Flames engulfed Marco and Ghiberti, the two men becoming a twisting, writhing mass of fire and screams and burning. They staggered towards the open shutters . . .

Strocchi closed his eyes. He had seen one man tumble from such a height before.

Ghiberti's screams lasted a few moments, fading as the two men fell.

Then came fresh screams from those passing by below.

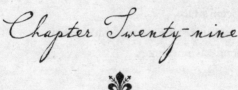

Chapter Twenty-nine

$\mathscr{S}$trocchi raced down the stairs inside Palazzo Ghiberti, hurrying by Uzzano as the maggiordomo demanded to know what had happened. By the time Strocchi reached the street outside, a crowd was already gathering where Marco and Ghiberti had fallen. Ghouls, eager to see what had happened.

'Clear the way,' Strocchi shouted, but none of them listened. He shoved through the throng, announcing himself as an officer of the Otto when anyone protested. Eventually he reached the two men, their burnt bodies lying at impossible angles, limbs bent in unnatural positions. The wool merchant was dead, his head twisted in a way that made Strocchi's belly weak. But Marco was still gasping his last through charred lips and bloody teeth.

Was he trying to say something?

Strocchi crouched over Marco, straining to hear him against the excited babble of voices from those standing close by. 'Shut up!' Strocchi snarled at them before leaning an ear nearer to Marco's mouth, trying not to breathe in the stench of burnt meat. 'What is it you want to tell me? I can send for a priest if you wish to make a last confession.'

'One more . . .' Marco rasped.

'One more? One more what?'

'One more . . .' Marco repeated between hacking coughs. 'One more . . . will die.' He coughed again, blood and spit flecking the side of Strocchi's face.

There was a dry rattle deep inside Marco.

Then there was nothing.

He was dead.

The sun was disappearing behind the hills as the cart left the estate. The driver, his apprentice and the guard had wasted no time unloading it and taking Ruggerio's things inside the villa, knowing they would not be staying overnight. Cassandra had arranged for them to sleep at a barn down in the village before returning to Florence in the morning.

When the cart was out of hearing Ruggerio told Cassandra to retire for the night. Making the villa ready at such short notice must have been challenging yet she had achieved it with her usual diligence. He was fortunate to have such a skilled housekeeper, a considerable improvement on her predecessors from the village. When in doubt, employ a Florentine. He might even consider making Cassandra his maggiordomo in Florence, should Alberti continue pouting and sulking. The behaviour was neither becoming nor entertaining.

Once Cassandra had descended to her room, Ruggerio went to his own bedchamber, retrieving a key from its hiding place. Taking a lit lantern, he unlocked his private ufficio and slipped inside. All was as he recalled, nothing out of place. The small chest sat atop his table, as did a neat stack of papers, two corners of the third document down still turned over.

Ruggerio strolled round the table to his chair. He reached beneath the table where a key was tucked inside a niche carved into the wood. But when Ruggerio slid that key into the lock of the small chest, he realized it was already open. Impossible. He always locked the chest whether he planned to be back within moments or not for months.

Ruggerio held the lantern closer to examine the lock. There were fresh scratches in the metal, a few days old at most. He dismissed the possibility that the women who'd come up from San Jacopo al Girone to prepare the villa might be to blame. They had no obvious reason to break into his chest, and limited opportunity. Nor was Cassandra a credible suspect. She possessed a key to the office, and had lived at the villa more than a year; her having forced the chest open in the last day or two seemed unlikely.

The one-armed thief – Lippo, that was his name – could be responsible. He had been watching the villa, observing it for someone eager to know the residence's vulnerabilities. Could Lippo have found a way inside, perhaps when Cassandra was busy in her walled garden behind the villa? Maybe. Yet the door would still be locked, and there was no sign that it had been interfered with or forced. Lippo had been a skilled pickpocket when he possessed two arms, but picking a lock with a single hand seemed unlikely.

That left one obvious suspect.

Ruggerio opened the small chest, pulling out all the papers to put them atop his table. Reports, letters, more reports . . . Gone. It was gone. The document he had laboured for so long to secure, the evidence that had threatened to undo him so many times . . . Taken.

Only one man would dare do this.

Aldo.

Curse that man and his impudent curiosity. No wonder he had been so smug when they met on the hillside. Aldo had the proof of what the five had done more than forty years ago. But he did not have all of it. The ink on the paper was faded, especially on its reverse. Ruggerio knew every word that had been written on it as if the ink was etched on his own skin. But time and sun had spirited most of the text away, leaving only hints behind. Enough for Aldo to guess the rest, but not enough to know. Not enough to be certain.

Ruggerio slumped in his chair. He could send two mercenaries to reclaim the document. Aldo would not give in without bloodshed. Killing an officer – no, a constable – of the Otto was likely to cause problems, but coin and whispers in the right ears would remedy that. Yet, were such measures necessary? Even if Aldo took the document to Florence, if he convinced the Otto to investigate further, what damage might that do? In truth, very little. Three of the others were already dead. Ghiberti might well have joined them by now. Besides, it was all so long ago. Who cared about the follies of five young men, led astray by the teachings of a mad monk? Most of Florence had been in thrall to Savonarola. Better for everyone to move on . . .

Yes, that would work.

They were lies, of course, every word. But lies would suffice.

The question of how to deal with Aldo, now that was another matter.

The man was a thief, creeping into this room and stealing a document that did not belong to him. How had Aldo got in? Ruggerio could not imagine Cassandra admitting him by choice. She must have been distracted, left her key in the door. An unhappy accident, but one that offered an opportunity. An invitation could be sent, asking Aldo to dine at the villa. Let him speak his accusations and go, put an end to this matter. But there was no need. Aldo would come of his own meddling volition soon enough. He could not help himself.

It was in his nature.

* * *

Bells were chiming for curfew as Bindi returned to the Podestà, yet the air was somehow more uncomfortable than the day had been. The segretario was a man of faith, but his prayers were not often answered. Would the procession of the Impruneta bring the rain everyone craved? Could a painting of the Madonna vanquish this heat? Perhaps . . .

At least the business of procuring the procession had distracted the duke from other concerns. But Cosimo's mind was too sharp to be so occupied for long. Come the morning he would soon recall Bindi's rash promise to capture or kill the murderer of Dovizi and Uccello. Bindi could argue his men had been busy protecting Palazzo Medici, but it was a weak excuse. Barring a miracle, a new segretario would be assisting the Otto before long.

Bindi sighed. So be it.

Waddling into the courtyard he found Strocchi slumped by the wide stone staircase. The young officer appeared broken, as if someone had beaten him without leaving a mark.

'He's dead,' Strocchi said. 'They both are.'

'Who?'

'The murderer you wanted us to capture. Marco killed himself rather than be arrested, but he took Signor Ghiberti with him. They're both dead.'

A thrill of hope made Bindi stand a little straighter, a little taller. 'How?'

Strocchi gave a brief report: colliding with Marco in the street, realizing the killer was heading to Palazzo Ghiberti. Racing there, finding Marco with the wool merchant at knifepoint. Pleading with the killer. Marco cutting Ghiberti's throat, setting himself ablaze and taking Ghiberti with him out the window, their fatal fall to the stones below.

'Did this murderer explain the reason for his vendetta?'

Strocchi shrugged. 'Ghiberti and the others did something sinful, long ago. It didn't make much sense, but Marco wasn't sound of mind by then . . .'

Bindi nodded. Most murders were crimes of passion or grievance, fuelled by money or lust or madness. This was no different, despite the extreme nature of the killings. 'Very well. You should go home. Rest. You have earned it.'

Strocchi pulled himself up, one hand on a stone wall for support. As he stumbled away, Bindi could not resist asking one final question. 'Tell me, how did you know this Marco was not going to attack the duke as he threatened in those proclamations?'

The young officer turned back. 'I suspected Marco could not read or write. That meant someone else wrote the proclamations for him. Those final pages were left for us to find. But it was a letter from Aldo that held the answer. He warned me the killer might try to divert our attention. The five founders were always the true target. Everything else, those claims about the spirit of Savonarola, that was all a stratagemma.'

'Did Marco confirm that?'

Strocchi shook his head. 'No, but I went down to the street after he and Ghiberti fell. The wool merchant was already dead, but Marco whispered four last words to me: "One more will die". Ruggerio is the last survivor. I believe someone plans to murder him, perhaps the person responsible for writing the proclamations. Aldo's letter said he suspected there were two killers, one in Florence and another out in the dominion. Marco is dead, but his murders made Ruggerio flee to the countryside . . .'

'Where the second killer is waiting,' Bindi said.

'Yes. With your permission, I will hire a horse in the morning and ride to Ruggerio's estate. He needs to be warned of this danger.'

'Very well,' the segretario agreed. 'But there is no need to waste coin on a horse. You may walk there tomorrow. Aldo is responsible for stopping crimes near San Jacopo al Girone. If Ruggerio dies, the blame for that would stop with Aldo.'

'But, sir—'

'Ruggerio is no fool. As you say, he is well aware of the threat to his life, otherwise he would not have fled from the city. Knowing Ruggerio, the signore will have mercenaries protecting him and his villa. But the court should still be seen to have warned him. If this other killer does succeed, it would not reflect well on the Otto that it failed to notify an important citizen of such danger.'

Strocchi did not protest further, his shoulders slumping. 'Yes, sir.'

Bindi watched the young officer depart. So the killer of Dovizi, Uccello and now Ghiberti was dead. That rash promise had been fulfilled after all, meaning there was hope the Duke would see no need to appoint a new segretario for the Otto.

Bindi smiled. For once his prayers had been answered. Miracles did happen.

Aldo leaned against the doorway of his rented hut, a cup of wine in one hand, staring up at the stars. Had Ruggerio found the broken chest lock in his ufficio yet? If not, he was bound to discover it by morning. The man was a true son of Florence. He had not survived and prospered for so long without sensing a threat as it grew closer.

How would he react to the document's disappearance?

Anger. Rage. A desire for retribution, followed by an urgent need to reclaim what was his. That the document had come to Ruggerio by criminal means – theft, extortion, or blackmail – would not matter. He would consider it his property and his alone.

Aldo adjusted his grip on the stiletto hidden behind his back. He had been waiting for a visit from one or more of Ruggerio's mercenaries. The men were strangers to San Jacopo al Girone and unfamiliar with the village, whereas Aldo had lived here for a year. He would have an advantage, especially at night. Yes, they had superior numbers and long-distance weaponry, but an arquebus was of little use if the man firing it could not see his target.

So far, no attack had come.

Once Ruggerio's immediate anger passed he would consider other options, other responses to this intrusion. He would soon realize the torn document was no longer the threat it had once been. The loss must still be punished, Ruggerio would require Aldo to pay a price for such impertinence. But it could always wait until tomorrow . . .

Then there was the matter of Vincenzo. Aldo had no direct proof that the stable hand was a killer, even if those burnt papers and inkpot in the stable were linked to events in Florence. But all Aldo's years with the Otto made him believe Vincenzo was responsible for murdering Scarlatti and setting fire to the dead man's villa. It was the answer that made the most sense. Evidence would have been reassuring, but Aldo was still certain.

That being the case, would Vincenzo wait until morning before striking against Ruggerio? Perhaps not. The stable hand had lived near the villa for months. He would know every path on the estate, every way in and out of the residence. Ruggerio's mercenaries were armed but they had come from the city, whereas Vincenzo was accustomed to the countryside. He would not stumble in the darkness, or signal his presence. He could have a knife at Ruggerio's throat before the mercenaries knew their paymaster was in danger. If Vincenzo wished, he could burn Ruggerio tonight.

Aldo would not weep if that happened.

Ruggerio was a murderer, though blood never touched his hands. Lippo was killed for daring to spy on Ruggerio's country villa.

Bernardo Galeri died because he was sent into the Convent of Santa Maria Magdalena to steal the document Aldo now had. So many others had been murdered on Ruggerio's orders or had died as a result of his decisions, of his malign influence, because of his willingness to sacrifice others to protect himself.

No, few would weep if Ruggerio died tonight.

What about Cassandra? Should she be warned of the potential danger from Vincenzo? Perhaps. But whoever killed Scarlatti made great efforts to ensure nobody else would perish in the fire at the villa. The same was true of Dovizi's murder, and – from the little Aldo knew – of Uccello's death. The killer or killers was taking care about whose life they ended so no innocents would suffer. No, Cassandra was not the target of this fiery vendetta.

Should Ruggerio still live tomorrow, it was past time he and Aldo had a reckoning. The silk merchant would want his stolen document back, and Aldo wanted answers. A simple exchange was possible, but knowing Ruggerio there would be blood, or pain, or sacrifice. Someone was going to suffer.

Aldo looked west. He could not see Florence's silhouette from down here in the village, that view was reserved for those with grand residences up in the hills. But Aldo was still able to picture the city in his head, was still able to imagine Saul standing in his own doorway on via dei Giudei, looking up at the stars. Was Saul thinking of him, wishing they were together? Aldo hoped so. If he survived tomorrow, that wish might still come true.

Aldo had a letter for Saul which he would entrust to Father Ognissanti before returning to the villa, along with enough coin to see it delivered and a warning that all those in the village should stay away from the estate tomorrow, no matter what they saw. There were things that needed to be said. Far better that nobody else put their lives in danger.

Chapter Thirty

⚜

Wednesday, May 29th 1538

Tomasia was already nursing Bianca when Strocchi woke. He had expected another restless night, his thoughts haunted by what had happened to Marco and Ghiberti. Instead, he had slept. Tomasia must have got up to feed the bambina, but he could not recall it. How had he witnessed the violent deaths of two men and yet still been able to sleep with untroubled dreams? Was he becoming hardened to such horrors? Maybe. More likely it was the exhaustion of the last few days claiming him. Eventually, a body had to rest.

Strocchi rose, preparing for the day ahead. He had told Tomasia everything last night, including Bindi's order that he go to San Jacopo al Girone. 'Good,' she had said. 'It will give you and Aldo a chance to settle your arguments.' Now she was watching him while rubbing a hand against the baby's back. 'I know you are going for the Otto, but promise me you will listen to Aldo. Hear what he has to say, yes?'

'I listened to him before—'

'No, you didn't. You told Aldo one of you had to stop working for the Otto, or leave the city. That isn't listening, Carlo. It's imposing your will on another person.'

'But Aldo is the one who—'

'It doesn't matter what Aldo did, or who he loves or what he believes,' she said, laying Bianca down in the cot before taking Strocchi to the front half of their humble home. 'The two of you have been as stubborn as each other. Yes, Aldo is a flawed man, but so are you. He doesn't belong out in the dominion. Florence is his home. It will be up to Bindi whether Aldo is allowed to work at the Podestà, but you can bring him back to the city.'

Strocchi knew Tomasia was right, and her words were always persuasive. Yet he struggled to accept everything Aldo did. Their differences were too much to . . . No. He did not want to argue with Tomasia. Not when he was having to leave her and little Bianca, unsure when he would return. Marco was dead, but if Aldo was right, a second killer could be at San Jacopo al Girone, waiting for the chance to attack Ruggerio.

That person might not care about who got in their way . . .

'I will try,' Strocchi said. 'I promise.'

Tomasia smiled, putting a hand to his face. 'That's all I ask.' She glanced at the morning light streaming in through the shutters. 'When do you have to leave?'

'Now.'

She pulled him into a hug, kissing the side of his neck. 'Say goodbye to Bianca before you leave. She will miss you while you're gone. We both will.'

Cassandra shivered when Ruggerio called her upstairs. She had been in the walled garden, gathering herbs and leaves for an insalata. But when she came back inside the signore was calling out, summoning her to the upper level. There was a hint of steel in his voice, the edge hidden by a simple request. No, she was being foolish. Coming into the cool air of the villa from the garden was what caused the shivering.

Wiping both hands on her apron, Cassandra went up the wooden steps, several creaking beneath her feet. Ruggerio was waiting at the far end of the hall, outside the closed door to his private ufficio. He did not usually wear a ring but this morning had a silver band on his right hand. 'Do you have your key to this room?' he asked, a forced smile stretching those thin lips. But there was no light, no sparkle in his eyes.

'Of course, signore.' Cassandra approached him, lifting the leather cord necklace over her head, the key warm from her skin. She offered it to Ruggerio.

'No, please,' he said, stepping to one side. 'Open it.'

She did as he requested, pushing the door open for him to enter.

'Let's both go in.' Ruggerio ushered her into the ufficio, closing the door behind him. 'Do you notice anything out of place?'

Cassandra shook her head.

'No, I also found nothing unusual when I came in last night. Not at first.' Ruggerio put a hand to the small of her back, guiding Cassandra to stand by the table. The signor had never touched her before. It was unpleasant. 'But what do you think I discovered when I opened the small chest I always keep on this table?'

'I—' Cassandra's hands were trembling, and she couldn't seem to stop them. 'I do not know, signore.'

'Is that so?'

'Y-yes, signore.'

'Well, why don't you open it?'

'I don't understand—'

'Do it,' he urged, handing her a key.

Cassandra did as he wished, but the key would not turn inside the lock. 'It's broken.'

'Because someone has forced it open. Who did this?' Ruggerio demanded.

Cassandra shook her head. 'I don't know.'

'Not one of the women who came up from the village to clean my villa?'

'No, signore. None of them had the key.'

'What about the one-armed thief who came here a few days ago?'

'I know he stole your good boots, but I don't see how he could have got in here.'

'Then that leaves only two people who had an opportunity to break into this chest. You' – Ruggerio moved behind Cassandra, leaning over one shoulder to whisper in her ear, so close that she could smell his stale breath – 'or Cesare Aldo. You let him into my villa, yes?'

She nodded. 'He was overcome by the sun, so I—'

'You let him inside my villa,' Ruggerio snarled.

Cassandra swallowed; her mouth had gone dry. 'Yes, signore.'

'Could he have borrowed the key without you knowing?'

'I don't see how . . .' She stopped, her words dying away. 'One of the girls from the village kept needing my help. I left my key in the ufficio door, but not for long.'

'Long enough, it seems.' Ruggerio drew away from her. 'He took advantage of your foolishness. Now he has something important of mine, taken from this room.' Ruggerio slammed a hand down on the table, startling Cassandra. She stepped back, almost colliding with him. 'Going somewhere?' he asked.

'No, I . . .' She shook her head. 'I'm sorry, signore, I did not realize – I apologize for my mistake. I will leave your service immediately, if that is your wish.'

Ruggerio put his hands on Cassandra, twisting her round to

face him. 'No, that will not be necessary. Not today, at least. I have a task for you to complete this morning.'

'Yes, signore.' She waited, but he offered nothing further, instead releasing her.

'You may leave me.'

Cassandra nodded, turning to go, grateful that—

'But there is one thing I must say first,' Ruggerio continued.

She glanced back—

—and he slapped her across the face.

The blow was so shocking, so unexpected, it almost knocked Cassandra off her feet. She staggered back, something warm trickling down her face. When she put a finger there, it came away red. The rough edge of his ring had cut her cheek.

He advanced on Cassandra, glaring at her, his hand drawn back, ready to strike again. 'Never fail me again. Do you understand? Never.'

She nodded, unable to escape the hatred in his eyes.

'Good.' A smile split Ruggerio's face, the change disturbing as it was sudden. 'Then we shall say no more about this. Return to your duties and I will call when I'm ready.'

Cassandra stumbled from the office, clutching a hand to her face to staunch the bleeding. Whatever Ruggerio was planning, she wanted no part in it.

When Bindi approached Palazzo Medici to make his morning report, he was gratified to find no crowd outside the ducal residence, no angry chanting citizens. The mob had dispersed the previous evening as curfew came, the promise of Savonarola's return come to nothing. Cosimo de' Medici was still Duke of Florence. For now, the streets around Palazzo Medici were quiet and safe.

Campana waited in the internal courtyard, clutching an armful of papers. Bindi's good mood soured. No, not fresh proclamations. Strocchi had assured him the killer responsible for posting them was dead, there should be no more . . .

'Good, you're here,' Campana said, smiling at the segretario. 'What do you think of these?' He handed Bindi one of the pages and the cause of his happiness became evident.

It was a proclamation in the same style and written by a similar hand to that which had promised the spirit of Savonarola was risen. But this page told a different story, inviting everyone to watch a procession of the Madonna of Santa Maria Impruneta that day.

'These are being put up across the city,' Campana said. 'As you suggested, we shall use the weapon of his enemies against them.'

Bindi expressed his admiration for the ploy, but could not help wondering what would happen if the procession did not bring rain. He had assured Cosimo any ill will would fall on the beloved painting. Yet he had stated the opposite to Monsignor Testardo to secure the Impruneta for this procession. If rain did not come, Bindi feared he would be the one both men would blame. After all, few people ever got rich gambling on the weather.

Campana reclaimed the page from Bindi's grasp. 'Are you coming to give the duke your report?' he asked, gesturing at the stairs to the upper level.

'I was going to,' the segretario replied, 'but I have little new to tell him, and spent much of yesterday here. Perhaps you could pass my best regards along to His Grace?'

'But this procession was your suggestion, after all.'

'Nonetheless,' Bindi said, 'I am needed at the Podestà to prepare for the court's next sitting.' He hurried towards the entrance, but a voice he could not ignore called out.

'Segretario!'

Bindi stopped, cursing himself for not leaving sooner. He twisted round to find that Duke Cosimo was standing beside Campana. 'Your Grace.'

'I hope you are not leaving us?'

'Well, I have matters to prepare for the Otto . . .'

'Come, come.' Cosimo beckoned, forcing the segretario to return to the courtyard. 'I'm sure whatever business the court has can wait a few hours. I want you by my side as the Impruneta moves through the city.'

'That is most kind, Your Grace—'

'I'm so glad you agree,' Cosimo said, beaming. 'This procession was your notion, after all. I wouldn't wish you to miss what comes of it.'

Bindi forced a smile. 'Indeed, Your Grace. It will be my honour.'

Aldo had waited outside his hut since dawn. The building was dilapidated, yet possessed one quality he valued: strategic positioning. It stood at the eastern edge of San Jacopo al Girone, meaning the road to Florence passed by. The hut also offered a clear view of the track up to Ruggerio's estate, enabling Aldo to keep watch on all those going to or coming from the villa. The unladen cart had already passed by, the driver and his apprentice returning to Florence with the guard riding on the back. Aldo expected to see Ruggerio's mercenaries stamping down the hill, bringing a message, a threat or an attack . . . but, so far, nothing.

The day was cooler, a few wisps of cloud creeping over the hills while a brisk breeze teased the promise of cooler air to come. It might be a lie, tempting farmers and the faithful to believe their prayers for rain might soon be answered. Aldo placed little hope in such efforts. If there was an Almighty, would he be concerned about rain in this one particular valley?

It was the road from Florence that brought a visitor to Aldo's door. A messenger had ridden past on horseback earlier, hurrying up the hill to the Ruggerio estate. He trotted down to the village soon after, heading back to Florence. But Strocchi was the first person on foot. He stumbled into view, boots kicking up dust as he approached the village.

'Carlo?'

Strocchi stopped, raising a hand to shield his eyes. 'Aldo?'

Soon Strocchi was quenching his thirst in the shade outside the hut and sharing the events of recent days in Florence; the murder of Ghiberti, the death of his killer, Marco, and the surge in those believing the spirit of Savonarola was responsible for all of it. 'As I was leaving,' Strocchi said, 'there were new proclamations being posted. A painting called the Madonna of Santa Maria Impruneta is being processed across the city.'

Realizing Strocchi had not heard of the Impruneta, Aldo explained its history. Twice he had seen the painting carried through Florence, the faithful praying for relief from plague the first time, and flooding the second. 'Using the Impruneta to distract people from Savonarola is a cunning stratagemma,' Aldo said. 'She has always been seen as a gift that benefits the whole city, not merely the Medici. If rain falls during or soon after the procession, it will prove the Madonna truly blesses Florence – or so the fervent will believe. If this drought continues, the people will have someone else to blame besides the duke.'

Strocchi took another sip of his wine. 'You speak as if you don't believe.'

'I speak about what others believe,' Aldo replied. 'My faith is my own business.'

The young officer nodded. He was still not twenty-five, but there was caution in his eyes that had not been there a year ago. Anyone working for the Otto encountered the worst of Florence, the worst of people. Enforcing the city's law was not an easy job, but coping with what that meant was the true test. Deciding what was just and how best to balance that against the rules and demands of the court was even harder.

'Tomasia made me promise to listen to what you have to say. According to her, it doesn't matter what you did in the past, or what you believe . . . or who you love.'

Aldo smiled. 'Your wife has more wisdom than the two of us combined.'

'Tomasia thinks you belong in Florence.' Strocchi finished his wine.

'And what do you think?' Aldo asked.

Strocchi hesitated. 'I used to be so certain, so sure of what I knew. But . . . Things are not so simple. The more I learn, the more I witness . . . How can I trust my own judgement when it is challenged every day?'

Aldo rubbed a hand across the stubble on his jaw. 'It isn't easy,' he admitted. 'You know in your heart what is right, what is just. Yet the laws of Florence are designed to protect those with money and influence while others with little or nothing suffer.' Aldo gestured up at the villa. 'Men like Ruggerio do what they wish without consequences for their actions. Now he and his fellow founders are reaping what they sowed more than forty years ago.'

'Are you saying Marco was right to murder Dovizi, Uccello and Ghiberti? That whoever killed Scarlatti was justified?'

'No. I'm saying this is a vendetta, someone taking the law into their own hands. Often – too often – justice fails us, all of us. We do the best we can but . . .'

'It's never enough,' Strocchi said.

Aldo nodded. Yes, the young officer was not the same as he had once been. But learning there was more than one answer to many questions would make him a better man. Movement on the track down from the estate caught Aldo's eye. Someone was coming.

Strocchi stood up, brushing dust from his hose and boots. 'Before he died, Marco whispered four last words to me: "One more will die". I suspect someone plans to murder Ruggerio. He should be warned of that danger.'

'Ruggerio already knows. He is paying four well-armed mercenaries to protect him.'

'Nonetheless, Bindi commanded me to tell Ruggerio to his face.'

'Let me guess,' Aldo said. ' "The Otto must be seen to be doing the right thing".' Strocchi nodded. 'Typical Bindi. His priority is always protecting his own position first, then that of the Otto, with everyone and everything else a distant last.'

'Will you come with me to warn Ruggerio?'

'Yes, but not yet.'

'Why?' Strocchi asked.

Aldo gestured at the lone woman approaching them. 'Because Ruggerio has sent a messenger to us.' Cassandra was wearing a skirt and blouse as usual, but her hair was loose, falling forward to cast her face in shadow. The housekeeper always kept her hair tied back, why the change? He introduced the young officer to Cassandra.

'Signor Ruggerio requests the pleasure of your company for a meal,' she said. 'He invites you to join him as the sun is approaching its highest.'

'Does he?' Aldo laughed. 'How delightful. And to what do I owe this unexpected invitation? Should I be thanking the messenger who rode through earlier, bringing news from the city that Ghiberti has been murdered?'

'How did you—?' Cassandra glanced at Strocchi. 'Ahh.'

Aldo spied an angry red line across one of her cheeks. He stepped closer, reaching out a hand to touch her hair. 'May I?' Cassandra nodded. Aldo tucked her hair behind an ear. She had a nasty cut across the skin, a bruise forming around it – a fresh wound.

'Who did that to you?' Strocchi asked.

'It was Ruggerio.' Aldo sighed. 'He found the broken chest.'

Cassandra stared at Aldo. 'Yes.'

'He knows I have the stolen document, and blamed you for that.'

'Yes,' Cassandra said.

'So Ruggerio hurt you and sent you down here so I would see that.' She nodded. 'Very well,' Aldo said. 'Please tell the signore I am delighted to accept his invitation, but I will be bringing my colleague Officer Carlo Strocchi with me.'

*B*indi doubted the wisdom of this. The duke had sent a messenger to Testardo, requesting a variation to the procession of the Impruneta through the city. In the past such journeys carried the painting to major piazze, pausing at each main church so the faithful could offer prayers. But Cosimo had proposed adding a further station to the procession. After the Impruneta departed the cathedral, he wished it be brought north for a final stop outside Palazzo Medici.

'Are you sure this is . . . necessary?' the segretario asked when he and Campana were summoned to Cosimo's ufficio with news that Testardo had agreed to the request.

'You mean do I think this is wise?' the duke replied.

'I . . .' Bindi was still not used to the young Medici's bluntness. Cosimo appeared to enjoy puncturing the pomposity of others, cutting through their worthy words to get at the truth. It was an admirable quality, but far from the approach favoured by previous Florentine leaders. 'Yes, I do. Is this wise?'

'Perhaps not,' the duke said, 'yet there are times when you must put caution and wisdom aside. When you must be willing to risk what you have for the braver choice.'

The segretario had never heard the previous duke speak in such a way, but that was no surprise. Alessandro de' Medici had been more interested in the spoils of being leader than in actually leading the people of Florence. Cosimo was a very different man.

A knock at the door summoned Campana away, but he soon returned. 'Your Grace, I have news. You asked for any reports of a change in the sky. It seems there are clouds gathering over the hills to the east of Florence – dark clouds, heavy with rain – and a strong wind is blowing them in this direction. There might be rain soon.'

Cosimo frowned. 'There could be rain,' he said, 'but it is still far from certain. Let us not become too excited by what has not yet happened.'

'Of course, Your Grace,' Campana replied, bowing his head.

'Very well,' the duke said. 'I've reports to read. You and Bindi may go.'

Campana led Bindi from the office. The segretario glanced back from the doorway to see Cosimo already hard at work. Yes, this was a very different man.

Strocchi could not recall when he had last been cold, but he was shivering as Aldo led him up the hill. They had waited outside Aldo's hut after Cassandra returned to the villa, watching dark clouds gather overhead. Having grown up in the Tuscan country-side, Strocchi knew a rainstorm when he saw one coming. These clouds carried enough rain to satisfy every farmer nearby, but whether the downpour would reach Florence was another matter. They might well empty themselves on the hills, frustrating those in the city. Strocchi did not wish to think what would happen if Florence had no relief from the heat soon.

While they were waiting Aldo shared what had happened since his return from Florence, and his suspicions about the missing stable hand Vincenzo. Aldo showed Strocchi the torn document recovered from Ruggerio's office, explaining the significance of its faded text. 'I can't be certain what Ruggerio and the other four did, but I believe this vendetta stems from that incident.'

Strocchi suspected he was correct. Whatever his other flaws and frailties, Aldo had an ability to understand what drove people to kill. Strocchi was not sure he would ever possess the same insight. Finally, Aldo announced it was time for them to visit Ruggerio.

'What did Marco look like?' Aldo said as they reached a bend in the track.

The question surprised Strocchi. 'Why do you ask?'

'We've been pursuing two killers,' Aldo replied. 'You were hunting Marco in the city, while I was searching for whoever murdered Scarlatti.' He pointed to the next hill where there was a gap around a cluster of buildings. 'That's where my suspect tried to burn the evidence of his killing. But the fire only claimed Scarlatti's villa, not his corpse.'

'You're sure Ruggerio's stable hand Vincenzo is the killer?'

Aldo paused. 'I have no direct proof—'

'You don't?'

'But Vincenzo is the most likely suspect,' Aldo continued. 'He is known on both estates, so nobody would question him or probably even notice him coming and going. Vincenzo lied to me about an itinerant cooper coming to the area to create a false suspect. And he disappeared yesterday when I was close to the truth. That makes him a suspect. These murders could be linked to two killers from the same famiglia.'

Strocchi described Marco, both when he was Uccello's servant and after cutting off his hair and beard to avoid capture. 'What did Vincenzo look like?'

'Much the same,' Aldo replied.

'You think they're brothers?'

'It would explain them working together. They could even be twins.'

That was feasible, but something about it still itched at Strocchi. 'Why wait so long? Savonarola died decades ago and his Fanciulli ... it's all so long in the past.'

'Something or someone must have stopped Marco and Vincenzo from pursuing their vendetta. How old would you say Marco was?'

'Perhaps forty,' Strocchi replied. 'And Vincenzo?'

'Much the same . . .' Aldo looked around him, seeming confused.

'What's wrong?'

'Nothing, but—' A smile split his face. 'Of course.'

'What?'

Aldo laughed. 'I couldn't understand what was missing. Ever since spring came I've been listening to the sounds of insetti, day and night. Now I can't hear them anymore.'

Strocchi listened. Aldo was right. There were no insetti to be heard, nor were there any birds in the sky. 'A storm is coming,' he said. 'Everything is taking shelter.'

'Come on.' Aldo strode onwards. 'We need to reach that villa before the rain does.'

Ruggerio licked his lips, enjoying the view from the loggia. He could see Aldo and Strocchi approaching, the severe slope stealing the strength from their legs. Most days the relentless sun added to the oppressiveness of the track, heat sapping the life from those trudging up the hill ... but not today. Angry black clouds had spread across the sky, stretching towards Florence in the distance, putting a chill through the air and promising a torrential downpour soon. Perhaps the rain would come while Aldo and Strocchi were still making their way uphill, turn the track into a river of mud and misery. Yes, that would be equally effective.

Ruggerio savoured moments like this. That catch in the breath before plunging in, the last delicious minutes before minds or bodies came together. Then the grappling would begin, the battle for control, for dominance. One would emerge on top, prove themselves stronger, force their will on the other. When it was done, there was a lingering sadness. Victory was to be savoured, yes, yet it could never again be claimed for the first time. The excitement, the lure of a fresh conquest was lost. The conquered held no interest, had nothing left to offer.

He would mourn besting Aldo. Their skirmishes, barbed exchanges full of hidden meaning, were always a pleasure. But Aldo stealing could not pass unpunished. Wounding Cassandra's face and sending her down for Aldo to see . . . It was a crude ploy, but one certain to bring him here. And Ruggerio wanted Aldo angry.

It made for a better opponent, and that made the—

'Signore,' Cassandra said, interrupting his thoughts.

'What is it?' Ruggerio snapped.

'One of your men is gone.'

'Gone where?' He had been watching the track down to the village. None of his hired men had used it, and there was no other way to leave the estate without knowing the hillside paths around the villa. His mercenaries had only been there one night.

'I'm not sure,' Cassandra said. 'The one on watch said the missing man went into the olive grove to piss and never returned.'

'Had either of them been drinking?' That often dulled Ruggerio's senses, sending him to sleep. This lost fool could simply be slumped against a tree, snoring.

'They asked for wine, but I only gave them water.' The housekeeper had fear in her eyes, and a tremble in her voice. 'When I was down in the village earlier, I heard Aldo saying there was a killer close by. Do you think this disappearance could be their work?'

Ruggerio feared Cassandra was correct, but would never admit it. Fear was for other men. 'Doubtful. Still, wiser to be wary than wounded. Where are my other mercenaries?'

'Resting in the stable,' she said. 'I will—' Cassandra stopped, her eyes widening as she stared past him. He twisted round to see what had taken her words.

The stable was on fire.

Smoke billowed from the building, flames reaching out through the door and shutters. Three horses ran out of the stable, bolting across the courtyard before racing away down the hill. How had the blaze taken hold so fast? Someone must have primed the stable to burn. Ruggerio knew it was full of dry hay and woodwork. Once fire claimed it—

A man stumbled from the stable. It was one of the mercenaries, confusion on his face. He looked up at the loggia, mouth opening and closing but no sound coming out. The mercenary fell forward in the courtyard, a finger of metal protruding from his back.

No, not a finger – a blade.

'Cassandra, lock all the doors,' Ruggerio struggled to keep his voice calm. There were footsteps below the loggia – Cassandra was already out in the courtyard, crouching by the fallen mercenary. She made the sign of the cross.

'He's dead, signore.'

Fire was claiming the stable as its own, flames escaping through the roof. If another mercenary was still inside the building, he must be dead or dying.

'Come back inside,' Ruggerio called.

'But signore—'

'Come back inside!' Ruggerio swallowed, struggling to keep panic out of his voice. 'I need you to lock all the doors, my dear. Do it now.'

Cassandra stared at him a moment before hurrying back into the villa, the front door slamming behind her. Fire roared from the stable, clouds of smoke making things difficult to see. But above the noise Ruggerio heard footsteps running towards the villa – one, no, two sets of them. He peered through the smoke. A familiar figure appeared from it, someone Ruggerio had never thought he would be grateful to see.

Aldo neared the last steep incline before Ruggerio's estate when he saw black smoke rising into the air, joining the dark rain clouds looming overhead. He quickened his step, Strocchi keeping pace. But the sound of approaching hooves made Aldo pause. Three horses came racing round the corner, hurtling down the hill. Aldo threw himself to one side, pulling Strocchi into a shallow gully by the track. The horses charged by, eyes wild with fear.

Strocchi helped Aldo back to his feet, the young officer's hand trembling. 'Those beasts would have trampled us to death.'

'The fire must have terrified them,' Aldo replied. 'Come on, we need to get to the villa.' The two of them hurried up the hill, Strocchi telling Aldo about Marco freeing the horses before setting Uccello's carriage ablaze.

'Vincenzo also cares for animals,' Aldo said. 'I doubt Ruggerio will be so fortunate.' When they reached the estate Aldo expected to see fire consuming the villa. Instead, flames were belching from the stable, clouds of smoke choking the air. Aldo put an arm across his nose and mouth, gesturing at Strocchi to do the same.

A man was sprawled face-down in the courtyard, a blade in his back. Aldo crouched by the body. Ruggerio? No, this corpse still had hair. Aldo rolled the body over. It was one of the mercenaries. That meant Vincenzo was still alive, still a threat.

'Aldo!'

Ruggerio was leaning out from the loggia. 'That man, he came out of the stable. Another of my men is still in there!'

Aldo got as close to the burning building as he could, but the heat was too intense to go inside. There was a shape sprawled amid the flames. Aldo crouched to peer beneath the smoke. Ruggerio was right, his other mercenary was in the stable – but there was blood across the man's face, and his lifeless eyes stared at Aldo. Two pistols beside the corpse were surrounded by fire, out of reach.

'He's dead as well,' Aldo shouted.

'Where are the others?' Strocchi called to Ruggerio.

'One went into those trees,' Ruggerio replied, pointing to an olive grove by the track, 'but he never came back. I think the other went to look for him.'

'Palle,' Aldo muttered under his breath, retrieving the stiletto from his left boot. 'Carlo, do you have a weapon?'

Strocchi shook his head. 'I was only sent here to warn Signor Ruggerio.'

Aldo pulled the blade from the dead man's back, wiping it on his tunic before offering the knife to Strocchi. 'Take this.' The young officer hesitated. 'Take it,' Aldo insisted, forcing the blade into Strocchi's hand. 'That could determine whether you go home to Tomasia and Bianca alive when this is done.'

Strocchi stared at the knife, his hand trembling.

'Ever used a blade to defend yourself?'

'N-no.'

Aldo suspected as much. 'Where's Cassandra?' he shouted to Ruggerio.

'Inside with me, locking all the doors.'

'Good. Tell her to secure all the ground-level shutters too.' Aldo rested a hand on Strocchi's shoulder. 'You'd better stay here, guard the front door. If anyone tries to get inside, yell for me. If I don't come . . .' He put a hand to his belly. 'Stab here, or between their legs if you get the chance. Don't be a hero. Your wife and child need you, yes?'

Strocchi nodded, face ashen, eyes wide.

Clutching his stiletto, Aldo strode towards the olive grove.

Cassandra shoved the final bolt into place, locking the back door of the villa. Ruggerio was calling her name from the upper level, a tremor in his voice. She hurried to the main staircase.

'Yes, signore?'

'Aldo is outside. He says to secure all the shutters down there.'

'Yes, signore.' Cassandra did as she was told. The villa was already dark from the storm clouds outside, and closing the shutters made it even harder to see. She was grateful to have been housekeeper long enough to know where every chair, table and piece of furniture stood. A sudden noise above made her jump.

'Signore?'

'I'm fine,' Ruggerio called. 'I knocked a table over, that's all.'

She felt her way to the main staircase before hurrying up, two steps at a time. But there was no Ruggerio in the hallway. 'Signore? Where are you?'

'In here,' he called from his bedchamber, a tremor in his voice.

Cassandra approached the doorway, wishing she had brought a knife from the kitchen. She pushed open the door, peering inside—

Ruggerio was on his bed, both hands nursing one of his shins. A side table was tipped over on the floor. The signore smiled. 'I thought, what if the killer was already inside the villa? What if we were locking ourselves in with him?'

'Don't worry. We're safe here,' Cassandra said.

'I hope you're right,' Ruggerio replied. 'Have you closed all the shutters?'

'Most of them, signore.'

'Then go and secure the rest.'

Cassandra withdrew from the bedchamber. She could not help noticing Ruggerio was happy to send her back downstairs. If the killer did get inside, she would be the one facing him.

Bindi watched from the windows on the middle level as the procession approached Palazzo Medici. The painting of the Madonna of Santa Maria Impruneta was being carried north along via Largo, surrounded by clerics on all sides. Monsignor Testardo strode in front of the procession swinging an incense burner on a golden chain, plumes of smoke billowing from the metal censer. The faithful followed the procession, clutching their rosary beads, while more were waiting opposite the palazzo on via Largo.

'Word has spread about the final station of the Impruneta's journey,' Bindi said.

'It was well leaked,' Campana agreed.

'Where is His Grace?'

'Downstairs, at the palazzo entrance. He intends to kneel in prayer when the procession reaches us.'

'I trust you tried to stop him?'

Campana glared at the segretario. 'The duke knows his own mind. He would not be dissuaded or gainsaid, no matter how I argued.'

Bindi leaned forward to peer at the sky. Dark clouds were thickening above Florence, promising rain, teasing rain . . . but so far giving none. 'This was folly.'

'Indeed,' Campana said, 'but it was your folly. His Grace will remember that.'

Below them the procession came to a halt outside the palazzo. It was dark, murkier than twilight as Cosimo strode out into the street, dropping to his knees in front of the sacred painting and the clerics carrying it. The sound of praying swelled up into the air, Testardo making the sign of the cross. Cosimo did the same, a moment after the monsignor.

Bindi closed his eyes. Lord, he prayed, have mercy on us. Give us rain and you will know this city's love for a hundred years. Amen. The segretario reopened his eyes—

A white flash lit up the city, following by an almighty clap of thunder.

Then came the rain.

Fat, single drops at first, followed by more and more until it was a downpour.

Bindi shook his head, struggling to believe what he could see and hear.

It had worked! It had worked!

Beside him Campana was making the sign of the cross, so Bindi did the same.

Below the clerics were scrambling to pull a heavy cloth up and over the Impruneta to protect it from the downpour. Cosimo got up from his knees, reaching out a hand to Testardo. The two men made the sign of peace. Bindi could see the duke speaking, but it was impossible to know the words passing between Cosimo and the monsignor.

That did not matter.

The drought was broken, the intolerable heat that had driven Florence and its people near to madness had been vanquished, beaten by a bold gamble and divine intervention.

Bindi smiled. His esteem had been restored.

Chapter Thirty-two

Strocchi stood with his back against the villa's front door, clutching the knife in both hands, willing them not to tremble so much. It was getting darker by the moment, smoke from the fire in the stable blotting out most of the sky. What little Strocchi could see was all black cloud, heavy with rain, a downpour coming at any moment.

A sudden flash of light made him cry out. Lightning, it was only lightning! A crack of thunder came moments later, booming overhead, so close it was near deafening. Strocchi pushed himself back against the door but there was nowhere to go.

Across the courtyard the stable was still ablaze, flames bursting through the roof tiles. An almighty groan rose from the building, as if it was crying out in pain. Then the roof gave way, falling down into the stable. Fresh clouds of smoke and ashes billowed outwards. Strocchi twisted his face to one side, hacking and coughing. The smoke surrounded him, stealing away Strocchi's breath, until he feared he might never breathe again . . .

Eventually the cloud thinned, leaving a mass of grey snow falling from the sky. A flake caught in Strocchi's mouth, bitter on his tongue. That wasn't snow, it was ash. He spat it out, wiping more ashes from his eyes and face.

As the air cleared, a lone figure emerged from the clouds.

'Aldo?' Strocchi asked. 'Is that you?'

The man – it was a man, but not one Strocchi knew – came closer.

'Are you one of Ruggerio's mercenaries?'

Still the man did not speak. Aldo had said each of the mercenaries was carrying a firearm, but the figure coming close had something else in his fist.

A burning torch.

Strocchi held up the knife in his own hand.

'You will not get by me,' he warned. 'I . . . I know how to use this!'

Aldo discovered the third mercenary in a ditch near the olive grove. Dead, throat cut, hose round his thighs, the stench of piss rising from him. The fool had been emptying his bladder when death came. Aldo scoured the surroundings, and soon found the dead man's arquebus leaning against a tree trunk. A quick check proved it wasn't loaded. Even if the guard had seen or heard his killer's approach, the weapon would have done him little good.

Why didn't Vincenzo take the firearm? It was effective at a distance in skilled hands, but little use for close fighting except as a bludgeon. Aldo decided to leave the arquebus where it was. A good blade was quieter, and needed no reloading. Besides, a stiletto had saved Aldo's life more than once.

It was getting darker by the moment, black clouds overhead making it harder to see. Aldo could not find Ruggerio's last guard in the olive grove. Had the mercenary fled, decided his pay wasn't worth dying for? Aldo wouldn't blame him. Whatever the—

Everything turned white for a moment. Then came thunder almost on top of the lightning, the boom so close it made Aldo cover both ears till the sound faded. Rain was imminent, he could taste it on the air. Another noise demanded his attention, the creaking groan of something heavy giving way, followed by a clatter of tiles smashing. The stable roof must have collapsed, flames burning through the supporting beams. Aldo hurried back between the olive trees, struggling to see his footing.

A frightened voice called out in the distance: 'Aldo? Is that you?'

It sounded like Strocchi, fear in his voice.

Aldo ran, arms up to shield his head from the sharp branches.

'Are you one of Ruggerio's mercenaries?' Strocchi's voice came again, not far off now.

Aldo burst from the olive grove, emerging close to the courtyard, struggling to see through all the smoke and falling ashes.

'You will not get by me,' Strocchi shouted close by. 'I . . . I know how to use this!'

A gust of wind parted the smoke, revealing Strocchi with his back against the villa's front door, brandishing a knife, and Vincenzo with a burning torch in his grasp.

'It's over,' Aldo called to the stable hand. 'Your brother Marco is dead.'

Vincenzo swung round to Aldo, his face riven with fury. 'You're lying! I would know if Marco was dead!'

'Aldo's right,' Strocchi said. 'I saw Marco die yesterday, in Florence. He perished killing Roberto Ghiberti. Both of them are gone. It's over.'

'Not while there's still one of those bastardi to kill,' Vincenzo hissed.

Aldo edged closer, determined to put himself between Vincenzo and Strocchi. 'You don't need to die here today. You can leave, or surrender yourself.'

'Never.'

'You can't get into the villa.' Aldo stepped in front of Strocchi, stiletto in hand, shielding him from the killer. 'The villa's doors and shutters are all locked and secure. Ruggerio is inside, you'll never reach him.'

'I don't need to reach him.' Vincenzo ran at Aldo and Strocchi, swiping the burning torch through the air, driving them back against the door. The flames seared Aldo's face as they passed, threatened to set his hair ablaze. He searched for an opening to lunge at Vincenzo with the stiletto, but the burning torch was too quick, too close—

Lightning cut through the smoke, thunder coming a moment later.

Then came the rain.

A single fat drop hit Aldo in the face.

Then another, and another, and another . . .

'No!' Vincenzo screamed at the sky. 'Not when I'm so close!' He dashed sideways, leaving Aldo and Strocchi by the front door. The rain was coming faster now, more and more of it. Vincenzo disappeared round a corner, heading for the back of the villa.

'Why did he leave us alive?' Strocchi asked.

'We're not his target,' Aldo replied. 'He was keeping us busy here, that's all. Palle! Whatever he's done, it must be behind the villa.' Yelling at Strocchi to go round the other side, Aldo sprinted the way Vincenzo had taken. He stopped at the corner to peer round, not wanting to run straight into a burning torch – Vincenzo was not there. Aldo scurried along the western side of the villa, rain lashing down now, turning long dry paths to treacherous mud beneath his boots.

As he neared the back corner, Aldo saw the fourth guard slumped on the ground. Dead like the others, arquebus by his side. Rain hammered at Aldo as he looked round the next corner, ignoring the walled garden. Vincenzo was hunched behind the villa, thrusting his burning torch into a stack of tinder and small branches. The pile was already blackened by fire but the downpour had put that out. Vincenzo didn't seem to notice Aldo creeping closer, the rainstorm drowning out all other noise.

Squinting, Aldo could make out another figure beyond Vincenzo. Lightning flashed, revealing Strocchi. Vincenzo twisted his head from side to side, seeing them both. 'Ruggerio deserves to die!' he snarled. 'He should suffer for what he did, what they all did!'

'I have proof of what they did,' Aldo said, shouting to be heard over the downpour.

'It won't do any good,' Vincenzo replied, shaking his head.

'We can make sure Ruggerio faces justice,' Strocchi offered.

'There is no justice,' Vincenzo insisted. 'Not in Florence. Not for my famiglia.'

Aldo knew this was true, but confirming it would only make Vincenzo more desperate, more reckless – and he had already killed four men since dawn. 'You're not old enough to remember what happened when Savonarola ruled Florence. How did you discover who was responsible for the suffering of your famiglia?'

'She told us, Marco and me. What those five did.'

Vincenzo must be talking about his mother. If he and Marco were twins, the two of them were born after what happened to their mother – possibly as a consequence of that. Aldo knew Ruggerio could not be their father, but the silk merchant was still part of it, still culpable. No wonder Scarlatti was haunted by his actions all those years ago . . .

'When did your mother die?' Strocchi asked.

'Two years ago,' Vincenzo said, throwing aside the rain-drenched torch, abandoning his attempt to burn the villa. 'She believed in forgiveness, no matter what. To her, only God could decide the punishment of sinners. She made us swear never to pursue a vendetta, and we kept that promise – while she was alive.' He shook his head. 'We failed her. I failed her.'

'You did what you believed was right,' Aldo said. Empty words, but perhaps they would hide him edging closer . . .

No. Vincenzo glared at him through the rain. 'Stay back,' he warned, pulling a knife from a sheath at the side of his drenched tunic. 'I don't want to kill you, but I will if I must.' He pointed at the dead mercenary behind Aldo. 'Men like that took Ruggerio's coin to protect him. They left me no choice.'

The guard who had died pissing in the olive grove had been no immediate threat, but Aldo kept that to himself. 'Nobody else need die here today.' Through the rain he could see Strocchi edging closer behind Vincenzo, knife raised. 'Carlo, don't!'

Strocchi heard Aldo's warning too late. Vincenzo had already spun round, one fist smacking the blade out of Strocchi's hand, the other putting a knife to his throat. Strocchi stopped, standing still as a statue in the pouring rain, the edge of the knife digging into his neck. Vincenzo stared at him, eyes wide, teeth bared.

'You . . . You don't have to kill me,' Strocchi said, swallowing hard. 'I have no weapon now, no way of hurting you, no way of stopping you.'

Vincenzo moved closer, keeping the knife in place. 'You were ready to kill me.'

'No, I wasn't. I've never taken anyone's life.'

'You're an officer of the Otto.'

'Only for a few days,' Strocchi said. 'I'm not a soldier, not a mercenary. I was sent to warn Ruggerio his life could be in danger, that's all.'

Vincenzo was studying him, head tilting to one side. 'Is that true?' he called out.

'Yes,' Aldo replied from behind him.

'Then why carry the blade?'

'I told him to,' Aldo said. 'For his protection, nothing more. Carlo isn't capable of hurting anyone. He doesn't have the instincts of a soldier, or the resolve of a killer.'

Keeping the knife against Strocchi's throat, Vincenzo slid past to stand behind him, so close his breath was warm on the back of Strocchi's neck. 'But you do?' Vincenzo asked.

Aldo nodded.

'He does,' Strocchi said. 'I've seen him—'

'Be quiet.' Vincenzo pressed the knife closer to Strocchi's skin. 'Nobody asked you.'

Strocchi nodded, closing his eyes. This was not where he wanted to die. Not at the whim of a killer, not while being lashed with rain. Not when he was so far from Tomasia and little Bianca and Mama. Not like this.

'Carlo,' Aldo said, his voice quiet amid the pounding rain. 'Do you trust me?'

Strocchi opened his eyes. What was Aldo asking?

'This isn't about the two of you,' Vincenzo said.

'Do you trust me?' Aldo repeated, rubbing a hand on his belly. Strocchi struggled to reply. 'I . . .'

'No!' Vincenzo moved to one side a little, pointing his blade at Aldo. 'You—'

'Now, Carlo!' Aldo shouted.

Strocchi snapped his elbow backwards into Vincenzo's gut. The killer staggered, folding forwards, a hand on Strocchi's back for support. Seeing Aldo pull his stiletto, Strocchi threw himself sideways into the villa wall. The blade flew through the air, raindrops flicking off the twisting metal as it turned over and over –

– and buried itself in Vincenzo's throat.

He gasped, surprise taking him.

Vincenzo's own knife tumbled from his grasp as he clawed at the blade killing him. He sank down on his knees, rain mixing with the blood seeping from the wound, his lips opening and closing but no words coming out from them.

Then he stopped, both hands falling down, mouth no longer moving.

The rain kept falling but Vincenzo was dead.

Strocchi leaned against the villa wall.

It was over.

Chapter Thirty-three

*R*uggerio did not want to die. All his achievements, all his thoughts, all of him stopping, decaying, rotting . . . It was too much to bear. When he first realized his own mortality, it terrified him. Being beaten as a child by his father, attacks from other boys for being different, the shame of being scorned by those he wished to love . . . Those had all been painful, humiliating moments in his life that haunted him.

But those moments shaped him too, made him the man he was now. They taught him strength and resilience, when to be careful and when to be cunning. They showed him how to control others, how to conquer those who challenged him, and how to punish those who wronged him. His whole life from the age of twelve had been an act of revenge.

Now the world was coming to revenge itself on him.

Ruggerio pulled the covers on his bed closer. It was cold inside the villa, colder than he'd ever known. A sudden chill in the air could explain the trembling in his hands and feet, but it was fear that had taken hold, that was responsible for the cold and remorseless grip threatening to empty his bowels, to steal his dignity.

He could hear noises outside: roaring flames, wood creaking and breaking, shouting voices, lashing rain, booms of thunder that shook the bedchamber around him. Then most of the sounds stopped, and that was worse. Relentless rain pounded at the villa roof, but that was all. No more voices, no threats or cries for help. No shots from the mercenaries' arquebuses. No shouts of triumph. Just rain, and more rain . . .

A sudden knock startled Ruggerio.

'Signore, are you there?' Cassandra asked from outside the door.

'Yes,' he replied, struggling to keep the fear from his voice. 'What's happened?'

'I don't know. I wondered if—'

'Cassandra! Ruggerio!' A voice was shouting in the distance. Aldo's voice.

Ruggerio cast aside the covers. If he was going to die, it would not be cowering in bed like a timid child. If he must face his end, let it be with some dignity. 'Where is Aldo calling from?' he asked Cassandra, rising from his bed.

'Outside,' the housekeeper said. 'In front of the villa, I believe.'

Ruggerio swept from his bedchamber, passing Cassandra on his way to the loggia. Rain was still falling heavily, but the worst of the downpour had moved towards Florence. A bolt of lightning flashed from the black clouds, striking close to the city. The intolerable, blistering heat of the past days and weeks was gone, banished by this abrupt change of weather. But Ruggerio's attention was drawn across the courtyard to the stable.

The roof had fallen in, and its wooden shutters burned away. The fire was out, beaten into submission by the sudden rainstorm. Clouds of black smoke rose from what was left. The stone walls appeared sound, but the rest of it would need to be torn out and replaced, rebuilt, recreated. How tiresome.

'Open the door!' Aldo shouted. He and that young officer from the Otto were beneath the loggia, drenched by rain but otherwise unhurt. Behind them a guard's body was still sprawled in the courtyard. So much for Alberti's assurances that the mercenaries were the best coin could hire. The maggiordomo would have to answer for this mistake.

'Where are my men?' Ruggerio asked as Cassandra joined him on the loggia.

'Dead.' Aldo pointed past the body on the ground to the stable. 'One's in there, another in your olive grove to the east, and the last died near the walled garden. All four were stabbed or had their throats cut.' Beside him the young officer – Strocchi, that was his name - rubbed a hand to his own neck.

'Who killed them?'

'Your stable hand,' Aldo replied. 'Vincenzo.'

Cassandra gasped. 'No, that's impossible!'

'He was the one who strangled Benozzo Scarlatti,' Aldo said. 'And Vincenzo's brother Marco was responsible for the murders of Dovizi, Uccello and Ghiberti in Florence.'

'You said "was",' Ruggerio observed. 'Where is he now?'

'Dead,' Strocchi said. Cassandra made the sign of the cross, but Ruggerio did not bother with such indulgences. 'He threatened to kill me,' Strocchi went on, 'so Aldo—'

'I did what had to be done.' Aldo folded his arms. 'What was necessary.'

Ruggerio shook his head. 'So much death, so many killings . . .' Yet he had survived. If there was a God, it seemed the deity was smiling on him today. 'You must be congratulated, both of you. I shall write a letter to the Otto di Guardia e Balia commending your efforts, and another to Duke Cosimo himself. If that fool Bindi has any sense, he will recall you to the city immediately, Aldo.'

'Most kind,' Aldo replied, though there was no gratitude in his face.

'Rest assured, I will also arrange a handsome reward for you both when I return to Florence tomorrow,' Ruggerio went on. 'It's the least I can do in the circumstances.'

Aldo and Strocchi glanced at each other. 'No reward is necessary,' Strocchi said.

'But I insist—'

'We don't want your coin,' Aldo cut in. 'Give your blood money to a foundling hospital or an orphanage, if that soothes your conscience, but we've no need for it.'

Ruggerio's joy curdled at this insult. He straightened his back. 'Very well.'

'Signore, may I make a suggestion?' Cassandra asked. He gave permission with a curt gesture. 'Why don't you come inside and take shelter from the rain?' she called to Aldo and Strocchi. 'You can borrow some clothes until your own dry out.'

'Yes,' Ruggerio agreed, 'do come in and take advantage of my hospitality.' He enjoyed the twist of anger that sent across Aldo's features.

'And I shall cook a warm meal,' Cassandra added. 'You must be chilled to the bone. Let me feed you both before you leave San Jacopo al Girone.'

Strocchi was about to reply but Aldo murmured to him, words too quiet for Ruggerio to hear. Strocchi nodded, and Aldo smiled. 'That would be most welcome, Cassandra.'

'How gracious of you to accept,' Ruggerio said. 'I look forward to breaking bread with you both. I'm sure there is much for Aldo and I to discuss after recent . . . events. Questions to which he craves answers. It should make for an entertaining meal.'

Wearing another man's clothes made Strocchi uncomfortable. It was good to be out of his own sodden tunic, hose and boots, good to escape the rain still falling outside. But this borrowed doublet and hose were an awkward fit, made to flatter the narrow-chested Ruggerio who stood half a head shorter than Strocchi. The fabrics were far grander than anything he was used to, silks and satins and the softest wool rather than the usual rough cloth.

Dressing in the finery of a man who ordered murder to protect his reputation, taking any kindness from such a venal creature was wrong, but Aldo had been persuasive. Yes, Marco and Vincenzo were dead, but there were still questions that remained unanswered, matters about these killings that needed to be resolved. The chance to question Ruggerio in his own villa when he owed them a debt was too good to deny.

Strocchi emerged from the guest bedchamber, tugging at the borrowed hose to stop them rolling down from his hips. But all that did was push the doublet sleeves back up his forearms. The sooner he was in his own clothes and away from here, the better. Let Ruggerio decide what to do with the bodies. More than anything, Strocchi wished he was in his own home and in his own bed with Tomasia while little Bianca dozed in her cot. He wished he was back in Florence . . . That made him stop. He wished he was back in Florence. Yes, he did. The city was his home. It was where he belonged now.

Still pondering that, Strocchi went downstairs. Rich cooking aromas guided him to the kitchen, the scent of stew making his mouth water. Cassandra was busy stirring the pot, tearing fresh basil leaves into the stew. Aldo hunched in a chair by the kitchen table, using a whetstone to sharpen the blade of his stiletto. His borrowed clothes were far plainer, and a better fit. Aldo glanced at Strocchi, laughter bursting from his mouth. Cassandra also struggled to hide her amusement.

'I look ridiculous,' Strocchi lamented.

'Comical, certainly,' Aldo agreed.

'Oh dear,' Cassandra said. 'I hadn't realized . . .' She set her wooden spoon down. 'Should I fetch you some of Vincenzo's clothes? Those are what Aldo is wearing.'

Strocchi had little wish to put on a dead man's things, especially having witnessed his killing a short time earlier. 'I'm sure my own will be dry soon.' He took a seat next to Aldo, still tugging at the short hose and ill-fitting tunic. 'Will we eat in here?'

'No,' Cassandra replied. 'The signore has a sala along the hall for meals eaten inside, but he usually dines on the loggia or outside in the courtyard.' She glanced through the shutters at the rain. 'I suspect you'll be in the sala today.'

Satisfied with the sharpness of his stiletto, Aldo returned it to his left boot. 'That stew smells good,' he said. 'I'd have thought Ruggerio preferred grander dishes.'

'He does,' the housekeeper conceded, 'but I had little notice of his arrival. Normally, I know weeks in advance. That gives me time to have game birds caught, the finest formaggi sent from Florence, for the best fruits and vegetables to ripen. But this is not the weather for insalata. You two need something to warm you up.'

Aldo nodded. 'Grazie.'

A question had been troubling Strocchi. 'Cassandra, was Vincenzo able to read and write?'

'Why do you ask?' she said.

Strocchi described the false proclamations that Marco had posted across Florence, leading to a rise in religious fervour and anti-Medici anger. 'But I could find no evidence that Marco could write or read, meaning somebody else created those for him.'

'Vincenzo could be the person responsible for the proclamations,' Aldo said. 'It makes sense. Besides being stable hand here, Vincenzo also took messages to Florence. That would have given him opportunities to deliver the proclamations to Marco. And I found an inkpot and scraps of paper burnt in a brazier at the stable.'

Cassandra set down her spoon. 'I believe Vincenzo could read a little,' she said, 'but I never had cause to ask if he could write.'

It was not the confirmation Strocchi had hoped to hear, but nor did it rule out his notion. 'Marco worked as a servant for Uccello. That put him close to one victim, and helped him become familiar with the others. Marco got that job thanks to a letter of recommendation supposedly written by Signor Ruggerio . . .'

'Ruggerio is among the most ruthless men in Florence,' Aldo replied. 'And if Marco had been the only murderer, I could well believe he was acting on behalf of Ruggerio. But Vincenzo killed four mercenaries and tried to burn down this villa with Cassandra and Ruggerio inside it. For once, I don't think the signore is the man behind these deaths.'

'How reassuring,' Ruggerio announced from the doorway, startling Strocchi. He had not heard the silk merchant's approach.

'Signore,' Strocchi said, rising from his seat. 'I'm sorry, we did not—'

'Hush,' Ruggerio cut in. 'It is not often I hear Aldo absolving me of blame.' He smiled at Cassandra. 'My dear, is the food ready? I wouldn't wish to detain our guests here a moment longer than was necessary . . .'

The housekeeper nodded. 'Yes, signore. If the three of you will go through to the sala, I shall serve the meal immediately.'

In the sala, Ruggerio took the seat furthest from the entrance, light seeping through the shutters behind him casting the merchant in silhouette. Aldo sat at the opposite end of the long table, wanting to keep a clear view of Ruggerio during the meal, even though it meant his own back was to the door. Strocchi was last to sit in the sala, taking the chair on Aldo's left as Cassandra brought in steaming bowls of her stew.

'How quaint,' Ruggerio said, a thin smile on his lips. 'Peasant food.' The housekeeper apologized but he dismissed her with a wave of his hand. 'No, this is quite adequate for our guests, my dear. I would not wish these incorruptible officers from the Otto to think I was bribing them with fine food and drink. Well, one officer . . . and one constable.' Ruggerio raised his cup of wine first to Strocchi, and then to Aldo. 'Salute.'

Aldo ignored the wine, and the mockery. 'You must be relieved, signore.'

'Why? Because the two of you managed to stop Vincenzo killing me?'

'That, and the fact that the other founders of your confraternity are now dead. None of them represent a threat to you or your reputation anymore.'

Ruggerio put down his cup. 'None of those good men were a threat. Far from it.'

'Good men? An interesting choice of words. I have the document you stole when the convent was dissolved. I know what the five of you did, as does Strocchi.'

'You have suspicions, but nothing more. That document is torn and faded, all but impossible to read now.' Ruggerio laughed. 'You and I both know it would never convince the Otto. I was granted a pardon from prosecution. What took place is long gone.'

'Not to Marco, it wasn't,' Strocchi said. 'Nor to Vincenzo.'

'And both are dead,' Ruggerio replied, his face souring. 'It is over.'

'Then tell us what happened,' Aldo suggested. 'If you have such faith in the strength of your pardon, give us an account of what prompted all of this. Many men are dead, four of those you claim to have been good. Convince us.'

The silk merchant glared, his thin lips whitening. But instead of replying he sipped some of the stew, smacking his lips in appreciation as Cassandra came back into the room. 'I take it back, my dear, this is most delicious. Well done.'

'Thank you, signore.'

Ruggerio gestured at Aldo and Strocchi. 'You two must try it. I insist.'

Aldo swallowed a mouthful of the stew. It was well made, with a tangy aftertaste that lingered on his tongue. Strocchi was also enjoying the stew, eating as if he hadn't seen food all day. Aldo took some more. 'This is very good, Cassandra. Thank you.' He pointed to a chair on his right. 'Why don't you join us? I'm sure the signore won't object . . .'

Ruggerio grimaced. 'Of course not. Please, my dear, have a seat . . . if you wish.' He took another mouthful, his face souring.

The housekeeper shook her head. 'Grazie, but no, signore. I have things to do.'

'Very well.' He dismissed her without saying another word. Cassandra left the room, closing the door behind her. Ruggerio pushed his bowl of stew away, the thick liquid slopping onto the table. 'Do you truly wish to know what happened, all those years ago?'

'Yes,' Strocchi replied, all too eager.

Aldo hid a sigh. The young officer was becoming more adept at the courtly intrigues of Florence, but Strocchi was still no match for the scheming Ruggerio.

'Then I shall have to disappoint you,' the merchant said, smirking. 'Alas, it was so long ago that I struggle to recall the details. Who did what to whom, how the home of that poor famiglia caught fire, the screams that could be heard . . . All lost to the past, I'm afraid.'

The bastardo was teasing them, taunting them. Strocchi's hands clenched into fists on the table, his anger at this gloating merda rising fast. 'What a pity,' Aldo said to stop Strocchi replying first. 'As you are the only person left alive from that encounter, it would have been valuable to know what you saw and heard . . . and did.'

'Perhaps, but it would do you no good,' Ruggerio replied. 'As a wise man once said, let the past bury—' He stopped, a frown settling on his face. 'Let the—' Ruggerio shook his head. 'I don't feel at all well,' he said, struggling to rise from his chair. 'Cassandra?'

The door opened behind Aldo and the housekeeper glided into the room. She seemed to shimmer beside him, a coil of rope clutched in her hands. Strocchi slumped back in his chair, mouth moving but making no sound. Aldo stared at the bowl in front of him.

The stew, there something in the stew!

Aldo pushed the bowl away but it was too late. At the other end of the room Ruggerio collapsed to the floor, his face slack and empty.

'I'm sorry,' Cassandra whispered.

The room swirled around Aldo.

Then all was darkness.

The stew had worked faster than Cassandra had expected. Had she put too much sleeping draught in the stew? Ruggerio could not escape his reckoning, not after so long, so much preparation. She leaned close to Aldo. His breathing was shallow, but steady. Good, good.

Cassandra lifted Ruggerio back into his chair, using all the rope she had to bind him and Aldo to their seats. She fetched a hand-cart from the garden, tipped the senseless Strocchi into it and rolled him outside. He had no part in this. Better to remove the young officer from what must be done. By the time he woke, it would be over. She locked the doors and secured all shutters on the palazzo's lower level to be certain.

Now it was just Ruggerio, Aldo and herself.

One to make his confession.

One to hear it.

And one to burn the bastardo alive.

Cassandra brought oil, tinder and dry hay into the sala. She was patient. She could wait a while longer for the men to recover. Then the truth would be told . . .

Chapter Thirty-four

*Aldo's eyelids were heavy. He wanted to wake, knew he needed to, but his eyes would not obey. Why did he have to wake? Sleep was so comforting. But a familiar voice kept repeating one phrase: sleeping men make easy targets . . .

Ruggerio. Cassandra. 'I'm sorry.'

Aldo snapped awake.

He was still in the sala of Ruggerio's villa, still in the same sturdy wooden chair. But his arms and legs were now bound to it with well-tied ropes. Strocchi was gone, his seat empty, but Ruggerio remained at the other end of the table, head tipped forward onto his chest. Asleep, or feigning it. The bowls were gone, but the tangy aroma from the stew lingered in Aldo's nostrils. His belly lurched, wanting to empty itself of the tainted broth. Aldo swallowed hard, struggling to keep it down.

'You're awake,' Cassandra said as she came in, closing the door behind her. 'Good.'

'Cassandra . . .' Aldo's tongue was still heavy with whatever she had put in the stew, his mouth clammy and slow. 'You . . . You wrote those proclamations. You were the one directing Marco and Vincenzo . . . Telling them who to kill, how to do it.'

'I guided them,' she replied. 'They were eager to have their vendetta. But I persuaded them there was another way, a better way. One that was more likely to succeed. One requiring both patience and resolve.'

'Where's Carlo?'

'Outside. He's quite safe. The doors and shutters are all secured. When he does awaken, he will not be able to get inside or intervene. It's just the three of us now.'

Aldo hoped she was wrong. Carlo was resourceful, he might still find a way. Best to keep Cassandra talking, keep her occupied. The longer she was delayed, the better their chances. 'You've worked here at the villa more than a year,' Aldo said. 'You could have had your revenge before now.'

'True,' Cassandra agreed, strolling to the other end of the table. She rested a hand on Ruggerio's bald pate. 'But simply killing this bastardo would not have been enough. It would not have been justice. All five men deserved to suffer. I want Ruggerio to confess his sins. To admit what he and the others did to my famiglia. To beg for forgiveness.'

'And then?'

She ignored the question, instead tipping Ruggerio's head back to slap him across the face. He opened both eyes, glaring at her. 'There you are.' Cassandra bowed low. 'Signore,' she said, mockery in her voice, before striking Ruggerio again. This time the slap was harder, much more vicious. Her nails dug into the skin, drawing blood. Ruggerio spat a curse at her, fighting against his bindings without success. Cassandra whispered in his left ear, words Aldo could not hear. That brought more curses and threats but Aldo recognized the emptiness of the words. Ruggerio was terrified, with good reason. They were both at Cassandra's mercy.

'Why target Scarlatti first?' Aldo asked. She would soon tire of questions, but every moment of delay was useful. 'He was the weakest of the five. Why not one of the others?'

'I chose Scarlatti because he was weakest, the one most likely to tell us all we needed,' Cassandra replied. 'His housekeeper was most helpful in sharing what she knew about the signore. Poor Federica, she had no notion what she was doing.'

'You were there when Scarlatti was being questioned,' Aldo realized.

'Of course. I needed to hear in order to make best use of that information. Vincenzo was capable of many tasks, but he lacked restraint. That proved . . . problematic.'

This confirmed Aldo's suspicion. The strangling of Scarlatti was accidental, if no less a murder. 'You wrote the letter about a dispute between farmers that took me away from San Jacopo al Girone. You didn't want an officer of the Otto stumbling on what you were doing.'

'You're not an officer anymore,' Ruggerio interjected.

Aldo ignored the remark, keeping his gaze fixed on Cassandra. 'Am I correct?'

'It seemed a wise precaution,' she replied.

'But why hire a thief from the city to study this villa for weaknesses? You know every door and pathway on this estate better than anyone.'

'The thief was a distraction,' she said, 'as were the proclamations in Florence. Ways to keep you, the Otto, the duke and the signore busy looking elsewhere. In truth, I had little hope my proclamations would stir up so much anti-Medici anger in the city. Marco proved himself most adept in how he used that anger to mask his true intentions. The spirit of Savonarola still lives on in the hearts of Florence's people.'

'Enough!' Ruggerio snapped. 'I have heard far too much from both your mouths. Cassandra, I command you to release me. Untie my bonds and I will let you leave this estate unharmed. No denunzia shall be made against you with the Otto. You are free to depart Tuscany without fear of imprisonment or execution, both of which are likely otherwise.'

The housekeeper did not reply, shaking her head with a wry smile.

'What is so amusing? I said release me,' Ruggerio raged, the veins on his temples throbbing. 'Do it, or you shall suffer the consequences.'

Aldo willed him to be silent, but it did no good. Ruggerio ranted at Cassandra for several more minutes before exhausting himself. She stood through it all, ignoring everything he said. When he did stop, Cassandra pulled out a chair and sat at the table, midway along its length. 'I'm going to tell you a story about what happened to a good, honest famiglia in Florence more than forty years ago. I was only eight then, but these memories are burned into me. Of course, that was not the only thing to burn . . . but I get ahead of myself.'

Ruggerio was staring at Cassandra, his eyes wide. 'No . . . it's impossible.'

'What is?' Aldo asked.

'This will go quicker if I am not interrupted,' Cassandra said in a sterner voice.

'Nobody else was there . . .' Ruggerio insisted, ignoring the warning in her tone.

'It seems I have to convince you both.' Cassandra rose from her chair, approaching Aldo to extract the stiletto from his left boot. 'So kind of you to sharpen your blade for me,' she said before approaching Ruggerio. 'This should prove I'm a woman of my word.' She stabbed the stiletto down through Ruggerio's right hand, the tip of the blade burying itself in the arm of his chair. Ruggerio howled in pain, curses and anguish pouring from his thin lips.

Cassandra waited until he paused for breath. 'Now, as I was saying—'

'Strega!' Ruggerio snarled, his face pale. 'I'll see that you suffer for this. I'll see that everyone you care about suffers for this!'

'You already have,' Cassandra said, twisting the blade inside his wounded hand before pulling it free. She wiped the stiletto clean on Ruggerio's sweat-soaked tunic before returning to her chair once more. 'Now, where was I?'

'Telling us a story,' Aldo replied. Better to placate Cassandra than antagonize her. She bore a lifetime of hatred. Ruggerio would not be leaving this room alive, not if Cassandra could help it. But Aldo had no wish to die here. 'Please . . . tell us more.'

Strocchi woke and immediately emptied his belly. It was the churning in his gut that forced him awake, demanding he roll on his side. Spasm after spasm tormented him even when there was nothing left to disgorge until, finally, the retching stopped.

He rolled away from the mess of stew on the ground, spitting to clear the acrid taste from his mouth. Strocchi looked around, trying to make sense of why he was outside. He had been in Ruggerio's villa with Aldo, the two of them having a meal with the merchant. Now he was in the courtyard; the smouldering ruins of the stable stood opposite, the body of a dead mercenary was still on the ground close by. Strocchi struggled to his feet, the world whirling and spinning before settling itself.

Why was he back out in the rain?

The villa's front door was closed and locked. Strocchi hammered a fist on the sturdy wood, calling for Cassandra or Aldo to let him in. No response. He stepped back, peering through the rain at the upper level. There was nobody up on the loggia, and no reply when he shouted. It did not seem that much of the day had passed. Aldo had mentioned that Cassandra grew medicinal herbs in the walled garden behind the villa, how she dreamed of being an apothecary like her father . . . Had the housekeeper given them a sleeping draught?

The food, she must have put it in there. All three men had supped the stew. Yet he was the only one outside . . . Strocchi shivered, and not because the rain was soaking through his borrowed clothes. When he'd asked if Vincenzo could read and write, that moment of evasion in her answer . . . He did not have many facts, but a suspicion was fast growing: Cassandra was behind it, all of it. The proclamations, the murders. She had killed nobody herself but, like Ruggerio, she'd made it happen. Her weapons – Marco and Vincenzo – were gone, dead. So she was finishing what she had started.

If Cassandra had instigated and planned the vendetta, Ruggerio was her final target. Both of them were inside the villa, Strocchi was certain of that. Why else would the door be locked and all the ground-level shutters be bolted shut? Yet Cassandra had chosen to put him outside while – it seemed – keeping Aldo inside. That made no sense, unless . . . Cassandra intended to force a confession from Ruggerio, and she wanted Aldo as witness. Such an admission of guilt would never satisfy the Otto, but Ruggerio had escaped justice before. Of course, this assumed Cassandra intended to let Aldo live . . .

Strocchi shoved all that aside. Getting into the villa was what mattered, there must be a way. He hurried to the back of the building, loose stones jabbing into his feet through the wool of his borrowed hose. A pity Cassandra hadn't thrown his boots outside with him. Reaching the back entrance meant climbing over the rain-drenched corpse of Vincenzo, blood still trickling from the stiletto wound in his throat. It resembled a small, sad second mouth, ready to sing a lament or whisper a curse. Strocchi looked away.

He reached for the back door of the villa – locked. Beating fists against it brought no response. Aldo and Ruggerio could still be suffering the effects of that stew. Cassandra might have gagged them to ensure both stayed silent . . . or they might already be dead. No, Strocchi refused to accept that. Aldo always found a way to cheat such outcomes, even if it meant taking a life. Vincenzo's corpse was proof of that, and so were other bodies Strocchi had encountered in the past. Aldo would find a way . . . but he might need some help.

Strocchi paused. Ruggerio's stable had been set on fire, and his horses had bolted down the track. Why had nobody from San Jacopo al Girone come to help, or at least to discover what was happening on the estate? Knowing Ruggerio, it was unlikely the villagers cared much for the merchant, but Strocchi still would have expected them to be curious. Unless someone had told them not to come, not to get involved . . . Whatever the answer, it was clear he would have to find his own way inside the villa.

Strocchi leaned back against the garden wall to see the shutters on the upper level. Some were closed, yet a few remained open. If he could reach one, he could get inside. But the sides of the villa were wet from the downpour, while his fingertips were cold and numb, unable to get much grip on the stonework. He needed another way to scale the wall.

Cassandra leaned back in her chair, Aldo's stiletto still in her grasp. 'Papa was an apothecary in Florence, making remedies to help those less fortunate. Mama died giving birth to me, but Papa raised me and my older sister Polonia as best he could. He taught us how to read and write, encouraged us to learn his skills as an apothecary. We were happy . . .'

Her words trailed off, seeming swept away by memories. Aldo stopped testing his bonds. He'd been straining his arms and legs against the ropes, seeking some escape, but they were well tied, without excess or slippage. At the other end of the table sweat dripped from Ruggerio's nose and chin. His face was etched with pain from the wound to his hand.

'Papa was against the Medici,' Cassandra went on. 'He believed our city had fallen into folly by ceding power to that family, by turning away from its true path as a republic of the people. He rejoiced when Savonarola urged everyone to remake Florence as a true city of God, a new Jerusalem. Then the Fanciulli appeared, boys and young men in white robes demanding donations for the Church from anyone who passed. Still our papa believed that Savonarola was doing God's work. But then these boys began hammering on the doors of good families, demanding the surrender of whatever the Fanciulli deemed unholy or profane. Papa worried that putting too much power into the hands of young men was a mistake . . .'

She paused, rubbing at her eyes. 'Twice one particular group of Fanciulli came to our home but Papa refused to let them inside. He told them our house was a holy house, with nothing to hide and nothing to fear. The third time' – Cassandra stared at Ruggerio – 'the third time you and your friends came, Papa was not there to protect us.'

Aldo had heard many stories of excesses and abuses by Savonarola's young acolytes, but never from someone who had been there. Never from someone who had lived through it.

'Before opening the door, Polonia made me hide,' Cassandra said, 'made me promise not to come out until it was safe. She told me Papa would be home soon. She was wrong.'

Ruggerio cleared his throat. 'We never meant—'

Cassandra slammed a fist on the table. 'I said no more interruptions!'

Ruggerio closed his mouth. He looked at Aldo, raising both eyebrows, as if to ask how they would escape. Aldo shook his head. There was no escape. Not for Ruggerio, and perhaps not for him. Cassandra's anger had eaten away at her. Now she had no reason to hold back.

'The five of them came into our home as if they owned it – Dovizi, Scarlatti, Uccello, Ghiberti and this merda,' she said, waving a dismissive hand at Ruggerio. 'They demanded coin, but we had none. They demanded gemstones, but Polonia would not let them take anything. Finally, they demanded her.' Tears ran down Cassandra's face, but she did not wipe them away. 'I watched from my hiding place as she fought for as long as she could. But there were five of them . . .' She shook her head. 'Do I need say anything more?'

'No,' Aldo replied. Of all the crimes reported to the Otto, none made him more ashamed than when men forced themselves on others. Murder he could understand, but violating another person . . . it was beneath contempt. He had no wish to make Cassandra tell them what had happened next. Aldo could picture it all too well.

'I did not touch her,' Ruggerio said. 'If you were there, you know that.'

Cassandra nodded. 'I know you have no interest in women or girls, signore. But you were laughing as she fought for her dignity, and you urged the others on. Perhaps you were doing it to hide who you were, but I saw how much you enjoyed that cruelty.'

Ruggerio shook his head, but Aldo believed Cassandra was right. Ruggerio was a selfish man, someone who rejoiced in the suffering of others. He cared only for himself, his own comfort, his own needs, his own wants. The hopes and desires of others held no interest for Ruggerio. Now the price of that cruelty was to be paid.

'Besides,' Cassandra said, 'you were the one who suggested burning my sister.'

'I would never—'

'Do not deny it!' she shouted, rising so fast her chair toppled over. 'You told the four others to set our home ablaze. You said it would stop my sister making a denunzia. You did not start the fire, but it was your idea, signore.'

Ruggerio kept shaking his head, as if denying the truth would protect him.

'What happened to your sister?' Aldo asked, keeping his voice low and unthreatening.

'She burned,' Cassandra snapped. 'We both did.' She twisted round, lifting her simple top to reveal a back covered in skin stretched taut and ugly by flames, a lifetime of pain and discomfort. Cassandra lowered the cloth, hiding her scars again. 'Polonia suffered worse but she did not die. When this bastardo and his friends had gone, I helped her escape the flames. She spent weeks in the ospedale, we both did, Papa praying by our sides each day. Nine months after the Fanciulli came to our home, Polonia gave birth to twins.'

Vincenzo and Marco, Aldo surmised, but kept his silence.

'Papa insisted Polonia make a denunzia against the Fanciulli, knowing Savonarola would never condone such behaviour, and certainly not in his name. But much had changed in those months. Savonarola no longer held the same sway. The Church and the city wished to be rid of its troublesome monk, and needed testimony from those willing to accuse him.'

'Which Ruggerio and his friends gave,' Aldo said, 'in return for their pardon.'

'What we did was within the law,' the merchant said, self-pity in his voice.

'Was it?' Aldo asked. 'Attacking Cassandra's sister and setting fire to their home, was that within the law? Accusing Savonarola of being complicit in your crimes – crimes about which he can have had no knowledge – to save yourselves, was that within the law?'

Ruggerio did no reply.

Cassandra righted her chair but did not sit. 'Papa took his life a few years later. He could not bear what had happened to us. After we buried Papa, I swore to see the five of them suffer, but Polonia was a better woman than me. She forgave the Fanciulli their sins, their trespasses. She was in pain the rest of her days, but forbade me from pursuing a vendetta against the five Fanciulli. But as her boys got older, I told them what had happened to their mother, why they had no father. Polonia found out what I was doing. She made Marco and Vincenzo vow not to seek revenge for what she had suffered. They promised not to do so – not while she was alive – and so did I.'

Aldo nodded. That was why their revenge had been so long in coming.

'By the time Polonia died I was a servant at the signore's palazzo in the city,' Cassandra continued, 'learning all I could about him and the others. I discovered the five were bound together by their sins. That had motivated them to form the Company of Santa Maria, using the confraternity to atone for their actions as Fanciulli. I wondered if my sister had been right. Perhaps what they did to her had changed the five, made them better men. But the closer I got to the founders, the more I realized it was no more than a mask they wore to hide their true faces, their true natures.'

'We did many good works,' Ruggerio protested.

'Papa often said this about men like you,' Cassandra sneered. 'In Florence, it is not enough to do good. It is far more important to be seen doing good. That is you, signore. An empty man, a callow creature who delights in the suffering of others and only cares about himself, his reputation.' She stabbed the stiletto into the table. 'If I could, I would set fire to your skin but keep you from death for years and years, so you could suffer as I suffered, as my sister suffered. But I am not as much a monster as you.'

Ruggerio sank back in his chair, the relief evident on his drained face.

The fool actually believed she might let him live.

'Instead,' she said, 'I am going to burn you alive like Dovizi, Uccello and Ghiberti. But first you will confess your sins to Aldo. Confess, and you might suffer less.'

Strocchi searched and scoured all around the villa without finding anything that could help reach the upper level. There might have been something inside the stable, but that building was lost to fire. Where else . . .? He stopped by the mercenary's corpse in the courtyard. The walled garden, he hadn't looked there. Strocchi raced round the side of the villa, jumping over the dead mercenary with the cut throat.

There was no gate in the wall that faced the villa, but Strocchi found an entrance on one side. He hurried in, glancing around – there! A simple wooden ladder, its two sides coming together to form a single joint at the top. Such ladders were common in the village where Strocchi had grown up, farmers using them to tend the tallest branches of their olive trees. Hopefully this one had enough height to reach the upper level.

He carried the ladder out of the walled garden and round the side of the villa. The shutters on the upper level were all narrow, liable to make too much noise as he got through them. Better to clamber up onto the loggia, and get inside there. Of course, that assumed there was no door between the loggia and the rest of the upper level. Strocchi realized he'd never been upstairs in Ruggerio's villa. It was a chance worth taking.

Reaching the front of the villa, he stood the ladder against the wall beneath the loggia. The highest point of the ladder was just short of the loggia, but if he stood on the top rung, he might be able to stretch and reach the balustrade – it would have to do. Strocchi put a foot on the bottom rung and pressed down, forcing the bottom of the ladder's legs into the mud. That stole a little height but hopefully fixed the ladder in place.

Pushing rain out of his eyes, Strocchi climbed upwards. The higher he went, the more unsteady the ladder became, bowing in towards the villa wall. It seemed to tremble beneath him, though Strocchi couldn't be sure if that was due to its instability or his own fear. As he got near the top, the ladder abruptly shifted below him. A glance down confirmed it: the ladder had slid backwards, away from the wall. The mud was not firm enough to keep it in place. Strocchi went higher, gazed fixed on the top of the ladder as it threatened to slip down. This was madness, but descending seemed as dangerous as continuing up.

The ladder gave another abrupt lurch as Strocchi put a foot on the highest rung, preparing to stretch for the balustrade. More tremors ran through the wood, accompanied by new cracking sounds. It was giving way, Santo Spirito, it was giving way!

Strocchi threw himself upwards, hands grasping at the air.

Aldo gagged on the overwhelming scent of lavender oil. Cassandra had emptied a bottle of it across the wooden table, filling the room with a cloying aroma. Now she was slapping both hands in the oil before wiping them on Ruggerio's face, scalp and clothes. 'Confess your sins, signore,' she urged him. 'Admit what you did to my sister.'

'Tell me,' Aldo chimed in. 'It will be better if you do.' It was a lie, of course. Aldo had no power of absolution to offer Ruggerio, no prospect of redemption. But it was better to agree with Cassandra, and hope Ruggerio had the wit to do the same. The longer the merchant talked, the more chance there was of Strocchi finding a way inside.

Aldo did not blame Cassandra for what she was doing. He had long hoped to be there the day Ruggerio faced the consequences of his actions. The fact that Cassandra had used her own sister's sons as weapons, sacrificing them to achieve her goals, proved how far she would go. Vincenzo had been willing to burn the villa with Cassandra still inside it. He wouldn't have done so unless she had told him to. That suggested she would stop at nothing to have her revenge, even if it cost her her own life. Cassandra would kill anyone who tried to stop her.

'Please,' Ruggerio spluttered through the oil running down his face, 'I can't breathe.'

'What did my sister say when you suggested burning her alive?' Cassandra asked.

'I was young and stupid,' he replied. Were those brimming tears of remorse, or a response to the oil getting in his eyes? Knowing Ruggerio, probably the latter. 'I never meant things to go so far. We were drunk on our own power—'

Cassandra backhanded him across the face. 'Liar! The only thing you regret is that I witnessed what you did, and survived to hunt the five of you down.'

'No, it's not true . . .' Ruggerio's voice was a snivelling whine.

She stepped back from him, disgust curdling her face. 'Yes, it is.' Cassandra brought tinder and dried hay from a corner of the room, piling most of it around Ruggerio but putting some in his lap and the rest inside his tunic. He cried out in protest – to no effect. When she was done, he resembled a straw effigy of himself, waiting to burn on a pyre.

Seeming satisfied with her work, Cassandra looked around herself.

'What have you lost?' Aldo asked.

'Flints,' she replied. 'I must have left them in the kitchen.' Cassandra strode out, Ruggerio screaming at her. Impotent rage was all he had left now.

Aldo ignored him, listening to her retreating footsteps. Once he was sure she was out of hearing, he hissed at Ruggerio to be quiet. 'You'll be dead soon unless we can find a way out of this. Can you move your chair at all?'

But Ruggerio was too far gone, tears streaming down his face. The stench of fresh piss billowed in the sala, colliding with the aroma of lavender oil – the merchant must have lost control of himself. Fear had taken Ruggerio.

Aldo rocked his chair from side to side, determined to topple it over. That might break apart one of the furniture joints, freeing him from the bindings. But before he could complete that task, the sound of approaching footsteps made Aldo stop. Cassandra was coming back . . .

Strocchi dangled from the loggia as the wooden ladder slid to the ground below. There was no way back now. After a moment to catch his breath, Strocchi hauled himself upward, clambering atop the stone balustrade before tumbling over it. He dropped to the floor, landing hard on his hands and knees. Fortunately, the loggia did have an open doorway leading into Ruggerio's villa. Strocchi wished he had a weapon, any weapon.

Once inside he paused, listening. Faint voices drifted up from below, guiding Strocchi to the main staircase. He crept down the first few steps, stopping as sudden shouts cut the air, a bellow of curses and rage: Ruggerio, screaming in anger at someone. Cassandra swept by, heading towards the kitchen. God be praised, she didn't glance up the staircase. Once she was gone, Strocchi descended the remaining steps, praying none would creak. They didn't.

Strocchi could hear Aldo close by, murmuring to someone else. The sound came from the sala; he and Ruggerio must still be in there. Strocchi hurried closer, staying on the balls of his feet. He smelled the sala before reaching it, a ripe mixture of stew, piss and lavender oil. What had been happening in there?

What Strocchi found inside stopped him cold. Aldo was still in the same chair, but his arms and legs had been bound to it with rope. 'Carlo! Thank God you're here.'

'What happened?' Strocchi asked, coming closer.

'Quick, untie me,' Aldo replied. 'It's Cassandra, she was behind everything.'

Strocchi did as he was told, but struggled to undo the taut knots binding Aldo's right arm to the chair. Ruggerio stared at them from the far end of the table, his skin glistening. Was that oil dripping from his nose and chin? Strocchi glanced under the table. Dried hay and tinder was piled round Ruggerio. Cassandra was making a funeral pyre for the silk merchant, but she intended to burn him alive. 'Santo Spirito, why is she doing this?'

'We don't have time,' Aldo hissed. 'She'll be back—'

A sharp pain exploded in Strocchi's head.

Darkness embraced him.

Aldo saw a hand flashing through the air, but before he could shout a warning Cassandra had smashed the flint down on Strocchi's head. The sound was sickening, like an egg cracking open on a stone. Strocchi slumped to the floor, no sound escaping his lips, no movements from his body. Cassandra stood over him.

'I was wrong. He did find a way back inside. Better if he had remained where I left him.'

'What are you going to do with him?' Aldo asked. 'With us?'

Cassandra pointed his stiletto at Ruggerio. 'That bastardo is going to burn for what he did.' She stabbed the blade into the table, the tip burying itself in the oil-soaked wood.

'Please, no,' Ruggerio whimpered. 'I don't want to die. Not like this!'

'As for you and this young officer' – she glanced down at Strocchi – 'I haven't decided. Not yet. If I let you free, I know you will try to save Ruggerio.'

'Then you don't know me very well,' Aldo replied, fixing her with an unwavering gaze. 'Trust me, I'm happy to watch that merda burn. I can be ruthless as you when required.'

Cassandra returned his look, studying Aldo's face. 'Yes. Yes, I believe you could. But I can't risk letting you go free. Not until I know the signore is beyond saving.' Ruggerio burst into tears at the other end of the table, losing what composure he had left.

'Ruggerio is beyond redemption,' Aldo said, before nodding. 'Do what you must.'

'Have you lost your senses?' Ruggerio spluttered. 'This strega is going to kill us both! Do something! Stop her!'

Aldo shook his head before smiling at Cassandra. 'I put my life in your hands, and in the hands of God.' He closed his eyes.

It was a lie, of course.

Aldo was doing no such thing. But he needed Cassandra to believe he had surrendered himself to whatever decision she made. He needed the housekeeper to let her guard down, to stop thinking of him as a threat, someone she must keep watching. If she did, there was the faintest chance somebody might still get out of this villa alive.

He heard Cassandra move towards Ruggerio.

It had worked.

His sudden acceptance distracted her from checking his bonds. She didn't realize how close Strocchi had come to untying one of the knots. Aldo lifted his right wrist from the chair arm, straining and stretching that knot still further. One end of the rope pulled free, loosening the rest of it. But the sudden movement made Cassandra stop.

She glanced round at Aldo, flint and striker in her hands.

'Do it,' he urged her. 'Do it.'

Cassandra turned back to Ruggerio, hitting the striker against her flint, sparks landing on the terrified merchant. 'Please, no,' he begged. 'I'll do anything, say whatever you want! Don't burn me – not like this – please . . .'

She ignored him, her blows with the striker faster now, more urgent. Spark after spark flew at Ruggerio, landing on his face, his tunic, the tinder piled on his lap. One of them must catch soon and when it did, he would become a human torch in moments.

Aldo pulled his right arm free, reaching across to untie his left arm.

'Please, you have to help me,' Ruggerio said. 'I don't deserve to die like this!'

'Tell that to Lippo,' Aldo replied as more sparks rained down.

'Who?'

'The one-armed thief you had killed in the Podestà because he dared to spy on this villa,' Aldo spat. 'Or try telling all the others whose lives you ruined. Do you think they would agree with you? Would they say you don't deserve to die?'

A spark jumped from the flint, glowing as it arced through the air, landing in the clump of dried hay piled on Ruggerio's lap. A curl of smoke rose up, taunting him. 'No, no, no, no, no!' Ruggerio started puffing at the spark that had landed, trying to blow it out. The fool had clearly never built his own fire; blowing on the ember would only make it—

A flame appeared in front of Ruggerio, the fire taking hold.

He screamed, an eerie sound full of panic and fear.

Cassandra stepped back from Ruggerio . . .

. . . but she kept staring at him.

Aldo got his left arm free – and lunged for his stiletto on the table. Cassandra did the same, the two of them scrambling to grab the blade first. But they reached it at the same time, their hands knocking the stiletto free from the wood. It slid away from them, tumbling over the far side and falling to the floor. Cassandra threw herself after it so Aldo sat back in his chair, reaching down to unbind his legs. He had to get free if he was to –

Ruggerio screamed again, but this time it was all pain.

The fire had taken him.

It was burning his clothes, his oiled skin, his eyebrows.

He roared and screamed and burned, the sight of it transfixing.

A blade sliced through the air in front of Aldo as Cassandra rose from the floor. Aldo flung himself sideways, toppling over the prone figure of Strocchi. The chair gave a satisfying crack as it tumbled, the joints breaking apart, loosening Aldo's legs from their bindings. But Cassandra was still coming for him.

He kicked out at the air and caught her on the chin, sending her sprawling back onto the oily tabletop. Aldo clawed at the rope binding his other leg with one hand, the other hand slapping Strocchi on the face. 'Carlo, wake up!' But there was no response.

Ruggerio was a burning mass of fire, smoke filling the air. Aldo coughed as a sickly aroma forced its way into his nose: roasting meat. Ruggerio was burning alive, being cooked by the flames.

Soon the dining room would be an inferno of fire consuming everything and everyone inside. They had to get out of here. Now.

Cassandra came again, a murderous gleam in her eyes. 'I should have known you would want to save yourself,' she hissed, soot and blood smearing her features.

Still on his back, Aldo swiped a boot in the air, kicking his stiletto from her grasp.

Cassandra howled with rage, all reason leaving her.

Aldo got his other leg free just in time.

She leapt at him –

– but Aldo pulled both knees back to his chest.

Cassandra landed atop him, Aldo's legs between them.

He kicked out, pushing backwards towards the burning mess of Ruggerio.

She stumbled, teetering, fighting for balance . . .

. . . then fell into the fire.

A howl filled the air, full of rage and anguish.

Aldo rolled onto his knees beside Strocchi, slapping the young officer across the face. 'Wake up, Carlo! We have to get out of here!' There was blood on the floor by Strocchi's head, but not too much. There was still hope. 'Carlo, wake up!'

Strocchi stirred, his eyelids fluttering. 'Aldo . . .?'

'Yes, it's me. We have to go!'

'Go? Where?'

Abandoning efforts to get Strocchi on his feet, Aldo dragged the younger man to the doorway instead. He paused to retrieve his stiletto, glancing back . . . Half the room was ablaze, the heat searing at Aldo, threatening to set his borrowed clothes and hair on fire. The table was burning, but smoke made it impossible to see Cassandra or what was left of Ruggerio.

* * *

Strocchi drifted awake and wished he had not. Pain throbbed through his head with the fury of a thundering horse's hooves, while every part of him was cold and wet. He was lying in the open on rain-soaked grass. How had he got here? They had been inside the villa, he and Aldo and Ruggerio. Strocchi remembered struggling to untie ropes and then . . .

Pain.

Strocchi forced himself to sit up, wincing all the way. 'Ughh, my head.'

Aldo was crouching beside him. 'It could have been worse,' Aldo replied. 'Look.'

Fire had claimed most of the villa now, roaring out through the shutters on both levels. Part of the roof had caved in, flames licking up at the sky, black smoke billowing towards the moody clouds overhead. At least the rain had stopped. There were drag marks in the dirt where Aldo must have pulled him away from the villa.

'Santo Spirito.' Strocchi put fingers to the back of his head. They came away bloody.

'Careful,' Aldo warned. 'You took a blow that would have killed some men. Good thing you have a strong head. Give yourself time to recover, yes?'

Strocchi nodded, wincing again. He closed both eyes. 'What happened?'

Aldo recounted what Cassandra had done, the burning of Ruggerio, the desperate battle as flames consumed the dining room, how she fell into the fire.

'She's dead?'

'They both are, she and Ruggerio.'

Strocchi looked around. Despite all that happened, they were still alone on the hillside. 'Why did nobody come up from the village to help us?'

'I told Father Ognissanti to stop anyone else intervening.'

'Why? They could have helped stop—'

'I didn't want anyone else risking their lives,' Aldo cut in. 'Not for me. Certainly not for Ruggerio. But then you arrived this morning . . .'

Another section of the villa roof gave way, sparks flying into the air.

Strocchi struggled to make sense of all that had happened. Murder, and murder, and more deaths. 'How did you know Cassandra was a killer?' he asked.

'I didn't,' Aldo admitted. 'But I had suspicions. The discovery that Scarlatti's murder was probably committed by Vincenzo suggested he was working with the killer in Florence. Yet the stable hand had seemed a simple, direct man – far from the cunning mind required to co-ordinate killings in different places. There were other signs, other clues to what she was doing, but it took me too long, far too long to notice them. That nearly got us killed.'

'You saved my life,' Strocchi said.

'You would have done the same for me.'

'But still . . .' The young officer puffed out his cheeks. 'If I can ever do anything for you in return, just ask and it will be done.'

Aldo smiled. 'There is one thing.'

Aldo got up and helped Strocchi to his feet. The young officer swayed and lurched at first, but soon steadied himself. Once he was able, the two of them stumbled down the muddy track towards San Jacopo al Girone. Aldo waited until they could no longer see the remains of Ruggerio's villa burning before speaking again.

'I want to come home. To be back in Florence.'

Strocchi hesitated before replying. 'I . . .'

'It's where I belong,' Aldo continued. 'Where I am at my best. I know you do not agree with all that I do . . . with all that I am . . . but I also believe you can see the sense in me returning to the city. We work well together, you and I.'

Strocchi nodded. 'I can make a case for your return to the segretario, but you know what Bindi is like. He will take some convincing to allow you back at the Podestà.'

'The fact that we found the killers should help.'

'True.'

Aldo knew that even if Bindi agreed, the segretario would be even more vindictive than usual. But it would be worth that to be back in Florence, nearer to Saul. To be home. 'Think of it this way,' Aldo suggested. 'What would Tomasia say if she was here?'

That brought a smile to Strocchi's lips. 'She would tell me to say yes.'

'And what do you say, Carlo?'

Strocchi stopped to look down at the dead man's clothes clinging to him, the shredded hose and smoke-stained doublet. 'We can't go back to the city looking like this.'

'Good answer.' They continued down the hill, Aldo smiling to himself. But every now and then the acrid stench of that hellish dining room filled his nostrils.

Cesare Aldo could still smell flesh burning, even from this distance.

Historical Note

Ritual of Fire is a work of fiction, but the story is based in part on real incidents and people. For example, the Madonna of Santa Maria Impruneta was a revered painting – supposedly the work of Saint Luke – that citizens of Florence believed could give them special protection. It was carried into the city to ward off plague, pestilence, drought, war and flooding. *The Medicean Succession* by Gregory Murry details how Duke Cosimo de' Medici had the painting carried through Florence while dealing with his first drought in the summer of 1538. The Madonna apparently obliged, and the city was blessed with rain.

Girolamo Savonarola attracted thousands to hear his sermons, many of them believing his promise that Florence could become a city of God. The monk turned unruly youths into his Fanciulli, sending them out on the streets in white surplices to confront gamblers and drinkers. If someone shouted, 'Here come Savonarola's boys!' gamblers would flee. The youths set up altars at crossroads where they sang hymns and encouraged citizens to join them, while others went door to door seeking alms for the poor. Some of those youths went too far after being entrusted with too much power. You can read more about Savonarola in *The Florentines* by Paul Strathern, and *The Pope's Greatest Adversary* by Samantha Morris.

Savonarola over-reached himself and was executed in the Piazza della Signoria on May 23rd, 1498, as Bindi recalls. Indeed, it was the Otto that officially condemned the monk to death. The next day, women were found kneeling and praying where he had been burned. The familiar Florentine vices of sodomy, gambling and whoring returned after Savonarola's death, but his supporters still believed. They became aligned with the anti-Medici political movement, as Lorenzo Polizzotto reveals in *The Elect Nation: The Savonarolan Movement in Florence 1494–1545*, making them a target for Cosimo after he became duke.

The unfortunate Cristoforo da Soci whom Strocchi visits in Le Stinche was a real person. He was a member of the Capi Rossi, a group of laymen who became increasingly fanatical in their religious beliefs. The notary made the mistake of sharing his prophecies about Duke Cosimo being overthrown with someone who brought these to the attention of the Otto. The magistrates sentenced da Soci to public humiliation and imprisonment in the area of Le Stinche reserved for the mentally unwell.

The arquebus firearms and wheellock pistols carried by Ruggerio's guards were often used by mercenaries during their period. Gun proliferation and gun control were becoming issues of increasing importance on the Italian peninsula during the sixteenth century. Indeed, the Beretta company was first documented as a maker of weaponry in Gardone during 1526, though the name is more popularly associated with handguns of the twentieth century. For more on this topic, read *The Beauty and the Terror* by Dr Catherine Fletcher, or her paper 'Firearms and the State in Sixteenth-Century Italy'.

The small village of San Jacopo al Girone stands where it has for centuries, tucked alongside the Arno, a few miles east of Florence. It remains a quiet place, though the truffle festival in early September is a popular event that draws people from miles away. Where the journey between San Jacopo al Girone used to require a horse or at least two hours on foot there is now a regular bus service. For a few euros it will transport you to Piazza San Marco, where Savonarola first rose to prominence more than five hundred years ago.

Acknowledgements

𝒥 am indebted to everyone at Pan Macmillan for their faith in my Cesare Aldo novels, for making *Ritual of Fire* read so well and look so splendid. Special thanks are due to my editor Alex Saunders, cover designer Neil Lang, publicity director Pips McEwan and everyone else at The Smithson for believing in this series of historical thrillers.

Thank you to all the historians, academics and authors whose work informed my writing of place and time in *Ritual of Fire* – any errors are my own. A special mention must be made of Dr Catherine Fletcher for sharing her paper on sixteenth-century firearms.

I owe an enormous debt of gratitude to booksellers and librarians for spreading the word about Cesare Aldo. Special shout-out to my local independent bookshop Atkinson Pryce and its partners in the Wee Three Indies, The Edinburgh Bookshop and Far From the Madding Crowd, who helped launch this series. A big wave to Wardini Books, Unity Books and Scorpio Books in New Zealand for pressing my paperbacks into the hands of Aotearoa.

A doff of my digital cap to all the book bloggers and wonderful book cheerleaders on Instagram, Twitter and BookTok for raising me up. In a world where social media can sometimes seem a forbidding place, people like Dan Bassett, Riley Klabunde and Andy Wormald make it much happier and more hopeful. Thanks to the podcasters and YouTubers who have let me talk about Renaissance Florence, especially Dani Vee at *Words & Nerds*, Mark and Mark at *The Bestseller Experiment*, and the ubiquitous Craig Sisterson.

Thank you to all the literary festivals that welcomed me – Theakston Old Peculier Crime Fiction Festival in Harrogate, Bloody Scotland in Stirling, Chip Lit Festival in Chipping Norton, Aye Write in Glasgow, Lyme Crime in Lyme Regis, Outwith Festival in Dunfermline, Newcastle Noir and Bay Tales in the north-east, and many more. I'm especially thankful to all the crime writers who welcomed me into their community with open arms.

I'm grateful to colleagues past and present on the creative writing programmes at Edinburgh Napier University – Sam, El, Dan, Noelle, Katie, Ally – for their patience and goodwill.

I remain blessed to be represented by the wonderful literary agent Jenny Brown, who guides and supports so many writers with her skill, wit and enthusiasm.

Lastly, thank you to my better half who listens and nods when I talk or grumble about how the book is going. Past time for another research trip to Florence, yes?

A Divine Fury

By D. V. Bishop

Read on for an extract from the next
book in the Cesare Aldo series . . .

Chapter One

Wednesday, October 29th 1539

In Cesare Aldo's experience, the citizens most likely to break curfew in Florence were the drunken, the deceitful and the dangerous. The challenge was knowing which was which while following one of them through the city in the hours before dawn.

Only a select few were permitted to use the streets after nightfall: Duke Cosimo de' Medici, the city's ruler, and his guards; anyone carrying a letter of permission signed by the duke; and the unfortunate men of the night patrol, enforcing the curfew for the city's most feared criminal court, the Otto di Guardia e Balia. Aldo was one of the unfortunates on night patrol, a purgatory he had endured since returning to Florence almost a year and a half ago. His experience of those who broke curfew was now, therefore, extensive.

The drunken usually blamed wine for still being outside long after the bells had tolled for all good citizens to return home. Some drunks were friendly, others belligerent and a few even violent, but most were no match for the night patrol. The deceitful were those citizens using the darkness as a mask to hide their illicit behaviour: generally theft or fornication. Aldo had little sympathy for anyone arrested while succumbing to lust or avarice. Yes, he had been guilty of both – but was not fool enough to get caught.

The dangerous, they came in many guises. There were those who had lost all reason, ready to harm themselves or others without warning. Some were looking for a fight, seeking somebody to hurt. And there were those with darkness in their hearts or murder in their heads. Once a person chose to kill, a fear of breaking curfew was unlikely to stop them.

The lone figure ahead was neither lurching nor staggering. That suggested they were more deceitful or dangerous than drunk. A heavy cloak and cap hid their face and build. But the care with which they used the shadows of alleyways and narrow streets to shroud their journey made Aldo crouch to pull the trusty stiletto from his left boot.

'What are you doing?' Benedetto asked. Like Aldo, he was stuck on night patrol, but the young constable made no effort to conceal his disdain for it. Benedetto had been an eager, even enthusiastic recruit to the Otto three years ago. However, serving the court had soured him so much that every task now seemed a chore, and every question a cause for argument.

'When trouble arises,' Aldo whispered, 'a blade is better in the hand than the boot.' He rose to his feet. They were close to Piazza Santa Croce, the largest square in Florence's eastern quarter, having followed the curfew breaker from near the convent of Le Murate. Now their quarry must cross the piazza, or make a much longer journey to avoid the wide, open space. Either choice would reveal something about them.

'What trouble? It's just someone creeping home in the dark.'

'Lower your voice,' Aldo hissed.

'Why should I? We've been following them since—'

Aldo put a hand over Benedetto's mouth to silence him, but it was too late. The curfew-breaker twisted round to stare at them – and then sprinted into the piazza.

'Palle!' Aldo raced after the suspect, leaving Benedetto to swear and splutter. By the time Aldo reached the piazza his quarry was halfway across, getting further away with each moment. Cursing Benedetto for not doing as he was told, Aldo pressed on.

The suspect disappeared into a nearby alley as Aldo reached the far side of the piazza. He stopped to catch his breath, spots dancing in front of his eyes. Running was for children and dogs, not grown men of forty. Benedetto soon caught up to him. 'Where did they go?' he panted. Aldo pointed to the alley. The passageway was dark and narrow, allowing only one of them to enter at a time – the perfect place for an ambush.

'Where's your knife?' Aldo asked.

'I didn't bring one. Didn't know I'd need it.' No wonder Benedetto was stuck on night patrol. He lacked the imagination for anything better.

A fat drop of water hit Aldo in the face, making him look up. The moon had been visible earlier, but now it was mostly hidden behind ominous clouds. Another drop fell on Aldo, and another and another. In moments it was a downpour, soaking into his cap and tunic.

'We should go back to the Podestà,' Benedetto shouted through the sudden, torrential rain. 'Anyone who wants to be out in this is welcome to it!'

'We have a curfew-breaker to catch,' Aldo replied. He stamped through the puddles forming on the ground to the alley. 'If they get past me, it's your job to stop them.' Gripping the stiletto in his right hand, Aldo entered the inky darkness. Once inside the alley he paused, letting his eyes adjust. The walls on either side were solid stone, two sturdy palazzi with no shutters at ground level. No means of escape there. Aldo edged forward, shoulders brushing against either wall as he advanced.

Up ahead, the alley opened into a small courtyard; a dead space between buildings. Again, no shutters, and no apparent way out. Despite a brief glimpse of the crescent moon above, it was dark and gloomy, difficult to make anything out in the pouring rain. Piles of rubble and broken stones seemed to fill much of the courtyard, providing several places to hide. Aldo peered round, searching for any sign of the fugitive . . . Nothing.

Had he been mistaken? Or was there another way out, some hidden door or—

A movement to one side caught Aldo's eye. Then he was shoved backwards into a stone wall, all the breath knocked out of him. Fierce eyes glared at Aldo, a fist rising up—

Aldo jabbed his stiletto forward, the blade finding his attacker. They howled, stumbling back. Male, definitely male. The fugitive lifted a hand to stare at his own blood before lurching back into the alley. Aldo wanted to pursue, but his legs crumpled beneath him. The blood on his stiletto was reassuring. The fugitive was wounded; they wouldn't get far.

A voice cried out – Benedetto, shouting at the fugitive to stop. A knife would have been more use. Aldo was getting to his feet when Benedetto rushed into the courtyard.

'Aldo? You in here?'

'Yes.'

Benedetto came closer, eyes widening when he saw the blade. 'Are you hurt?'

Aldo shook his head. 'It's the fugitive's blood, not mine.'

'He knocked me flying,' Benedetto confessed.

'Where did he go?'

'Toward Piazza della Signoria.'

'Then let's get after him.' Aldo pushed Benedetto back along the alley, turning west when they reached the other end. If not for the rain they might have tracked their quarry from the drops of blood his wound left behind. Instead, they had to rely on the likelihood that his injury would force the fugitive to take the most direct path to wherever he was going.

Piazza della Signoria was the most important square in Florence. It was there that its citizens gathered to praise and protest, and it was where condemned men were publicly executed. Tall stone buildings surrounded the piazza, Palazzo della Signoria the tallest of them all. The city's laws were debated there by the Senate, though true power was held by Duke Cosimo de' Medici. The likelihood of the fugitive being foolish enough to linger here was low.

Yet when Aldo and Benedetto reached the piazza, a figure was lying prone beneath the statue of *David* in front of the grand palazzo. 'There,' Aldo said. 'Must have cut him deeper than I realized.'

They moved closer, Aldo keeping his blade ready in case of another ruse. The rain was passing, making the way easier to see. The statue towered over the body, its bold white marble a stark contrast to the silhouettes of surrounding buildings. Aldo was a young boy when the *David* was first brought into the piazza. Forty men had taken four days to move it there, such was its colossal size and weight. Seeing it that first time was the moment Aldo knew to whom he was drawn. It was the statue's shapely buttocks that caught his eye; the modest cazzo proved far less impressive, and was now hidden behind a cluster of copper leaves to spare anyone embarrassment.

The nearer Aldo got to the figure on the ground, the less certain he became it was their quarry. He had not seen much of the fugitive, but the man beneath the statue wore no cloak or cap. He looked heavier, too. There was an angry red line round his neck.

Lifeless eyes stared at the thin moon at it reappeared from behind thinning clouds.

'This is someone else,' Aldo said.

'You think the fugitive killed him?' Benedetto asked.

'Unlikely. The fugitive was trying to move through the city unseen. Why would they flee this way after killing someone here earlier?' He put a knee down on the wet stones by the body to look closer. It was a corpse, there was no doubt about that. The clothes were soaked through, meaning he had been left here before the rain came. Aldo searched the face but did not recognize the dead man. There was something curious about the way the body was positioned on the ground. Both arms were stretched out sideways, while the legs were close together, one crossed over the other at the feet. Almost as if he was—

'There!' Benedetto pointed across the piazza. Someone was limping away in the shadows on the far side: their fugitive. 'Should I go after him?'

'No.'

'But before you were—'

'That was before,' Aldo said. 'We can catch them another time. A man has been murdered. That matters far more now.'

Contessa Valentine Coltello politely stifled a yawn behind one hand. Her gesture was not caused by the lateness of the hour – nor indeed by its earliness, since dawn must be close by now. Her weariness could not be blamed on a lack of sleep, despite having been kept awake all evening, as she had taken the precaution of resting through much of the previous day. Besides, the hours before sunrise were her domain, a world where she was at her finest.

No, the reason for her yawning was all too predictable.

The cause, inevitably, was a man.

She had invited Signor Federico Dandolo to dine with her alongside several other far more interesting guests, artfully chosen to avoid arousing suspicion or encouraging unwanted gossip. As curfew approached and the other guests rose to depart, the Contessa contrived a reason for Dandolo to stay longer, claiming a need for his wisdom. She had led him to this richly decorated salone to assess the worth of certain tapestries left by her late husband. Dandolo knew nothing of art and even less about tapestries, but flattery and his own arrogance persuaded him to profess an expertise he did not possess. More than an hour passed while he blustered and bluffed. Once that was done, the Contessa had patted the chair beside her own and invited Dandolo to share the story of how he came to be so significant, so important and so admired.

Few men were immune to flattery and Dandolo was no exception, despite his receding hair, dull features and a belly running to fat beneath his gaudy silk tunic. But the Contessa had not expected him to be quite so in love with the sound of his own voice. Hour after hour he droned on, regaling her in quite excruciating detail with the dreary, unimpressive events of his life. Most men possessed enough wit to realize they were being flirted with, courted, even lured. Somehow Dandolo had remained unaware or unable to grasp this simple fact.

Of course, there was no question of taking Dandolo to her bedchamber; the very thought was both repulsive and hilarious. No, she simply wished to learn whatever he might know about Duke Cosimo de' Medici and those around the leader of Florence. That mixture of secrets and gossip would be thoroughly sifted before the most useful morsels were duly reported to her paymasters at the Council of Ten in Venice.

In other circumstances – had Dandolo been more attractive or more intriguing – the Contessa would have taken matters into her own hands. Alas, Dandolo possessed an opinion of his own magnificence that far outweighed whatever merits he might have below the waist. But to get what she wanted, it was sometimes necessary to tease and tempt the ugliest of wits.

'Please, tell me more,' the Contessa murmured when Dandolo took a rare pause for breath while explaining his importance within the ducal court. She stroked one finger down the back of his left hand as a test. The fool's nostrils flared, and his eyes widened. It seemed what she was apparently offering had finally become obvious to him.

'Well, Juan de Luna is as tactless as he is haughty,' Dandolo said, licking his thin, unsightly lips. 'Typical Spaniard. Since being appointed to lead the garrison at Fortezza da Basso this idiota has managed to offend almost everyone he encounters. The duke is so frustrated that he wrote to his father-in-law for advice after de Luna insulted one of Cosimo's segretarie and his mother, Maria Salviati, both in the same afternoon.'

That confirmed what the Contessa had heard from others within the ducal palazzo. Cosimo had been married to Eleonora de Toledo but a few months, yet the young Medici was already making deft use of this connection with her father, Pedro de Toledo. The Viceroy of Naples was close to Charles V, the Spanish king and Holy Roman Emperor, without whose approval Cosimo would never have been appointed ruler of Florence. Seeking counsel from de Toledo demonstrated what the Contessa had concluded about the young duke: Cosimo had the guile of a much older man, despite being no more than twenty.

'And what of the duke's new bride?' the Contessa whispered, letting her gaze wander to Dandolo's groin before looking into his muddy eyes once more. 'I have heard whispers she is pregnant already. Can this be true?' The Contessa knew it for a fact, but the question was a snare to see how much Dandolo was willing to divulge, how compliant he might be.

'I . . . I am not supposed to speak of such things,' he stammered, before licking his lips once more. It was an irritating habit. The Contessa doubted his lovemaking was any better.

'Of course not,' she said, resting a hand on Dandolo's thigh. 'I have no wish to do anything that might make you . . . uncomfortable.' Her fingernails slid along the hose, edging closer to the growing bulge that lurked between his legs.

Dandolo swallowed hard. 'No, I'm sure it would be . . . fine.' The fool's voice rose higher with each word. Soon it would be the equal of a soprano. 'I've heard tell that she—'

A sharp knock at the door interrupted them, stopping whatever tedious utterance had been about to spill from Dandolo's mouth. He half rose from the chair before sinking down again, face flushing crimson, both hands clasped between his legs.

'Come!' the Contessa called, suppressing a smirk.

Her maggiordomo Pozzo entered, bowing low, hands behind his back. 'Forgive my interruption, Contessa, but a message of utmost urgency has arrived.'

'A message? So late after curfew?' Dandolo asked.

Truly, the man had less wit than the chair on which he sat, and none of its charm.

'Forgive me,' the Contessa said, rising to her feet. 'I must discover what this matter concerns. Please, remain here. I shall return as soon as I am able.'

Dandolo rose in a half-crouch, still struggling to hide the excitement in his hose. 'Of course, Contessa. It will be my pleasure to—'

'Good,' she interjected, sparing herself any more of his words by marching to the door. Pozzo held it open so she could depart, following her out into the hallway before closing the door behind him. 'Diavolo, where have you been?' she demanded. 'We were supposed to be interrupted long ago.'

'Forgive me, but I was actually busy with a messenger.' Pozzo produced a letter from inside his tunic, the folded page sealed with black wax. The Contessa noted crimson beneath his nails on both hands. 'A night patrol pursued him through the city in the rain,' Pozzo continued, 'and one of the constables wounded him.'

The Contessa snorted her disbelief. 'I've watched better tales at the teatro. Night patrols are all fools and dullards, everyone knows that. It's why I send letters after dark.'

'It seems at least one of these constables was no fool, and also handy with a blade,' Pozzo said. 'I've spent the last hour sewing the wound he made.'

'That explains the stains beneath your fingernails, at least. Tell me, if this night patrol is so adept, how was it the messenger escaped while wounded?'

'It seems the constables were distracted by a corpse in Piazza della Signoria.' Pozzo hesitated before clarifying. 'The corpse was not of the messenger's making.'

'I take it back,' the Contessa said. 'That story is better than anything I've seen at the teatro this year.' She snatched the letter from Pozzo, tearing it open to read the words within. The fact it was written without any ciphers was surprising, but the content of the letter was shocking. If this was true . . . 'Is the messenger still here in the palazzo?'

'Yes, Contessa.'

'Are they capable of taking a letter back to who sent them?'

Pozzo nodded.

'Good. Fetch me ink and paper. This can't wait.'

A few minutes later she swept back into the salone, her face a mask of wistful regret. 'My dearest Dandolo, I am so dreadfully sorry, but you must leave at once.'

'I must?' he asked, rising to his feet.

'Yes.'

'But I thought we . . .'

The Contessa waited, letting the fool stumble over the folly of his imaginings.

'I thought that perhaps you and I might . . .'

He might still be useful one day, she supposed. Better to let him down gently now, in case that day came sooner rather than later. Besides, if the letter brought by the messenger heralded what she thought, Dandolo could serve another purpose. The Contessa glided across the salone to him, cupping the left side of his face with a delicate hand. 'And perhaps we might, perhaps . . . but not tonight. Not now.' She used the same hand to gesture at the door. 'My maggiordomo will see you out and advise on the best way to avoid the night patrols.'

'Oh. I see.' Dandolo appeared quite crestfallen, as if there had actually been some hope that she would allow a minor functionary from the duke's court to visit her bedchamber. He really was quite the fool.

She watched him dawdle to the door. 'My dear Federico?'

'Yes?' he replied, twisting round, fresh hope obvious in his face.

'I wonder . . . But no, it is too much to ask.' She looked aside. 'Forgive me.'

Dandolo hastened back to her, eager as an animal for the lure, unaware of a trap closing around him. 'Contessa, whatever you wish, please ask me for it.'

She suppressed a smirk of triumph. It was almost too easy.

'Perhaps you could write me a letter . . . if time allows. Once a day should be sufficient.'

'A letter, once a day?'

The Contessa fixed her gaze on his eyes. 'I want to know more about you, Federico. I want to learn everything about you. What interests, what intrigues, what excites . . .' She glanced down at his groin so he would have no doubt what that meant. Dandolo had already proven himself insufferably dim in such matters. 'Tell me all the gossip from your day and I am certain I shall find some way to . . . reward you.'

Dandolo was quite crimson now. Yes, even he had understood her. 'And will you write to me in return?' he asked, perhaps hoping to read about her lusts and desires.

'Alas, no.' The Contessa smiled at him. 'I am still a widow, and it would not be seemly for me to maintain any kind of correspondence with a gentleman, no matter how important and significant he might be. You understand how it is.'

'Yes, of course.' Again, a crestfallen expression haunted his face. Most unappealing.

'Then, it is settled. I look forward to reading your first letter later today.'

'Today?'

'It will be dawn soon, my dear Dandolo. You really should be getting home.' She ushered him to the salone door, a gentle but firm hand in the small of his back propelling the fool out. 'By the way, my maggiordomo tells me it had been raining quite heavily tonight,' she said once Dandolo was in the hallway. 'Do try not to catch your death out there.'